u

JESUS OF INDIA

JESUS OF INDIA

His Unknown Years and Travels

Maury Lee

This is a work of fiction. Names, characters, places and incidents either are the product of the author's imagination or are used fictitiously, and any resemblance to any actual persons, living or dead, events, or locales is entirely coincidental.

This book was printed in the United States of America.

To order additional copies of this book, contact:
Xlibris Corporation
1-888-7-XLIBRIS
www.Xlibris.com
Orders@Xlibris.com

CONTENTS

This book is dedicated to all on the spiritual path.
My friends and family who have contributed their support,
know well my indebtedness. I thank them all.
To all living and dead, who by their struggles and
willingness to share, have taught me, I offer gratitude and praise.
If the dead could talk, books would speak
and I would answer, "Yes, you taught me that."

767-ENTW

ACKNOWLEDGEMENTS

I am grateful to all of those who have approached the spiritual realm with an open mind. This is never easy, for psychological security is something we strive to maintain. It's a rare bird who doesn't falter.

Frederick Nietzsche, Carl Jung, Fritz Perls, readily come to mind. The great Eastern thinkers, Ramana Maharshi, Sri Nisargadatta Maharaj, and J. Krishnamurti, also come to mind. Without these, my journey would have been quite different.

Foremost of all, Jesus Christ, like many others, gave his life for his efforts. All of these great spiritual leaders risked psychological security, and physical death, in order to find that rare perennial jewel, mystical union.

However, it was Holger Kersten's book, *Jesus Lived in India,* which was the inspiration for this book. Without his work, his research, his openness and willingness to risk it all, the passion for this effort would have remained unleavened. It is with great admiration and respect for Kersten's work that I have taken on the task of imagining Jesus' travels prior to the recorded Gospels.

I have very loosely, and for my own enjoyment, created many events, experiences and talks. I claim no special knowledge or archeological background which would allow me to make any factual claims. This is a work of fiction, a personal journey I took, using Jesus as the vehicle.

Many have done this before. Jesus is just too great a figure, and too far beyond easy understanding, to be left alone. Whatever truth is in this work, is for you dear reader, to decide. I have no special hold, lock or key, on which to claim special dispensation. My hope is simple. If through this story you are inspired to seek a deeper truth, I and you will benefit.

(1)

The Monk and the Virgin

"What are you going to do about it?"

"I don't know."

"Well, I know what I'm going to do! I'm going to go to Qumran and talk to the abbot."

"Please Father. Don't do that! At least let me see him and talk to him."

"What can he do now? Isn't it a little late?"

"It's not too late! If I go to him. Tell him he is the father, maybe he will leave the monastery and marry me."

"Oh Mary. Do you really think it will be that easy? God forgive us! He's been living as a monk for ten years. What does he know about living in the world? He's useless. I think he ought to be kicked out of the monastery and driven into the desert. Let him really learn to be alone with God—if God cares to know him."

"Father! You're walking way ahead of the camel. Slow down and listen to me! There's still time."

"Time for what? You're going to start showing soon. I will have to deal with your mother then. That will be a day in Scheol."

"Father. I know you are angry with Joseph. As a monk he should have known better. He should have shown restraint. But, it is not entirely his fault. It was I who went out to see him, to hear him talk. It was I who stayed after the others left. And it was I who went out more than once to his tent."

"I'm angry at you too. You have just squandered all the freedom I have given you. Where are your choices now? You could be stoned for this! The last one I saw was several years ago, but you and a monk! There are grounds."

"Father. What you say is true. But this need not fall into the hands of the elders. Let me go to Qumran. See Joseph. Ask him to marry me. If he agrees, we can have a wedding soon. You could even send me off and say I am betrothed to someone in another town. I could come back in a year or two. Who would know? Perhaps we can keep this a secret between the two of us."

"Not for long. Once you are gone a day or two there will be questions. When it turns out you're not at a relative's, explanations will be in order. "All right, but Mother does not have to know now. We'll tell her after I've met with Joseph."

Jaochim sat on the large boulder outside the stable's entrance, his head in his hands. "I feel defeated, defiled. How long have I loved the Essenes? How long?"

"Forever, Father."

"Yes, forever. And this is my reward? A monk impregnates my daughter. Where is the justice? I thought I was doing you a favor by taking you there. Do you remember?"

"Of course I remember. I loved taking those trips to Qumran, riding on the camels, seeing the desert, watching the stars. And Qumran, how I love that place. So different. All those men and no women."

"And foolish me. I took you there and introduced you to your fate. This is fate you know—pure and simple."

"Our whole history is wrapped in destiny. Why should my life be different? It's a Jewish right of passage."

"Don't make jokes, Mary."

"I'm not joking. Do you think I've been laughing the past two weeks? I've cried myself dry. I wish to act now. If this is my destiny, let me face it!"

Jaochim sat, still with his head in his hands, looking at the dirt. "What choice do I have?"

"Send me with the next caravan passing by Qumran. Give me a camel and some provisions. Send me with a gift or something to trade. You know they will let me in. I will talk with Joseph, and God willing, he will return with me. What other choice do we have?"

"None, Mary. I only wish I had never let you out of my sight. I thought I was doing right by giving you a little freedom."

"This is not over yet. Let me try."

"All right. I'll let you go. You can take a camel. Ride with the next caravan. Hadar will probably be coming through tomorrow. I heard from an advance rider yesterday that he was only a day away. I'll send some cloth and incense—a gift for the abbot. What do we tell your mother?"

"Tell her you're sending an offering to the Essenes. After I'm well on my way, tell her the truth. She'll have a couple of days to think about it."

"I guess I could do that. Save you some grief. By the time you get back, with or without Joseph, we can make the next step as a family."

"Yes, Father."

"Tell me, Mary. How did this happen? Didn't your mother or sisters notice your being gone?"

"No. They thought I was with friends or relatives. They didn't realize I was alone. Do you remember last month, when Joseph was here, teaching on the outskirts of town?"

"Vaguely, I do. I was so busy. It didn't really register." "Well, I went out with my sisters, to listen and show support. He was sleeping in a tent just outside our village by Olive Stream. He was sent to do some recruiting, reminding the villagers that they took in orphan boys. He also answered questions about the monastic life. There were no large crowds there, Father. A few people came and went. They asked questions, listened and gossiped with their neighbors. Nothing much. My sisters left early that first day. I stayed behind. They were not concerned. Others were still there. But the others soon left and I was alone with Joseph.

"I was completely enthralled with his teaching. I can't explain what happened next. I'd never known a man before. I didn't know how easily it could happen. It was neither of our intention."

"Perhaps not yours. But I know men!"

"Believe as you will, Father. He touched my shoulder as a friend, then everything changed. There is nothing for me to explain to you. You have six children. You must know."

"You should have known better! Our laws are very strict. You should not have been alone with him. Even so, a little restraint would have been enough."

"It's too late to go over this. I can't say any more."

"But you went back out! More than once! How did you manage that without anyone noticing?"

"It was easy. I would say I was going to visit a girlfriend. Or Mother sent me to market. I just asked if I could take time to visit Sarah, or Ruth. That was all. The time was not missed. It's not like crowds of people were always out at Joseph's tent. He was alone much of the time."

"No more. Enough of this. Go now. Help your Mother with supper. Tomorrow or the day after Hadar's caravan is due. He can take you on to Qumran. But, you must be back within a few days. Your Mother will be suspicious. Follow my lead at supper tonight and we will ease our way into this."

"Thank you, Father."

"Go now."

Mary turned and walked briskly down the slope. The scene behind her was of her Father's stables. They were built of stone, mud and timber, on a slight rise behind their home. They were his pride and joy. He was prosperous, with land and a business to leave to his sons. Though he could not leave her any of that, Mary felt that he had always favored her in other ways, taking her on trips and confiding in her. She felt she held a special place in his heart.

She saw the smoke from the evening cooking fires and could smell the meat, the fat dripping into the fire and filling the air with its aroma. She pondered her Father's kindness in granting her wish. She took her usual spot in the courtyard, sitting on the granite bench. She picked up a rolling stone and began to grind the rye to flour. Her Mother said nothing and Mary was soon far away, reliving the past. She thought of the first time she had traveled to Qumran. It was a business trip with her Father. She thought of how she had first entered Qumran years ago. As far back as she could remember, her father had taken her along on the short run from Nazareth. He had wanted her to see and hear the Essenes. Observe how they lived, what they taught. She had never turned him down.

As a small child she had been allowed to stay overnight with her Father. As time passed, a tolerance among the monks had developed and Mary was one of the few grown women allowed into the monastery. But this was only during daylight. To this day, she remained intrigued by the white-robed Essenes. They were mysterious, even now that she was grown. They were different from other men and Joseph in particular had always attracted her.

She remembered meeting him when he was still a boy, an orphan, adopted by the Essenes. She had learned of the Essenes' need for orphan boys because the community was celibate. No women were permanent members. New recruits were needed to fill the ranks. Young boys were adopted for their labor, and with the hope that they would join the community as adults. She had seen how few of the adopted boys ever left, how difficult it was for men not brought up in the community to stay. Without women, the community had a peculiar atmosphere, and those not adopted into the community as children found it quite difficult to adjust. It was a supportive community, but if one were used to a woman's touch, there was little to compare.

The Essenes were a strict lot, with regimented roles. The work was hard and all their property was held in common. Personal belongings were meager, consisting of a robe, a bowl and a walking staff. The staff signified their commitment to the One God. It also helped on long walks up and down the steep, stony ravines.

Mary thought of the first time she met Joseph. She was tending the camels by the well while her father transacted his business. Some scruffy boys approached, offering to help. Not seeing many young girls, they were surprised to see her.

"How is it you are in here?" one of the older boys asked.

"My father trades here. I came with his caravan."

"Why does he bring you along?" another boy asked.

"Because I beg him. I don't like being stuck in the house, seeing nothing but my mother and sisters!"

"Oh, you are a lucky girl to have a father who takes you with him. I have no father," the boy said bluntly.

"How is that?"

"I am an orphan, as are all of us boys. My father was killed by the Romans and my mother died soon after. They say her heart was broken."

"I'm sorry. I feel very lucky. What's your name?"

"Joseph."

As Mary relived this conversation she felt tears running down her face. Ever since that day she had always kept a special place in her heart for Joseph. Over the years, while her father chatted with the Elders, Mary and Joseph had met at the watering hole or gathered wood together just outside the community walls. They had talked briefly many times about nothing in particular. But, something beneath the surface, unseen, unheard, connected them.

At supper that night Joachim told the family that he was sending Mary to Qumran with gifts for the abbot. He explained that it had been some time since he had been able to go there and he did not want them to feel that they had lost his support. "As you know, Mary has most often been the one to accompany me. Since she will be traveling with Hadar, her safety is assured."

No one objected. Her sisters had never had much interest in Qumran and her brothers even less. Even when Joseph was in Nazareth, they had only gone out once. Mary was surprised that no one, not even her mother said anything or sensed anything out of the ordinary.

Alone on her mat in the corner that night, Mary's mind brought back the images of that first day—Joseph, beyond the confines of Qumran, his tent just outside Nazareth. That afternoon, Mary had become increasingly aware of an intense connection with Joseph. His soft voice expressed so well the teaching of the Essenes. He constantly stressed the direct experience of God, over and above any explanation. When he said, "Men and women, look into your own heart and listen there," she had felt as if he were speaking only to her. A warmth enveloped her and she longed to spend more time with him.

When the others unexpectedly left, she and Joseph were overwhelmed by something much more powerful than the friendship of childhood. As she had looked into Joseph's eyes, a passion she had never felt before, took over. When their bodies met, all resistance had vanished.

Though Mary had never made love before, all her feelings, her very nature, said yes! The sweaty smell of Joseph's skin became foreground, leaving the smell of the camel hair tent behind. Outside, the desert air blew away the smoke and ash of the cooking fire. With Joseph's movements she had felt the sand shift under her back. The goat hair blanket on which she lay rubbed her back, the stiff fur reminding her of her nakedness. With ardor, she knew Joseph and herself in a new way. Her passion had no resistance or shame. She had wanted to stay all night. But, the thought of her father and brothers waiting up for her, had drawn her home.

She had kissed Joseph goodbye. But he had insisted on walking her to the edge of town. That long walk back to town and the quiet conversation sealed their union. At the first sight of stone walls, the shadowed outlines of the mud and stone abodes, they kissed and parted. She had walked through the village lanes alone, wrapped in joy. A dim light had shone through the crack of the doorway. She was grateful to find only a single lamp burning. The family had gone to bed. No one spoke as she entered and blew out the flame. As she lay down on her bed, she was grateful no one had spoken. She feared that she might give herself away. She had lain awake, feeling the hardness of the mat, reliving the smells, the sounds, the feelings she had had with Joseph.

In the morning, as she packed to leave, she went over the past few weeks. She could not condemn Joseph, for again and again she had gone out to see him. Each time they were alone, they had joined as one. She had risked all in these encounters, but the risk paled each time she had been in his presence. A sense of wholeness had bonded her to Joseph. It was bliss until the night he left, returning to Qumran. Before he walked off into the desert, leaving her, he told her, "Mary, I must return to Qumran. Our passion is such that I cannot teach. In truth, I can barely think. I must return to the monastery to gather my wits and pray for forgiveness." Mary listened in silence as Joseph continued.

"I have lost control and can no longer claim to be the man I thought I was. I am an Essene, a monk, sworn to celibacy. Yet I prove to be no different from other men. My spiritual inheritance I have thrown away! My flesh is weak. Both of us are now in danger. Not six weeks ago, in Galem, I saw a woman stoned. There was nothing I could do to stop it. At this moment, it's as if it is I who hold you before the crowd, encouraging them to stone you. So I must leave before we are both driven out of town, into the desert or stoned. My heart is yours, Mary, but I must leave. Pray you are not pregnant."

Mary did not protest. She was used to suffering in silence, like most of the women she knew. It occurred to her that she might never see Joseph again. With that, he had kissed her and walked off into the night.

Within a couple of weeks, Mary was certain she had missed her time of the month. Her cheeks were flushed and her taste for food had changed. It was then, after several days of heavy crying, that she had approached her father, telling him of her situation. She knew her only hope was to persuade him to let her see Joseph before she began to show. She approached him when he was alone because she knew he would object. With every

"No!" she had stood her ground. As she recalled her father finally giving in, she drifted off to sleep.

That night, in another part of the house, Jaochim thought of Mary. She was his favorite daughter. As a wealthy trader, it had been his joy to bring Mary along with him on short trading junkets. Since childhood she had always been precocious, independent, qualities Joachim prized. He had done the best he could with her, but it had been difficult, as assertive women were frowned upon. Without verbally admitting his dislike for certain customs, his leniency toward her spoke volumes.

Joachim thought often of Mary—how average she was in height and weight, no stronger than the other women of Nazareth. She had the same brown hair, brown eyes and sun darkened skin as all the local women. But he was proud of her high cheek bones and prominent nose, so Jewish. He thought how you could pick her out from among a crowd by watching the way she moved. In movement, her nature proclaimed itself—an assertion of confidence, of grace in contact with earth. Her face in expression, likewise stood out. There was a spark, a flash in her eyes that arrested the casual glance. Her smile, inviting, drew people even closer. Her hands spoke, accentuating her presence, communicating an uncommon aliveness. Even those who did not know her were often drawn into her sphere.

The young people of the village, when needing someone to confide in, sought her out, for she had a quality of listening and discerning without judgment. Her insights, he was told, were elegant, simple, without condemnation. She answered spontaneously from her heart. Jaochim thought what a blessing she had been. He hoped that this was not the end.

As Mary prepared to leave for Qumran, she wished there were someone to confide in besides her father, but that was not possible. Instead, she prayed that Yahweh reveal his mercy.

She remembered that first night. Wasn't that just what nature wanted? The walk to his tent, the expanse of desert sand, the free blowing wind—all had made her feel so open, so willing.

She finished packing her small leather bag, having stowed care-fully, cheese, flatbread and a bladder pouch of water. She walked to the well at the center of town and waited, watching for Hadar's caravan. Hadar was a friend of her father's. Mary would know him by sight, as she was familiar with many of the camel drivers. She knew the camels and the routes.

The sun began to beat down. She sat against the wall of the well, speaking casually to the women who came to draw water. But her mind was elsewhere, thinking about the first time she had gone to Qumran, begging her father to bring her along. Joachim continually reprimanded her for her independent ways. But she always sensed at heart, he didn't really mind. He had allowed her some privileges not commonly condoned. He had let her learn from her older brothers, some reading and writing. Secretly, she had practiced with a stick in the sand. An educated Jew, Joachim had passed on to her, knowledge and understanding.

Sweat poured from Mary's brow and the heat brought human and animal smells to her nose. She looked down the road and saw a small caravan approaching. She could see the blankets on the camels' backs. From the size, shape and color of the blankets, she knew this would be Hadar's caravan. She stood up and watched them approach the well. She greeted Hadar and could barely wait for the camels to finish drinking. At Hadar's prompting, Mary mounted a sorrel-colored camel and was on her way to Qumran. The camel swayed, tilting Mary left, then right, with its rhythmic gait. Her legs moved in and out with the camel's breathing. Soon she was thinking again of Joseph. How would he feel? What would he say? What would he do?

Late in the day, the caravan stopped at Qumran. There was a small watering hole that made Qumran a common stop. It made trading with the community viable. Mary dismounted, took down her bundle of cloth, incense and food. Mary was thirsty and tired, but having arrived, she could feel tension stirring. She was glad to be off the camel's back and on her feet. It took a minute or two for her legs to adjust after the long ride. She thanked Hadar and straightened her tunic. Then she approached the gate. Although the walls were stone, the gate was made of split wood. She knocked loudly. After waiting patiently for several minutes, she knocked again, this time louder. Finally she heard the scraping of wood and the screech of rusted hinges. An old face, wrinkled with time and sun, peered through the slats of the viewing hole.

"What's your business?" he asked.

"I am Mary of Nazareth, daughter of Joachim the trader. I would like to speak with Joseph. I have with me some cloth and some incense for the abbot."

"But child, Joseph is in meditation now and can't be disturbed."

"Then I will wait."

"No harm in that. You may wait."

"Sir," said Mary, holding up her arms, "I am tired, sweaty and dirty, and I could use a drink. Could you let me wait inside?"

"It is not customary to let women inside. But I recognize your face. You have visited here before, have you not?"

"Yes, with my father. He has traded with you since I was a child."

"Very well, I will ask the abbot's permission that you may enter."

"Thank you kind sir. I will wait."

The face disappeared from the hole in the gate. Mary found a large boulder several yards from the gate and sat down. She could smell her body and the smell of the camel lingering on her. Mary hoped she could clean up some before Joseph saw her. She waited, staring at the gate. She could feel the mingling of sweat and the patchouli oil she had brushed on her cheeks. Suddenly, her reverie was broken by the sounds of the wooden gate opening. A voice called out to her.

"Young woman, you may enter."

"Oh thank you, thank you."

Mary stepped forward and entered Qumran for the first time by herself. She felt exhilarated and her tiredness began to fade. She was led to the well.

"Get yourself cleaned up and fill your water pouch. Then report to Caleb in the kitchen. Understood?"

"Yes, kind sir!" When the old man left, Mary drew water from the well and washed her face and hands. She felt the nearness of Joseph and contemplated his situation. He had been in the community since he was eleven. He was immersed in the society, well liked and respected. But Joseph had experienced family life as a young boy. He had those roots. Mary felt sure that though Joseph had lived in the community for over ten years, he could still be a family man. She would ask Joseph to leave the community and marry her. She knew this was a big thing to ask, as Joseph had already taken his vows. But Mary knew that he had also broken them, and that when he found out she was pregnant, he would feel obliged to leave. She was counting on it, praying on it.

Being aware of her predicament, Mary knew that if Joseph didn't leave the commune and marry her, they would both be in serious trouble. For despite her father's protestations, the townspeople might stone her, and Joseph would be forced from the monastery. As she washed, she prayed. Strength came to her and she let go of some of her doubts. When she was finished cleaning, she put some fresh patchouli oil beneath her chin and strode toward the kitchen.

As she walked across the quad to the kitchen, she thought about the community, what it meant to Joseph, and what it would mean for him to leave. She knew that the main reason men left the community was that their attraction to women was too strong. This made it difficult to stay. Joseph was now in this position. But he would soon have the added complication that she was already pregnant. She was not quite sure of the abbot's stance on this issue for he was a foreigner. She had heard that he was from Tibet. Her father had caravans that passed through there, but she had never been there. The foreigner looked different and spoke Aramaic with a strong accent.

Joseph had explained that although the Essenes were a Jewish sect, with esoteric knowledge, they were not exclusive when it came to a certain level of understanding. Joseph had tried to explain to her about the oneness of the mystical traditions, but she already felt that and didn't need an explanation. Her knowledge, she had always felt, was intuitive, and Joseph sometimes seemed overly intellectual. But she did understand that the foreign teacher had brought to the community, methods of more deeply understanding the Jewish mystical tradition. Joseph had explained that the Kabala, though new to the abbot, was not foreign to his understanding. His yellow skin, bald head and accent, did not prevent his knowledge from being shared. She hoped he would be tolerant of Joseph's decision.

Mary had seen the abbot only a few times. Each time she had felt that she was in the presence of a deep, gentle being. It was an odd feeling, as if everything she was and thought, was immediately accessible to him. But it was a peaceful acceptance, without fear or shame. She had seen how the monks treated him with awe and reverence. Whenever she had looked in his eyes she had felt it too. There was an aware but far away look in his eyes. His smile, as broad as his face, was dazzling. His few yellow teeth, the rest missing, did not detract from the smile. The monks had told her that he was an enlightened being.

As she passed under the fig trees, Mary recalled the many times she had been here. It was a good feeling, giving her confidence. Just like the confidence she had felt when she was alone with Joseph. She walked past the vegetable garden. The monks were primarily vegetarian, so the garden was well kept. As she approached the stone kitchen, she could see Caleb, the cook, hunched over the stove. The smell of burning dung filled the air, changing the smell of the food cooking over the heat. Caleb was tasting broth from a large pot when he noticed her.

"Hello Mary," he said. "What brings you here?"

"My very own self. I've come to help you cook."

"Oh, you come all the way from Nazareth to help me cook? How sweet. I don't believe a word."

"Suit yourself Caleb. What have you got cooking?"

"Why, vegetables. What else? Here, taste this."

Mary put her lips to the ladle held out to her. "Very good," she said. "May I stay and have some?"

"I'd be delighted," Caleb said."

Mary knew the Essenes had their evening meal late in the day, after prayers and meditation. She knew she would be seeing Joseph soon, but she would not be able to talk to him till after dinner, for she would not be allowed to eat with the men. She would be relegated to the kitchen.

"Tell me again. What brings you here?" asked Caleb.

"Some business."

"For your father?"

"Yes. He sent me with some gifts for the abbot. Some cloth and some incense."

"I see. You're now your father's emissary. Very good!" Mary smiled, for Caleb had always enjoyed teasing her.

"Don't worry. My father does not let me go far. Nor does he allow me to travel far alone. I came with Hadar's caravan. He will pick me up on his return trip."

"I don't know what to think, it seems so unconventional to see you here alone. I'll have to speak with your father the next time he's here."

"As you wish, Caleb. My father often treats me like a son. My brothers are even jealous of me!"

"I see," said Caleb, not knowing what else to say against this onslaught.

"Look. Here I am in the kitchen with you, in Qumran, where no woman is allowed. What do you think of that?"

"I don't know what to think. You amaze me. You must be chosen by God or for sure you wouldn't be here."

"Thank you." Mary smiled to herself. She quickly went to work helping Caleb get the evening meal ready. He made no more teasing remarks. Working with him was a pleasure, for he enjoyed cooking. Mary could see that Caleb enjoyed her presence in the kitchen. The two of them sang hymns and folk songs until the call went out for supper. The monks filed in, quiet, serene from their meditations.

Mary was left in the kitchen while Caleb got a message to Joseph that he should come there to see her. This was after another monk, whom Mary did not know, had informed Caleb that Mary was to be allowed to see Joseph.

"I have unloaded your camel and given the bundle you brought to the abbot. He says to tell your father he appreciates the gifts." Mary nodded in gratitude that her request had been delivered. She waited anxiously to see Joseph.

When he entered the kitchen, Mary's heart jumped to her throat. The look on Joseph's face was enough to break her will, for he appeared frightened. Caleb quickly left the room.

"What are you doing here?" Joseph asked. He stood before her as if he had seen a ghost.

"I have something to tell you. I am with child." Joseph stood mute. The silence was deafening.

Mary spoke again. "I am with child, your child. I have come that you may know. I don't have to tell you that this is not something I can do alone without grave consequences. I am asking you to marry me."

Finally Joseph spoke. "I am in shock at your appearance here, but I cannot deny that what you have just told me stands on solid ground. This was the possibility. I had hoped it would be otherwise. Still, it is a shock. Our lives will never be the same."

"They will never be the same. But we can make the best of it. We are not bad people."

"In my own eyes, I have fallen. But as for you, your passion was not disgraceful. I have thought much about you since I left. Most likely, had you not conceived, I would have left the community anyhow. But you have taken away my longing to wait, to ponder, to ease myself out. I must act!"

"So, will you leave with me?"

"Give me a day to still my mind and take my leave. Yes. I will marry you."

"Oh Joseph, thank you, thank you." Mary stood and embraced Joseph and he held her tight. But they did not embrace long, for should they be seen, it would cause trouble.

"Mary, I must leave now, for to stay too long will cause concern. I will form my request and present it to the abbot. He will want to know the reason for my leaving. I want to say it right."

"I understand," said Mary. "Go in peace. In my breast I feel the strength of a rock. I am calm and ready. Thank you Joseph."

"Where shall I meet you after tomorrow?"

"I will be at Salem's house, in Gabatha. He is a trader and knows my father well. He will put me up."

"Very well Mary. I will see you there. God keep you well, I honor the divine in you."

"And I in you," said Mary.

Joseph turned and was gone in an instant. Mary stood in the kitchen, awestruck at the understanding between them. She saw Joseph walk briskly neither looking back nor to the right or left. She felt how much she loved him, a love she had never expected to feel. She lifted her blouse to her nose, Joseph's smell was still there. She would have his smell to sleep with and that was enough for now. Mary was brought out of her reverie by Caleb's voice.

"Well Mary, did you get your business handled?" In the pale moonlight, Mary thought she could still see a twinkle in Caleb's eyes.

"Yes Caleb, I did."

"Where to now, Mary?"

"I must go to Gabatha, up the road. It's not far."

"But I cannot let you travel outside the walls at night. You must stay. I know it is very unorthodox, but I cannot let you go."

"What do you propose, Caleb? There are no women's quarters here."

"You can sleep here in the kitchen. I'll bring you a mat. The headmaster, should he find out, will not begrudge this breach of code. He let you in, didn't he?"

"Yes, I have his permission. He did not ask when I was leaving."

"Very well then, Mary. I shall return with a mat."

Mary thought how well she was treated here. She was over-
come with gratitude and felt how lucky she was. She knelt on the
floor between the dried dung and the oven and prayed. "Thank
you God, thank you. Your presence is like a cool breeze to me.
How have you ever failed me? May my child bless you and all of
us. Amen."

Caleb returned with a mat. He spread it on the floor and pat-
ting her on the shoulder, said, "Goodnight Mary."

"I will leave before daybreak so you needn't worry over questions in the morning. Goodnight Caleb, and thank you."

As the moon shone through the window, giving contour to
the shadows of the kitchen, Mary laid down on the mat. Everything seemed perfect, even the pile of dung waiting to be burned
in the stove. Goat and sheep pellets she thought, were easy to
handle and an excellent fuel, but the smell was not appealing.
Tonight, however, with the moon full in the sky and her future
secure, Mary could think of nothing that wouldn't work out.

She dreamed that night, a dream she would never forget. She
saw her father standing on a hill, and God came to him, speaking
from a face in the moon. "Behold. You have a daughter in whom I
am well pleased. She is blessed among women and I have given her
a son. A son of the Most High. But, you will call him 'The Son of
Man,' for he is one of you." Mary saw her father kneel and thank
God, with praise and song, reveling in his good fortune.

The dream changed and now Mary saw Joseph, alone in his
room, and God came to him, appearing as light, and said, "Behold, you have been chosen to have my son. He will speak for the
Most High, teaching the multitudes and demonstrating my power.
His life will bring freedom and joy to many. He will be a wise man
among the wise, compassionate among the compassionate. He will
bring men together in understanding. They will call him wonderful, but he will call himself, 'The Son of Man.' He will bring the
Jew and gentile together, teaching them the oneness of being. The
world will be blessed by him."

Suddenly, the dream changed again. Now Mary saw Magi from the East, coming on camels. They came to her and her new-born, with gifts of gold, frankincense and myrrh. They told her they had followed a star from the East that had led them to her and her child. "Your son," they said, "is the embodiment of a great spiritual teacher. We come to praise him and tell you his name. He is to be called 'Jesus, the Christ,' as he is to be a light unto the world."

Then Mary saw shepherds in their fields, and the sky opened, and a host of angels appeared. Through the clouds they spoke to the shepherds, stunned and rooted in place. "Behold, a child is born, a son of the Most High! He shall be blessed among the many and he shall be called the Christ. He will be a leader of men, a King to the wise, and a light to seekers of truth. Those who hunger for truth will find it in him. He points the way to all men's hearts."

Mary now found herself in a strange place, a cattle barn, and the shepherds came to her where she lay sleeping, her child in a manger. And they said to her, "Praise be to you and this child. Take good care of him, for he is a child of God. He brings light and wisdom to all who have ears to hear." When the shepherds left, Mary was full of joy.

She awoke, her heart full. What has transpired? she thought. It was still the middle of the night. Mary pondered her dreams in awe and wonder. She saw that she was in a lowly kitchen. But, could it be, that this place, Qumran, was enchanted? Among these spiritual souls, did spirits walk and talk and speak in dreams? As deeply as she pondered, Mary could not shake the feeling that the future was foretold. There, by the pile of dung, she rose to her knees and praised God.

"Now, before you, God almighty, I vow to you this night. I shall not rest till this child is grown, safe and secure in the knowl-edge of you. I will call him 'Jesus,' but 'The Christ,' I will leave that to your people. I will leave his revealing to you. Thank you God." With these words in her heart, Mary fell asleep, full of joy and hope.

(2)

Joseph Meets Quan Yin

Joseph lay awake on his mat in the stone room. Though the desert air blew softly through the open window, sweat poured off his body, soaking his bedclothes. His loincloth was moist, as though washed and just wrung out. But, he ignored his physical body—his mental state absorbed all his energy, thinking of Mary, his passion for her, and what that meant for his life.

Everything was different now. What had seemed set, secure, was now turned on its head. He knew he must leave the monastery, but life as a married man, in the world, that was a different matter. He was frightened. Though it was hot, it was the anguish of his soul that caused sweat to pour from him.

What Mary had already given him, what she was propelling him into, seemed fated, pure, natural. But, it was so different from what he had expected. He had not imagined this happening to him. A new Joseph, embodied, with passions, was now the self he confronted. Pushing against his fear was an aliveness, a pulsing of life renewed. How was he to blend his training, his mental and spiritual life, with this new experience? It was too late now to pull back. His vows of compassion, love and responsibility now included Mary and a child. His whole life as he had known it was now behind him, never to be touched again.

When Joseph finally let go of his anguish, accepting what was to be, he became acutely aware of his body, dripping sweat, soaking his mat. He got up and stood before the window looking out at the moon. "What do you say, oh silent one?" he murmured.

"What do you say?" With no answer forthcoming, Joseph left his room and wandered in the courtyard. Again he went over in his mind the interludes he had spent with Mary. Every thread of the blanket, every wrinkle, was etched in his mind. So were every inch of Mary's face and body. Her form, her smell, her feel, was as clear to him as the moonlit courtyard.

All in the same moment, he felt cursed and blessed. These two states mingled in his mind like two opposing fighters. How could he explain what he had done to the headmaster? What would he say? He phrased and rephrased words, but nothing seemed to satisfy. Finally, he knelt and prayed, looking up at the moon which was silently observant.

"Oh Holy One, blessed be your name. Give me the words to express what I must say. Give me the peace I want and thought I had. I know that you and I are not separate. Let my desires be your desires, my mind as your mind. So, Dear One, guide me, direct me, give me peace. But, Your will, not mine, be done. Amen."

Joseph felt much better. He saw his shadow in the pool. He thought, "I am good looking, tall and strong. I can get what I want." But immediately, an intrusive thought stepped in, "You shall not want." He shook his head, as if to shake it out and walked back to his room. He fell into a deep sleep and dreamed. Out of the pond in the courtyard, a female form, larger than life arose. She was a beautiful woman. Her clothes, exotic. On her head was a crown of rubies, diamonds and pearls, inlaid with gold. Her top garment was of fine silk, as red as blood. Around her neck, a golden chain. Her skirt was blue like the sea, with animals of all kinds, leaping and chasing each other. On her feet were leather sandals. Her form was that of soft curves.

She stood before him, taller than he, so that he had to look up. "I am Quan Yin, Goddess of nature and compassion. You have too long denied me. But you see me now and you have experienced my power. I am not to be denied. Did you think you would escape me? Oh, but only for a while. You are mine now. But do not think I take away from you. It only appears that way. I bring you many blessings and joys. But you will have to struggle with me, wrestle with me, embrace me.

"You are to keep me in your heart, for I do not dwell in your brain, where you can analyze, discuss and dilute me. So, when you feel your heart, know that I am there. I am with you always. Trust me. I will bring you deeper awareness than you could ever know with that mind of yours. Now sleep and never leave me."

When Joseph awoke, he felt refreshed. It was as if a great burden had been lifted. He knelt by his bed and thanked God for his visitation in the night. He looked at his legs, his arms, his body. What a beautiful sight, what delight. I have never had thoughts like this before. But I do not mind them, they are me also. Joseph walked across the courtyard as the cocks crowed. He entered the meditation hall, smelling for the first time, the musty, earthy, smells of the room. The size and shape of the room felt like a being, a body, a warm friend. Why had he never felt this before? He did not know, but it was a welcome feeling. Then he noticed his heart, he could feel it there, in the center of his chest, open.

Meditation was easy, and very different this morning. Joseph noticed that while his heart was open, his mind was still. What a welcome relief. The hour was over before Joseph had a thought, but the experience, he couldn't describe it. There was joy, laughter, knowing, it seemed absolute, yet inexpressible. At the sound of the gong, Joseph looked around for Sri Rancoche. He needed to set a time with him to talk.

Joseph spotted him leaving by a side door and walked briskly to him. "Sri Rancoche, I have need to speak with you today? Could you set a time?"

"Come now," Rancoche said, motioning with his head. Joseph followed. They walked in silence to the master's quarters. Taking a seat on a small platform, sitting in lotus position, Sri Rancoche closed his eyes and sat for a few moments before his spoke. "Speak, Joseph," was all he said.

"Mary, the daughter of Joachim, was here last night. She has made a request of me. She says that she is with child and that I am

the father. I cannot deny it. My vows of compassion and responsibility demand that I leave the commune and marry her. I ask your
permission to do so."

There was a very long silence. Again, Sri Rancoche closed his
eyes, and finally, Joseph saw a smile on his face. Sri Rancoche
began laughing and laughing. Joseph was stunned. This was not
what he had expected. "Did a Goddess come to you in the night,
Joseph?"

Joseph was surprised. How could he know? After a moment,
Joseph said, "Why yes sir, but how did you know?"

"Was her name Quan Yin?"

"Yes."

"In the Far East we know her well. She comes to those who are
to live in the world and share her spirit. Her appearance gives you
her blessing. Take what you learn from her and apply it in the
world. She releases you from your vows of chastity and monastic
life. Her presence is a gift. You do not need my permission to go,
she has given it to you directly. You are blessed."

Joseph was awed, this was nothing like what he had expected.
Sri Rancoche's laughter washed over his soul like a cool breeze.
Truly, Joseph thought, this man is gifted of God. He knows more,
sees more, than I ever imagined. And how I looked down on him
when he first arrived.

"Sri Rancoche, I must apologize, for I have not held you in the
regard that I should have. I see that you know more than I imagined. I ask for your forgiveness. I ask this to expiate myself, not
because I need to get it from you, for I know it is given."

"You are correct, Joseph, you needn't ask it of me. As for yourself, your asking has cleansed you. Your mirror will reflect purely
now, so the world will not contaminate you. You are free. There is
no need for you to stay, you need not practice further, for you are
the practice. Just let yourself be and follow your heart."

Joseph rose, bowing. He had never bowed before to a man,
but it did not feel unpleasant, for Joseph was truly humbled.
"Thank you, sir. Thank you."

And so Joseph passed this crisis in a manner unbelievable to him. He crossed through the courtyard, smiling, to attend his daily duties. They were effortless, his thinking was still. He felt his heart, present, open, quiet. There were no disturbing thoughts, no questions, just the peace of existence.

After the noon meal, Joseph could see members giving him sidelong looks and whispering among themselves. He knew they knew something was up. He should nip this talk in the bud. He found two of his closest friends and sat them down. He told them everything. Even this was easy. They listened and were dismayed.

"You know we need to keep as many members as possible, Joseph," one said. "Without orphan boys we could barely survive. Must you go?"

"Yes," said Joseph. He explained no more.

He thought his friends would ask him what it was like to be with a woman, but they did not ask. Joseph knew that he would not have to tell anyone else of his leaving. His friends would spread the word. By evening, Joseph was getting strange looks from many, but few spoke to him. He didn't mind, with the peace he experienced now, and with Rancoche's blessing, no one could disturb him.

Joseph began to think about what life would be like out in the world. Having to make a living, having a wife, raising a child. But the thoughts were not overwhelming, just there. He thought how wonderful it would be to have someone sharing every evening. He thought about the prospect of more children. For with Mary, there was no doubt, more children would come.

The next morning, at the first glimpse of day, Joseph's departure ceremony began. In the great room, in front of the entire community, Rancoche spoke.

"Dear friends and members. We have today released one of our members to the world. It is a big world and there will be many challenges for Joseph. But he is ready. A vision from the Goddess Quan Yin has come to him. Her presence will bless and guide him. She has drawn him to her. Not all of us are so drawn. But, neither those of us remaining, nor Joseph should feel condemned. There are many ways to be in the world. Our way is only one. Though Joseph has been with us and now he leaves, he is still with us, for our spirit is in him. Though he is released from his vows, his spirit remains. Spirit reigns supreme and Joseph's spirit is firmly established. Let those of you who harbor ill feelings, regret or condemnation, meditate on that, for your very own self is in danger by hanging onto those feelings. Polish your mirrors that the true spirit remains to be seen. Thank you."

There was a long silence. Joseph was again impressed with Rancoche's presence. I must carry that light with me wherever I go, thought Joseph.

His white robe was taken from him and he was given a new loin cloth and a camel hair coat. He was allowed to take his staff and a cloth satchel. He was given a leather bottle of fresh water, some cheese and flatbread. The members bade him farewell.

There was some pain in leaving, but no regrets. At his last meal with the commune, Joseph sat with his friends. They gave him their blessing and wished him well. Others, Joseph could sense, harbored ill will and looked away if he turned in their direction. He let them go in peace.

"Stop by when you can," his friend Jesse stated.

"I will if I can," answered Joseph.

"We would love to hear about the outside world from one who has lived among us. It would be refreshing to hear it from someone who understood our point of view," said another.

"I will," said Joseph.

The afternoon was well underway when Joseph placed his bowl, his leather water bottle and quilted cloth in the pack he was given for his journey. His friends walked him to the gate. Rancoche was nowhere to be seen. Rancoche would be all right, Joseph knew, but others would be bereaved. For to loose a member was a calamitous event. The community's existence depended on keeping members. No child had ever been born in the community.

Joseph walked through the gate looking back at his friends as he stepped forward onto the path to Gabatha. He walked away, seeing that the gatekeeper's eyes were full of tears. There was nothing more that he could say or do to ease their pain. The sun beat down, but Joseph didn't notice. He was on his way.

The sun was on a downward slope and Joseph knew that he had to walk fast to get to Gabatha before nightfall. As always, it was dangerous to be on the road alone at night. Bandits and thieves preyed on lone travelers. Fear and elation accompanied Joseph's every step. The world was open, fresh, new. The unknown was there. The miles passed, almost as if by magic. Freedom was here and now.

Over the dust on the road and glimmer of the sun the outline of buildings rose from the earth. In the forms pressing up from the earth, Joseph saw the Goddess and Mary as if joined in one being. They are calling to me, Joseph thought. His steps sped up. This new-found energy delighted Joseph. He accepted it with pleasure.

At Gabatha, Joseph asked direction of an old man, humped over a basket full of whips. "Could you give me directions to Salem's house?" Joseph asked.

"If you buy one of these fine whips, sir, I will walk you there."

"I have no need of a whip," laughed Joseph. "I have neither home, nor bed. A stable or an animal is far more than I have ever owned."

"For a friend. Buy it for a friend."

"That's a thought," said Joseph.

"Take a look at this one, see the tip, it's a pig's penis. It's a fine whip, supple yet strong."

"That's very nice, I can see, but alas I have no money either, so your talk is wasted."

With that the old man placed the whip back in the basket. Pointing to a large house at the center of the village, he said, "It's that one, the largest house in town. And you say you have no money. I don't believe you!"

Joseph smiled. "Well, sir, believe as you will, this world is a strange place. Farewell."

Joseph approached the heavy wooden door. By the brass hinges and metal furnishings, Joseph could see that this was the house of a wealthy man. Mary's father, Joachim, was a wealthy man. Wouldn't they be friends, both traders? Joseph knocked.

A young woman opened the door.

"Ah, you must be Joseph. We are expecting you. Mary says you have business with her father."

"Well, I am sure I have some business to attend to with her father. It will be soon enough I assure you. What is your name?"

"Rachel. I will go fetch Mary. Please come in."

Joseph entered, admiring the fine workmanship of the door. It was not unlike the carpentry work he had done for the monastery, but the wood was of a better quality. He had seldom been able to use metal parts. How much stronger to use metal for hinges than the large wooden bolts he had made.

Mary came running to the door, and Joseph's heart leaped. "Oh Joseph, I am so glad to see you! Please come to the courtyard. We have wine and fruit. You must be tired after your trip."

"Actually, I feel rather good," Joseph said.

"Come, come," said Rachel.

In the garden, Joseph was introduced to a white-haired man, short and stout, with a well fed, but harried look on his face. "This is my father, Salem," said Rachel.

"Glad to meet you, Salem," said Joseph. There was a confidence about Salem that Joseph admired. He wished he had it. But, then questioning himself, Joseph thought, I think I do have that, but I am not familiar with it yet.

Joseph shook Salem's hand and was led by him to a table well stocked with baskets of fruit and jars of wine. "Please, Joseph, eat," said Salem.

Everyone ate. All of it was good. Joseph drank a little wine, but he was careful not to drink too much as he was not used to it. Feeling elated and welcome, Joseph talked quite freely, but did not divulge his and Mary's secret. The goat and chicken Joseph had eaten lay heavy on his stomach.

After dinner, Mary led Joseph to a corner where they could talk. "Please, Joseph, do not talk too much. I have been discreet, and they have not pried, though they must suspect something. So, please do not say more than you need to. Talk about the monastery."

"All right, Mary. Do not worry."

(3)

A Wedding Condoned

It was only later that evening that Mary and Joseph had some time alone. Dinner and the mandatory banter were now over. In a quiet corner of Salem's courtyard Mary and Joseph spoke softly.

"Joseph, I know you are concerned about my family, what they know or don't know. But you needn't worry; I can handle my father. He knows I am pregnant. I told him. But he suspects you will not return with me. Your coming will be a surprise. He let me come to get you, thank God."

"So, my coming home with you is going to create a difficult situation."

"Yes, but don't worry. What will my father do? He loves me! When I tell him you came willingly, he will be glad to let us marry. How else will he get out of this situation?" She took Joseph's hand and led him to a stone bench. "Sit Joseph. Now listen. I have my father's approval. He agreed to talk to my mother while I was on this trip. So, that will be done. Consider this! He does know you. We have both known you since childhood. It's not like you're some interloper, someone he doesn't know at all. Look what you bring to our family, your carpentry skills and all your knowledge of the Essenes which my father loves dearly."

"But I have no other worldly skills or knowledge."

"Joseph, Father has used benches and chairs you've made. He has eaten on the grand dining table at Qumran. He was impressed that you made it. When I remind him of your skills he will see the benefit of having you around. Joseph, I think your carpentry skills can provide us a good life. Don't you?"

"Keep talking, you may convince me."

Mary could see the hope in Joseph's dark eyes. She thought of them as mongrel because they weren't a solid brown, there was a touch of blue-green in them. "Just keep listening, Joseph. You are the youngest Master Carpenter ever at the community. You were relieved of other duties because your carpentry skills were so valued. You have a special talent for wood. Right?"

"Right."

"So, count on it. Believe me, Father has plenty of carpentry work to be done. None of my brothers have the skill you have. You will be valuable. Think of his stables. There's enough work for several men."

"I would like working in the stables. That sounds good."

"See!"

"Thank you, Mary. Your confidence is reassuring. I have fallen into a new world, while you are still in yours. Inside the community I knew what I was doing, I knew my place. Out here, I know nothing."

"You'll learn."

"I hope so. What about money? I have no means to pay your father."

"You'll pay him with your work. Remember, he's a wealthy man. He doesn't need money."

"What about your mother? She doesn't know me."

"She'll be fine. She won't take the unexpected as well as Father, but with his consent, she'll be fine."

"Your brothers and sisters?"

"My brothers will object. But again, they can argue, but my Father's word is final."

"We'll have to marry soon, won't we, before you begin to show?"

"Yes Joseph, we will. Remember Joseph, Father loves the Essenes. Although he could never live that life, he admires it.

Just think of the pleasure he will have, asking you questions, discussing spiritual matters."

"That I can believe. He has always loved coming to Qumran, staying longer than necessary, speaking with the headmaster. I think this will be my pass into his good graces. There will be no one in Nazareth with the training I have."

"Now you're talking Joseph. I like to see this confidence in you."

"Thank you Mary. I do not wish to bring any shame to your household. I want to be an asset."

"You will. You will. I must be off to bed. We have talked long enough. I'll see you in the morning. The traders I came with will be passing through on their return tomorrow. We'll ride with them. Hadar will be looking for me by the well. We'll have plenty of time to talk on the trip. Good night, Joseph."

"Good night, Mary."

As she left, Mary squeezed Joseph's hand tightly. He returned the squeeze. Mary was glad to be off to bed, for traveling alone, unmarried, was bad enough; being alone with Joseph was really pushing the limit. Mary settled in on her mat in the daughter's quarters.

Joseph had been given the guest room. This house was plush, compared to what he was used to. He watched through the doorway as the fires in the courtyard died down. Through the small window he saw the full moon. His heart filled, thinking of all that had transpired. He felt, despite his troubles, that God was with him.

Joseph drifted off to sleep and dreamed. He dreamed that Mary gave birth to a son. He taught his son the ways of the Essenes: their esoteric mystical understanding, their code of conduct, their prayers and meditation. He saw his son sitting across evening fires, discussing all that he was learning. He taught his son to read and write, to think for himself. Joseph told his son, "I could not live the letter of the law, but I will teach you the spirit of the law."

Suddenly, the dream changed. He saw his son being taunted

by crowds, beaten and flogged. He saw him, dragged to a cross and nailed on it. Joseph woke, a scream in his throat. Sweat flowed from every pore. He lay there, unable to move, wondering what could have brought such a terrible image. Guilt? His guilt? Could a father pass on such a fate because of his failures? No, thought Joseph, I will teach him to be careful, true but wise. This dream is to remind me to teach my son humility, to praise God and not himself. With this comforting thought, Joseph was able to fall back to sleep.

In the morning, after eating breakfast with Salem's family, Mary and Joseph walked to the well to wait. They sat in the shade of a small tree. It was hard for Joseph not to touch Mary. She would soon be his, but this was a public place. Joseph looked into Mary's face, lovingly, longingly, and she returned the gaze.

It was close to noon when they spotted the caravan, single file, spilling over the ridge of a hill. They waited excitedly until the caravan stopped at the well. Young boys used as camel drivers were the first down from the camels. They fought playfully over the water bucket, spilling and splashing. Mary watched the boys with pleasure. If her dream were true, she would have a boy soon. She hoped her boy would be just as joyful and carefree.

Mary approached the well where Hadar leaned against the edge, drinking from a leather bucket.

"Hadar," she exclaimed, "I am here!" Hadar looked over the bucket, squinting his eyes. His tanned skin wrinkled at the corners of his eyes.

"Ah, I see that it is you, Mary. Does your father approve of these excursions, traveling by yourself?"

"Hadar, you know very well my father does not approve, but he tolerates. All fathers should be more tolerant. Don't you think?" Mary gave Hadar a disarming wink, nodding her head to suggest his response.

"No, I don't think so, or I would have young girls along with me, like these boys, traveling up and down the Silk Road. Can you imagine the troubles I'd have? No, I think you women should be kept at home so that you don't end up in the hands of someone like me." A broad smile crossed his face.

"And you, Hadar, are such a terrible boss, such a pain to work for. I can see how these boys are burdened and beaten down. Would you treat me worse? Look, they are free as birds. You just think you own them. They're just out for a caravan ride, taking advantage of you! They don't even consider this work and think you're a fool to bring them along.

"Ah, you are so right, Mary! I thank God every night that I don't have a daughter like you! If I were your father I would already be dead and turning in my grave."

"Lucky for you Hadar that you only have to put up with me when I travel with you. My poor father always has me with him, even if only on his mind." Mary placed her hand on Hadar's shoulder and gave it a tight squeeze. "I have a friend that will be traveling with me back to Nazareth, his name is Joseph." Joseph stepped forward extending his hand.

"Glad to meet you," said Hadar.

"Glad to meet you," said Joseph.

"Do you have business with Mary's father?"

"In a way yes," said Joseph.

"Oh, I see. You have business with Mary," Hadar said with a smile.

"Quite right. I see you are a man of insight."

"Enough of this talk," said Mary. Let's get on our way."

"Before I move from here, Mary, you must tell me, is this someone you intend to marry?"

"Yes Hadar, now can we go?"

Hadar pulled Mary aside. "You know girl, you do not show enough respect for your father. It should be he, not you, bringing some man home."

"Yes, yes, Hadar. But, what about the heart. Isn't the heart important?"

"What of a woman's heart? Aren't you bought and sold just like camels? And you, you should fetch a high price."

"You are an insult to all women. You should be sent to China and left there!" Mary kicked sand with her foot at one of the camels. The camel moved away from her, making a huffing sound. "I have no price. My father would never sell me. It would break his heart."

Suddenly Joseph spoke up. "I am her price. She has chosen me. I will work for her father till he is paid off."

Hadar was surprised that Joseph spoke. He did not know this well-built young man, with strong pronounced features. Hadar did not want to get involved in a dispute with him. He loved to tease Mary, but he did not want this to get out of hand.

"Come Joseph," said Hadar "Take your woman and let's go. You can handle her I am sure." With these words, Hadar settled the conversation. Mary seemed satisfied with his acceptance of Joseph.

Approval having been won, Mary and Joseph got on one of the camels, a female, laden with goods. Nazareth was a day's journey away. Mary wanted to arrive as soon as possible. At this point, every day mattered. She wanted to have her marriage arranged before she began to show. Mary knew that Hadar did not want to stop long at mid day. There was another watering hole they needed to reach before nightfall.

The sun beat down relentlessly. The camels swayed side to side as if hypnotized by the sand and sun. Their pace never varied, their gaze fixed on the horizon. Mary and Joseph sat together, Mary in front and Joseph behind. Joseph kept his hand around Mary's waist, and spoke to her quietly, seeing mostly the back of her head. He found her hair arousing, sensuous, feminine. He smelled his armpits and hoped that he wasn't too offensive. He reassured himself that Mary was sweating too. He could smell her. Yet the smell was delicious. Everything about her was appealing, especially her confidence, which had disarmed him. He found himself unable to worry and marveled at her ability to calm him.

"Joseph, when we get to Nazareth, I want you to wait for me

at the market, by the well. I will speak with my father, make sure
I have his approval and then come get you."

"I guess there's nothing for me to do but wait. You waited for
me. I see no problem in waiting for you. Do you really think you
will get his approval so quickly?"

"I am sure of it. What can he do? He's a liberal man—well
traveled. He knows our customs are not common elsewhere. He
appreciates other ways."

"Very well, I will wait for you at the market. I will even sleep
there if it takes you longer than you think."

"Thank you Joseph. Your trust in me gives me strength."

How Mary could get strength from him, Joseph could not
understand. He had failed in so many ways. But he was glad she
felt it, for he certainly felt hers.

A breeze was stirring as the caravan arrived at Nazareth. Mary
dismounted near the outskirts of town close to her father's property. Joseph remained with the caravan which headed for the well.
Joseph looked forward to walking the streets of his new environment. He knew he might very well spend the rest of his life here.

Mary approached her home, smiling at the thought of her
father's response. She carried a parcel full of spices with her, a
goodwill gesture from Hadar. Mary passed her mother, grinding
wheat in the yard. Neither said a word. Her mother did not approve of Mary's travels. She never had. And this time, Mary had
taken off on her own. To her, this was a commoner's behavior,
nothing a woman of class would do. Mary thought her father had
spoken to her mother, but she couldn't tell.

Mary spoke with her sisters long enough to feel free to slip off and
speak to Joachim alone. They said nothing either, but their smiles
gave Mary confidence that her father had kept his part of the bargain.
They knew. Her mother had avoided joining the conversation with
her sisters, but excitement was in the air.

It was now late afternoon when Mary wandered off in the direction of her father's stables where he spent most of his time. She
found him in his tent, working on his accounts.

"Father?"

"Oh, Mary, I'm so glad to see you back safely. Did your trip go well? Did you meet with Joseph?"

"Very well. I must tell you all about it."

"I'm all ears. What have you got to say?"

"I told you that I would get Joseph's approval. I have!"

Now Joachim's brow furrowed and he put down his quill. He decided to give Mary a hard time.

"Speak child, what did Joseph say?"

"He agreed to marry me. Did you keep your part of the bargain?"

"Yes. What did you expect?"

"How was mother with that?"

"Well, she wanted to know where was our say in this? You know it is my prerogative to find a husband for you."

"Yes Father, I know the custom. But I am in love with Joseph. He is the man I want to marry. I am pregnant and he has agreed to marry me."

"Joseph the Essene monk, who has taken vows of chastity, now agrees to marry you. I must say, you are a lucky girl?"

"He has already broken his vows. You know that. You needn't give me such a hard time. He says he will marry me."

"A monk is going to marry you? Who would have ever thought? On your own you have found a man, with no help or input from me. And now you ask for my stamp of approval."

"But this is a man I know you respect. You know him, you have seen his carpentry work. His skills will make a good living and benefit you."

"Now that's a thought! A benefit for me. Let me see. What about payment? Have you thought of that?"

"I do not have a price, Father! I would rather live alone."

"How is this monk, ignorant of the ways of the world, going to take care of you? So he has some skills. He's been living in an isolated environment, saying prayers, meditating. What besides carpentry does he have to offer?"

"You forget, Father. This is a man who can read and calculate. He is quite well educated. That's more than you can say for most of our neighbors."

"That is true," he said, shrugging his shoulders and standing up. "What prestige will he bring to our family?"

"Why, religious prestige. The Essenes are well respected."

"You know the Essenes take a vow of poverty and that they hold everything in common. He will only have the clothes on his back."

"Yes, but he will work for you to make up for his lack."

"That's to be expected."

"Joseph is only twenty-five years old. There is plenty of time for him to learn your business and be an asset. He will bring you his carpentry skills, which are better than any I see around here. You already agreed. Why are you giving me such a lecture?"

"Because you deserve it. Tell me more about the benefits."

"You have seen his work at the monastery. You have sat on benches and eaten on tables he has made. Remember how you commented on his wooden hinges, how fine they were?"

"Yes, I remember."

"Father, think of all you will be able to discuss with him. Remember how you like to talk with the monks. How you always overstay when you go to Qumran. You will have someone steeped in the tradition, right here, under your own roof."

Joachim sat. He was tired of this barrage. He had always had trouble keeping Mary in line, or getting her to change her mind. She was just too persuasive.

Mary could see that her Father was latching onto the possibilities she had presented. Joachim sat a long time before he answered. Mary knew that she had convinced him that this was not a rash decision, even though she was already pregnant. Joseph did indeed have much to offer the family.

"Your words are convincing, Mary. I cannot argue with your logic. You are of age. Joseph is of age. You have just relieved me of a burden. Choosing a man for you has not been something I ever felt would be easy. Though I love you very much, you are a difficult child, independent, stubborn, strong-headed. I have often sat, arguing with myself, how I could make this decision for you. Now, you have taken this burden from me. Has Joseph left the community?"

"He has already left. He is here in Nazareth. Did you tell mother? From their treatment of me today since I got home, I believe you have."

"Yes I told her. She thought this falling in love was pure delusion. She feels slighted."

"Did you tell her how we met again, when he was here a month ago, teaching on the outskirts of town?"

"Yes. We spoke and discussed these matters. I told her you could want no other man, that you would be a good wife to him. She struggled with the idea, but she is resigned. But, I am not sure I like having a daughter who talks monks into leaving the monastery. Where is this man?"

"He waits at the market for your approval."

"Truly, I will be glad to see you married. Let someone else try and keep you in line."

"He will."

"Mary, you have my blessing. Go fetch him. Bring him here." He knew Mary was strong-headed, but not rash. He had raised her in a more liberal fashion than was customary and this was the price. Now, with this situation, Joachim trusted his daughter. There was not much more he could do. His job was done. At least, Joseph could be of use around the stables. Good carpenters were hard to find.

"Mary, we'll make a room for him. I will announce the wedding tonight at supper."

"Thank you, Father!" Mary gave Joachim a long happy hug. "You will not regret this, Father."

Mary walked and skipped to the marketplace. Suddenly she realized that she had not skipped anywhere in a long time. As she approached the market, she looked at her clothes and realized she had not bathed since she got home. She smelled, and her clothes were sticking to her. Oh well, she thought, Joseph won't look much better. She looked forward to supper, for the wedding would be announced.

(4)

The Wedding Feast

Mary walked briskly toward the market. As she thought of seeing Joseph again, her pace quickened. The patchouli oil mixed with her other scents as she broke into a sweat. She didn't mind, Joseph had told her the smell of her skin was arousing. She couldn't wait to be married so she could sleep with him again. She began to sing a traditional love song she had known since childhood. It made a lot more sense to her now. The longing was hers.

As she neared the market, she saw Joseph running toward her. She ran too, falling into his arms. Heads may have turned, but Mary didn't notice. Nor did she care. She had a Father sanctioned relationship now! Nothing could stop them. Holding hands, they strolled, in no hurry, to her father's home.

As they approached the house, Mary's sisters came running across the yard to greet them. They wanted to get a closer look at Joseph now that he was going to be a member of the family. They could speak now, of what they had heard in Mary's absence. Her sisters had barely disguised their knowledge earlier, now they were ecstatic. Mary had returned from Qumran with a man! At least her dad had broken the news to them, making Mary seem a proper daughter.

The sisters were all smiles, gesturing to one another. Sarena was holding her hand over her mouth, staring at Joseph, making him uncomfortable. He smiled politely in return.

"I'm Joseph," he said.

"Glad to have you here," said Julia, the oldest sister.

They all gathered round, pressing in on Joseph. The attention made Joseph blush. He could feel his ears getting hot and his armpits starting to run.

"Come Joseph," said Mary, "let's go meet the rest."

Joseph followed obediently. Anne, Mary's mother approached. She was not smiling. She was a small woman with a stern face and her brows were creased. "Is this the man who is to be my Son-in-law?"

"Yes he is. Meet Joseph."

Anne made a slight bow, her hair falling forward over her shoulders. Mary could see that the bow was restrained. Her mother's eyes were downcast. "I don't like being the last to know," she said.

"I'm sorry, Mother. But I had to keep it a secret till Joseph was sure he would leave the monastery."

"Oh, I see," said Anne. "Seems rather hurried to me." Turning to Joseph, she said, "Pleased to meet you, Joseph. This is a bit of a surprise to me, but Mary has never ceased to surprise me. I'm sure she'll have a few surprises for you."

"She's had a few surprises for me already," said Joseph.

"My life has never been the same," Anne said, "not since the day she was born. My what a precocious child! Always wanting and getting her way. Why if Joachim wasn't so doting, she'd have been married off a long time ago."

"Oh, I see," said Joseph. "Well, I'm glad she waited. I can't imagine marrying anyone else. You do realize that Mary and I have known each other since childhood?"

"How's that?"

"From her visits at Qumran. We're not entirely unknown to each other."

"Well I'm glad of that. I thought Mary had just recently picked you up at the market."

"Well, in fact she did, but we've been working on this for a long time." Joseph was hoping to ease Anne's concern. He wasn't sure how good he was doing because he wasn't used to being in social situations with women. "How much have you been told about me?"

"Little to nothing, really."

"May I bring you up to date?"

Mary gave Joseph a disapproving look. "Why don't you come with me? We have other's to meet."

Joseph ignored Mary and continued speaking. "I'm from the Essene Community, originally from Bethlehem. I was orphaned as a small boy and the Essenes took me in. I've been the community's master carpenter for a number of years—a trade I learned from my father."

"Well that sounds promising," said Anne, for the first time smiling. "Joachim could use a good carpenter. Lot's of work here with all this livestock. I'm just glad we have the stables now, so we don't have the animals in the courtyard under foot. I'm pleased you have a trade. What's your lineage?"

"I'm of the lineage of David. I don't think you could have a problem with that!"

Anne smiled. Joseph could see that he was doing well and was pleased with himself. He saw Mary giving him another angry look, but he kept on talking.

"I can make almost anything from wood. I can calculate angles, squares and circumferences. I've made tables, chairs, even wheels." Anne put her arm around Joseph's waist and directed him to a corner of the room.

"Sit down, tell me more."

Mary gave Joseph a final disgusted look and stormed off to another part of the house, looking for her father. Not finding him anywhere near, she went to the stables. He was watching his caretakers mending leather harnesses, tending the horses and camels.

"Father! Mother has cornered Joseph and is asking him all kinds of questions. He's telling her everything!"

Turning to Mary with a smile, Joachim said, "Is that so?"

"Yes, and I don't like it."

"Well Mary, you have just turned this household on its head and you wish to complain? Dear child, I think your anger is a little out of order."

Mary stood staring at him, pouting her lips, thinking.

"Sit down Mary, let me tell you something."

"All right. But you can't keep me from being angry with Joseph." Mary sat on a bench near where her father stood.

"Earlier this week you announced to me that you wanted to marry, and that you had the man already picked out. Now, that is contrary to our custom and you know it. It is I, the father, who is supposed to decide when and whom his daughter is to marry. This has not been the case. But, you and I have had a special understanding for a long time—a relationship that gives your mother grief. I've not treated you in a typical manner. In fact, I've let you have privileges usually accorded only to me. I've treated you more like a son than a daughter."

"Yes Father. That's true. But haven't I deserved it?"

"I don't know if deserve is the right word. You've been very independent and strong headed for a girl. I've just let you get away with it. You always pleaded and begged me to take you with me everywhere, even on those trips to Qumran. You, riding horses and camels, hanging around the men instead of your mother. As much as I've enjoyed your company, you've been very hard on us both. Especially on your mother. You have never really been a daughter to her."

"But Father, I've just followed my heart."

"That's reserved for me. In another family, you would have been held under lock and key, not catered to. So, you should have a little consideration. I could ask you what you thought you were doing to put our family in this position, but I won't. However, your mother, who has never met this man, has the right to get acquainted with him. Believe me Mary, she will be much easier to deal with if you leave her be."

Mary sat for a long while considering the wisdom of her father. Finally she answered. "You are right. I have little justification for being so irritated. I'm just afraid Joseph will say something which he will later regret."

"I think Joseph can take care of himself, Mary. Remember, he has had to fend for himself since he was very young. I am sure living in the community was not easy. And there were few opportunities for him to talk with women. Give him his day in the sun."

"Thank you, Father. You have been most kind. I am a lucky woman. I will always be grateful to you." Mary got up from the bench and went to Joachim, giving him a warm embrace. They held each other for a long time.

"It's all right Mary. You have always been a joy for me."

"Father, I want the wedding to be soon."

"You see, one thing solved and you throw another at me. It's no wonder your mother has fits!"

"How soon can we have the wedding?"

"Well, let's see. There are messengers to be sent, people to invite, travel time, purchases to be made. How soon are you asking?"

"Next week."

"Next week?"

"Yes."

Joachim stepped back and began to pace, stepping around a mound of camel dung. Finally, without asking for more time, he said, "All right."

Mary jumped up from the wooden bench and gave her father another hug. "You're the sweetest Father in the world."

"Now you see Mary. It is good that your mother is spending time talking with Joseph. She will feel much more familiar with him and a wedding next week will not be so unpalatable. Please, be kind to your mother and patient with Joseph."

"Yes, Father, you have my word."

"Your word is good, my child. Now go. I need to finish here."

Mary danced off, much happier than she had been. She was ecstatic to have a wedding date. Someday, Mary thought, I could run a trading business. I'm as good a deal maker as my dad. Short of that, I could certainly help Joseph run a carpentry business. He has the carpentry skills and I have the business and negotiating skills. Together we could run a business and raise a wonderful son. A girl was out of the question, hadn't her dream foretold a son?

When Mary arrived back at the house, Joseph was still talking with her mother and sisters. It seemed that Anne was enthralled. But this time, Mary was not concerned. As her Father had said, this would break the ice with Anne, and the wedding date was set. Mary sat next to her sister, Ruth, and listened. There was nothing she hadn't heard already. She sat quietly for awhile and then set about preparing supper. This was the least she could do.

It was after dark when supper was ready. Her brother Canaan lit the oil lamps. When everyone was seated around the table, Joachim stood and said, "I have an announcement to make."

All eyes were upon him. "Joseph and Mary are engaged with my approval. The wedding will take place next week."

Several gasps were heard. Mary tensed a little, wondering what would happen next. But silence reigned. Finally, Joachim said, "The speed of this wedding may be a surprise to you. Nevertheless, I have known Joseph since he was a child, and so has Mary. They have been friends for years. That Joseph would leave the monastery to marry is a surprise, but that he has chosen Mary is not. I have much business to do next month. A quick wedding will be necessary. Let's eat."

Mary was impressed with how her father passed over the major issues and took responsibility for the quick wedding. No one would dare challenge his reasoning. With Father's admonition, everyone started to eat. As the food was passed and people began to chat, Joseph relaxed and dared look at Mary. She was smiling. This was all the reassurance Joseph needed. He ate too. After a while, the conversation picked up, much to his relief. Mary gave Joseph a wink, and Joseph smiled back. "The food is good," he said. To himself, Joseph thought, Mary is quite some woman. I can see that she is used to getting her way. How will I keep up with her? At least I don't need to worry that I won't have guidance. She always seems to know what she wants.

The meal went smoothly which pleased Mary very much. Her

father hadn't had to field a bunch of questions. Her brothers' silence was telling, but they didn't bring up any concerns at the table. This was good. Joachim gave Mary a knowing smile and she returned it. Mary knew that Joachim would have to do some fast talking with Mom tonight. But at least she wouldn't have to listen. Mary knew that though her mother would protest the suddenness of the marriage, there was nothing she could do about it. Her father's word was law.

Mary went to bed with her sisters. Mary longed to be with Joseph, but the longing was sweet and hopeful. At least she didn't have long to wait. Mary slept soundly.

Later the next day, Joachim informed Mary that he had spoken with her brothers and they had decided the terms of Joseph's staying on with the household. Joseph would have to work for Joachim for three years at half pay and would have no financial interest in the family business. Joseph would have to make his own way.

"If he proves himself useful, after three years we can make other arrangements. Fair?"

"Yes, Father, that seems fair."

Joachim didn't tell Mary that her brothers were happy to see her married. They actually were looking forward to seeing Mary under some man's wings. They didn't envy Joseph, for they knew what a tough job lay ahead of him. None of them would wish to marry a woman such as her. Now she could bother Joseph and leave them alone.

For the rest of the week the women were very busy. There were many things that needed to be done, passing out the word at the marketplace, at the well, to traders in town. Messengers were sent to the relatives nearby. Food was purchased and prepared. Surprisingly, by the end of the week, all was ready and the wedding took place. There were at least a hundred people there, friends, guests and relatives. No one said a word about the hurriedness of the arrangement, for Joachim had brushed it all aside.

A week later, Mary and Joseph were settled into a room of

their own, and life returned to normal. Joseph went to work for
Joachim, and Mary's mother, to her surprise, seemed happy with
her choice. Joseph was a serious and hard worker, taking responsibility easily and quickly. Soon, most of the repairs needed around
the house and stables were complete and Joseph was able to take
on extra work. Half the proceeds went to Joachim. The added
income more than made up for the new addition to the family.
The benches, tables, chairs and animal troughs that Joseph
made were singular and unique. There was pride of workmanship
and creativity evident in each piece. The other stable hands quickly
accepted Joseph and came to him with the problems they had
with wooden structures.

Mary settled into her marriage much better than Joachim or
Anne expected. Mary, the precocious child, sometimes wild, seemed
to be the consummate wife, dallying over Joseph's affairs and helping Anne as best she could. She even began to treat her sisters as
equals, which surprised Joachim and Anne immensely. Even friends
at the well and market marveled at the change in Mary. As she
began to show, no one spoke a word about the suddenness of her
pregnancy.

Joachim was very pleased with his decision to allow Mary's
marriage. He felt that he had gotten a good bargain for himself.
Often he had wondered how he would find a man that could
handle her. For she had been more than a handful for him. All in
all, Joachim and the rest of the family, got along well with the new
member. Even Mary seemed to get along better with everyone.
Business was going well for Joachim, except for the tax collectors,
who could be harsh at times. There was talk in the town of a new
tax incentive that had Joachim worried.

As the months passed and Mary grew larger, she told Joseph of
her dreams the night she stayed at Qumran. Joseph told her his
dream of the Goddess. He also told her about the nightmare he'd
had, where he saw his son being hung on a cross. But Mary brushed
that aside saying, "That was not in my dreams, and why should

such a thing happen to our Son? No, we will raise him well. He will not have the death of a criminal."

Mary enjoyed being pregnant and with the foresight of her dreams, had great hope and confidence. She believed what her dreams foretold, that her son would bring joy and wisdom to the world. Several times, Mary went to visit her cousin Elizabeth and her husband, Zechariah. He was a priest and minister to the people, a good and wise man. Like Mary, Zechariah had a vision. It was an angel which appeared to him and told him that Elizabeth would conceive and bear a child. Zechariah objected saying she was "too old." But the angel brushed his disbelief aside and told him that he "would have a son and that he would be called John, a preacher to the lost of Israel. He would lead many of the people of Israel back to the Lord. He would clear the way for righteousness and repentance, a sign of what was to come."

Mary had heard this story before she had slept with Joseph. She had wondered if such a vision could come true. But Elizabeth had in fact become large with child, and Mary believed that dreams and visions could come true. So Mary too was confident in her dreams, her vision of what was to be for her and her baby. Mary told Elizabeth her dreams from Qumran, and Elizabeth believed, for though she had been a skeptic, and had mocked Zechariah, she was now full with child and could no longer doubt. Elizabeth told Mary to keep her and Joseph's dreams to themselves, for telling would bring much attention and cause problems. Mary felt that Elizabeth was right and she promised Elizabeth that she would keep her dreams and visions secret. "The Lord's time will come," she told Elizabeth, "I do not need to forecast it." Mary and Elizabeth got on their knees and thanked God together for what he had given them.

In the evenings, before bed, Joseph began to teach Mary how to meditate. He explained some of the teachings he had received from the headmaster at Qumran. "These are rare and powerful teachings," he told her, "they come from the Far East." Mary did her best and meditation became a silent bond between them. Mary admired Joseph's knowledge and training. She felt that she had received a man who was far advanced spiritually for his age, one who would bless her and her child.

Over time, though Joseph did not tell Mary of the secret aspects of the esoteric knowledge, he could see that Mary was picking it up, simply from being with him and meditating. This pleased Joseph very much. For he wanted Mary to know everything he knew, except for the privileged secrets he had vowed never to reveal.

There was talk in the village that King Herod would soon call for a registration of the whole Roman world. The rumor was that everyone would have to go to the place of his birth to register. This would mean a great deal of hardship for many people, especially those who no longer lived in the town of their birth. For Joseph, this meant that he would have to go to Bethlehem. He discussed this with Mary. Her response had been, "Where you go, I go. I am not going to have this baby away from you."

Mary checked the rumors out with Joachim. He said everything he heard from the tax collectors was that the rumor was true. So Mary prepared to go with Joseph, though everyone begged her to stay. Still, Mary hoped that Jesus would be born before the great registration, for the baby was due soon. Mary passed her days, hoping that the rumor was untrue, and that she could have her baby at home, with Joseph and her family.

(5)

Mary, The Gypsy And The Wise Men

Joseph began to hear rumors that Emperor Augustus was about to decree that everyone must return to their home towns and register. Joseph was quite concerned and sought out Joachim. He found him, talking with a stable hand, looking at a camel with a bad leg. As Joseph approached, Joachim turned to him.

"How do feel about eating camel for the next couple of weeks?"

"That would be all right with me. Haven't had any recently."

"Well, this old camel's gone lame. She's no good for travel and I can't sell her."

Changing the subject, Joseph asked, "Have you heard the talk about a registration for everyone?"

"Oh yes, I have. The tax collectors are quite pleased. They should all be getting bonuses soon."

"What do you mean?"

"Well, we have a few good laws. One of them is that a traveler cannot be taxed outside his home town. But a lot of people have been staying away from home and avoiding taxes. Rome doesn't even know where they are. If they can get everyone to go home for the registration, taxes can be collected while getting a head count. It'll be hard on the people, but Rome and the tax collectors will be happy."

"I see," said Joseph. "But do realize that I will have to go to Bethlehem and I may miss the birth of my son?"

"Oh, you're going to have a son. Are you sure?"

"I believe so."

"I've thought about your situation. You'll have to talk with Mary about it. I know she won't be happy."

Joseph left and found Mary grinding wheat. "Have you heard," he asked, "about the registration?"

"I've heard rumors. Nothing more."

"Well, your father thinks it's coming, and maybe soon. The tax collectors know all about it."

"It means you'll have to go to Bethlehem. I'll go with you."

"But Mary, that's three days away. Look at you! Why we could end up having our baby on the road!"

"So be it. I'm not having the baby here, without you. God is with us. I feel it in my heart. Whatever happens, God will protect us."

Joseph didn't argue any further. He knew Mary well. He went back to the stalls he was working on. He prayed that their baby would be born before the registration was announced.

Within the week, word came that the decree was made. Joseph, being from Bethlehem, knew he would have to go there. He spoke with Mary, but she would hear nothing of remaining behind. In her ninth month, she felt very close to Joseph and wanted to be with him. Joseph, despite his reluctance, made ready to take her with him. Mary, for her part, was not put off by the difficulty. Some things you just put up with. She felt Joseph would manage, and that if the baby were born on the trip, they could handle it. She was certain that God had introduced her to Joseph. The child of their union was protected. Her faith was strong.

Joachim helped with arrangements. Mary and Joseph would lead a small caravan to Bethlehem. He gave them two camels and four donkeys for their trip. He suggested taking spices and pottery to Bethlehem, so they could make a profit. Mary did not object.

Joseph had not been back to Bethlehem since his childhood and was anxious. He had no way of knowing if any of his relatives would still be there. He doubted he would know them. Fondly, he remembered playing with his cousins, but they were children then, now they would be grown.

Joachim's backing for their trip helped alleviate some of Joseph's fears. He knew that the money they would make from the sale of goods would help pay any taxes. Joachim let Mary and Joseph know, that if need be, they could use all the profits made to pay taxes. But he didn't think Joseph would have to pay, for he had lived his whole life in the commune at Qumran and had no land or property to speak of.

On a hot windy day, with Mary riding a donkey, the small group set off for Bethlehem. The roads were full of people traveling to their homes of origin. It seemed to Joseph that the whole world was traveling. It was a hot and sticky three days journey. Mary struggled to stay comfortable, and though she complained to Joseph, she did not wish that she had stayed behind. They made it to Bethlehem without major difficulty. Joseph knew he was lucky that Mary was tough, and full of faith.

In Bethlehem, Joseph searched for hours looking for a place to stay. There was none to be found. Weary, covered with dirt and sweat, he returned to Mary and the group, empty handed. "There is no place left," he said. "All the rooms are full!"

"We'll make do," said Mary. "Don't worry. Even if I have to sleep in the street with the animals, I will manage."

Joseph, encouraged by Mary's statement, said, "Thank you." The men gave them forlorn looks.

Mary said, "Why don't you look for a stable where we can feed the animals? At least they won't get stolen."

Joseph was not pleased with this, but he could think of nothing else. "Very well, Mary, I will look for a stable."

Joseph spent the rest of the day searching for a stable. He did find one, though the price was steep. For the extra money, the owner told them they could sleep in the stable with the animals. Joseph was only too pleased at the proposition. It was the best offer he'd had all day. He paid the owner and returned to Mary. "This was all I could find, he said."

"It'll do," said Mary. "I have slept with animals on the road before. I can do it now."

"What if you give birth tonight?" said Joseph. "What a sorry place to have a child."

"Don't, Joseph," said Mary, "God is with us, appearances can be deceiving."

With these words Joseph accepted the situation and led the group through the dusty town to the stable he had found. There was a pile of fresh straw in one corner, so Joseph and the men made separate areas for them to sleep. Soon, the weary travelers were laying on their blankets on fresh straw. It was passable.

"This is all right," Mary whispered. "The fresh smell of straw is wonderful! Smell it, Joseph. Forget the rest."

Joseph took Mary's advice and settled in to sleep. He thanked God that he had found such a strong and pleasant wife. He prayed that he would have the goods sold and the taxes paid the next day. Maybe, they could get back to Nazareth before Mary had the baby. With this thought in mind, Joseph fell fast asleep.

Mary lay beside Joseph and tried to sleep, but sleep would not come. The vision she had seen nine months prior, at Qumran, returned. It was so clear in her mind that she felt as if the vision were happening now. She felt her womb tighten and release. She had experienced this occasionally for several weeks. But now, the contractions were stronger, and more frequent. As the pressure grew, Mary prayed that all would go well. It was the middle of the night when she could ignore the pain no longer. She leaned over and shook Joseph. "Joseph, the time is here. Our baby is coming."

Joseph woke with a start. "What?"

"The time is now. The baby is coming!"

Joseph sat up. Mary took his hand and placed it on her stomach. Joseph could feel the tightness of her womb. He got up and went to their bundle. He lit a lamp and pulled the swaddling clothes Mary had packed from the bundle. Returning, he placed the cloth on a fresh pile of straw. He saw Mary's face in the lamplight, straining. He wished he could do more.

Mary strained as the baby burst into the world. She gave a great sigh of relief. Joseph immediately saw the veins in her neck and forehead relax and disappear. The baby lay between her legs. It was over.

Mary reminded Joseph that he needed to take his knife and cut the umbilical cord. Joseph, having attended the birth of animals, knew what to do.

"Go ahead, cut the cord!" Said Mary.

Joseph did as he was told. Then he picked up the baby, and saw that it was a boy.

"It's a boy, Mary," he said, holding it in the lamplight.

Mary smiled, "A boy! His name will be Jesus. My dream is fulfilled!"

Joseph knelt in awe at the miracle he had just witnessed. A strong sense came over him that he was part of a process, a grand mystery. Though he was the biological father, he knew he was not the ultimate father. The baby sputtered and gasped for air, but did not cry. His breathing settled and his body relaxed. He looked the image of serenity. Joseph placed the baby in Mary's arms and embraced them both. Mary's eyes were full of a joy, a bliss Joseph had never seen.

Joseph returned to their bundle and brought a jug of fresh water. With one of the swaddling cloths he helped Mary wash the baby clean.

"What a serene expression," said Joseph.

"Truly a child who can bring peace," said Mary. "Like in my vision."

Mary and Joseph looked at each other, acknowledging that this must truly be the work of God. They rejoiced that they were chosen to be the parents of this healthy, wonderful promise.

An hour or so later, Mary and Joseph had checked every part of the new baby and each had held him many times. Mary placed the newborn at her breast. The baby Jesus nuzzled her nipple for several minutes without much interest. Then, suddenly, as instinct kicked in, he made a snorting sound and began sucking with gusto. It surprised Joseph to see the force of nature so displayed. Mary held Jesus to her breast, enjoying the freshness of his skin. He fell asleep. Mary lay awake with the baby sleeping next to her. Mary and Joseph's eyes met and Mary could see tears running down Joseph's cheeks.

Neither Joseph nor Mary got any sleep during the rest of the night. Morning came and the stable woke. Cocks crowed, a donkey brayed, and the men, sleeping in another corner woke, rubbing their eyes. Mary took her baby outside for some fresh air. She also wanted to see him in the daylight. Finding a stone bench by the side of the road, she sat down. She watched the travelers passing by. No one noticed that the world had changed.

Joseph left for the market to sell their goods. Mary was still sitting on the bench as Joseph turned a corner and was out of sight. Up the road came a Gypsy woman carrying a water pouch. She stopped at the nearby well. In mid motion, leaning over the well, the Gypsy lady noticed Mary and the baby. She stood still. Then she dropped her water pouch to the ground and came over to where Mary sat. She stared at the baby.

"Forgive me, woman, but I must tell you, your baby is surrounded by a blazing white aura. It covers both of you. Do you see it?"

Mary looked up at the dark haired woman. She noticed her dark luminous eyes and the carved ivory hanging from her ears and the beaded necklaces around her throat. "No, dear woman, I do not. I am not one who can see these things. But I have heard that some people do."

"Oh, dear one, the aura of this child is the brightest I have ever seen! Your child must be truly blessed."

Mary was thrilled to hear these words, but she did not know what to say.

"Tell me," said the Gypsy. "Have you had dreams or visions concerning this child?"

"Oh, yes I have," responded Mary. "Wonderful visions."

The Gypsy moved to Mary's side and sat down. She looked intently into Jesus' face. "Dear woman, please tell me your vision."

Mary hesitated a moment, this was a stranger asking these

questions. But the sincerity of the woman's inquiry melted Mary's concern. She hadn't spoken to a woman in three days and this was the first woman with which she could share her child. "My first vision occurred nine month ago, just after I knew I was with child."

"Pray tell me more. This child is surely special!"

"In a dream I saw my father, and a voice came out to him from a cloud. 'Blessed are you for you have a daughter in whom I am well pleased. She will have a son of the Most High and he will be a blessing to the world. And the world will rejoice and be lifted up by his presence.' And then my husband appeared in my dream and an angel came to him and said, 'You will have a son of the Most High, and he will be counted among the wisest of the wise. And he will be a healer among men, the world will rejoice that he is born.'"

"Yes, yes, I believe you, dear woman, for your child's aura is like the sun!"

"And then three magi came to me, worshiping the child. They told me they had followed a star from the East searching for a child, an enlightened soul that would bring many to an understanding of God. And there were also shepherds who saw angels telling of his birth, and they came to me also, and worshiped my son."

The Gypsy woman covered her mouth in amazement. Finally she spoke. "The three magi and the shepherds are with my caravan! Your vision is prophetic! Your child is the one! You see, we have been on a long search, following a star to find a great spiritual leader promised to us. During the last two weeks, the star changed course and led us here. A group of shepherds recently joined us, telling us that one of them had seen a vision in which angels appeared, announcing an important birth. I must go quickly to tell the magi that I have found the child whose birth was foretold. Pray tell, where will I find you when I return?"

"I am staying with my husband in the stable across the street. My baby was born there just last night."

Before leaving, the Gypsy gazed at the baby for a long time.

She gently touched his forehead with her index finger. "I will see you later today, dear woman. The wise men will want to see you. They can see auras too. They will verify my seeing this. I doubt they have ever seen an aura like this!"

The Gypsy left and Mary was alone in her amazement. She drifted back to the time when she went to Joseph at Qumran. She thought of the precarious predicament in which she had found herself. If Joseph had denied her and refused to marry, she might have been stoned. Now she was with her newborn, and he was already having visitors from afar. How could things have turned out so well? Looking at Jesus, she looked for the light, the aura, but saw nothing. Many travelers passed by, none of them noticed either. She waited for the Gypsy to return with the wise men, for she had heard that they could see special things, such as auras, read the stars, people's palms, and follow omens.

Mary knew that people from the Far East often passed through Jerusalem. It fell along the Silk Road and was a popular trading area. People with special talents performed. Some had rare and exotic animals which did tricks for money. Traveling musicians attracted great crowds. Mary had often traveled, watching the stars that her father pointed out, using them as guides. For Mary, the magi following a new star, taking it as a sign of a new birth, was not altogether strange.

Mary made several trips to the stable for water and to check on her belongings. There were many people coming and going. She had the men keep the animals away from her corner of the stable. She wanted to keep it free of animal dung.

About mid-afternoon, Mary saw the Gypsy woman riding a camel coming her way. Behind her, a small caravan of weary travelers straggled along. As they came to the place where Mary sat, they gathered into a group along side the road. Mary observed the unusual bridles, saddles and blankets. She could tell that this caravan had come from afar. The leaders, several older oriental looking men, dismounted with the help of several young boys. They approached Mary reverently.

The foreign-looking men bowed before Mary holding their palms together. Straightening up, the taller of the three men spoke.

"Dear blessed woman, we have come to look at this newborn child. We have been traveling for many months, following a star that appeared in our sky. We are spiritual elders from a land far from here, in the Himalayas. A land your holy book refers to as 'the land of milk and honey.' We come from a monastery in Kashmir."

"Very well," said Mary, "Have a look." She was in awe that these dignified men from afar were stopping to see her. The men looked at Jesus, smiling, especially the tall one.

"Many years ago our great Lama died. A conference of our wisest and most learned priests convened and meditated on where our great leader would reincarnate. They determined that he would be born in a far away land, and that a new star would appear to guide the way. We have been waiting a long time. We believe your child is he!"

Mary gasped, "Do you think so? This is beyond belief!"

"Not so dear woman, for I see a great light, shining around your child. And so do they," he said, pointing to the other two elders. They smiled at Mary.

"We have watched the stars for years, and last year, in the early Spring, one of our elder astrologers spotted a new star. Within a week it began to move. We were chosen to follow it and it has brought us here. In our country we often search for a reincarnated leader, but never before have we followed a star, nor traveled so far."

"I am very much in awe of your story," said Mary. "It seems so wondrous, and you have come so far. But how can I be sure that what you say is true?"

"The Gypsy has told us that you had a vision concerning this child. Is it not so?"

"It is so."

"And did you not see in the vision that your son would be a great spiritual leader?"

"Yes, that is what the vision appeared to show."

"There is no doubt in our minds that this is so. Once in Israel, the star headed straight for Jerusalem. As that is the seat of learning here, we thought surely, the child would be there. But, several days ago, from Jerusalem, we saw the star was hovering at a distance, lower to the ground over this valley. We spoke with several religious elders about our search and inquired as to what town was in this valley. The told us, Bethlehem. They informed us, they too, were expecting a messiah to be born, of the lineage of David, and that Bethlehem was the town of David. Does this mean anything to you?"

"Yes, what you say is true. A messiah is to be born, a king of the Jews. And he is to be born in Bethlehem. But surely, my son is not to be the King of the Jews?"

"Maybe more than that. A great spiritual leader perhaps?"

"I would like that better. My visions were more along that line."

"May I have a closer look?"

"Yes," said Mary, as the tall gentleman leaned forward. She unwrapped some of the swaddling clothes. The other two men also stepped closer. All three bowed before the child and then knelt before him. The eldest of the three men, small with very white hair and a flowing ochre colored robe, stared at the baby. He spoke excitedly to the other two in a language that Mary could not understand. The Gypsy who had stayed back until now, stepped forward and said, "These men also, can see the light of your child. You need not be afraid. They can see that your son is the reincarnation of a great Lama."

The tall one spoke again to Mary. "Your child is the reincarnation of our great Lama, Sri Tautoga Rancoche who died several years ago. We have been guided to you and your child. Now we can return to our monastery and report that we have found our master."

"Tell me again Sir, where are you from?"

"We are from Hemis, in an area known as Ladakh, in the land

of Kashmir. We are emissaries from a monastery close to a town called Leh. I am telling you this so that you may know where to send your son when he is older. You may tell him of our visit and give him directions."

Mary was overwhelmed with this information and would have been frightened, but these events were so in line with her dreams at Qumran, that she felt this must be true. Seeing her unease, the tall one continued.

"Dear woman, we do not ask you to give up your child now. You have been chosen to be his mother. It is your task to raise him. By divine revelation, you have been chosen to raise him. We only ask that you tell him of our visit. When he is ready, he will come."

"That is reassuring," said Mary.

"We trust the divine revelation and your choice as a mother. We only convey to you the knowledge that your son is destined to be a great leader of men, a wise man, a healer, an enlightened teacher. He is destined to teach us as well.

"We will send an emissary from time to time to check up on this child. So please, take note of our names and from whence we come, so that you will know who has visited you. When the child is of age, if he asks, you may send him to us. There is no force needed, for this is destiny." Holding up his arms, the tall man pulled a parcel from under his coat. "We have a map here, it's on a leather scroll in India ink. It is a map to our monastery. Our names and the way to our territory is well marked. We give it to you today. It will be returned to us by your son when he comes."

"I will keep it for him," said Mary.

"Very well. But, tell no one what you have heard today or show them the map."

"But I must tell my husband. We are as one."

"Very well, keep this among the two of you, but no others. Take good care of the scroll and give it to your son when he is ready."

The tall one gave Mary a small wooden box. He showed her that inside was the scroll. He bowed again with the others. The

Gypsy woman then stepped forward and touched the baby Jesus'
forehead with her index finger. Noticing Mary's concern, she said,
"Dear woman, your child has a blazing white light. I touch the
place where the light emerges on his forehead. The light is confirmed by master, Kyopo Swadami, the head of the Dukpa
Kargyupa. Your child is destined to be an enlightened master. I
have touched his forehead as he will someday see the third eye.
You are truly blessed."

Mary took this all in. She placed the wooden box beside her.
"Guard the scroll well," said the Gypsy. "Your son may have
need of it one day."

The third gentleman that had not spoken, motioned with his
finger to one of the young boys tending the lead camel. The boy
approached with a woven bag, bulging at the seams. The boy handed
the bag to the man and stepped back. The man opened the bag,
showing Mary that it contained gifts, gold, frankincense and myrrh.
"For you, my child," he said, "to keep him safe."

Mary took the gifts. "Thank you," she said.

The tall one spoke again. "There is one last thing before we
leave. While in Jerusalem, we were approached by a messenger
from the King. Apparently, the elders with whom we spoke, informed your king of our quest. Being one enamored with astrologers, he had sent his messenger to us with a request. He asked if
this leader we were looking for could be called the 'messiah' of
which your books prophesy. We told him that we did not know.
The messenger told us that, if we found this child, we were to
report back to the King and let him know where this child was
found. We do not believe your King Herod is to be trusted, so we
do not intend to return by way of Jerusalem. We feel you should
be aware of this."

"No, you should not report what you have seen," said Mary.
"Neither that you have found a child, nor that we are from
Bethlehem. Please, do not return by way of Jerusalem, but go
directly home. I fear my child may be in danger!"

"That we guessed, dear woman. Your request is granted. In

order to pose as little danger as possible, we will tarry no longer, but be on our way. We are satisfied."

Before the wise men departed, the shepherds came forward and knelt before Mary and her baby. One by one, clasping their hands in a display of worship, each one blessed him and returned to the caravan. When the last shepherd had paid his respects, the members of the caravan mounted and were quickly on their way. Mary watched them as they fell out of sight. She could see that they were headed away from Jerusalem.

Mary was full of awe and amazement. She knew that she truly was blessed and that her child was one who would bring great things to the world. She thanked God in the silence of her heart.

(6)

The Trip to Alexandria

Joseph found buyers at the market for the spices and pottery. With the money, he felt confident that he could take care of any taxes due. He set off for the tax collectors tents, set up at one corner of the marketplace. It was noisy and hot. Dust was constantly being churned up by the crowds. He heard a lot of yelling and screaming as many people were aghast at the amount of taxes they owed. Many had stayed away from home for years to avoid taxes. Now they had to pay.

Joseph entered the line at the tent where everyone had to register. When he got through that line, he was sent to another tent to pay.

"You Sir. Where have you been living?"

"At the monastery in Qumran," Joseph replied.

"And what have you in the way of assets?"

"I have none. Only my robe, these sandals, my staff and pouch."

"Ah, so we have a monk here, do we?"

"Yes."

"You like that life?"

"Yes."

"Good for you. I like an honest, simple man. I see that Qumran keeps all property in common. It is taxed as a unit. Therefore, I do not believe you owe us anything."

"Thank you, Sir," said Joseph.

"Next!"

Joseph was greatly relieved, a three-day trip, but no taxes. He was registered and could go home. He returned immediately to the stable. He found Mary sitting on the bench. He told her of his success in selling the goods and registering with the tax collectors.

"And I have something to tell you," Mary said.

"What's that?"

"A gypsy woman saw Jesus' aura, she brought monks from the Far East. They claimed Jesus was the reincarnation of their Lama. Look at this! A map with directions to Kashmir. They left it for us to give Jesus when he is older."

Joseph was amazed. They discussed the events in hushed tones, Mary going over everything that had happened in Joseph's absence. When Mary showed him the gold and rare scents, he was frightened. "We must leave at once, Mary. We could be robbed!" They agreed to tell no one and leave Bethlehem at once. Joseph walked briskly to the stable, paid what was due and gathered his men. He was nervous being in a strange town with the gold, but mostly he was afraid that the wise men may have been followed.

Within an hour they were on the road. Three days later they arrived back in Nazareth. Joachim was pleased that the trip had brought a profit. "You have performed better than I expected," Joachim exclaimed.

"Thank you," said Joseph.

On the eighth day, as was the custom, Mary and Joseph took Jesus to the temple to be circumcised. Joseph wanted his first son designated as holy to the Lord, as was common. As Mary and Joseph entered the temple an old man who was there saw the baby. He approached Mary and Joseph, and dropping to his knees, prayed aloud.

"Lord, now you can dismiss your servant in peace, for I have seen your face. As you promised me in a vision, I would not die till I had seen one that would be a light unto the Jews and the gentiles alike. Glory be to the God of Israel. The light of this child fulfills your vow to me, Lord. Now I may go home to die in peace."

The old man turned to Mary, "Dear woman, this child is to be a light and a revelation to all the world. Sweet woman, your child is appointed to bring a message that will cause the rise and fall of many in Israel. For there will be much debate and dispute over the message this one brings. And you, dear mother, will feel as if your very heart were pierced. The thoughts and hearts of many will be revealed.

"Who are you?" Mary asked.

"I am Simeon. I came here from Jerusalem to finalize my affairs. My wish is to be righteous, and fearing God, I came to set my affairs right with my children. Here I came to pray and let God be the judge of what I have done. When I saw your child, there was a light shining around him and I heard a voice saying, "Here is the one, here is he of whom I spoke to you in a vision. So, out of the joy of my heart, I knelt before you, your child and God. I am at peace now. Take care that you raise this child well, for he will bless many."

Mary and Joseph were amazed and frightened at this spontaneous outburst. What kind of child was this that evoked such spontaneous occurrences? "How will I protect this child?" Mary thought. "Even now he is noticed and praised by strangers." Before she had collected her thoughts, a woman rose, advanced in years, and spoke.

"Oh, Lord, my God, I am blessed to be here today and see this child. I have waited many years, even without a husband, for this day. But you Lord, you have not forsaken me, for I am now in your presence." Turning to Mary, she said. "Praise God for this child who will one day bring wisdom beyond his years, even to these guardians of the temple." The old woman approached all who came to the temple, telling them of the presence of a child who would one day preach to all the people of the world, a wondrous and powerful message.

Mary and Joseph stepped forward and asked the priest to hurry, as they were frightened by this attention. The priest performed the circumcision and blessed the child, officially recording his name as Jesus. On their way out, Mary asked the gatekeeper, "Who is this woman that speaks so about my child?"

"That is Hannah, the prophetess, the daughter of Phanuel. She is a widow who prays day and night to be reunited with her husband. She claims that the Lord will not let her die till she sees his son. She spends day and night here at the temple praying. She praises the Lord ceaselessly and begs for him to take her. Believe me, if this woman tells a thing, such as what she has said today, believe her, for she is wise and has prophesied many times before."

Having named her son, Jesus, as in her dream, and having dedicated him to God, Mary was satisfied. Joseph too was pleased. But they were both wary of the unexpected recognition of their son. Joseph was especially concerned that Simeon would return to Jerusalem and tell of their son. Joseph feared that should King Herod hear of these proclamations, he might send soldiers to kill Jesus. For Herod was known to be jealous, cruel, and ruthless towards anyone that might threaten his throne.

Joseph knew that Herod, not being a Jew, was not even allowed in the temple. But he was powerful and had contacts among the priesthood. Mary and Joseph determined to pay close attention to any word coming from Jerusalem. If any threatening news came their way, they decided that they would leave Israel for Egypt.

Mary and Joseph settled back into life on Joachim's estate. Mary worked with her sisters while tending Jesus and Joseph worked as the chief carpenter under Joachim's watchful eye. Jesus grew and Mary saw that Jesus was a precocious child, much as she had been. She spent a great deal of time telling him stories, stories from the Torah and also the traditional folk tales. Sometimes Mary made up stories that related to the visions she had at Qumran. She wanted to instill in Jesus the portent of what her dreams had revealed to her.

Mary was careful though, not to tell Jesus directly of her visions, nor of the Gypsy woman, nor of the wise men and shepherds. She knew a time would come when he would be ready. Mary did not speak of Jesus' light, but she did tell him that some people did see light emanating from people, that the light could be different colors. She told him, "Some people have a gift to see

JESUS OF INDIA 75

these colors. The color, hue and shape, shows a person's nature. Sometimes, a white or yellow light is seen around people of a deeply spiritual nature."

As time passed and Jesus grew, word came from Jerusalem that King Herod was searching for the Messiah. In the marketplace, rumor had it that Herod had sent emissaries to Bethlehem, asking the whereabouts of a child, one visited by wise men from the East. It had been some time since Mary and Joseph had worried that danger was immanent. But now they were frightened again. Mary went to her father and spoke to him of her fear. Joachim calmed them both, stating that he would provide a caravan for them to travel to Egypt. Twice a year Joachim sent goods to the Jewish community there and he would gladly send them along.

Mary and Joseph prepared to go. The choice of Egypt was confirmed by a dream Joseph had. An angel appeared in the dream saying, "Joseph. King Herod is going to kill all the first born male children under the age of two in Bethlehem. Rise, take your child and his mother and flee to Egypt. For Herod is furious that the wise men did not return by way of Jerusalem and inform him of Jesus' birth and location."

Mary and Joseph, having seen how their dreams foretold the future, did not hesitate once Joseph had this dream. They worked diligently and quickly with Joachim and soon had the goods and camels ready. A caravan on its way to Alexandria was coming through soon. Mary and Joseph would join it.

Jesus was now two years old. Mary was still nursing him, so there would not be a problem with food. She felt Jesus would be able to travel safely. Joseph, though he liked Joachim very much, was glad for the opportunity to be out from under his shadow. Mary was even more pleased to be able to get away from her mother. Anne was just far too traditional for her taste. She had the audacity to tell Mary how to raise Jesus. That was more than Mary could stand.

Joseph had heard that Alexandria was an exciting and stimulating city. Being interested in esoteric teachings, he had always

7-ENTW

wanted to go there. That an opportunity had arisen was like a dream come true. He knew there was a large population of exiled Jews there. Although they spoke a different dialect of Aramaic, he did not think that would be much of a problem. They would manage. Joseph was now quite confident that he could make a living anywhere with his carpentry skills.

Mary liked to travel and she had not done so to any great extent since Jesus was born. As caravans of traders plied through town, Mary and Joseph asked many questions, especially about the Jewish community in Alexandria. The answers were encouraging, for they were told that the Jews in Egypt were highly regarded and protected. They were some of the biggest traders and merchants there.

Joachim soon had a caravan of local traders organized. Several caravans on their way to Egypt stopped and were glad to join with the local group for the rest of their journey. Caravans of large groups often traveled together for there was safety in numbers. When all was ready, Mary and Joseph had a quiet send off, not wishing to draw attention to their reason for leaving. Joachim told everyone that Joseph and his family were going as business emissaries. This was not unheard of and no one was the wiser.

Early one morning, as dawn broke over the horizon, four caravans, now joined as one, took off down the route through Ascalon, the shortest route to Egypt. Mary and Joseph were well placed to maintain some independence from the other traders as they had their own camels and donkeys. They were responsible for their own animals. Joseph knew that his carpentry skills would be of value to the caravan, as well as to locals in the towns and villages where they would camp.

On the first few days of the trip, Jesus had difficulty adjusting. He didn't like being stuck on the camel's back all day. Mary kept him on her lap much of the time, keeping him occupied with songs and stories. Mary's legs sometimes went to sleep, and she struggled to hold Jesus and change position at the same time. But, for the most part, they got into a routine that they both could live with.

The sun was scorching, and often they went days without a bath. The smells were sometimes overwhelming, but then they were often very pleasant as well. It was the sand that was the most tiring, for it was everywhere. It stuck to the sweat on their skin and could only be washed off at river crossings which were few. Meanwhile, the days passed. Mary made some clay figures for Jesus to play with, which he loved very much. He was soon making up his own stories, telling them to Mary.

When the caravan stopped at night, Mary took walks with Jesus and encouraged him to run. There were a few other children on the trip, and they and Jesus were soon fast friends. Sometimes the caravan stopped for several days. They all bathed frequently, enjoying the time on the ground. Some traders reached their destination and left the group, while other traders joined the caravan. During the stops, Joseph plied his trade, fixing plows, yokes and wheels. Once he did a small house project. Joseph paid close attention to the various woodworking techniques he encountered. He kept a scroll of notes, and drew pictures of new and interesting tools and joining methods.

Some areas they traveled through had been settled for many hundreds of years. Joseph found beautiful wood carvings at religious shrines and temples. He learned about the pagan gods depicted and watched ceremonies when he could. Mentally, he looked for the common ground with his own religion. He and Mary spent many evenings discussing religion, its ramifications, source and result.

The main trading route of the Silk Road ran close to the sea coast. Several times Mary and Joseph were able to take Jesus to the shore and let him wade in the water. They enjoyed the sea very much and loved seeing Jesus' enjoyment of it. They were awed by its vastness. It made them feel close to God.

Mary and Joseph were impressed with how intensely Jesus saw things. His reactions were immediate and his perceptions original. His perspective on things, and his comments, often made them think. Jesus loved laying in the sand, looking at the sky or sitting and staring at the distant horizon. One day, he pointed out to Mary that the caravan resembled a rope. "A living rope, made up of people and animals."

"Yes," she said.

"See how every living thing is joined, moving together. Camels, donkeys, dogs and even monkeys, all in this rope, moving as one. This is the biggest living rope I have ever seen!"

Mary laughed. She was very proud of the analogy Jesus had made. She told Jesus that the monkeys were from a distant land called India. "I would like to go there some day," said Jesus.

"Maybe you will," she answered.

Later, Mary told Joseph about Jesus' remarks about the living rope. "He does have a way with words," she said.

"Yes, Mary, he does," answered Joseph.

As the weeks progressed, members of the caravan changed. By the time they crossed into Egypt, Mary and Joseph were old-timers. It seemed like an eternity had passed when they finally reached the city of Alexandria. As it rose over the horizon, it seemed huge compared to Jerusalem. Once closer, the variety of buildings and design showed a great conglomeration of cultures. They passed great temples, the Sphinx, the pyramids. It was wondrous. They found the Jewish quarter and made their tent. Soon, Joseph had work, and not long after that he bought a small shop on a busy street. The family settled in behind the shop and home was now in Egypt.

(7)

Alexandria

Alexandria was a godsend as far as Mary and Joseph were concerned. Since there were no close family relations here, had they not been such independent individuals, it might have been much harder. However, the large community of Jews in Alexandria provided much needed support. Mary and Joseph, having come from the holy land, were well received and well liked.

Alexandria, as Joseph and Mary found it, was approximately 300 years old. The city had been laid out by Alexander the Great after his conquest of Egypt. Because of the Greek influence, the Jews in Alexandria had been introduced to Greek culture and literature. Both the Egyptians and the Jews absorbed much of the Greek culture. Hellenistic philosophy and religion were known and of considerable influence.

One of the things that Mary and Joseph found desirable about Alexandria was that it was a seaport. Alexander The Great had created the port by turning a small village, between Lake Mareotis and the sea, into a highly productive port.

Alexander's workmen had laid a strip of land about a mile long between the shore and the small island of Pharos. This created a sea break with relatively quiet seas on either side. Soon Alexandria was the most productive port in this corner of the world. Sailors from all the known world landed here, staying for brief or long periods of time. Traffic from Africa, Europe and Asia was heavy. This cosmopolitan effect brought tolerance of different cultures to the city.

On Pharos' Island, the first lighthouse in the entire world had been built. It was almost 500 feet tall and could be seen at sea, miles from shore. There were white marble columns standing on each successive story, with balustrades and statues as ornaments. It was called by some, one of the seven wonders of the world. Jesus, as he grew older, was able to walk the entire strip of land that led out to the lighthouse. It was thrilling to see the strange sea fish caught by the men fishing from its banks. Sailors of many nations came ashore and were accommodated by both the natives and members of their own nationality. Over time, groups of foreigners had made enclaves which catered to their own likes and dislikes. Due to the heavy volume of trade, the Egyptians were quite tolerant of foreigners and let them practice their respective religions. One eighth of the population was Jewish and the Jews had their own section of the city, where Joseph and Mary felt quite at home. Mary and Joseph did not flounder, but prospered in this new land.

In time, Joseph and Jesus explored the city. They quickly became familiar with its streets and quarters. Predominant groups lived and carried out their lives in particular quarters, according to their own customs and culture. Joseph made sure that Jesus was open and tolerant of the different cultures and encouraged him to visit these other areas of the city. Jesus, being the precocious child he was, did not need much encouragement. The city of Alexandria covered about fifteen square miles and had a central avenue, five miles long. Five different sections of the city could be reached by traveling down this one central avenue. It was more than one-hundred feet wide and Joseph and Jesus loved to walk it's length. Jesus, even on his own, found it easy to get around. Every kind of hawker and trader had his wares laid out on mats, tables or baskets. The sellers yelled at passers by to stop and look.

The "Body Quarter" was so named, because it was here that the body of the Great Alexander was buried. It was also the most highly developed and prosperous section of the city. Here, the Royal Mausoleum stood, which housed the embalmed body of Alexander. One day Joseph and Jesus visited the Mausoleum. Seeing the place where such a great man's body lay, Jesus gained a sense of history, a feeling for the long term effects of a great leader. Conquerors, he thought, had a tremendous effect on the lands they conquered. What about spiritual leaders? Did they have the same effect? Jesus took this all in and pondered these things deeply.

There were many large edifices, buildings and walls in Alexandria at this time. The city was known for its magnificence and beauty. Over a period of time, Joseph took Jesus to see the Royal Palace, the Temple of Neptune, the Great Theater, the Gymnasium and the sprawling magnificent Necropolis. Jesus wondered what caused such magnificence to be created.

The Museum interested Joseph and Jesus the most. This was unlike anything Jesus had ever seen for it was not a place where the past was locked up and displayed, but a place of active learning. Here, teachers, the most learned of the time, taught students from all over the world. They taught the fine arts, philosophy, and religion. There were plays in an outdoor theater and literature readings. Cartographers gave lessons in geography and mapmaking.

Having been there once, Jesus went back often. Even though others thought he was too young to be interested in such talk, they tolerated him because of his enthusiasm and intensity. He was not afraid to ask questions.

Alexandria at this time had one of the most respected libraries in all the world. Its halls and rooms were filled with manuscripts from all over the world. It contained texts from Greece, Rome, Asia Minor, Palestine and even India. Maps, even of Antarctica, where on display. Eventually, Jesus was able to worm his way into the library by befriending teachers at the Museum. Even at his young age people in his adopted city responded to his intelligence and grace. In discussing this very young man, people would shake their heads, thinking, I don't know why I make exceptions for this boy.

But Jesus learned early to step forward, to ask questions and speak his mind. He was not at all shy. Sometimes Joseph would have to go looking for Jesus as he did not come home. Usually,

Joseph would find him, deeply involved in listening to some great teacher speaking on the public steps of the Library, the Museum or some other place of learning in the city.

Alexandria, was often compared to Rome. Although Rome was bigger and therefore the greatest city in the world, Alexandria was known as the philosophical and intellectual capital of the world. For Mary, Joseph and Jesus, this made Alexandria the most precious city in the World. Compared to the towns and cities in Israel, Alexandria was a giant of intellectual freedom.

The tolerance and freedom of the people here was a blessing for Jesus; it enabled him to blend, mold and expand his knowledge. His way of looking at the world opened up. As time passed and Jesus grew, he too became tolerant of all kinds of people, those of his race and culture and those of other races and cultures. When he had free time, he explored the streets, the seashore, the markets, the bazaars, but especially those parts of the city where he could listen to the great orators and teachers.

Jesus also spent a good deal of his time helping his mother and father, running errands and doing chores around the house. He was learning a good deal about his father's carpentry, but this was not one of Jesus' main interests. There were many things for Jesus to do, but listening and asking questions on philosophical and religious matters was his greatest pleasure.

Joseph's business was prospering. But business came easily to the Jewish quarter of the city. The Ptolemys had favored the Jews for their business and trading abilities. Being a busy seaport, the business acumen of the Jews was highly valued. The Jews were given their own special quarter in the city and operated their businesses there. In fact, an eighth of the population was now Jewish and the bulk of the trade ran directly or indirectly through their hands. Many of the Jews were very wealthy, owning their own ships and trading vessels. They imported and exported wheat, wine, gold, precious stones, pottery and all manner of spices. Mary and Joseph were able to help Joachim bring several caravans a year to Egypt and were able to give Joachim advantages in his trades in Alexandria.

The central gathering place of the Jews in Alexandria was the main Jewish Synagogue. It was an immense and imposing building in the center of the Jewish quarter. There were over seventy trade guilds operating from the temple, which made it as much a place of business as a place of worship. Even the Jewish governor came to meetings there and presided over Jewish affairs, only reporting to the Egyptian authorities in response to some inquiry or special problem. Each guild had its own elder and each guild had a bejeweled chair in which to preside over their meetings.

The synagogue was involved in many activities that would later influence much of the world. As Greek was one of the main languages for trade, most of the Jews in Alexandria spoke Greek, and the Hebrew bible was translated into Greek, here in the city. The Jews were very pleased with the spreading of their religious texts and worked to keep the translations pure. But this was impossible, and many unintended nuances and misinterpretations came about. Joseph and Jesus often sat in on discussions of the translations. Jesus learned to appreciate the enormity of the task, and his critical thinking sharpened.

High level interfaith discussions were common. Bazaar keepers and food vendors often ran shops to earn a living, but dealt with the public, primarily to satisfy their delight in observing and discussing intellectual and religious issues.

It was during this time that a new school of thought arose, which tried to blend the Hebrew tradition with that of Greek philosophy. Attempts were made at reinterpreting the Hebrew texts to yield Platonic and Stoic doctrines. But much of this attempt was really a defensive maneuver on the part of the Jewish scholars. They wanted to show that Greek and other gentile religious thought had originated with them. However, in this process, the Greek philosophy infiltrated Jewish thought as well.

It was in this environment that Jesus found himself. Mary was very supportive in all this, and in her quiet way took part in these discussions.

Joseph continued to be amazed at his good fortune in coming

to Egypt. As far as he could determine, there were approximately a quarter of a million Jews living in and around Alexandria. Other larger cities in Egypt also had Jewish communities. There were three Jewish temples in Alexandria alone. So, there was no difficulty in attending services and observing the Jewish rites and holidays. And the Jewish temples were always open and available. Mary and Joseph took Jesus to the Synagogue every Sabbath and many evenings. Jesus learned the Jewish traditions, enlightened by Jesus' father, who had rather different views than those of more traditional Jews, especially the Pharisees and Sadducees.

As Jesus grew older, Joseph took great pains to show Jesus how and why his views differed from the typical Jewish traditions. Mary and Joseph continued to take Jesus to the many local museums, art markets and even to the great pyramids. All of the religious variety was explored. Alexandria at that time provided an awesome scope for awareness of other views. With Mary and Joseph as parents, Jesus was allowed unusual openness and liberty to listen, explore and come up with his own conclusions and insights.

Mary and Joseph watched Jesus grow to young adulthood. They prospered. Mary was busy with the home life as her family increased. She carried great influence with the family and she pushed Joseph and Jesus to look out for the rights of others, especially the deploring plight of women. She gave Jesus the freedom to walk the streets, visit the various quarters of the city and the encouragement to learn as many languages as possible.

In time, Jesus had friends in every corner of the city. Although he enjoyed playing with friends his age, everyone recognized that Jesus was far advanced for his age. His intellectual insights were far beyond his young years. So, when he was bored with his friends and their play, Jesus would stop and listen to the teachers, speakers and shop owners talk about their views, beliefs and philosophies.

Had Jesus been older when he arrived in Alexandria, he might not have spent so much time in other quarters. But Jesus had arrived in Alexandria very young, and his parents, although well received, did not have a clan of close relatives to take up their time. So Jesus walked and played where he willed and grew in wisdom and in spirit.

What surprised Mary and Joseph most, was Jesus' great liking for the Buddhists who had several large missionary schools in Alexandria. Jesus loved to go to the Viharas, as they were called, and listen to the ochre colored priests discuss their religion. Initially, Jesus sat outside their school and stopped the monks as they entered and left the academy. Since he was so young, they were not inclined to invite him in to participate in any of their activities. But Jesus' imagination had been captured by these monks: their dress, their simplicity, their smiles. There was just something very different about them. So, he persisted in sitting at their gate and accosting them coming and going, asking questions and countering their answers with sometimes startling insight.

Jesus did not know at the time, that what he was doing, had already become standard practice at most Buddhist schools. That is, one had to wait outside the gate of a monastery and live the life of a monk to gain entrance. This practice was a very simple method for the Buddhists to eliminate those who did not have the patience to take up this form of practice. But, this is exactly what Jesus did.

While his father worked in his carpentry shop making wheels, tables, stools and chairs, and while Mary mended clothes and tended the younger children, Jesus wandered up and down the streets close to their home. As Jesus was a very responsible and careful child, and obviously quite intelligent, neither Mary nor Joseph worried much about him. In fact, when they did want to find him, they went to his usual haunts, which were the churches and synagogues and religious schools in the neighborhood.

(8)

Jesus Reads The Tao

Over time Jesus learned to seek out teachers from the Far East. Among the Far Eastern people that Jesus met were Chinese laborers, sailors and ship Captains. Their calmness, manner of speaking and instruction, were quite different, yet appealing. These men taught by example even when they were not teaching. Who, and what they were, simply came through.

Many of them could not give a name for what they expressed through their presence, but Jesus felt it. Sometimes in conversation, Jesus would hear them refer to the Tao. But when he asked them to describe it, they would say that it could not be put into words, one could only see it's effect. What could be described was not the Tao.

Jesus could relate to this, in a sense, as the Jews did not say the formal name of God openly. That was blasphemy. But the Chinese had a different perspective, perhaps more subtle. It was not that to say the name of God was blasphemy, but that even the best name could not describe the Source. No name was adequate. Besides the Tao, Jesus often heard of an individual, a philosophical, quasi religious leader, named Confucius. He was generally known as having set down a philosophy of social mores, but it was debatable as to whether it was a religion.

So, Jesus did not get all his ideas from books. He sought out spiritual masters. Sometimes, a friendly local who had traveled to China or elsewhere, brought him word of other lands and cultures. However knowledge came, Jesus devoured it. From a Chinese ship captain, Jesus first heard the tenet, "A man should love others as himself and their parents as his own." On questioning, the captain said that the saying was attributed to Lao Tzu.

Some time later, after many discussions, the captain copied down some of the sayings from Lao Tzu and gave them to Jesus. The gentle captain explained that the selection had come from a collection of sayings called, the Tao Te Ching. He explained that many of these old sayings were common Chinese understandings, but that they were often attributed to Lao Tzu, as he had collected them and written them down. The Captain read Jesus the opening passage of the Tao Te Ching.

> The way that can be spoken of
> Is not the constant way;
> The name that can be named
> Is not the constant name
>
> The nameless was the beginning
> of heaven and earth;
> The named was the mother of the myriad creatures.
>
> Hence always rid yourself of desires in order
> to observe its secrets;
> But always allow yourself to have desires in order
> to observe its manifestations.
>
> These two are the same
> But diverge in name as they issue forth.
> Being the same they are called mysteries,
> Mystery upon mystery -
> The gateway of manifold secrets.

"This passage," said the Chinese gentleman, "should keep you thinking for a long time. It's hard for me to believe, that you, so young, and a foreigner, are interested in this. Usually, such subject matter is only of interest to older men."

"Sir," answered Jesus, "If you knew the passion with which I search, you would not question my interest. Even I sometimes, wonder at my obsession with these matters. For me, the search for this kind of knowledge is instinctual. I surprise myself with the questions I ask. I don't even know where they come from."

"Young man. You are truly destined to be a great teacher. May I live to visit here when you are grown."

"You too are blessed," said Jesus, "I intend to spread the truth from any source. And I find this passage a great one. I will study it diligently, and meditate on it."

"Very well," said the captain, "You do that." The seaman got up and took his leave. "I have many duties to attend to before I get this ship headed back to China."

Jesus read the text which had been translated into Greek. Reading Greek was easy, for he had a facility for language that many said was truly exceptional. On his way home, Jesus found a tree in a deserted field, off the beaten path, and sat down under its shade. After putting the text to memory, he began to meditate. Meditation came easily to him after a long walk. Though physically tired, his mind was active.

Since Jesus had been very young, he had learned what his mother had taught him, of prayers and visions and the importance of dreams. If she said there was power and knowledge in prayer, meditation, dreams and visions, it was so. So Jesus was attuned to these things. He thought about his mother and father and how much they encouraged him in his pursuit of spiritual knowledge. Now, under the shade of this wonderful tree, Jesus put his mind to this purpose.

Soon, he was far into his inner self, totally unaware of a separate world. He felt his physical body became one with his mind as he drifted inside. He felt the breeze outside come in—the rustle of leaves and the singing of birds drifted into him. Jesus felt one with the tree, the bird; the bird's song was his song. The breeze was him, as were the leaves rustling in the tree above. He felt himself expand until everything around him was a part of him too. Soon he was in ecstasy. It lasted for hours.

By the time Jesus woke from his altered state, the sun had passed steeply down from the sky. He jumped up and ran home, full of youth and energy. At supper that night Jesus showed the text to his father. Joseph read it, haltingly, and then said the phrases aloud in Aramaic. "This sounds very similar to some of the Gnostic mystery texts I read at Qumran."

"How, tell me how, Father?"

"Well, I can't tell you everything about them, for much of it is secret, but I can help you understand. As you know, we have our standard texts. But there are other texts that are mystical interpretations of these. Interpretations of a wholly different nature. There is a name for them, but for now, I will just call them mystery texts. This is a good name for them, because even at Qumran, this type of text was kept in a secret code. Even numbers have meanings in those writings. This is so the knowledge is kept hidden. The reason is very simple. Back home, people can be stoned for heresy, for interpreting the scriptures in a different way.

"These secret mystery texts speak of mental states that the common man knows nothing about. Very few people experience them other than accidentally. These states, you might say, are like dream states, but they are not terrifying in any way. Much the opposite, they are a kind of knowing ecstasy. When these states come, one senses that one is in touch with the Absolute. One knows, whatever one experiences, absolutely. Yet, when the experience passes, it is a mystery how it happened and what you know you cannot adequately express in words. This text talks about the mystery of the One behind everything. It is the One, always mysterious but that can be known, that this text is talking about."

"Well, Father. As you know, I have been meditating the way you taught me to since I was six. For me, this state is not uncommon. I have been meditating ever since that time and continue to this day. I even meditated on this text today."

"And what did you experience?"

"I experienced a oneness with everything around me! I was not separate from anything: not the tree, not the wind, not the birds, not their songs, nothing was not a part of me! I rose from meditating with a surge of energy which caused me to run all the way home. I still feel full of energy."

"Well, Jesus, you are still very young, maybe your energy is just youthful zest."

"No, father, this is a different kind of energy. It is as if I die and another essence takes me in. Like a silent spring, deep inside that invigorates and whispers secrets."

"Dear child, you are into much more than I could expect from a son your age. I believe you will contribute great things to this world. Your intentions are way beyond your years. The fact that the teachers here offer you training and give you access to their books is beyond anything we could have expected. You are blessed. We are blessed. Someday, you must return this blessing to the world."

"I will, Father. I will."

"Now go fetch water for your mother. I can see that baby Naomi, over there, needs cleaning up."

Jesus ran off to get water from the well. Usually there were a number of women at the well. He might even get to talk to them. Jesus liked talking to the women. They had a different perspective on things that he enjoyed very much.

When he arrived, a gathering of women stood chatting by the well. They were in no hurry to get home to their chores, so they were standing around talking. Jesus stood at the edge of the well and listened. They were complaining about their husbands and their children and all the work they had to do. But they were smiling and laughing while they talked about their troubles.

Jesus said, to no one in particular, "Must be something in the water."

"What?" several of them said, turning in his direction.

"Must be something in the water."

"What do you mean?" said a woman with a child slung on her hip.

"Well, I see a lot of smiles and laughter, all while you are complaining. Must be some laughing potion in the water."

Some of the young girls who had come with their mothers laughed and giggled. Jesus was fun. He said a lot of off beat things that made people laugh. Sometimes though, he said things that upset their mothers.

This time the women just shrugged him off, saying, "Go home to your Mama and tell her not to send you to the well."

"Very well," said Jesus skipping off with his jug of water.

After Jesus helped with the chores and his younger brothers and sisters were all asleep, he stayed up and talked with his mother. He had a very special relationship with her, every bit as good a relationship as he had with his father. They talked about the business, the other children, Jesus' adventures, and what he had learned today. He told her about the text from the Tao he had received and how he had meditated on it and the experience he'd had.

Mary took it all in and although she didn't mention it, she thought again, as she often did, about her visions, the Gypsy lady, and the Wise Men from the East. She was amazed at how Jesus was attracted to the wisdom of the East. She listened and encouraged him.

When Mary saw Joseph blowing out the lamps, she went to bed and sent Jesus to his. Jesus lay awake listening to the night sounds and letting his thoughts drift into the oneness that he was becoming ever more familiar with.

(9)

Jesus Trains At A Buddhist Academy

There was one monk in particular at the Buddhist academy, Sri Sygoroyal, who was Jesus' favorite. He was middle aged, stocky, and stooped in the shoulders. He was approachable, and Jesus had often wished to speak with him. On this particular day, when Jesus tugged at his sleeve, the monk responded.

"Dear child, would you like to walk through the gate and see our academy from the inside?"

"Yes!" said Jesus. And so the monk invited Jesus in.

"I will give you a complete tour. I am tired of seeing you, like a stray dog, hanging around the gate. Maybe if you see what we do here, I can help you decide if this is a place for you."

Jesus was shown the dormitory and the beds, the pond where strange plants floated, the tea room, the garden and its well-manicured sitting area, the bathing pool and the carvings and pictures that hung on the walls. Jesus was astounded by the beauty and simplicity of the place. There were no women here, only men. The monks not in the meditation hall or sitting in small circles talking, were all busy, sweeping, cooking, cleaning, raking and tending the garden. It was a quiet but busy place.

At the end of the tour, Sri Sygoroyal asked Jesus if he would like to study with them and learn to meditate.

"Yes I would," Jesus answered.

"Very well," said the monk, "will you be able to get your father's permission?"

"I believe I can Sir," said Jesus.

"When is a good time to visit with your father?"

"After work, about seven or eight in the evening. Mornings there is no time, but after work my father is quite inclined to talk. That is the best time to approach him."

"Very well child. Come back this evening after supper and I will come with you and speak to your father. But there is one last thing. Instruction here is not free. You will have to work, as you see the others doing, for we maintain this place ourselves. Except for bartering and trade for items we do not make, all our food and utensils are made here. There are no women here to cook. You will have to work in the kitchen to earn your training."

"That's fine with me," said Jesus. "I'll work hard!"

"Well, I guess we have a deal." The monk led Jesus back to the gate. "Good bye, my friend. I'll see you tonight."

"Thank you, Sir," said Jesus, as he skipped off down the street. The street scenes passed quickly as Jesus ran all the way home. Running immediately to his father's shop, he waited for the right moment to approach his father. That time came, when Joseph sat to whittle on a spindle.

"Father," Jesus said, "You know how I like to discuss the various religions with the elders. Well, a monk at the Viharas has asked me to study with them. It is not free. I will earn my training by doing chores for them."

Joseph whittled for a long while before answering. "This is something you really want to do?"

"Yes, Father!"

"Maybe this would be a good thing. At least we would know where you were. As it is, you wander from synagogue to synagogue, to this church and that!"

"Yes, Father. It would be good for me to be in one place. You wouldn't need to worry!"

"Well, do I need to speak with anyone?"

"Yes, there is a monk. His name is Sri Sygoroyal. If I have your permission, I would like to invite him here tonight, after supper. He would like to speak with you."

"That will be fine. I am sure your mother will approve. She will be relieved to know exactly where you are. I suppose, you will get a different type of training there. Something that you are not getting now. This could complement what you have been learning from our priests. I'm sure they have some texts you've never seen before."

"Yes Father. I think this could round out my education. May I bring Sri Sygoroyal here tonight?"

"Yeah. I think that would be a good idea."

After supper, Jesus ran down the streets, still crowded with people. Jesus was amazed at how many people lived on the streets, eating and sleeping there, with no permanent home. He was glad that his father was able to do so well.

At the Viharas, he pounded on the wooden gate, loudly. The gate keeper ushered him in. Shortly, he was walking ahead of Sri Sygoroyal toward his family's home. Jesus was eager for Sri Sygoroyal to meet his parents. He hoped they would approve his entrance into the academy. Jesus' whole family was seated in the one large room behind the shop, lamps lit, waiting. Mary was nursing her youngest child and telling another to quiet down.

Sri Sygoroyal bowed, clasping his hands together. "I am pleased to meet you," he said. "I salute the divine in you."

It warmed Joseph's heart to hear this familiar phrase. He had heard it used by Sri Rancoche, long ago at the Essene Community. Joseph returned the bow and the phrase. He motioned for the monk to have a seat across from him, on the mat on the floor. When the monk was seated, he spoke to Joseph. Jesus could tell that it was difficult for Joseph to understand the monk. He spoke with a heavy accent. The common language was not the one Joseph had grown up with. However, Jesus knew his father would judge the man, not by his use of language, but by his presence and demeanor.

"I was raised in a community somewhat similar to yours," Joseph said. I was taught to meditate as a young child and still do. Meditation is not a common practice for us Jews, but in the Essene community where I grew up, that was accepted. We had a headmaster who brought us teachings from the East."

"I am surprised to hear this. But I am pleased," said Sri Sygoroyal. "The training we offer then, is not so dissimilar to what you yourself have practiced?" said the monk.

"No, I do not believe so."

Jesus listened intently to the conversation without interrupting. He had not explained to the monks that his father knew of similar practices and beliefs. So he listened carefully when his father explained his life as an Essene.

"I was orphaned as a child and was given to a community that was dedicated to God. There were several branches of the sect, some more ascetic than others. All of us took vows to serve God and to lead spiritual lives of service. Knowledge of the truth was our highest priority. I was somewhat more liberal than many and favored a branch called 'Nazarenes.' We wore our hair long and did not shave, but we did not practice the severity of asceticism that some other community's did. I only left the Community to accept the responsibility of caring for my wife." Joseph pointed in Mary's direction.

"You seem to have had some practices very similar to ours," said the monk. "I am pleased. It will not be so strange to your son. He seems to have learned a lot from you."

"Yes, that is true. We Jews have been traders and lenders for many years. So we have always had contacts with other cultures. Also, we have often been the subjects of foreign powers, invaders who have promulgated their ways in our midst. Often, we could not own land or houses, so we have been a people on the move, always looking for a better place to live. So, you find many Jews here in Egypt.

"All of this contact with other groups has made us extremely divisive. Some groups, seeing something of value in a different religion, either adopted the other religion, or adopted their teaching or practice into theirs. The particular group I belonged to had picked up meditation from traders from the Far East. At our community, we appointed a man from Tibet to lead us. We did not agree with everything he taught us, but he was so advanced in wisdom, that he was made the headmaster."

The monk listened to all this and a great smile spread across his face. "Jesus will have no trouble learning with us. You have provided him with a background we do not usually find here. I, too, am from the East, although not Tibet, and would be happy to teach your son all that he is capable of learning."

It was late in the night when the monk left to return to the academy. Joseph and Jesus walked with him back to the school out of respect and appreciation. Joseph, although pleased with the training Jesus had received so far from the Jewish priests, felt that this broadening of Jesus' learning would be of great benefit.

He was also very pleased that he had a son, an oldest son, that had genuine interest in learning all he could of spiritual matters. Joseph looked back in his mind over his life, especially the move to Egypt. He was delighted with how things had turned out. All the pain and struggle seemed to be rewarded.

Once back home, Jesus went to bed. Joseph spoke with Mary of his thoughts and feelings, especially his joy at the promise of Jesus. In whispered tones they talked about the events surrounding his birth. They remembered the visions and what they had seen in person. Mary mentioned the scroll, but Joseph noted that it was not yet time to tell Jesus of it. As usual, Joseph was a little more cautious than Mary. He thought to himself that Jesus had a lot of Mary's traits. This was good. Mary was a competent and responsible wife, yet daring; and the best business partner he could have found.

The next morning, bright and early, Jesus was off to the academy. He was excited and full of energy. Glad to have this opportunity. He had found the priests at the synagogue, too contentious and argumentative. They, he thought, wanted to win arguments more than they wanted to know the truth. Jesus, already, because of his travels and wide exposure to different cultures, did not readily accept anyone's truth. He felt, even in his childish way, that truth was something beyond anything he had yet seen or heard.

Jesus thought about his parents. They appeared much more open and inquisitive than most. They, unlike many, seemed to relate to many people, with an openness which brought them, not only a lot of business, but also a wide variety of friends. Jesus listened to them all. He listened to the arguments in the streets, watched the various groups and their religious leaders, finding many were arrogant and stuck in their own minds. He wanted to be able to move into that which was beyond.

Meditation, which he had learned early, had opened up vast new possibilities, and these Buddhists knew about this. These were teachers that might be able to explain some of the experiences he was having. Jesus pounded on the gate and was let in. A thrill ran through him as he walked onto the grounds. This time he was a student. He vowed to himself that he would work hard and learn all he could. He felt this place was home.

(10)

Work And Meditation

The first thing that Sri Sygoroyal showed Jesus was the tool shed. The monk informed him that "Serving the community will be your first priority. What you will learn here is very valuable to you and the world, therefore, one who is not able to serve is not taught."

Jesus listened intently, saying nothing, but taking it all in. The tool shed had brooms, buckets, wooden shovels, axes and all the tools needed to keep the school clean and functioning. Next, Jesus was taken to the kitchen. "Here you will work every day, carrying water, making tea, cooking vegetables." Jesus looked the kitchen over carefully, taking note of where the various utensils were kept. "Since you have arrived in time for morning prayers and meditation," said the monk, "you may join us in the meditation hall."

Jesus followed the monk to a large room. Thirty or forty men were seated on the floor, legs crossed. Jesus noted that they each held their palms, open faced, on their knees. "You must sit at the back, Jesus. You are the newest member and you are not to draw attention to yourself. I will take a position up front. Wait for me when we are finished. I will take you to the kitchen to help prepare lunch."

"Yes, Sri Sygoroyal." With that, Jesus quietly took his place at one corner of the last row. He mimicked the position of the others, bowed his head and closed his eyes. The monk on the raised wooden platform began to speak.

"We perform these prayers, these mantras, and these chants in order to bring us to the One. However, we must always keep in mind that these words, these mantras, these rituals are fingers pointing to God, they are not God. What we practice are the vehicles to God. Let no one in this room feel that they have achieved anything of consequence simply by being present and performing these rituals.

"As our great teachers have always made clear, all these practices are only fingers pointing at the moon, neither the hand nor the finger is the moon. No hand, no finger, no words, can place your heart in God, for you are already there, though you may not know it. But, these words, mantras, chants and prayers, may open your own inner path to the light which is hidden there. Every one of you in this room is chosen by your dedication to God, to wisdom, to truth. Now let us pray." With that, the leader's voice dropped an octave and Jesus felt the voice as if it came from within his own heart.

"Our Father, of one mind and many aspects, deliver us from the attractions of this world, for the world has led many astray. Forgive us our many transgressions as we pray likewise to do, and leave us not in ignorance, for thine is the power, the glory and the oneness behind all. So it is, for all who know the truth."

Jesus was struck dumb by this wonderful prayer. He had never heard any prayer so succinct, so heartfelt, so perfect. He hoped that he would hear the prayer again. In the silence, however, after the prayer, Jesus remembered the phrases, line by line. He repeated them over and over to himself.

Jesus was caught off-guard when chanting began. The words were not in a language Jesus understood. As he listened to the words and the rhythm of the chanting, the words were repeated over and over again. There were many chanters, but only one voice. It seemed to Jesus that the words were, "OM MANI PADME HUM. OM MANI PADME HUM."

Silently, at first only to himself, Jesus began to repeat the phrase in his head, then, with confidence gained, he began to repeat them, audibly. As he fell into the mood of the chanting, a spell came over him. It did not matter what the words meant, he felt at one with himself and all the others in the room. He felt only one presence, the One.

Jesus had no idea how long the chanting lasted because he did not feel anywhere physically present, but everywhere present. Present in a different dimension. Suddenly, all the other voices stopped. Jesus repeated the mantra one last time before he stopped. Apparently he had missed some cue. No one said anything about his lapse, so he didn't feel that he had committed some grave error. He opened his eyes and looked around, everyone was still seated, and looking straight ahead. He could not tell if their eyes were open or closed. Jesus too, just sat and waited with eyes closed.

Again Jesus felt that he was in a different world. He saw lights flashing before his eyes and strange geometrical shapes of various sizes and colors. His heart felt open and aware of something beyond his normal awareness. It was similar to his experience under the shade tree meditating on the Tao. Could this be feeling the presence of God?" he thought. Whatever this feeling was, Jesus stayed with it. He did not open his eyes until he heard the clanging of a loud gong.

It took several minutes for Jesus to come back to his surroundings. But no one was rushing to get up. Finally there was a stirring. Some of the men in front of him appeared to be loosening their postures. Slowly, men got up and filed silently out of the room. Jesus waited until the last man was on his way out. It was Sri Sygoroyal, his mentor. Jesus followed him straight to the kitchen where the monk introduced him to the cook.

"This is Vinda Govanga, Jesus. He will be your instructor in the kitchen. You are to do as you are told. You will be able to eat when all of the others are finished." With this, Sygoroyal turned and was gone. Jesus was on his own. The cook motioned to Jesus and Jesus stepped forward.

"This is the water-carrying bucket. Take it and follow the path to the center courtyard. There is a well next to the pond. Bring me water until I tell you to stop."

"Yes Sir," said Jesus as he picked up the buckets. There were two buckets, one at either end of a leather strap. Jesus was familiar with this system, and he knew to put the strap behind his neck and over his shoulders. The two buckets then hung on either side. Jesus headed out the door, and having seen where the pond was earlier, headed in that direction.

The sun was out and Jesus was in a rather ecstatic state, so he minded neither the buckets, nor the work that lay ahead. He was keenly aware of the sounds around him, of the birds and the various insects, singing and humming in the morning breeze. The kitchen was not far from the well and Jesus soon had the buckets full and started on his way back. "Water is very heavy," Jesus thought to himself. "But I will not be lax." And so, this first morning of training at the Viharas, Jesus worked very hard. But it didn't seem like work to Jesus, because he was in a place, to him, magical.

After all the others had eaten, Jesus was given a half-hour to eat his own meal. It was simple, grain, vegetables and tea, similar to much of what he had eaten since arriving in Egypt. Yet, Jesus was satisfied. For another hour or so after he finished eating, Jesus cleaned the clay and wooden dishes, and the other utensils. About the time he finished, Sri Sygoroyal appeared in the kitchen doorway. "Come, Jesus," he said, "It is time for your afternoon class." Jesus followed him without a word.

At the head of the class sat a monk, white haired and thin, but with obvious energy. His eyes were lively and he spoke with eagerness. Jesus took a position on the floor and listened.

"The mantra is not God speaking to you. It is you imploring God to speak to you through your inner eye and heart. It helps cleanse your thoughts, for it is difficult to have other thoughts while reciting a mantra. The phrases and the tones are of a special quality that helps bring you to spiritual awareness. But, there is no magic in them, no mystery that will not speak to you. But you must listen!" The monk pounded a palm to the mat.

"The mantras, the chants, lead you to the silence, which for most of you is not something previously experienced. You are all too busy with your inner chatter, what you will eat, what you will drink, what you will wear tomorrow. You are all so busy about tomorrow, you do not know how to live today! Do you think the turtles in the pond worry about the lilies being there tomorrow? I assure you they do not. But, you can be sure they are enjoying the sun today! They know full well their turtleness!

"So, we should all be like turtles, knowing our own present experience. Awareness is what we are striving for. Not what others think, but our own, moment-to-moment awareness. It is only in the movement from the past and the future into the present that we can begin to contemplate our own presence. If you sit quietly in your own presence, then, soon enough, you will begin to get a very strange feeling. The feeling is strange and yet somehow familiar. The feeling will reveal to you that your true sense of self is different from your thoughts and feelings. You have the experience of I Am, but that I Am is no longer a separate individual. It is God's Self. And that I Am is common to all."

There was a long Silence before anyone spoke. Then, members of the class, those who had obviously been there for some time and had some confidence, asked questions or made comments. The teacher responded quickly, almost spontaneously. The answers were often surprising to Jesus, and some of the questions he didn't even understand. But, he did listen and take in all that he could. When the class was over, it was time for Jesus to go home. He was not a full-fledged member of the academy, so he would not be sleeping there. Jesus walked slowly home, very much aware of himself and his surroundings. He felt peaceful and hopeful. He was happy with his first day's experience.

Jesus smiled to himself as he pictured the discussions he would now be able to have with his father. His father, he knew, had similar training himself. But that was a long time ago, in Israel. This was a different country, a much bigger city, and this was a school actually run by people of a different religious teaching. He knew his father would be interested, and they could compare notes. His mother, Jesus knew, would be equally interested, although she might have trouble keeping up with the discussion, since the younger children would be demanding attention.

Jesus thought again about his mother and father and how tolerant they were of people with differing views. He thought about the fact that his mother could read and calculate numbers. She had taught him to read at a very young age and this was a great advantage for him. He thought how his father, a carpenter, had such a wealth of experience due to his experiences in the Essene community. Jesus felt that he could really begin to relate to some of his father's knowledge. This, thought Jesus, is a great experience.

There were plenty of chores for Jesus to perform when he got home. His father had him go down the street to pick up supplies from the market: wood workers glue, grease and some sharpening stones. His mother had him pick up some vegetables for their evening meal. Jesus didn't mind the errands. The tolerance and opportunity his parents allowed him were more than he could ever repay. He returned with the supplies and helped his father and mother till the evening was late and the family could sit down to supper. After the evening prayer, they ate while Joseph asked Jesus about his day.

Jesus told his family about the academy, the way it looked, smelled, and felt. He told them about the teachers, the mantras, the chants and the teachings. His parents listened attentively, asking only a few questions before Jesus finally stopped talking.

"Seems like you've had a wonderful day," said Joseph. "I can see that you take to learning like I did, wanting to know as much as possible. I am glad."

Mary said, "You keep it up, Jesus. There are great things in store for you. More than you know. What you are learning will be of great value to you and many others. You too will some day be a teacher. I am certain of it!"

"I would like very much to be a teacher. I love to learn so much. And I am so lucky to be here in Alexandria, where they have teachers such as these. I cannot say what the difference is, but our own teachers do not convey the same feeling these teachers do. These Buddhists, they are not so argumentative and they smile more. They work, and yet they don't seem to be working. They don't complain. Even for me, the work seemed effortless, even though it was hard work!"

"Sort of like my work," Joseph said. "I work hard, but it doesn't seem like work because I enjoy it so much. It is almost as if I get meaning through my hands. Working with things, touching them, sanding them, sharpening them, gives me a feeling of awe and wonder. It's wonderful to make a living this way."

"And I like books and learning," said Jesus. "I shall always like them. I would rather read than work in a shop. There is so much to know!"

"Yes, Jesus," said Joseph, "There is much to know. But do not judge, my son, which is better, to work with your hands or with your head. That kind of judgment could lead to narrow views. I, too, have a love of learning. I love to read the scrolls, but I also love my carpentry work and the feeling I get from using my hands."

"Yes, Father, I know. I did not mean to be disrespectful. But I don't get the same feeling you do from working with my hands. I don't mind physical work, but thinking and listening seem much more important."

"Well, Jesus," said Joseph, "mind you study hard and please the monks, so you may one day teach. And mind getting married too young, as you may find yourself working very hard to feed others."

"I will not get married," said Jesus, "I intend to devote my life to learning."

"Very well," said Joseph. "Mind your learning and stay away from women. But you may find that rather difficult as you get older." Joseph smiled a knowing smile.

Jesus and his father talked well into the night, discussing the differences between the Essenes and the Buddhists. Mary joined in the conversation when she could. Joseph had to tell Jesus to go to bed. He was too excited to go to bed on his own. Jesus lay on his mat for a long time. He repeated to himself, as he drifted off to sleep, "OM MANI PADME HUM."

(11)

Jesus and the Prostitute

Jesus went to the Buddhist academy five days a week. He was now eleven years old. Since he lived nearby and was still young, he was not required to live on the premises. However, he would gladly have done so. But Jesus knew his parents would be upset if he did. He loved his studies, especially the ancient Vedic texts which were in the Library. With access to them on a daily basis, Jesus spent many hours, hunched over the wooden table, studying them. This was much easier than going to the main library in the city, where many thought he was too young. It was easier too, than getting scraps of text here and there from sailors or others who favored him with their attention.

The monks were quite surprised at how readily Jesus took to meditation. They had no way of knowing how much time Jesus had already spent meditating, but they did notice that he jumped right in without hesitation. Although the monks said nothing to him, they did talk amongst themselves about him. How interesting they thought, Jesus' face looked, at the end of the meditation sessions. They could see him experiencing considerable ecstasy. Some were envious, but Jesus never bragged about being better or further along than others. He simply asked appropriate questions and answered questions put to him.

Jesus was coming into puberty and the normal drives and interests of that age began bearing down on him. He wondered often, why so many preached that spiritual life and life of the flesh could not be integrated. For him, there did not seem to be a big division. His main concern was not to get so involved with externals that he did not have time for meditation and other spiritual pursuits. For him this was not a problem. But he could see that for many others it was. He saw how the common man did not possess the drive or the obsession for spiritual matters that he did. So, for them, Jesus thought, finding the time or inclination to meditate, was difficult.

Similar issues confronted Jesus in relation to the attitude among the monks, especially regarding renunciation. This included doing one's best to avoid women. Many monks espoused and lived celibate lives. They explained to him their reasons for promoting celibacy and showed him texts supporting their point of view. But, for Jesus, this did not seem necessary. He was aware that women had children, and that a man responsible for a woman and children, might not have as much free time. But, avoiding women excluded a large part of life. So, Jesus thought about these issues, on his walks, and in meditation.

Jesus often walked the neighborhoods around the docks. These neighborhoods housed the sailors, many far away from home and without family. Low class laborers and slaves were also prevalent. With these lonely men came the women who serviced them. A certain type of lamp was displayed by these woman, in their windows at night. Jesus was well aware of what went on in these houses and he had seen monks and other religious men, supposedly celibate, leaving such houses. Watching, Jesus noted these religious men often visited these places after a trip to the market during the day. Jesus figured that this was so, because, for a monk to be gone at night, would have aroused suspicion.

One day, Jesus saw his mentor, Sri Sygoroyal, leave one such house. He was sure it was he as his stocky body and hunched shoulders were still evident beneath his flowing robe. Jesus watched from around a corner till his teacher was out of sight. Then Jesus went to the door and knocked.

An aging dark-skinned woman came to the door. Jesus could see that she had once been handsome. She was tall, well proportioned, with large dark eyes and hair. Her eyelashes were thick and she had a come-hither look.

"I'd like to see the woman that monk just visited," said Jesus.

"Aren't you a little young?" asked the lady, looking Jesus over carefully.

"Yes, madam," said Jesus, "But I just want to talk to her." The madam stood in the doorway for a long moment.

"You just want to talk, not engage her services?"

"Yes Ma'am."

"Your father doesn't work for the authorities, does he?"

"Oh no. I just want to ask her what the monks do when they visit here."

"What do you think they do?" she asked, surprised.

"I'm just curious. Do they talk, or are they just like other men, doing what others do?"

Apparently that sounded like a plausible question from a young boy approaching puberty, for she let him in. "Just go to the last room, it's the girl behind the purple curtain."

Jesus did as he was instructed. He stood outside the curtain and whispered, "Madam. Madam." The curtain parted and an older woman stood, mostly naked, staring at him. She was full bodied, sumptuous, with almond skin and a warm face. She looked at Jesus, sizing him up.

"And what do you want with me, boy?" she asked.

"Oh no, Madam. I do not wish to use your services. I just want to talk to you about the monk who just left."

"You want to talk about him?"

"Yes. I want to know how the monks are."

The woman looked at Jesus, giving him a wide-eyed expression of incredulity.

"I was wondering if he, and other monks, are different from other men? I mean, do they do different things with you than other men?"

"Well," the woman paused, thinking. "You mean, do they do it?" she said, making a swaying motion with her hips. Jesus thought she was trying to scare him off. "The one who was just here. He isn't circumcised like the Jews. Does that answer your question?"

"No, that is not what I mean. I want to know if they are different, the way the act, what they do?"

"What a strange question, young man. Why would you want to know such a thing?"

"Because religious men are different. Well, I assume some are different. I am just wondering if you can see a difference. For example, the monk who just left, obviously he is a religious man. But he visits you. So he is not celibate!"

"How do you know he did not just come to talk, just like you?"

Jesus thought for a moment. "You just said he wasn't circumcised. I guess that means he does more than just talk."

The woman laughed heartily. "Come in young man, have a seat here," she said, pointing to the edge of a cot. "I will tell you what I can, but I do not know if I will be of any help."

Jesus sat and listened.

"Many monks come here, not just those in the ochre robes. I see religious men of all ages, even some very old ones that can hardly perform. I rather like them and have a certain affinity for them. That is why I cater to them. I am no longer young and wealthy men don't want me, since they can afford very young girls. So, I cater to those I can. These priests and monks, they can't afford much. So, I take them.

"But that is not all. These religious men, for the most part, have no wives. They can't mess around with their parishioners, so they come to me. I find them very gentle and appreciative."

"How so?" asked Jesus.

They aren't out to prove something. They just need some physical contact, some company, a hug. They are easy for an old woman like me to handle."

"But what about their character? That is what I am getting at. If they come here, they must be like other men! Is this just a sham, this piety, this fake celibacy, or does it make a difference? Tell me!"

"My dear young man. Why such concern?"

"Because, I am very interested in these religious men. I just want to know, however I may, if there is a difference in those leading a religious life."

The almond skinned woman sat on her cot, smiling. A musty smell pervaded the room. Her breasts were full and hung loosely in full view. Finally she said, "These are men, just like other men. They are just obsessed in a different way. Their thing is religion. Traders and businessmen are just as sincere as monks, priests and rabbis. They're just sincere in a different way. It's a matter of interests. Some of the highest religious teachers in Alexandria come to see me. Some of them are humble and wise, some are just as full of themselves as the Pharaoh. Does that answer your question?"

"I don't know. I guess I am asking for something you really can't give me. I will need to answer this for myself. Thank you very much for your time."

"I am pleased by your obvious inquisitiveness and the passion with which you ask. Please come see me when you are ready to see what a woman has to offer. I will give you your first visit for free."

"I will consider your offer," said Jesus. "But right now I have other interests. Thank you." With that, Jesus walked out of the house and back onto the street. There were so many things he wanted to resolve. He couldn't resist his own intellectual and heartfelt passion. Asking questions and prodding everyone whom he thought could help, was all he knew to do. He walked down the street, back toward his neighborhood, past the venders and hawkers in the marketplace and home.

That night Jesus asked his father about the religious men, priests and rabbis he saw visiting the houses of ill repute. Joseph listened and a deep smile crossed his face.

"Well, son, you are seeing this as either black like onyx or white like limestone. It is neither. Questions like these are more like many colored quartz. You see, many religious men, though not all religious men, who dedicate themselves to God, presume that they will not have the needs of normal men. For some, this may actually be the case; for others it is not so simple. They may start out full of zeal and commitment, but sooner or later, either curiosity or the normal human desires become a problem. The problem does not go away because they pray or run from their desires. So they give in."

"But then they have broken their vows!"

"Yes and no. They are still committed to God, and service, but they simply cannot be celibate. They haven't so much broken their vows to God as they have misjudged themselves and human nature. I myself would have liked to have stayed at Qumran and lived a celibate life. But, I too, had strong desires. Stronger and more instinctual than I would have guessed. My will power gave way. But, I am still a very religious man. And, in loving your mother, am I not loving God?"

Jesus couldn't answer right away. Finally he said, "Dad, I'll just have to think about this one for a while."

"Very well, Son. You ask very good questions. Your curiosity is good. Remember, stones come in all colors, their qualities are different, but they are all useful."

"Thank you, Father, I will remember."

The next day, when Jesus was at the Viharas, after he had finished washing the dishes from the midday meal, Jesus had the opportunity to question Sri Sygoroyal about celibacy. "Pray tell," said Jesus, "What is the advantage of being celibate?"

Sri Sygoroyal did not flinch, nor grimace, nor make any facial response that Jesus could read. After a few moments he responded. "I believe there are some advantages for some people, but not for all. The Vedas, and the Bhagavad-Gita, for example, call for renunciation. Part of the renunciation of material things is celibacy. For some this is extreme, for others, easily understood and accepted. I am surprised you are asking such questions now. It will be awhile yet before you can afford a wife."

"I am not thinking about a wife. I do not intend to marry. But this is an issue concerning how one lives. I want to know what is the right way to live."

"But this is not a simple question. It cannot be answered yes, or no."

"Then answer as best you can."

"The simplest answer is, if you can renunciate all, including material goods and physical desires, that is best. If not, it may be harder to attain the highest peaks of enlightenment, but it is not impossible. On the other hand, trying to put aside a strong desire can cause many problems. One may not be able to concentrate, or even meditate, because these desires come to the surface. In this case, it may be best to satisfy the desire so that one can at least have peace."

Jesus could sense that Sri Sygoroyal did not wish to talk about this subject any longer, so Jesus dropped it.

"Thank you, Sir," he said, "I will think about it."

Jesus went straight to the library. He told the librarian that he wanted to see the Bhagavad-Gita and the commentaries. Even though this was a Buddhist academy, they did have these Hindu texts, and Jesus preferred them over the Buddhist texts. The librarian was opposed to pulling these books as they were very old.

The books were stacked on wooden shelves of red cedar and the book covers themselves were of wood, with colored silk bands holding the pages inside. The pages were loose, that is, not strung together, and the librarian did not like getting them down.

"You don't need to look at the book itself, Son. Part of my job is to have as many of these books as possible memorized. Did you know that one of the reasons these books are in the form of stories is so that one can remember them without having to refer to the text?"

"No, I did not," responded Jesus.

"Well now, what did you want to know about, if it is in the Bhagavad-Gita, I will recite the verse to you. I like the Vedas too!"

"I want to know about renunciation and celibacy."

"Hum," the librarian seemed to be shuffling through his brain. "Chapter Eight, verse 11 says this. 'Persons who are learned in the

Vedas, who utter omkara and who are great sages in the renounced order enter into Brahman. Desiring such perfection, one practices celibacy.'"

Jesus had the monk repeat the phrases several times, till he himself had it memorized. Jesus could not have read it himself anyhow, since it was written in a far Eastern Language which he did not understand. "I will meditate on it," Jesus said, and left the library. Jesus liked the old monk in the library, but he also knew the books were very rare and the pages fragile. So asking to see a text, was asking a lot. Also, Jesus knew by experience that most people reacted strangely to his questions. As if, at his age, he should not be concerned.

In class that afternoon Jesus asked questions about renunciation and celibacy. There were answers and some debate, but Jesus wasn't satisfied. He knew they taught that human beings were God incarnate, God manifested; so why, he asked himself, should we reject our bodies and the senses through which life comes? Even the Psalmist said, "Know ye not, ye are Gods!"

These issues caused Jesus to probe deeper and deeper. He wanted to understand these issues, and how, taking all the various teachings together, they could make sense, without any conflict. What Jesus wanted was the utmost simplicity in seeing, understanding and living. He had already given himself this task in life, although he did not consciously recognize it at this time.

As Jesus walked home that night, he ran across an Egyptian temple. He read the words carved in stone. "Osiris lives. His suffering and pain are gone. He is resurrected. Now a God. Praise be to Horus who raised him from the dead." Jesus watched the people coming and going from the temple and thought about all the resurrection stories he heard. Each religion had its own God-Son; born of woman, fathered by a God, killed and resurrected. He wondered if all these stories could be true. He wondered where these resurrected beings were. He looked at the sky, but was unsure.

Jesus had tried to get into the Egyptian temples, but because he was Jewish, he often was not allowed. But he asked a lot of questions about their rituals and prayers. What he heard seemed very magical, but without the same emphasis on personal experience that he found among the Buddhists.

Time passed and many people wondered about the young Jesus. He seemed interested in subjects well beyond his apparent youth. He had gained the reputation of a child prodigy among the spiritual leaders of the community. But Jesus did not let this reputation go to his head. He was not striving for recognition, but understanding, and it was this depth of understanding that brought him to the attention of the spiritual elders. The elders of his own faith, however, were reluctant to take him into training for the synagogue, as he was disruptive with his questions and answers.

(12)

A Trip Back to Israel

At the age of thirteen, Jesus was considered by the intellectual and spiritual elite of the city, highly advanced. He had a reputation as a leader and was often allowed to participate in debates at the synagogue, even though they did not want to train him in their school. Jesus spoke at the Museum school too. He was considered the brightest student at the Buddhist academy, which pleased Mary and Joseph immensely.

It was at this time, that a caravan arrived from Israel, with the news that Joachim wished the family to come back for a visit. Mary and Joseph considered this at length, but there were five children now, including Jesus, and Mary did not think she could take them all with her. Joseph's business was going well, and he could not see leaving either Mary or the business. So it was decided that Jesus could go on his own and visit the family. Jesus was very excited to hear this, and he was eager to go. It had been more than ten years since he had been to Israel; he barely remembered it at all. He readily agreed to go, and was pleased that his parents trusted him enough to let him go on his own.

So it was that Jesus, a few weeks later, left with a caravan returning to Israel. The monks at the academy told Jesus to be careful and not raise too many challenges to the leaders at the synagogues in Jerusalem. They knew all too well Jesus' enthusiasm and penchant for honesty. They also knew that his level of honesty had caused him trouble in the past, and in a new environment, especially in Jerusalem, the Jewish religious center, he could be trouble.

But Jesus told them not to worry, that he would listen well before he spoke, and try to phrase any questions in a non-threatening manner.

Early in the morning after the good-byes were said, Jesus and the caravan took off along the shore route to Jerusalem. After several hours, Jesus settled down and took in the sights, guiding the camel he had been given as his responsibility. There was the typical ragtag band of touring magicians and Gypsies, which Jesus hoped would make the trip more interesting.

When camping near a village or town, people would come out to the caravan to barter and trade for jewelry and spices from Egypt. The magicians would perform for the crowd; the dancers would dance; and the palm readers would read fortunes.

At one of the many stops, Jesus had his palm read, and the lady was quite confused. She told Jesus that his life line split right in the middle. "You may have a terrible accident at mid-life and just barely survive," she told him. "It seems that your lifeline does, however, continue after that split."

Jesus thought about the reading for a while, but he didn't linger on it. He was going to live, wasn't he? At least he wasn't going to die at thirty. At other stops Jesus watched the shows and sometimes helped. He soon began to see through some of the magician's tricks and when he told them how they performed them, they didn't like it. But the magicians did respect Jesus' ability to observe. So, they let him help. He was figuring out their tricks anyway.

There was a young Gypsy woman, named Delilah, who was very attracted to Jesus. She was not a beauty, but she was quick, and also observant. She and Jesus got into many conversations about magic, dancing, and the spiritual world. She told Jesus, if he were older, she would like to marry him. Jesus told her that he did not intend to marry. She was not impressed by this statement and told him, "I could make you change your mind."

Jesus told her that she could not. So, she went about the business of seducing Jesus. It was more of a game to Delilah than it might have been for some other women, as she often serviced various members of the caravan. She reported directly to the leader of the caravan, and he made sure that no one claimed possession of her. He did not want fights breaking out. So, for Delilah, Jesus was just a special project. He held out for a long time, but eventually gave in. He was almost fourteen now, and many men his age, were already full time workers and laborers. He had reached puberty and was capable.

Somehow, Jesus was able to take this new experience in stride and did not become overly attached to the woman. He was not worried about her becoming pregnant, because there would be no way to say who the father was. Also, these Gypsy women had methods of their own, a secret of their trade, that, for the most part, prevented pregnancy. The rumor was that these Gypsy women knew how to put a small stone in their womb, and this prevented the pregnancy. However it worked, Jesus did not question her on her method. The Gypsies' special talents were well known.

Jesus worked hard on the trip, as a number of the camels and donkeys, belonged to Joachim. This also gave Jesus a special standing, as he was the only relative of Joachim on the trip. The caravan leader made sure that Jesus knew his responsibilities, and that he was protected. The caravan leader took a special interest in Jesus, not only because he worked hard and learned quickly, but also because he often carried goods for Jaochim.

At night, around the camp fires, Jesus was a real story teller. His ability to tell suspenseful stories was superb. He was able to tell parables that created wonderful settings and scenes that made the listeners think. He made the trip a lot more bearable for those who had traveled for many years, as he brought a fresh approach to things and events.

As for Delilah, Jesus was her favorite, but she could see that he wasn't ready to settle down; besides, he was too young, quite a bit younger than she. Still, Jesus' attitude about things, his way of looking, and his piercing eyes, were very attractive. She could see how he was interested in serious things, yet he could laugh with the rest of them. Although quite different, he was very human. She told him she would miss him when they parted in Jerusalem. Jesus told her he would miss her too.

Weeks had passed by the time the caravan arrived in Jerusalem. Jesus took Joachim's animals, and with the two members of the crew that worked for Joachim, split from the main group and traveled on to Nazareth. Jesus would have to see the sights in Jerusalem at a later time. First, he had to meet his relatives. The small band arrived at Joachim's estate, late in the afternoon of a sunny day. Caravans liked to arrive at stopping points in the early evening. This gave them time to set camp and get a good night's sleep before they had to barter and trade with the towns' people.

As soon as they saw the caravan approaching, Jesus' grandmother, her daughters and their children, came running out to greet him. They were glad to have visitors, especially a relative they had not seen since he was a little child. Jesus was led away to the family quarters while the hired hands took the animals to the stable.

"Tell us all about Mary and Joseph," said the grandmother. And Jesus told everything he could think of, answering all their questions. He told about his brothers and sisters and life in Egypt, and how well Joseph's business was doing. Supper was made and eaten and wine was drunk. It was late into the night before any of the family made it to bed. Jesus was tired, happy and full. He went to sleep easily once his head hit the mat.

The next several days were spent eating and talking, sharing stories and descriptions of places, events and people. Alexandria seemed to Jesus' relatives, a grand place, a place they would love to visit. Most of them were well aware that they would never do so. Jesus, being observant and gifted with words, kept the adults and the children spellbound with his descriptions of museums, temples, palaces, boats, and all the various peoples that converged in the port city. Although Jesus enjoyed all the talk, and the relatives, he was eager to get to the synagogue.

When the Sabbath came, Jesus went with the family to the

local temple. Jesus joined in the discussion readily and surprised the elders with his knowledge and his insight. In a discussion of man's place in the world, an elder, Michael, stated, "We should be fearful of God and especially on the Sabbath, to follow the letter of the law."

Jesus asked, "Is the Sabbath made for man, or man for the Sabbath?"

The elder was surprised at such a question from a young man. The elder didn't recognize Jesus. "Who are you?" he asked.

"I am Jesus, grandson of Joachim, of the house of David. I am in town visiting." This statement made the elder feel a little more at ease. This would not be someone he would have to deal with every Sabbath. He thought a long while before he answered Jesus. "Man was made for the Sabbath. For God made man to worship him."

Jesus answered directly. "Is it not written in your text, "Know ye not ye are Gods?"

The elder thought awhile, his brow knit. "Where is it in the text?"

Jesus responded, "Your very own King, the psalmist, said these words. If you will hand me the scroll, I will find it for you."

The elder handed Jesus the scroll, and Jesus turned to the Psalm and read the verse from the scroll. He also read the following two verses to show the elder that he could read. Then he handed the scroll back to the elder. As he checked the scroll to verify that Jesus had, in fact, read the text, Jesus said, "In the very beginning of our book, it says, we are created in the image and likeness of God. King David was simply expressing this fact in a direct manner. How would you explain his statement?"

Again the elder looked at the ground and then around at the small crowd gathered round. "I cannot explain it," he said.

Jesus responded, "The Sabbath was made for man, for we are the likeness and image of God. Just as God rested on the seventh day, so man rests on the seventh day. King David acknowledged that we are more God, than servants of God."

.ENTW

The elder immediately replied, "There will be no more discussion on this subject today. Go make your sacrifices and do your prayers." The crowd, in awe of what they had just witnessed, stood in silence. It was several minutes before the first person moved on to other business. Many of the crowd stared at Jesus. As others moved away, a few came up to Jesus and asked him to explain. As the elder had turned on his heels and walked off, Jesus felt free to explain.

"We are images of God, created in his likeness. We are even more a part of God than we are His subjects. The psalmist was expressing this fact. We have too little respect for ourselves. We have stooped too low and no longer own our own divinity. I ask you to dig deeply into the question, 'Who am I?' I assure you, if you dig deeply enough, in answering this question, you will know who you are."

The men gathered around Jesus were astounded at his teaching. He did not yell, he did not raise his fists, but the authority with which he spoke was very clear. The preciseness of his thinking, combined with some unknown inner authority, caused the men to wonder who this young man was. "Is he a God?" they asked themselves. But Jesus, knowing what they were thinking, said, "Whatever I am, you are, for I am in you, and you in me, and all of us are one in God."

With this statement Jesus got up and wandered off into the crowded streets. He made no sacrifices at the alter, nor did he say prayers in public. He went off by himself, and under the shade of a fig tree, meditated on what he had seen. He was appalled at how beaten down his own people were, and how their elders were not lifting them up. Jesus wept.

It did not take long for talk to circulate in town that Jesus had made a fool of the elder at the synagogue. Joachim was quite troubled at this, and didn't understand how this could happen. But he smiled as the situation began to remind him of Mary, his daughter. She had also created situations like this one, and his life had been much more peaceful since she had gone to Egypt. But he missed her. Joachim decided that he would not say a word to Jesus, but would defend Jesus' right to speak. He had practice defending Mary, and he had learned how to make light of such situations. Joachim hoped that Jesus wouldn't stay too long. He redoubled his efforts to get another caravan organized for the return trip to Egypt.

Before a return trip could be arranged, another Sabbath was approaching, and Jesus told Joachim that he would be going to Jerusalem, to the main temple, to worship. Joachim said nothing to dissuade Jesus from going, but he was not very keen on the idea. Finally, Joachim gave Jesus a donkey to ride, so that he wouldn't have to walk the entire distance. Jesus thanked him, and well before the Sabbath, he took off for Jerusalem.

The trip itself was uneventful and Jesus had plenty of time to find the temple. He had never been in Jerusalem before, except in passing on the way to Nazareth, so he took his time meandering through the streets. He spent the night on a side street, his donkey tied to a post. He slept well, as he was tired.

(13)

A Challenge to the Priests

Jesus woke up with the cocks crowing and the sun just peeking over the horizon. He could see the temple in the distance, atop the plateau, at the peak of the city. Its stone walls gleamed in the sun. It was not nearly as big or as impressive as the temples in Alexandria, but this was the main temple of Israel. As Jesus was looking, a young girl stepped out of the house which formed the part of the alley in which he had slept.

"Did you sleep here?" she asked. "Weren't you cold?"

"Yes I did. It was not too cold."

"Do you have food to eat this morning?"

"Nothing warm, but I do have some dry bread and cheese."

"Well, I cannot let you eat bread and cheese if I can feed you something warm. Let me ask my mother if we can spare you some warm cereal." With that the young girl turned, and smiling, went into the home. She returned several minutes later with her mother. She had a warm face on a slight frame—but Jesus could see that she was a strong woman. "Please come in," she said.

Jesus followed her into the home. He was asked to take a seat at the family table and eat with them. They asked him where he was from and what he was doing in Jerusalem. He told them of his wish to see the temple and to listen to the priests. The father, a confident man with easy grace, gave Jesus the local news. His perspective was one that only people living right outside the temple would have.

When the meal was over, Jesus felt enthusiastic about his plan to approach the temple, the priests, and engage them in dialogue. The family gave him directions and he left, well fed.

Jesus found the temple and stood outside, watching the proceedings until he had an idea of where he could best position himself. He went into the courtyard and took a place near a corner where he could listen unobtrusively. He watched the priests going through their early morning rituals: lighting candles, burning incense. He saw the money changers busily at their task, and he saw the herdsmen bringing in goats, sheep, pigeons and other small animals.

Jesus listened to the talks while several groups formed for discussions. Jesus picked a group to listen to, one in which the priest seemed especially enthusiastic. As Jesus listened, he was enthralled to hear that they were discussing scriptures which dealt with eternal life. Several heated discussions ensued, dealing with whether or not a particular verse proved the existence of eternal life. Jesus had been quiet, just listening, for several hours; but finally, he could contain himself no longer. He asked the priest, "What makes you think that you can prove eternal life from that text?"

The priest turned and looked toward Jesus. The look seemed to say, how dare you ask such a question. But there was silence from Jesus and silence from the small group listening. The priest then said, "Because this is our holy book, the guidebook of our people. Are you not Jewish?"

"Yes I am Jewish, but the question of eternal life can be answered by experience. Anyone, of any race or creed, can answer this question for himself. Words, even from this holy book, cannot give you that."

"Oh, so you have experienced eternal life?" said the priest, haughtily.

"Yes I have," answered Jesus.

"Have you died and been resurrected?"

"No," said Jesus, "I have not."

"Then of what experience do you speak?"

"Have you never been in a state of spiritual ecstasy, where you feel that you are one with all mankind, whole, and one with the entire universe, a place where even the birds and their songs are you and yours?"

"No! I have never heard of such a state!"

"Well, if you ever experience such a state, you will not spend your time debating lines of text; you will know."

The priest was now irritated at this young, tall, skinny lad. He said, "No experience negates or renders this text obsolete!"

Jesus answered, "I do not say the text is obsolete, only that, in this case, the book can only answer the question in your mind. But you may still have doubt. When you have the experience of which I speak, you will know beyond a shadow of a doubt that you are already eternal, that you have always been so and always will be."

The group standing around Jesus was fascinated by his words. They were even more astonished at the authority with which the young man spoke.

"Where are you from?" the priest asked.

"I am Jesus. I have just come from Nazareth."

"And since when do we have such learned children coming from Nazareth?"

"Experience is the great teacher, if one listens to one's heart, even a child can be wise."

With this, the priest rolled up the scroll and walked into the temple. A small group of listeners surrounded Jesus.

"Please, please, tell us more," they asked.

Jesus spoke to them, explaining, "All knowledge does not belong to the learned or priestly caste. Neither is all knowledge contained in any holy book. It is good to find solace from a passage in a holy book; it is worthy of consideration. But let it not be the sole source of your knowledge. If you do so, you become a slave to the author, to the priest, to the book."

He continued, "We are all children of God. Though some may still call me a child, I have my own inner knowledge. For me, I am simply stating a fact. When I proclaim that I have eternal life, I say so from experience. That experience can be yours."

As Jesus spoke, more people joined the discussion. The priest who had left in a huff could be seen periodically poking his head out the door of the temple, grimacing at Jesus and the people listening to him. Jesus stayed till late in the evening. It was then that he discovered that the young daughter who had invited him in for breakfast had been among the crowd, listening. Her older sister was with her and had been listening too. The older one, Salome, asked that Jesus return to their home for the evening meal. "We would like to hear more." So Jesus went home with the two young women.

At supper the girls' father asked Jesus how he was able to speak with the priests with such authority. Jesus thought a moment and then replied.

"It seems to come to me naturally, an assurance, a knowing that comes from inside. When I speak from that place, there is no question of not having authority. I know what I know with my whole being. With that knowing I am free to challenge anyone. For me, it is a simple thing. I assume that others have the same knowing, but then I discover they do not. The worst experience I have, is to hear the priests spouting verses and acting so pompous, when they do not feel the truth. There is no experience, no life behind their words."

The family listened intently. "How can we gain such knowing?" asked the father.

"That is a difficult question to answer. I've had this ability since I was quite young. But if it is not present for you, meditation helps."

"Is that like prayer?" asked the older daughter.

"Very similar, except in prayer, one is usually asking, beseeching, thinking, but in meditation, one simply sits and waits for the silence."

"What is this silence?" asked the younger daughter.

"The silence happens when you reach quietness of mind that

is undisturbed by thought. Feelings come up, and a knowing that one can draw from. It is not words and that state cannot be described in words, but the knowing one gets from that state is absolute. Others may question you regarding what you know, and you cannot prove a thing, but you yourself, know it absolutely."

"Tell us some more about this knowing." said the mother.

"You are an interesting family," said Jesus. "I am not always so well received. This knowing, I wish I could just pass it out to everyone, but I cannot. As a child I could easily get into this knowing, and it allowed me to converse with adults with confidence. But, as I grew, it started to fade. I knew I did not want to loose it, so I set about to practice how to get into the state. What I discovered was, that my personality was in the way. The person that I was beginning to think I was could not keep its ground in the presence of this otherness, so it resisted. But the feeling of this state, of knowing, of oneness, had such a pull, that it gave me the strength to question my personality. The process I learned is just something that works for me. To explain it to others, proves very difficult."

"Oh but please try," said the older daughter.

"One has to get to a place where the mind stops, where the chatter of the intellect, the person that you think you are, releases its hold. Then you are there. I have to tell you, this practice came about while I was still a child. It was a fairly natural inclination and might have gone nowhere, but my parents were very strong spiritually, and they encouraged me. It was a personal challenge. It is hard for me to see what others do not understand, and what needs to be explained."

"So, try with us. It is important to us, too." said the father.

"Well, there are people that practice meditation. They come primarily from the Far East. It is a science with them. I study with them now, in Alexandria. I do not know their science as well as I would like. I am still learning. But I can say this. If you sit alone and go deeply into your self, you can find this place. I am sure that if it is in me, it is in everyone."

"So, one just needs to sit quietly and try not to think?" queried the father.

"Well, it's not quite, trying to stop thinking. It is almost as if thinking looks at itself and says, 'I cannot go beyond this point. It is no use, I give up.' Then, suddenly, this other space is there. Over time, one learns how to get to this space, but, there is no single path that works for everyone. Each person must find their own."

The family sat in awe of Jesus, but he was hardly aware of the respect and authority that was accorded him. He had received this respect from others most of his life. Even this family, unknown to him until this morning, was asking him questions, and he was answering, with experience, with knowledge. It came easily to him, and even he could not explain why.

He talked with the family for many hours. When it was time to sleep, they offered him a place inside the front door to sleep, so that he wouldn't be out on the street. They showed him a place in the back where there was hay and dried grass for his donkey. For the family, Jesus was a breath of fresh air, one which gave abundantly from some inner source which they could not fathom.

Over the next few days Jesus returned to the temple every day. Mostly he listened, but he did speak up when he could no longer stand the rigidity of the knowledge propounded. The interpretations the priests made of some scriptures made it difficult to remain silent, even though he knew he was challenging their spiritual leadership. Again and again Jesus was questioned as to his authority to speak. Jesus repeatedly quoted the psalmist, "Know ye not that ye are Gods?" He let the priests struggle for an answer to the statement, but they could not. Neither could they accuse Jesus of blasphemy, because he was quoting scripture. This method, of quoting their own texts, almost always gave Jesus the upper hand. They could not answer him because they had not gone deeply enough within, to the source, the place from which Jesus spoke. The Pharisees and Sadducees, trained in the letter of the law, could not rise to Jesus' level, which was above the law, for it was the source of the law.

During the days he spent at the temple, the priests would occasionally hand him the scrolls and ask him to find a passage. When he did they were amazed. Jesus was previously unknown to them, and yet he could read and quote the scriptures. After several days, Jesus noticed that when he joined a group, the priest would adjourn the class and leave the area.

One young priest, however, found Jesus fascinating. He questioned Jesus on his background and experience. Jesus explained his visit to Nazareth and Jerusalem and his life in Alexandria. The young priest was extremely interested and spoke with Jesus at length. On the fifth day of his visits to the temple, the young priest informed Jesus that he should go home. "You are causing talk among the rabbis, and they will have some small charge brought against you to get rid of you. You will have a hard time because you do not live here, and you have no relatives or friends here to protect you. Please go home."

Jesus listened and said, "I will do as you suggest. I am a long way from home and I am very young. It would not be right to place myself in jeopardy while I am visiting my relatives. They would feel responsible. For your sake and theirs, I will go. Thank you for your advice. Your concern places you in my highest regard. God bless you." With this, Jesus left the temple grounds, said good bye to the family that had befriended him and prepared to leave. Before he left for Nazareth, the family told Jesus that any time he was in Jerusalem, he was welcome to come and stay with them. Jesus agreed to do so. He mounted his donkey and waving goodbye, headed back to Nazareth.

On arriving in Nazareth, he related his experiences in Jerusalem to his relatives. He told of the family that had sheltered him, and of his talks at the synagogue. Joachim was a little concerned to hear that Jesus had spoken at the synagogue.

"You spoke at the synagogue? To whom?"

"Why to the priests!"

"You talked back to them?"

"Of course, they were misinterpreting the scripture."

Joachim held his hands to his forehead in disbelief. "Did you get in trouble?"

"Oh, just a little. After a few days they didn't want me to come back."

Joachim shook his head. "Try to be a little more discreet here in Nazareth. This is a little town and if you get in trouble here it will reflect back on me. I'm a businessman, I don't need trouble from the townspeople about my guests."

"I'll do my best. I do not try to cause trouble. My questions just seem to disturb. I'm looking for honesty, that's all."

"Very well, but mind your honesty, especially in religious matters. They may not want to hear it." Jesus didn't respond, he could see that this conversation was not going to get any better.

After several weeks Jesus was again causing a stir among the religious elders. He could not stay away from the religious gatherings, and trouble just seemed inevitable. Joachim was well aware that this was not good for Jesus, or his family.

Joachim began to encourage Jesus to go home, to return to Alexandria and his mother and father. Joachim thought he would like for Mary and Joseph to return to Israel, but not with Jesus. With Joseph's skills, now so highly developed, he would be an asset, but Jesus would be a problem.

Jesus agreed to return home. In fact, the provincialism of the Jews in Israel, and especially the church elders, bothered him. So leaving would be a relief. He spent only another week with the family, staying away from the religious elders.

Early, on a bright morning, he left with a caravan headed back to Egypt. He had three camels and several donkey's belonging to Joachim in his care. The goods they carried were to be sold in Alexandria. Any profit could help pay for Mary, Joseph and their children to return to Jerusalem. But Joachim told Jesus, "If you return, you must keep quiet." Joachim made it very clear that Jesus was to relay this information to Mary and Joseph. Jesus agreed to deliver the camels, to help Joseph with the trading, and to give them the message.

Jesus understood, but did not think that he could live in Israel and not speak out. Herod was dead now. But, one of his sons was in charge. So danger was still present. The freedom and openness of Alexandria was not here.

(14)

Maleb Moab, the Kashmiri Trader

The trip back to Alexandria took four weeks. There were stops for trading, buying new animals and meeting up with new travelers as others left the group. Jesus especially enjoyed the crew of a small circus the caravan picked up along the way. At first he thought they were Jews, but it turned out that they were from Kashmir. Their language sounded very similar to Aramaic. This intrigued Jesus immensely and he began to list all the words that were similar. Every time he heard a word that was the same, he wrote it down.

He was fascinated to hear stories claiming that the lost ten tribes of Israel were in Kashmir. He pursued these stories with great curiosity, for the location of the ten lost tribes had been an important topic of discussion as far back as Jesus could remember. According to the Kashmiri, the "land of milk and honey," where Moses led the Israelites after leaving Egypt, was Kashmir.

Furthermore, these men claimed that Moses' grave was in Kashmir. Other, lesser prophets, also were buried there. This fascinated Jesus. He recalled that the scriptures described forty years of wandering before his people came to the promised land. The scriptures also said that most of the older generation, which had done the traveling, died before arriving. So, there might be, old Jewish graves scattered along the famous Silk Road and in Kashmir. In order to hear more of these stories, Jesus ingratiated himself with the circus crew, helping the magicians and caring for their animals.

In particular, a man named Maleb Moab, who had traveled the Silk Road for many years, captured Jesus' attention. He was over middle-age, small, wiry like a monkey and quite knowledgeable. He claimed to be originally, from the land of Moab, as mentioned in the Hebrew bible. Over camp fires, late into the night, Maleb, with his fiery eyes and lively gestures, spoke about the people of Kashmir. For Maleb, there was no doubt that his people were descendants of the Jews. Having traveled in both Kashmir and the Middle East, he proudly laid out a litany of evidence.

He told Jesus that in traveling throughout India, he had never found another people like his own. "For example, we look different from Indians, we look like Jews. Our way of life, morals and mannerisms are like yours. Once you have observed life in Kashmir and Israel, you can't help but see the similarities.

"We don't use fat or grease for cooking, we use only oil. We prefer boiled fish, called 'Phari,' in remembrance of the time before our exodus from Egypt. Our butcher knives are half-moon in shape, like those commonly used in Israel, and the rudders on our boats are heart shaped, like yours on the Sea of Galilee. (1) Our dress, our dances, so many things are the same. For this reason, I can easily travel this route through Israel. I don't feel like I am far from home."

"Tell me more," said Jesus.

"Well, if you want to look at it historically, I could point out, that many of the older graves in Kashmir point West as yours do here. Near Bijbihara, near a bath named for Moses, there is a cemetery with an old stone bearing a Hebrew inscription. There are many places in my homeland that have names that mean, 'Where Moses Slept, Where Moses Rested, Where Moses Ate.' And, inside some of our temples, where the structure is older, the architecture is typically Jewish. Once I came to Israel, I couldn't help noticing the many architectural similarities."

"Go on," said Jesus.

There is no other language in all of India like ours. The other Indian languages stem from Sanskrit; ours does not. I have found many words in common with your language. For example, your word for single is 'Akh,' just like ours; death 'ajal,' just like ours; 'Aosh' tears, just like ours. I could go on and on. You must come to Kashmir some day and see what I can show you. Come in the winter months, I don't travel then."

"I would love to visit you some day," said Jesus. "What town are you from?"

"I am from Srinagar. If you come see me, I will show you the grave of Moses."

"This I will have to see," said Jesus, "I have traveled quite a bit and live in Alexandria now, where people come from all over the world. But there is much yet for me to learn. If Moses' grave is in your land, surely we Jews must have been there. And you, though you are not Jewish, have the feel of one. I must come and visit you someday and discover my history. I have always been fascinated with history."

Suddenly, Jesus' mind turned to another concern. "You know Maleb, I hate the provinciality I find, especially here in Israel. It keeps the people down. I feel for them. The poverty here makes me weep. If they could see what I see, the similarities and connections, the oneness, beneath the differences, I would be happy. The more I travel, the more I see past the differences, to the subtler levels. For me the surface of things is continually receding into the One. We are more one, all of us, than different, but we refuse to see it. Even though it is right before our noses."

"Yes," said Maleb. "The more one travels, the more one enjoys the differences, but sees the commonalities."

Almost daily, Jesus and Maleb discovered similar words, similar cultural icons and idiosyncrasies. These convinced Jesus that his people's past was, in part, to be found in Kashmir. Maleb, jokingly said, "You know Jesus, I have a granddaughter that might make you a good wife. Come live in Kashmir and I will introduce you to some very nice women."

Jesus shrugged his shoulders. "I am not old enough to be thinking about marriage. Besides, I am not sure that my life is taking me in that direction. I am more interested in spiritual things than material things. I don't think women will go for that."

"Ah, but you do not see your assets, Jesus. You have an openness about you that will attract women. Believe me."

"Women are beautiful," Jesus answered, "but they tie you down. The only reason you have escaped, is that your wife died. Now isn't that the truth?"

"Yes," Maleb agreed with a sigh. He grew quiet. "I miss my wife terribly."

"I'm sorry," said Jesus, "I wasn't meaning to be rude."

"That's okay. I know."

Jesus felt he needn't go to Kashmir to find a wife, for there were women on this trip who found him attractive. They cornered him whenever they could. Jesus was careful, and he made sure that any woman he was intimate with, was not likely to claim him as her own.

Maleb took a long look at Jesus. He looked older than his years, but this was due to his demeanor of confidence and authority. He had a stubbly beard. His nose was strong, his cheek bones high and his high forehead made him look wise beyond his years. These features, Maleb knew, were also attractive to women. Above all, Maleb noted, Jesus' eyes were absolutely piercing. When he looked directly at you, it was as if your soul was known. He had seen that women liked to look into his eyes, then turn away, due to the intensity of his gaze. When they thought he was looking away, they'd look again. Maleb liked the fact that Jesus didn't make women his primary pursuit. Maleb saw Jesus continually having to keep them away. Maleb wished his personal power worked so well. Without effort, Jesus worked magic.

As the caravan moved along, they joined other caravans that had come all the way from China, bringing loads of silk. This fine cloth was so durable that it could endure months of being jostled and carried, even used on the way, and still sell at top price. In fact, the further they traveled, the more valuable the silk became.

Silk was one of the main sources of China's income and the silk trade was enormous.

Naturally, Jesus found people interested in discussing the customs of India and China. Those from India seemed to have the widest variety of beliefs and customs. Most of them called themselves Hindus. What Jesus found most intriguing about the Indians, was that whatever new beliefs they encountered, they simply incorporated them into their own, open-ended religion. This aspect of their faith inspired Jesus, as it seemed so different from the Jewish reaction to foreign faiths. Whereas the Jews prided themselves in keeping foreign influences out, the Hindus welcomed everything new in.

Another custom Jesus noted among the Hindu women on the trip, was that they put red clay, in the form of a dot, on their foreheads.

One day, Jesus asked, "What is the red dot for?"

The young woman answered. "It represents the third eye."

"And what is the third eye?"

"It's something our yogis see when they are enlightened."

"Oh, so it's a spiritual matter."

"Yes, very spiritual. The third eye is a light that is the spark of the soul in each man. It can be seen between the eyes in the middle of the forehead."

Jesus pointed to his forehead, just above his nose. "Here?" He asked.

"Yes, and that is why we put the dot here." And she pointed. Jesus pondered this awhile, then asked. "What do the yogis do to be able to see this third eye?"

"Meditation."

Jesus knew about meditation, but he had never heard about this third eye. He decided to look for this third eye when he meditated. He wondered why the monks at the academy had not spoken to him of this third eye. I will ask them about this when I get home, he thought. Late into the night, after others had fallen asleep, Jesus sat in his tent, meditating.

His obvious determination and seriousness, affected all those around him. Young as he was, very few people could say that they didn't experience something different about him, something intense, pure, good, and yet disturbing.

Sensing the soul of a yogi in Jesus, one of the Hindu women started making patterns with colored sand in front of Jesus' tent. She did this each morning, before camp broke. Bringing different colors of sand, which she had found, or made, she drew symbols in the sand. But Jesus would have to step over them each morning, or walk through them when he stepped out of his tent. At first this disturbed Jesus, and he tried to avoid stepping on the drawings.

But the woman protested, "Oh, but you must walk on the drawing, it will bless your feet on the path you take. If I were in India, I would be making this design each morning in front of my home, for my whole family to step on. Since I cannot do that for them, I choose to do it for you. Please accept my blessing, tread on it, do not reject a simple woman's pleasure."

So Jesus relaxed and did not resist the woman's devotion to him. He would wake and stand at his tent door, staring quietly at the symbol until he had it committed to memory. As he walked out and later packed his tent, he gave no heed to his feet, trampling the drawing. The patterns left behind, played in the desert sun, remnants of one soul's blessing of another. When he got the chance, Jesus would ask her what the symbols meant; she was always glad to tell him. The spirituality of this woman and others from India, amazed and fascinated Jesus.

Another engaging belief of these Indians was their firm belief in reincarnation. For them, reincarnation was as sure as the sun coming up in the morning. They explained to Jesus that all the souls in the world were going through stages until perfection was reached. At that point, which they called Nirvana, one reunited with God in the absolute bliss of the Godhead. They spoke of yogis who had reached this state and how their eyes shone like the brightness of the sun. They could make you feel, in their presence, as if you were the only person in the world. They had a depth of bliss in their gaze that made one feel they could see into the past and future at the same time.

These discussions on reincarnation made Jesus think. He did not reject the idea outright, but, he decided to meditate on it. His primary obstacle to accepting the idea was that he could not determine who it was that would reincarnate. He pondered how, the individual that had died, could retain his previous sense of self, in another body, of a different sex, with different parents and different experiences. For Jesus, the very sense of self, that wished to be reincarnated, was so dependent on sex, race, culture and experience, that in a different body, that sense of self would be totally alien. Jesus felt that reincarnation was a substitute for a true sense of the eternal. For, as he understood it, the true self wasn't an individual, but the One Universal Self. It was that One that kept reincarnating. Reincarnation, of the individual soul, Jesus thought, was just a way of hanging on to the little self—a lacking or partial understanding of God.

Especially difficult for Jesus was the concept of a personality or soul that could be in an animal and pass into a human, or vice versa. How could an animal soul become a human soul? For Jesus, this idea was unnecessary, all were just manifestations of the One. That One, was the personality of all, any reincarnation was simply that same One, in a different form. As he had told the priests in Jerusalem, he already felt eternal. His sense of being eternal was not dependent on his personality, it was something deeper. He already was, had been, and would be, eternal, whether this body existed or not.

By the time Jesus got to Alexandria, he had decided to tell his parents that he wanted to travel to Kashmir and India. He had changed and grown intellectually and spiritually. Already, he had made arrangements for Maleb to contact him before he left on his return along the silk road. For Jesus had informed him, "Unless I am physically restrained, I will go with you on your return to the Far East.".

Maleb informed Jesus that he would be in Alexandria at least

a month before starting the return trip. This would give Jesus time
to discuss with his parents his burning desire to travel further
East. As they approached the outskirts of Alexandria, Jesus took
the animals in his charge and headed for the Jewish quarter and
his parents' home. Jesus knew he would have to explain to his
parents that, although he loved the Viharas school, he was now
totally enraptured with the historical significance of the stories
about Kashmir. He felt a deep necessity to meet some of the Indian yogis he had heard about.

When his younger brothers and sisters saw him coming, they
ran out to greet him, screaming, "Jesus, Jesus, Jesus!" The sound of
their voices brought tears to his eyes. He leaped down from the
camel and hugged them all.

Mary came out and embraced him, not wanting to let him go.
Jesus went into his father's shop and gave him a big hug. Joseph
couldn't stop working, but he did ask Mary to make a special meal
in celebration of Jesus' safe return.

(15)

The Map to Kashmir

"Jesus," Mary said, "I have been waiting a long time to tell you something. I cannot wait any longer. You have asked to go East, so I must tell you now, for this was foretold. Since what I have to tell you is important to me and your father, you should know that I have his permission to reveal this secret to you. Much of what I have to say is personal, my experience, so Joseph values my sharing this with you alone. I have a gift for you too. One I am passing on for someone I met a long time ago. I will give it to you shortly."

Jesus did not say a word. He just sat obediently and listened. Mary continued. "When you were newly conceived and in my womb, I went to Qumran to the Essene community to speak with your father. We were not married at the time and Joseph did not know that I had conceived his child. I spent the night in the kitchen waiting for his decision as to whether or not he would leave the commune and marry me. During the night, an angel came to me in a dream and told me that you were destined to be a great spiritual leader, a man of wisdom and light. The vision was so real that I could not doubt it, and it gave me great peace of mind.

"Now, when you were born in Bethlehem, I was approached by a Gypsy woman who could see a clear white aura around you. She brought to me three Wise Men from the East. They were looking for the reincarnation of a great Lama. In seeing you, they were certain that you were the one. Into my hands they entrusted a scroll, a map really, of where you were to contact them when you

were ready. All these years I have kept the scroll, even though I
have never spoken a word of it to you.

"Even though you have never been told of these things, you
have grown into the kind of man that was foretold. There is no
doubt that you are destined to be a great spiritual leader. All your
actions point in that direction. Your father has observed this with
me over the years, and he is in complete agreement. Your request
the other day, to go East, was the key that unlocked this secret. We
grant your request to go East."

With this said, Mary walked to her trunk, a magnificent piece
made by Joseph himself, opened the lid and took out the mats and
cloth it contained. Then, deftly, she took out a false bottom and
pulled out a small wooden box. She handed the box to Jesus, saying, "Open it. Look at the map."

Jesus did as he was told. He opened the wooden box and looked
inside. Neatly rolled up, tied with silk, he saw an ancient yellowed
scroll. He took it out, untied the ribbon and carefully unrolled it.
Jesus' eyes grew big as he read the names on the map: "Kashmir,
Ladakh, Leh, Hemis and Srinagar," the very names that Maleb
Moab had talked about just weeks ago. Jesus was stunned. His
mind could barely take in the awesome significance of the parallels
between his desires, his wants, his wish to travel to Kashmir, and
this revelation by his Mother.

After a long time looking silently at the scroll, Jesus said, "This
is absolutely, beyond doubt, the most affirmative confirmation of
something I have always felt. It is as if I have always felt a destiny,
but did not know quite what it was. Now, with this revelation, my
desire to go East and this map, it is all clear. I have been handed
the exact mission I would have requested, had I known what it
was. Thank you Mother, the timing is auspicious." Jesus stood up
and held his mother in his arms for a long time.

"You know Mother, if you had shown me this map or told me
of this scroll as a young child, you would have spoiled this for me.
It would have been as if I were being told what to do. But, by
keeping this to yourself and letting me develop on my own, I can

now accept this scroll, this map and the message of your vision, without any hesitancy whatsoever. Thank you! Thank you."

"You're quite welcome Jesus. God bless you."

"May I leave and take this scroll with me, so that I may be alone with it?"

"Oh, but surely. Go and take it all in, let it take you to God."

So Jesus put the scroll under his tunic and walked out into the sun. He walked for several miles until he came to his favorite spot, under a large tree and sat. He took out the scroll and studied it, reading the names of the places along the Silk Road and the places in Kashmir and Tibet that Maleb had spoken of. The magnitude of his wishes, the thoughts and the portent of this scroll, filled him with so much passion, he could hardly contain himself. He felt ecstatic. For several hours he sat, feeling whole, complete, in harmony with all of his surroundings—every leaf, every tree, every blade of grass, whatever came into his awareness.

When Jesus got home that night he shared his thoughts and feelings with Joseph. Joseph was very pleased and related to Jesus, his dream, the one in which he was told that Jesus would be a light of wisdom and truth for the world. Jesus found it very hard to accept this from his father. He felt he was being given more than his father had ever received. For Jesus knew well of his father's wish to live in Qumran and to be a priest, studying the scriptures and living the life of one wholly dedicated to God. But Jesus accepted this wonderful gift from his father and he gave him a warm embrace too.

Over the next several weeks, preparations were made for Jesus' trip East with Maleb's caravan. In order to give Jesus protection for the trip, Mary and Joseph gave Jesus two camels and a donkey to take on the journey. This they thought, would give Jesus goods to carry and to sell, as well as something to ride on when tired, or ill. Jesus was glad to accept, knowing the value of the increased status of owning animals in a caravan.

Maleb came by late one afternoon and ate supper with the family. Mary and Joseph were pleased to have a man, older, obviously intelligent and well traveled, being Jesus' mentor and guide for this trip. It seemed that God was providing the means to carry out His plans. Although Mary and Joseph knew they would miss Jesus, they knew that his life was a mission of truth, and they felt honored to let him go.

In the morning, after good-byes, Jesus left with Maleb on his own pack animals, to meet up with the caravan that would take him to Kashmir and his future. Mary and Joseph watched Jesus ride off down the road out of town. They knew his destiny was God's call and that it must be fulfilled. Mary's eyes filled with tears. They were tears of joy, of loss and hope. Joseph comforted her, knowing his own heart was breaking too. When Jesus was finally out of sight, they knelt on the floor of their home and gave thanks to God.

At work that day, Joseph thought about losing a son who could take up his profession, his business, when he got old. But it did not trouble him severely, because, although Jesus had always been a good worker, it was not his interest to be a carpenter, a trader or a businessman. His destiny was to bring light to the world. Joseph went about his work with renewed enthusiasm, feeling that his contribution to the world was complete. His work seemed easy and light and he wished his son all the best on his journey.

Mary too went about her household duties, with a spring in her step and a song in her heart. She had been blessed to have a son who was destined to be a light to mankind. She gave thanks that she had been chosen to carry, deliver and raise this boy, a gift to the world from God.

Jesus too, thought about his parents, and although he would miss them, he knew that wherever he was, he was with his true father, and that was enough. The first day went fast, but not a lot of territory was covered as the caravan was just coming into its own. Each caravan had to find its own rhythm, its own pace, its own way of traveling in the world, just as each individual, animal, man, woman and child, had to find its rhythm and its place in the caravan. Jesus was now fifteen and considered a grown man. If he had stayed with his parents in Alexandria, he might soon be committed to some woman in marriage, but with this trip, he was escaping that fate.

Over the next few weeks Jesus settled into the flow of travel. He felt as if he were married to destiny, to the will of God. Paradoxically, this gave him a sense of absolute freedom. Jesus was what he was, complete and whole unto himself. This Self which he felt, was not separate from anyone or anything. The sense of security which he felt was perceivable to everyone that came in contact with him. Yet Jesus remained humble and profound, helping with the animals, the sick and the lonely, always ready and willing.

It took several months to arrive in Kashmir. Jesus was extremely excited to arrive as Maleb had been talking incessantly about the land. In the view of the Kashmiris, this was the promised land, where they, the lost ten tribes of Israel, lived. Maleb pointed out to Jesus all the various towns and villages with Hebrew names, many of them exactly as they appear in the scriptures. Towns with names such as: 'The Place of Moses, Moses' Bath, Where Moses Wept.' As Jesus saw these towns, Maleb explained the names and their similarity to those in the scriptures, thus: Beth-peor became Behat-porr and eventually, Bandipur; Heshbon became Hasba or Hasbal. All these biblical towns were here, and Jesus recognized them from the Hebrew scriptures.

Maleb easily convinced Jesus to take a detour and visit Moses' grave on the plains of Moab, where Maleb was from. They passed Bandipur, Ayat-i-Maulu, Aham Sharif and then came to Booth. Moses' tomb was "beneath Mount Nebo." Jesus knelt at the grave and was quiet for awhile. Maleb stayed respectfully still until Jesus got up. Maleb spoke to Jesus of many things while they continued on their way to Hemis. They were now in the hills at the base of the Himalayas and climbing. At Leh Jesus and Maleb left the caravan. Jesus left his animals and most of his belongings, except the scroll, with Maleb. He told Maleb to keep and use the animals, but to track and to record their offspring and the profit from their sale, so that there would be supplies and animals for Jesus' return trip to Egypt. At whatever time Jesus might leave, he wanted access to funds or animals, in order to have the means to return home.

Jesus and Maleb parted ways, and Jesus headed further up into the Himalayas. The monastery at Hemis was where the three Wise Men had come from. They had given the scroll to Jesus' mother. Now, Jesus carrying this very same scroll, was approaching the town of its origin. Jesus felt a tremendous responsibility as he approached, knowing the auspicious history behind his being here. But a monastery was just the place Jesus was longing to be, despite his fears and the strangeness of this place.

The air was thin and only a small path wound its way up. A monk was waiting outside the door of the monastery, which was high on the side of a mountain. Apparently Jesus had been seen approaching long before he got to the front gate. The monk asked Jesus, "What Sir, brings you here?"

"I have come to see the abbot."

"What is your concern with the abbot?"

"Tell him that I have word concerning a certain reincarnation of a great Bodhisattva, who was born in the West about fifteen years ago. Three wise men were sent out, following a star. They found a boy and gave his mother a scroll. I have word of that boy." Jesus had no intention of telling the gatekeeper, that he, Jesus, was in fact that boy, and that he had the scroll with him. After such a long trip, he wanted to be certain that this was the right place.

"Very well," said the monk, "Come in. I will make your presence known to the abbot." With that, a small wooden door to the side of the main gate was opened and Jesus passed through. Jesus was amazed at the beauty of the place. Not only was this place clean, with beautiful statues—many of the Buddha, but the Himalayas were its backdrop. Of any place Jesus had been, this was a place where the environment alone, would cause one's soul to leap. Jesus thought he would certainly love to stay here, if this was the place.

Jesus found a stone bench and sat down to wait. He could

hear chanting in the background, echoing through the stone walls, and out into the mountain crevices. It seemed like a thousand men must be chanting at once. Jesus later learned that 1,500 men lived and studied in the monastery. There were pine forests all about the monastery, hugging the hillsides. Further up the slopes, the tree line stopped. It was too cold and too high for the trees to grow beyond that point.

Presently, a very old man approached Jesus. He spoke in the local language, which thanks to Maleb, Jesus could understand.

"What message do you bring of the boy from the West?"

"I bring news of his whereabouts. But Sir, before I speak more of this, I humbly ask that you answer a question too."

"Very well."

"Tell me," said Jesus, "What was given to the boy's mother, that he would bring to this place?"

"Very well, I will tell you what it would be, but then, if you do not carry such a thing with you, you cannot use it as evidence that you are who you say you are."

"Very well," said Jesus.

"The mother of the boy born in the West would have a small wooden box."

"Right," said Jesus, "and what would be in the box?"

The abbot paused for a moment, then said, "It would be something that would provide direction, a map."

"Direction to here?" asked Jesus.

"Yes."

"And what form would it take."

"It would be a scroll of leather, preserved to last a lifetime. It would be a map written in India Ink."

"I have this scroll with me and I am the boy." With that, Jesus reached under his robe and produced the small wooden box. Handling it very gently, Jesus reverently passed it with both hands to the abbot. The abbot opened the box, reached in and carefully pulled out the scroll. He took off the silk ribbon and opened it up. He looked at it carefully. Then, with a delightful smile, showing a wide row of yellow teeth, the abbot bowed to Jesus, almost touching the ground. "You have arrived. We are so glad to see you. We have much to tell you."

The abbot quickly turned to the gatekeeper, barking orders so fast that Jesus could not understand. The gatekeeper left almost at a run. Jesus sat patiently, waiting for what would come next. It looked to Jesus as if the monk would pass out. He was very old, beardless, with a reddish yellow tint to his skin. In contrast, Jesus' own skin was very pale, even though he was well tanned. After the gatekeeper was well out of sight, the abbot turned to Jesus.

"So you are the son of the woman who received this map?"

"Yes, I am."

"Do you know what else was given to the mother besides this map?"

"Gold, Frankincense and Myrrh."

"You are definitely the one. Although, I shouldn't have had to ask, as there is a white light more radiant that the sun, shining all around you."

"I am glad you asked the questions," said Jesus, "I needed to be sure as well. This has been a long trip. I am glad that this is the place from which the wise men came."

"Yes, this is the place and you are most welcome. What a glorious moment. We will have a grand reception tonight. You will see."

Before Jesus could speak any more with the abbot, groups of ochre robbed monks came rumbling down the stairs from various rooms and halls. They were all very excited and all were headed in Jesus' direction.

(16)

The Hemis Monastery

Jesus was amazed at the excitement coursing through the monastery. Groups of monks came up to him bowing and gazing at him in awe. Some began kneeling and bowing with tears running down their cheeks. They were saying under their breath, "Buddha, Buddha, Buddha." Jesus could not believe what they were saying. Did they believe he was the reincarnation of the Buddha? Jesus said nothing, but sat quietly, looking into the monks' eyes, a soft smile on his face and compassion in his heart. Jesus considered what these monks were experiencing. He had studied reincarnation at the academy in Alexandria, but he was not sure he believed it to be fact. Even in Israel, part of the populace believed in reincarnation, but as yet, Jesus had not decided this issue for himself. He had his reservations.

Before long, a crowd of fifteen hundred monks were standing around him. An Ochre colored sea of robes flowed about him. Jesus was impressed with their interest. He knew that he made a formidable impression on people, even at his young age, but this kind of adulation he did not expect. Jesus' response to this honor was to feel humbled, hoping to return the honor.

"Rise," Jesus said, "go on about your business." But the monks were hesitant. They knew the abbot would want them to pay due respect and not treat Jesus like just another traveler. So they stepped back, but they did not leave. Presently the abbot returned with a number of older men. Jesus could see that these were the leaders of the monastery.

"Please tell these men to go on about their business," Jesus said.

"No, Master," said the abbot, "Please do not ask me to disperse them. This monastery has been waiting many years for your arrival. You are the reincarnation of the first Gautama Buddha, if we do not pay homage to you, we will not feel fit to remain here. Please honor us by your acceptance of our gratitude."

With this Jesus did not know what to do. How could he turn these men away knowing they would feel that they had been disrespectful. So, Jesus said, "Let me pray for us all and this monastery." The abbot was pleased with this and nodded his head in approval. So Jesus prayed.

"Dear Father, praise be to You, the only presence here. You are the One speaking and listening. Praise be to You for Your placement of each and every one of us here. Let each one of us, in our own way, perform Your will, according to our understanding. Let each of us be in awe of each other as a manifestation of You, the One, the Only, our very ground of being. Om." With this, Jesus ended his prayer.

The monks remained in silence. Each and every one of them was struck by the words spoken. This was such a young man, but what a powerful message. They stared at Jesus, looking closely for signs of his divinity. His appearance was almost as striking as his prayer, for he looked quite different from them. Jesus was tall. His skin wasn't yellow and his head was not shaved. Many of them could not grow a beard, yet Jesus, young as he was, already had one. It made him seem older. His piercing eyes, light skin and height, made him seem like a God to them. His prayer had sealed his coming as truly the one they expected—the return of the Buddha into their midst.

The abbot brought the elders of the monastery to Jesus. One by one, each bowed and paid homage to him. Jesus accepted as humbly and politely as he could. Little did these monks know that Jesus had trained in a Buddhist monastery and therefore knew how to be respectful according to their traditions. Jesus bowed in return. The monks were impressed. After these proceedings had gone on for an hour or more, the abbot led Jesus to a set of rooms at the very top of the monastery. As they entered, Jesus could see young boys taking covers off the furniture.

"This room has been preserved for you," the abbot said.

Jesus looked at the spacious room, impressed that this was obviously to be his home as long as he wished.

"Thank you," said Jesus.

The room was dusted and a fire lit in the fireplace. Jesus was asked to sit at the head of the table in the room, and food was brought. The elders, eleven of them, asked Jesus' permission to sit, and with a nod of his head, they all sat. The food came and being quite hungry, Jesus ate. He was aware that these men were studying him closely, but Jesus was used to this. He was often studied when he spoke in public. It had always been this way since he was a small child, so it did not daunt him in any way. He had learned early, how to be natural when people paid him attention. The interest of the teachers in Alexandria had humbled him, but had also taught him to speak his mind. Besides, Jesus felt that he was simply searching, doing his Father's bidding.

When Jesus finished eating, he was told that he would be presented to the town this very night. They would take him to the village center. This was necessary, for if they did not go there, the whole town would be coming up to the monastery to see the reincarnation of Buddha. Jesus agreed to go to the village with them. Before they left, there was a general discussion on his life, his mother, his father, his studies, his travels. Jesus told them everything he could. The monks nodded their heads in approval. Jesus would indeed grow into the great teacher they had expected.

The abbot informed Jesus that they had been concerned, when the three wise men, now dead, had come back from so far. They had been even more concerned when they found out that the reincarnated Buddha was from a foreign land, so far away. But, they trusted their elders, and over the years, had grown used to the idea. The abbot informed Jesus that as soon as he was ready, he would be given the top position at the monastery.

To this, Jesus responded, "I will let you know when I am ready, but it will not be soon. I am still very young and have a lot to learn."

"We will wait until you are ready. But you must teach us while you wait."

"I will teach," Jesus said, "I have been told by many to teach. Yet, I am young. It seems inappropriate that I do so. However, it looks like I will be unable to avoid it here. It is a gift, I'm told. I shall not refuse. I will share all I know with you. I will learn from you as well."

With this issue settled and night coming on, Jesus was led down the hill. He would not ride in the poled chair that was proffered him. As they approached the town, torches were lit, held high on both sides along the path. Young men and girls were waving the torches and singing praises. Jesus was a bit surprised at all of this attention. He recognized the amount of respect the spiritual leaders held, but did not like adulation. It seemed these people were missing the vital point, that each person had his own inner leader.

Jesus was concerned about how these people would respond if they did not want to hear what he wanted to teach. What was it going to be like when they found that he might not be, say, or teach, what they were expecting? Jesus thought to himself that he would be careful. He would listen and learn so as not to tread on their expectations. He also determined, that should things be expected of him, that were not true of his mission, he would leave.

Jesus was led to the marketplace in the middle of town. There was already a feast in progress. Meat was roasting on the fires, and vegetables too, some which Jesus had never seen. He was asked to stand and receive everyone. People came and bowed, and many kissed the ground on which he stood. Then he was brought more food and Jesus ate again. He was glad to see the people of the town having a reason for celebration, but he didn't say much as he was already getting more attention than he thought he deserved.

The party went on most of the night. Finally, Jesus said to the abbot. "The people must be tired. Let us leave and return to the monastery so they can get some rest."

The abbot agreed, and as they turned to leave, a roar went up from the crowd, cheering Jesus' presence. Some followed and some led the way with their torches. At the monastery gate, the people turned away. Jesus was shown to his room, where the fire was still crackling. His bed was neatly made. Jesus thanked the abbot and the elders for such a wonderful reception and went to bed. It was now approaching sunrise and Jesus fell into a deep sleep.

Jesus dreamed about his mother and father, Egypt and his homeland, about his travels and his arrival here. But there were no nightmares, he was relaxed. He felt called, being told from deep inside, that he was someday to lead. Words and prayers did come naturally to him and he knew they would be there when the time came for him to speak.

Over the next few weeks Jesus was introduced to the routine of the monastery. He himself was given no duties other than attending all the prayers and meditations. Although he was asked frequently to participate, he kept his participation to a minimum. He was listening deeply to what was going on, thinking about what he wanted to do and say. He was waiting for the right place and time. He knew well that if he listened, he would be respected and that when the time came for him to speak, he would be able to make his points clearly and respectfully.

For the next six months Jesus listened to all who came to him. He observed all the comings and goings at the monastery. He discovered the value of, and the greatness of parables. He knew that if each listener could glean his own meaning from a parable, each would have his own experience of truth. Listeners would consider him wiser than if he gave them a direct answer. In time, Jesus grew accustomed to the ways of the monastery and became deservedly well liked.

At this time there was a great assembly of monks, a festival of enlightened ones. The best and brightest of the monks from Tibet, China and India had come to Hemis for two weeks of camaraderie, lectures, talks and decision making. Jesus was asked to give a lecture at the end of the gathering. Even though he was now only fifteen years old, Jesus gave this talk.

"Dear men of God, we are gathered here in each other's presence and in the presence of God. I believe that the kindness and respect we show one another we do for God, because our neighbor is our Self. In this Eastern land you have a term for this, you call it non-duality. But, the word is not the thing. Even though I did not learn that word till I met people from the East, I knew the feeling, I had the experience.

"Now, many of you have this knowledge through personal experience. Yet even those of you who have not experienced this state, do see the difference it makes in those who have. It is honorable to seek this state, for to pursue it, is to become humble. For me, humility and the profound go together. May we all be so humble that we are unable to look at another without seeing ourselves. In this awareness, giving is receiving and receiving is giving. What a blessed state.

"For many years, even as a child, I questioned my experience of being. What is this I amness, this presence, I claim as myself. Who or what is responsible for this feeling of presence? Consider, is my experience of presence different from another's? Each and every one of us can say 'I am' and feel it. Yet ultimately, your 'I am' and my 'I am' are the same. My physical body and yours, my experiences and your experiences separate us, but this separation, on examination is superficial. Ultimately, your 'I am' is my 'I am,' and both are expressions of the one Source. The oneness this imparts, is to feel and be in the Kingdom of Heaven.

"Where I come from, very few strive for this oneness. They see God as separate from themselves. So, they find it difficult to understand how they are manifestations of the One. There is a big difference between being a part of the One and being an object.

The difference is between knowing that one is God, here present or feeling separation, as if God were an object. In truth there is only subject. Object is appearance only. For those lacking a sense of oneness, a longing sets in to find relief from that sense of separation. I no longer desire to be one with God as I am fully aware that I am. My only desire now is to do the will of Him who sent me.

"Thus, for those that are still struggling in duality, the first law of living, to love one's neighbor as oneself, becomes a code of behavior. This law will keep one on the right course. However, for those beyond duality, this is no longer law, but a living fact, unavoidably real. For one living in non-duality, following the law is as natural as walking. There is no question of treating your neighbor as yourself, for your neighbor is your self. Therefore, let us treat one another with the respect that we deserve, not as the children of God, but as God himself, here and everywhere present. What more is there to say?"

With this Jesus ended his talk. There was complete silence in the hall. Two thousand monks were gathered here and all were silent. Jesus said, "Let us chant this mantra until the gong sounds. Repeat with me together, I am, I am, I am, I am." The voices joined repeating the mantra in a vast chorus reverberating through the hall. The massive oneness of the voice carried down the halls and through the windows and echoed in the mountain crevices, spilling down into the village below. People in the village stopped and listened. Some even joined in the mantra, feeling full of awe.

When the gong sounded a number of the monks could not stop chanting. They were off in another world. Some had even fallen over in a swoon, their faces expressing great joy. Jesus sat down, looking at the room; many were full of joy and bliss. He wondered how these things happened. He had not prepared this talk. It was as if it came through him, but not of him. He truly felt that he spoke his Father's words, not his own.

Jesus' reputation spread far and wide. People came from all over the land to speak with him, to pray with him, to listen to him. Still Jesus mostly spoke in parables, except to the monks who could grasp what he was saying. Although the elders believed him to be the reincarnation of the Buddha, he refused to take the official leadership of the monastery. Instead, he played the role of teacher, lecturer, friend and scholar. When asked, Jesus always said that his role was not to be the authority for others, put to point to each and everyone's inner authority. For all authority belonged to God, and God was present in each and everyone.

Jesus lived at Hemis for three years, praying, meditating, working in the carpentry shop and teaching. But Jesus did have some time off from the monastery and its obligations. Since his position was elevated, due to monastery's belief that he was a reincarnated Bodhisattva, he had much more freedom than the other monks. Jesus came and went as he pleased. He did not take undue advantage of his position, but neither did he confine himself strictly to the rules.

In town, Jesus often spent time with a woman named Chaila. She was the daughter of the town's chief councilman and as such was very attracted to Jesus, as he was regarded with such awe at the monastery. Jesus was introduced to Chaila early in his stay at Hemis, for when he was at the feasts or festivals, Chaila's father was always presiding.

Chaila, approached Jesus herself when she noticed him looking at her. She did not know if Jesus appreciated her looks, but other men certainly did. She had the high cheekbones of the Mongols, yellow reddish skin and straight black hair. To test his interest, she walked up and said, "You like?"

Jesus looked her over, not sure of what his response should be. She did not look like a Jewish woman. She was shorter, stockier, with a broader face. Her nose was small. Her skin was smooth, her features fine, her eyes intelligent. Her breasts were small, but her legs were strong. "What are you referring to?" asked Jesus.

"Why to me!" she said.

"I like what I see," said Jesus, feeling that he might be out of bounds. But Chaila smiled and Jesus felt better. He soon learned that Chaila loved putting people on the spot. She had no compulsions against being pushy when she saw something she wanted. Because of her father's status she got away with it.

Chaila, like Jesus' mother, was an exceptional woman. She did not bend easily to the mores that kept other women down. She was independent, stubborn, and a free thinker. At gatherings, where Jesus was always the center of attraction, she would question him about his background, travels, thoughts and attitudes. He never failed to impress her. She was enchanted.

Chaila had difficulty with most men. Not that she didn't appreciate them, but they couldn't appreciate her. Being used to more docile, demurring women, Chaila was a handful. So, even though all the other women her age had married while still very young, Chaila had not. So Jesus, like her, being single, and of a similar age, was one of the few unmarried men around. Chaila's father had tried to get some of the older men, whose wives had died to marry Chaila, but neither they nor Chaila would have anything to do with each other.

In time, Jesus and Chaila began to spend more time together. Chaila's father hoped that Jesus would be the man to take her hand. However, Jesus was still searching and pursuing clarification of his mission. So, although he spent much of his time outside the monastery with Chaila, he had no inclination to marry her. Chaila suggested marriage to Jesus but he reminded her that he was a foreigner and would some day be returning home.

"I'll go anywhere you go," she responded.

"That means a lot to me. But, there is time. I have much yet to do, to learn. I intend to go to India sometime, probably before I return to Israel. I promise you will not be forgotten. I will keep you in my heart. Remember, the pull I feel from inside is one I cannot resist. I must go."

"I understand. I really do. And I will keep you to your promise."

Jesus appreciated her open invitation and eventually began to consider her proposal. Chaila and Jesus became intimate, and Jesus knew that he would likely become a father and have to marry. But, over time, the two of them became aware that Chaila was unable to conceive. Besides being unable to conceive, Chaila was often sickly and had to stay in bed. She looked good, and most of the time she was able to get around. But, when her illness struck, she was often bedridden. The local healers did all they could and were often of much benefit, but she never seemed completely cured.

When she was feeling well, she and Jesus took walks in the mountains, watching the wild animals play. Jesus liked Chaila's playfulness too. He often said, "You are a wild animal! People just think you're a woman." Chaila would laugh, for she was a wild woman, compared to the average fare in this community. But Chaila was also very smart and could defend herself so well in an argument, that few challenged her.

Jesus loved Chaila's wit. In discussing all that went on in the monastery, Chaila's insight was often very beneficial. She knew the customs and mores of the people well, which Jesus did not. He did not always catch the nuances that she did. So, when deeply perplexed, or perturbed, Jesus would seek Chaila out and take her council. He revealed to her the depths of his doubts and the strength of his calling. She encouraged him, assuaging his doubts and letting him know that a calling should not be ignored.

After long discussions of their respective trials and tribulations, Jesus and Chaila would walk into the hills and meditate. She and her countrymen had very advanced practices and Jesus was amazed at her dedication.

In time, although Jesus and Chaila never married, they were thought of, and when appropriate, treated as a couple. Women had their place, but they were not stoned for transgressions like they were in the Near East. Jesus grew very accustomed to the freedom the women had in Kashmir. It made them much more fun to be around, and certainly allowed more of them to excel.

In time Jesus again became restless, wanting to go to India for further study. He and Chaila discussed the consequences, were he to travel there without her. Chaila had always insisted that she should go with him, but Jesus felt that this would be asking too much. For he was well aware that there were places and practices which he would want to study, which would not be conducive to a relationship. This issue was never fully resolved, which bothered both Jesus and Chaila.

After several years, when Jesus felt more internal pressure to move on, Chaila was ill. At this time she had to stay home while her mother took care of her. Since Jesus lived in the monastery, he came often to visit her. When she did not get better, Jesus felt it was time for him to speak with her.

"Chaila," he said, "I have been waiting for some months now for you to get better. But your condition remains the same. I have been waiting to see if you could go with me to India, but I see now that this is not possible. Here, you have your mother and sisters to take care of you, and I live in a monastery. I want desperately to see and study with the great sages of India. I think this might be the appropriate time for me to go. Another level of my studies awaits me there."

Chaila, who loved Jesus very much, reached up from where she lay, and held his hand. "I hate to see it come to this, but I agree. I think you should go. I am in no danger of dying. We both know that. But I am capable of little right now. Traveling is out of the question. It may be some time before I am completely well. So, I feel that you should go, for you are a man of destiny, and you must find what you are seeking."

"Oh Chaila! Thank you. Thank you for understanding. I can feel your love. It is full of freedom as well as passion. I love you too."

"I will miss you," said Chaila, "but I would be remiss if I begged you to stay. But, be forewarned, when you return, I intend to follow wherever you go."

Jesus held her hand, and looking into her eyes said, "I understand." He kissed her goodbye.

(17)

The Mongols and the Cave-dweller

Jesus was eighteen years old and was feeling once again the urge to travel. He spoke with the abbot who gave Jesus his blessing to travel, to teach and to continue his learning. So it was in the Spring of that year, Jesus, now a fully grown man, learned beyond his years, took leave of the Hemis monastery to travel further East. It was to India that Jesus wished to go, for he had encountered many yogis from the East, with powers that seemed unbelievable. There were many different sects of the Hindu religion in India and Jesus wanted to understand them all, through his own experience.

Jesus went to see Maleb Moab as arranged to finish planning the trip further East.

"Well," said Jesus, "What do we have left to do?"

"Not much. I've decided that we will only need to take four camels and three donkeys."

"Will that make the trip faster?"

"Yes, and certainly easier—not so many men and animals to look after. I don't have much experience traveling in India."

"That's fine with me. What else do I need to do?"

"Let me give you an update on the animals you now own."

Jesus thought about his long standing arrangement with Maleb. When he had first come to Hemis, he had given his three camels and two donkeys to Maleb for safe keeping. He had also given Maleb all his funds. Initially, Jesus had just told him to use them as he needed. In time, the animals had reproduced abundantly and Jesus' funds, which Maleb invested, had also made good returns. Doing so well, in fact, that Maleb and Jesus had agreed that all the animals and funds be divided. Thus, Maleb ended up with camels and donkeys and an amount of money. With these, Maleb had started his own caravans and became a businessman and land owner.

"You now own fifty camels, seventy-three donkeys, twenty goats and one-hundred-fifty sheep. Your half of what we divided. I have purchased land in your name, from your half of the funds. I now have as many animals as you. My business is doing fine and I sometimes use your funds to help finance a caravan. Half the profits, thus go into your share."

"I never thought," said Jesus, "that I would become so well established. I only hoped to have a camel to ride on when I was ready to return to Israel."

"Funny, isn't it, how well we've done, but without the start you gave me, I would still be a camel driver and not a camel owner. I am well established thanks to you. My sons and daughters will have an inheritance. I am a happy man!"

"I am pleased."

Maleb thought about how he had blossomed under Jesus' trust. He would now be the leader of this expedition to India. He stood to make a lot of money. I would go anywhere for Jesus, he thought. Without him, I would have nothing.

"Now," said Maleb, "You know I don't usually travel to India, but rather from here to Alexandria. Where will I drop you off and when do I pick you up?"

"I don't know where I want you to drop me off. I will decide when I get there. You may travel on to the coast picking up whatever you can to sell upon our return."

"Sounds good to me."

Jesus thought there was a parable in his experience with Maleb. A parable about trust and stewardship perhaps. Jesus had learned much from the Eastern tradition of telling stories taken from everyday life. Common experience was easy for people to understand. So, Jesus worked at perfecting parables, creating them to meet his understanding. His goal as always, was that others gain insight into God's Kingdom.

Maleb knew he was not the spiritual seeker that Jesus was. But, he was an observant trader and he loved to travel. So he and Jesus made a wonderful team. Maleb thought often of the sincerity and genuineness with which Jesus treated him. He had truly blossomed through his association with Jesus. For the first time in his life he had a sense of himself as a free man, able to be always himself. Maleb didn't pray often, but when he did, he thanked God that Jesus was his friend.

Jesus and Maleb took off for Northern India. A number of stray dogs tagged along. There were three other groups of traders going with them. Each group had its own animals and goods. Their loads were rather heavy as much of what they were carrying were metal goods from Kabul. The craftsmen of Kabul were expert steel makers, molders and shapers. They made excellent knives, swords, pans and other steel utensils. These sold well in India. There they would pick up spices for the return trip.

Early one morning, as the moon still hung in the sky, Maleb's caravan began its trip to India. The mountains glimmered in the early morning dew and the animals, not yet used to each other, snorted and groaned. As soon as Jesus was mounted he thought about Chaila and how he was leaving her behind. She had been his only lover during his stay at the monastery. She had favored him with all the blessings a young man could desire. But Jesus could not take her on this trip with him. It was dangerous in the mountains and she was ill. He felt bad that she had sworn to wait for him until his return. He was not sure when that would be. He wondered if she had the same understanding of non attachment.

Chaila looked through the window of her room, watching the caravan carrying her lover away. There was nothing she could do. There was nothing she wanted to do to stop him. He was on his path, doing what he was passionate about. She only wished that it hadn't meant leaving her behind. She watched the caravan snake up the mountain pass and prayed that Jesus would return. She had never met a man like Jesus before, so serene, so confident. Before he had arrived she had been resigned to not finding a man to equal her. But she had found such a one in Jesus. She understood his passion to see and share the light and that he would go to the ends of the earth to do so.

She remembered what she had told him before he left, "Though you leave, my longing will sustain me. My longing will comfort me and keep me one with God." She said these words again, softly to herself. After the last animal passed over the ridge of a far hill, she returned to her bed in tears. They were tears of joy and sadness, for she knew what she had had, and also what she would be missing.

Over the first few days, the caravan, like a rope, wove between the mountain peaks, following the valleys. Jesus felt at one with nature, for it too, was a manifestation of God—the mountains and valleys were but extensions of His arms and legs. As he looked at them, he felt that were he to say to one of these mountains, "Rise and fling yourself into the sea," it would do so. But Jesus was not interested in challenging or changing his father's handiwork. He knew that his Father had placed them exactly where he wanted them.

Fifteen days into their journey, high in the mountains, the caravan rounded a curve in a steep ravine. Suddenly, a band of roving bandits appeared. They were standing on a rise, a small plateau. The caravan, strung out in a line at the base of the ravine, could not turn around and run. There were at least twenty warriors, well armed and fierce looking. They were Mongols, as could be seen from their faces and heavily woven blankets. Here and there, pieces of metal, sewn into the cloth, sparkled. Maleb stopped the caravan and sat, frozen in place, for the Mongol bands were known to be merciless. Maleb looked around, taking stock of the caravan's position and the advantage the Mongols had above them. There was no way of running from this confrontation.

Standing only thirty feet apart, the two groups eyed each other. It looked to Jesus as if the two groups were about to draw swords.

Without thinking, he stepped to the front of the caravan. He stood in front of the Mongol leader for a long time with his head bowed. The men in Jesus' caravan remained still, watching. This was a brash move and they could not understand. Maleb alone prepared to rush in. His hand rested on his sword.

Jesus, looking straight into the Mongol leader's eyes, said, "Let he be the first to swing his sword, who with impunity, would strike the very flesh of God." Jesus stood there, looking directly in the Mongol's eyes. The Mongol looked at Jesus in surprise. He didn't know what to think. This man, standing boldly before him, wasn't a Mongol or a native—his accent was bad. But, he was entranced with Jesus' statement and his boldness. He sat on his horse, expressionless. Minutes passed. The other Mongol horseman waiting behind their leader began to fidget. Maleb, though frightened, sat still. The caravan was bigger than the Mongol group, but they were mostly on camels. They were no match in a battle with men on horses.

Slowly, Maleb saw a change of feeling begin to cross the Mongol's face. The fierce warrior began to smile, staring at Jesus. The smile broadened and then, lifting his arm and sword skyward, the Mongol made a motion that they should pass. With Jesus leading the way on foot, the caravan moved passed the bandits. When he looked back, Maleb saw the bandits weaving their way up the plateau, back into the mountains.

Maleb was awestruck. He knew Jesus well, but he had never seen him do anything like this! Truly, Jesus was fearless. He jumped from his camel and approached Jesus. "What were you doing? How did you do that?"

"I really don't know," Jesus said.

"What do you mean you don't know? I thought we were all dead? What did you say to him?"

""Let he be the first to swing his sword, who with impunity, may strike the very flesh of God."

"That's what you said? That's all?"

"That's all."

"I would never believe this if I had not seen it with my own eyes. I was sure we were all dead."

"But you see Maleb, from the perspective of eternity, we are all already dead."

"I don't understand."

"Maleb, learn to meditate and you will understand."

Maleb knew that Jesus wasn't going to try and explain this right now. He looked tired. Maleb was just glad to be alive.

With this daring evidence of leadership, Jesus' reputation spread throughout the caravan. At villages along the way, stories were told and retold, making Jesus' name well known. At night, Jesus gave talks by the light of the campfire near his tent. His talks seemed to make life easier. People loved to listen. Often Jesus' tent was crowded late into the night. His stories were simple, yet could not be easily forgotten. Everyone found Jesus and his stories fascinating.

Within a month the caravan came to the first major city in India, Srindapur. As there was a great temple here, Jesus stopped to pray. It did not matter to him that the temple was in honor of a Hindu God. Here at the great temple of Shiva, Jesus walked the grounds and visited with the people and the priests. The caravan decided to stay for several days and rest. It was then that one of the priests took Jesus down into the cave beneath the temple, to show him a true yogi.

Jesus, holding a candle, followed his guide underground. In a dark natural cave beneath the temple lived a sanyasi who had not stood, spoken, or seen the light of day for seven years. Jesus had already seen much suffering. Yet here was one, deliberately torturing himself as a way to approach God. Jesus saw the man, thin and withered, sitting in a lotus position on the floor. He appeared to be a hundred years old.

"Someone is allowed to bring him food once a day." Said the priest.

Approaching the man, Jesus spoke. "Sir, I know that you believe you are serving God by doing this penance. But what you are doing is an abuse of God's very own body. In your meditations over the years, have you not experienced your oneness with God? Surely you have become aware that you are a manifestation of God? You must now understand that life is God's gift to you. A gift you are to cherish. Do you have no feelings for what He has created? You must know that this body, which is the very embodiment of God, was created for you to love and treat gently."

Jesus looked at the man to see if he was listening. Jesus could see no change in his expression. "Shall I continue?" asked Jesus. The man nodded his head ever so slightly.

"Your voice is the very voice of God and it is your right, your privilege and duty to use it. Your limbs are the very limbs of God, which He has given you to use for His work. I tell you. God would rather see you fling yourself off the top of this temple than to disown what he has created. Rise, go out into the sun, feel the warmth God has created! Let His light shine on you. Go speak to your mother. Tell her you are part of God's gift to her and that you must now do God's work, that you are through with this abuse."

As the priest looked on, tears began streaming down the man's withered face. In the candle light he turned his head and looked into Jesus' eyes. Slowly, with great difficulty, he said, "No one has come to me with such good will. And no one has ever spoken to me with such authority. You speak the truth. I hear you. I will come out."

With that, the man tried to get up, but he could not as he had not stood up for years. Jesus leaned over and touched the man. Trembling, the man tried again to stand. Jesus reached out his other hand and put it under the man's elbow, helping him to his feet. Then, with faltering steps, the sanyasi held onto Jesus. Great sobs racked the yogi's body. He held tight on Jesus' arm and took weak but joyful steps. Wobbly on his unused legs, the man leaned on Jesus. Slowly, together, they walked out of the cave. The yogi grimaced and covered his eyes from the daylight.

Several young boys, seeing the yogi emerge from the cave, ran to get the man's mother. A crowd gathered and whispered among themselves, "Who is this man that can convince a yogi to come from his cave? Who is this man that can cause a yogi to break his silence after seven years?" The crowd increased. Soon they saw the man's mother coming at a run. When she saw her son in the light of day, she fell at Jesus' feet and kissed them. Jesus lifted her up, placed her in her son's arms and held the two of them up. Neither had the strength to stand.

Jesus turned to the crowd and said, "Let each man and woman rejoice in spirit, without abusing the vehicle through which God presents himself. This body is God's expression of Himself as you. It is not a thing to despise or deny. Neither is it a toy to trash, simply because it does not suit you. For whether you are male or female, strong or weak, it is God's good pleasure to present Himself as you.

"If you want to know God, look around you, look into one another's eyes, faces, hearts. You will see that God is there. It is not necessary to sit in a cave doing penance. Get together in His name. Dance and sing. That you love one another is God's greatest wish. You cannot do this by denying yourself. Do you not see that each of you is a manifestation of the One? Your duty, if you want to call it that, is to love and respect yourself and to love and respect others as your very self. I tell you, meditating in a cave, denying oneself all pleasure, is not celebrating our Father. It is joyous celebration that our Father wants. Go son, eat, drink and celebrate with your mother, for you are free."

So the yogi left with his mother, his brothers and sisters and went home. There was a great celebration at the mother's house lasting the rest of the day and into the night. Before the night was done, the whole town was celebrating. By morning word had spread far that a man from the West had come, with great power and authority. Power enough to convince a yogi, with only a few words, to free himself from silence and self-denial.

The next day, Jesus was asked to speak in the temple to a gathering of the priests and elders of the town. Jesus loved these people and did not refuse. After the noon meal, Jesus was presented to the crowd with the elders and priests behind him. With great respect and awe, the chief priest of the temple asked Jesus, "By what authority are you able to speak such words, that even yogis respond?"

Jesus answered, "My authority is no different from your own. To find that authority which feels genuine and comfortable, seek God's authority within yourself. When you use God's authority you are standing on rock. God's authority is so real, it will convince even you."

The priests and elders were astounded at these words, so simple, yet elegant. Another priest asked Jesus, "Do you say that God does not mind for us to be selfish?"

Jesus answered, "Be selfish. Be as selfish as you like. But, I ask you, be deeply and seriously selfish, for if you are, you will find that all others are also your Self. Being truly selfish, with understanding, means you must respect others as your Self. So there is no question of taking advantage of another, for the other is you."

The head priest sat down as he was no longer capable of standing. To the priest next to him he whispered, "Who is this man? God come to earth?"

Sensing what they were thinking, Jesus said. "Each and every one of us is divine. The only difference between what I know and what you know, is the extent to which you know who you are. For there is a light in each of you, just as strong as mine. Only your light is covered up, hidden, deep within you. Uncover your lamps, light the darkness, for all have need of light."

With these words Jesus sat and spoke no more. The council members and the priests were silent and Jesus stepped down from the podium and walked out of the temple. He found Maleb. "Gather the animals, for we must be on our way."

Before Jesus was able to leave town, a number of the women had brought their babies to him to be blessed. Some of them were cured from illness by touching Jesus, though he did not know that this had occurred. Thus Jesus' reputation continued to spread, and even he could not see how it was accomplished.

Maleb did as he was told. The camels were loaded and the donkeys packed, and shortly they were back on the road. Jesus had not intended to begin teaching so soon. He knew there was much for him to learn as well. The man in the cave was trying so hard, but he was abusing himself. Jesus had simply responded, but he was surprised himself at the results. He was aware only, that when he responded spontaneously, from the authority he felt inside, a Great Source worked through him. At these times he felt like a vehicle for good, power and energy. It was not even in his will to disobey. These things, he thought, must be the result of my inner work.

This was a land in which people revered gurus, saints, yogis and holy men. Because of the spiritual focus of the people, Jesus felt very much at home. But as yet, Jesus was still curious about how he would be received elsewhere. It wasn't long before he found out. His caravan was approaching a much larger town, where word of the events in Srindapur had spread ahead of him.

A large crowd of people came out to greet him, led by a large animal which was decorated with brightly colored blankets, chimes and gongs. Jesus had never seen such an animal before. He was astounded to see such a huge living thing.

"What is that?" he asked.

"That's an elephant They are a revered here. An animal, both worshiped and used for labor." Jesus remembered that he had heard of such beasts, but had never believed that a living thing on four legs could be so big. He was intrigued that an animal so large could be so tame that people could ride on its back, even on its head.

Jesus was begged and cajoled into taking a seat on the elephant. Not being one to deny a celebration, he complied. So it was that Jesus rode into Gandipa on the back of an elephant. There was no way now for him to hide or take a break. The elephant was guided directly to the temple where Jesus was asked to speak. Elders, priests, women and children were gathered there. Many of them did not even know the reason for the gathering, but they stood, ready to participate. They had simply followed the celebrating crowd, joining the procession. Like traveling minstrels, a traveling holy man in India was always well received.

Maleb, having traveled in India previously, agreed to translate, as many here could not understand Jesus' language. So Jesus spoke, and the crowd was entranced with what he said. Jesus spoke again on the asceticism that he had seen that to him was so misguided. He said, "May it please each of you to hear the voice of God in your own heart today. I will speak, but you must listen to your own heart and receive from your own inner guru. God gives everyone the ability to commune with Him, to tap into universal wisdom. It is good to receive guidance from external sources but not to set those sources too high above yourself. Your trust in yourself must be raised, not lowered. Do no harm to yourself or others, and within this framework, delight in yourself and others. Certainly there is legitimate suffering. That is ordained. But please, do not look for more. For God wishes that each of us rise to our greatest joy and highest delight. Share your thoughts, your feelings, your very bodies, with those you love.

"Light your lamps. Keep them lit. You do not need to restrain your deepest nature, your true love of self. Truly I say, in order to please others, please your deepest self. For, it is your deepest self that is one with everyone else.

"To give love and joy you must possess it. You cannot show another the way by denying yourself. You need not sit in caves, not eating or speaking, to please God. It is for speaking that God gave you voices and for loving that God gave you bodies.

"The higher ground is not in ceaseless suffering, but is in pleasure, delight and joy. So take your stand with life, rise and be not afraid to seek pleasure, even if others do not, for you will be the way shower. Neither should we protect others from their pain by repressing our joy. But express your joy, and if this brings others to confront their pain, let them confront it and be done with it. For verily I say to you, there is only so much legitimate suffering in this world. Once through it, there is boundless joy.

"If we are manifestations of God, by what right do we deny ourselves. Are we not Gods? Let God be God by being true to yourselves. If others do not wish to do their work, so be it, your joy should shine."

With that, Jesus ended his talk. If he had any thought that he would get some rest, he was soon to find that India was not a place where his teaching would go unnoticed.

(18)

The Temple of Fertility

Late one night Jesus left the town of Gandipa alone on a donkey. The heat was still sweltering, even in the moonlight. Jesus was tired, but he did not want to be there when the town woke up. He knew there would be no escaping the crowds. He thought by leaving in the night he could regain his privacy. Maleb had agreed to go on with the caravan to the coast. He would have liked to remain with Jesus, but Jesus wanted to continue alone.

"It will be several months before I return this way," said Maleb. "If you wander off alone, I may not be able to find you."

"When you come back through," said Jesus, "wait here in Gandipa as long as you can. If I don't show up, go home without me."

"I would hate to return to Hemis without you."

"I know," said Jesus. "But it may come to that."

It was agreed that Maleb, in such a case, would keep Jesus' animals as before. On Jesus' eventual return, whatever profit was due him, would be paid. With this promise, the two parted company.

As Jesus traveled through the night, the moon shone brightly and the donkey did not stumble. Jesus stopped some distance from the town and bathed quickly in the river. Then he changed into new clothes he had brought along so that he would not be recognized. He left the clothes on the river bank for someone else to use. He rode hard throughout the night. It was not until he had passed several towns unnoticed and his donkey was tired that he dismounted. He tied the donkey to a tree and lay down to rest.

The land was lush and warm and Jesus had no difficulty falling asleep. Anonymity assured, he slept. When he awoke he saw a woman on her way to the market and was able to buy some food from her. Another passerby had some fresh juice from a fruit Jesus did not recognize. But Jesus drank the juice and was refreshed. He remained the rest of the day, under the shade of a great tree, watching the donkey graze and observing the people as they passed. Women came to the river to fetch water and wash clothes, bathing themselves and their children. The older children ran and splashed, providing a sense of joy which enlivened the scene.

The next morning, Jesus rode off down a wide dirt path, following the bank of the river Ganges. It was a vast river, with many sights and constant traffic. To the local people, this river was sacred. Jesus saw this reverence constantly expressed with ritual bathing, candle lighting, and other ceremonies held near or in the water. To Jesus, the whole world was sacred and worshiping this river seemed a natural part of this sacredness.

The following day Jesus took off again, down the river bank, passing more villages. As an anonymous traveler, he was able to observe, contemplate and take in all that he saw. He allowed his mind to wander, neither embracing certain thoughts nor trying to get rid of them. As he observed, he watched his thoughts come and go, looking for their source.

This he had learned, was one of the favored methods of internal knowing practiced by the sages. Already, he was impressed with the depth of spiritual and religious thought known here. The donkey's meandering, rhythmic pace, produced a meditative response in Jesus and he enjoyed the simple relationship he had with the animal.

Jesus made slow but considerable progress down the river. He did not stop until he was sure he had gone far enough that he would not be recognized. He had come to India to learn, to seek further depth, so he needed to be careful. The exalted position he

had inadvertently created at Gandipur, was not what he was looking for. He had become the teacher and lost his freedom to roam at
will, unobserved, anonymous. Jesus knew there was still much for
him to learn. He wanted to be seen as an equal, not held apart as a
teacher. He hoped to find an interesting place to stay for a while,
just observing and listening.

He was already impressed with the variety and depth of the
spiritual masters here—true spiritual Gurus from which he could
learn. Jesus wanted to open himself up to the great masters of
India, unencumbered with previous tradition. He was willing to
be quiet and listen. Jesus knew he had to be silent, for when he
spoke, the response of people, even masters, was too great.

At sunrise on the fourth day, still traveling along the river,
Jesus came to a temple shining brightly in the sun. It was of white
stone, glittering in the sun like a jewel. There was a large sun molded
into the front of the temple above the main entrance. It was covered
in gold leaf and reflected the sun's rays, scattering light in all directions. Jesus dismounted and tied his donkey to a stone pillar. He saw
and approached several men entering the temple.

"What is worshiped here?" asked Jesus.

"The sun," they answered, "The god of fertility."

"Who do I talk to, to find out more about this place?"

"You may talk to the steward, he will be glad to show you
around."

Jesus wasn't sure who the steward was, but he stood and
watched as people came and went. He stood quietly, waiting, looking at the wonderful people. He saw many of them bowing before
two large pillars that rose twenty feet into the air, one on either
side of the entrance. As he was looking, a man appearing to be a
caretaker, came up to him.

"Sir, I see that you are new here. What is it you are seeking?"

Jesus responded, "Right now I am looking at these pillars.
What do they represent?"

The grounds keeper smiled, "They are giant phallic symbols,
reaching up to God."

"Oh, I see," said Jesus. "And are these mounds the testicles?"
The caretaker smiled. "Yes and no," he said.

"What do you mean?" asked Jesus.

"Well, they are large and round and placed where one would expect the testicles to be, at the base of the phallus, but, as you can see, they are pear shaped and have nipples."

"So they are breasts! Right?"

"Absolutely. It's a play on the symbols of masculine and feminine. Here, in these phallic symbols, we have joined the male and female sexual organs, symbolizing the truth of oneness. The whole truth is the joining of male and female. We worship the sun here, and everything relating to the seasons and fertility. We are Hindus, but our emphasis is fertility and the sun is the single most important symbol of this. Please, come inside where you can see what we have plotted on the walls."

Jesus followed the caretaker between the two pillars under the blazing gold leaf sun and through the entrance. On the walls were large, highly illustrated, astrological calendars. In great detail, pictures showed a great variety of feasts and celebrations. All aspects of fertility were prominent as symbolic pictures and statues.

"These are the subjects of contemplation," said the caretaker.

"I see," said Jesus.

"These are very sexual objects for meditation. I have never seen this included in spirituality."

"We pride ourselves in the integration of sexuality and spirituality. God is fertile. She is fecundant. We worship her bountiful pleasure in creating."

Jesus found this blatant sexuality utterly foreign. Even in Egypt, where fertility was also worshiped, it was not this open or graphic. Israel certainly had a different idea of what symbolized God. Jesus decided that this place was different enough that he could learn something here. He decided to stay and see what he could learn. He liked the blatant, exhibitionistic atmosphere here, so open and unashamed.

"May I just stick around today and watch, absorb the atmosphere?"

"Surely you may. We enjoy having visitors. We enjoy watching their reactions to our symbols. Strangers' faces, when they look at the phallus and breasts, make us smile too!"

So, Jesus sat inside the temple and watched the men, women, children and priests, come and go.

He stayed the day, buying what food he needed and taking care of his donkey. He spent the night, sleeping just outside the temple. He waited until the morning rituals were over to approach a man, dressed in a long yellow robe, who appeared to be one of the temple priests.

"Sir," said Jesus, "What must one do to study here, to learn from the masters?"

"You want to study here?"

"Yes, I want to be taught your faith and practices."

"Wait here, I will get the elders. They will be glad to talk to you about it." The monk then disappeared into the temple. He came back a short time later with several older men, also dressed in bright yellow robes. A dark-skinned man, with gray hair and brown eyes, spoke to Jesus.

"So, you wish to study with us. Tell us about yourself. You do not look like you are from this area."

Jesus explained his travels, his experiences and training, his reverence for spiritual things. After further questioning and discussion among themselves, Jesus was told that he could stay and study.

"You must, however, give the donkey to the church staff. It will be theirs to use during your stay. Any funds you have with you will have to be kept in the temple office until you leave. No student can own anything other than his clothes while he is here."

Jesus understood perfectly well. This was a common practice everywhere, for it fostered community and helped keep favoritism to a minimum. This was the case in most temples and monasteries. As long as you were a student, your duty was to earn your keep through service. After accepting these conditions, Jesus was shown to a small room with a window, overlooking the temple grounds and a view of the river.

Jesus was assigned to work in the kitchen and vegetable garden. It was a welcome relief to be free of being the center of attention. Jesus was determined to be low key and not create a stir, for he did not want attention. So Jesus worked and remained silent. When he wasn't working, he sat for many hours in prayer and meditation. He watched and absorbed all the services, ceremonies and celebrations. He listened to the elders and made friends with other students. He was careful not to say too much, or to challenge the authorities. He found the teachers and elders much more open when they weren't put on the defensive.

What Jesus noted and liked about this place, and generally what he experienced in India, was the religious tolerance. Jesus observed that everything in India seemed to blend into everything else. Their diversity of beliefs was astounding. Whatever came in contact with the local religion was simply absorbed. Jesus thoroughly appreciated this unconscious, but obvious religious fact. Although there were conflicts, these tended to be more territorial and political than religious.

Jesus learned about the Sufi poets, with a long tradition in the Vedas. These were poets that sang hymns to the one God behind all the different religions. This religious tolerance curtailed conflict but did nothing to stifle debate. India seemed to be full of people pursuing a spiritual path. Giving oneself to God was a thoroughly respected and common practice. Men with begging bowls were prevalent. Sometimes, so omnipresent, they were a nuisance. Everything was spiritualized, but in a non-dogmatic, amorphous way. Particular practices were chosen and followed, but few proselytized that theirs was the only way.

Although ascetics were common, this temple to the sun and fertility was not a place where ascetics reigned. This was a place where people celebrated life, fullness, joy, physicality and sexuality. The acceptance of life, as it was, expressed through fertility and sexuality, continued to amaze Jesus. One night, he observed a ceremony which celebrated the harvest. It was held at the high point of a full moon. After a great feast a contest was held among pubescent girls.

The highlight of the ceremony, which Jesus observed, occurred when young, pubescent women, got to show off their physical prowess. To the rhythmic playing of sitars, drums and symbols, young girls lined up before the phallus at the temple entrance and danced. They were bare-breasted, with only a short cloth around their buttocks. The dancing was sensual, obviously sexual, and yet, without shame. To the sound of rhythmic drumming, the girls, one by one, approached the stone phallus and shimmied up the stone. Those, strong enough and agile enough to reach the top, perched there and gyrated their hips and upper body. Not all of them could reach the top. Some even fell and the crowd had to catch them. They were shooed to the sidelines as less than desirable.

Jesus was told, "Those who reach the top and sit there, are considered prime marriage material and fetch a higher dowry." Only a few, the strongest, could reach the top. Their victory dance was ecstatic, enticing. This meant they were healthy and strong. A girl who could work hard.

"I want that one!" a man yelled from the crowd. "She will make a worthy wife."

Fathers wanted their daughters to bring top price, so this event was well attended. Jesus was impressed by the people's lack of inhibition and felt that even though this might seem crude, it was a way to celebrate God. In his mind, he compared these pole climbing rituals, to the trials of the holy men sitting in caves.

He thought these rituals were closer to God's joy, but they lacked the inner work.

Jesus took all this in, consolidating all the variety he experienced at this temple. Although he enjoyed very much being here at the Temple of the Sun, it was rather external. This religion did not have the emphasis on inner life that Jesus craved. They did have texts, a branch of the Vedas, which they read and studied.

But it was a more exogenic religion, one the public readily embraced. Their acceptance of the physical nature of life was beautiful and innocent and it was sorely needed in other lands. But Jesus was looking for something more internal.

After months of living in this splendid temple, with its open sexuality, he decided it was time to move on. What else might he learn in this vast land of jungle and spirit, filled with people? As he contemplated leaving this place, Jesus vowed to himself that one day, he would return to Israel and teach his people of all he had learned in this great land. He felt the dogmatism of his own people keenly and it weighed on him. One day, he thought, I will free the souls of Israel.

Jesus spoke with the head priest of the temple, requesting his leave. The head priest was sorry to hear that Jesus wanted to leave, but acquiesced. Jesus' donkey and his funds were returned. The next day, to help him on his way, he was given a parting ceremony and a blessing. After it was over, Jesus mounted his donkey and headed down the banks of the river again. Following the river was the only way he felt he could not get lost. Many people informed him that if he wanted to see temples and rituals, the bank of the Ganges, was the best place to find them.

(19)

The Naked Jain

As Jesus traveled along the Ganges he witnessed a wide variety of religious beliefs. He experienced tremendous joy watching the religious ceremonies—some done unobtrusively and others for public consumption. The variety continued to astound him. Over and over again he was refreshed by the tolerance shown to different customs and beliefs. He could see that to truly live, one must let live.

After a particularly long day's travel, Jesus came across a white haired man sitting on a rock. The man was naked and carried only a bowl and a brush. He was so thin, he looked like a skeleton thinking of returning to life. Parchment thin skin, long white hair and a white beard that hung to his navel, added to the image of someone ancient, living, but ready for death. Jesus stopped. "What may I provide you with today?" he asked.

"If you have any food, that would be appreciated. I have not eaten since yesterday."

Jesus threw his donkey's rope around a rock and took some food from his woven cloth pouch. He took out a mango and a papaya, and a starchy substance, cooked, yet hard, which traveled well. He placed these in the man's bowl and sat beside him while he ate. When he was through Jesus asked, "What is your practice?" For it was obvious that this man was on some kind of a spiritual quest.

"I am a Jain. I gave up everything three years ago, to travel naked, beg for food and meditate."

"And what have you found?" asked Jesus.

"I have found that I can starve, that I can be sore and bug-bitten, and remain bitter despite this practice. In three years I have not yet reconciled with death. Hours and hours of meditation don't bring easy results. Yet, something good has come of this. I have found that I can survive on very little."

"What have you discovered from your meditation? Anything?"

"I have discovered that enlightenment is hard to come by and that I may not be able to do it."

"What is enlightenment?" Jesus had his own ideas about this, but it was a matter of common discussion in India. So the question wasn't too personal or out of line.

"Enlightenment is a state in which you no longer have any questions. None! A state in which there is no more searching. Where the seeker and the sought are united."

"Have you ever reached this state?"

"No, but I have met many who have."

"Many?"

"Yes many."

"And do these people have what you desire?"

"Yes."

"Please, describe these enlightened ones to me."

"Well, there is a look in their eyes that is unmistakable. If you see it, you will know they are in a place that is entirely different from others."

"Go on."

"It's as if they are looking far away, or very deep inside at some internal space, perhaps it is the same space that the universe sits in, but I myself don't know. When these enlightened souls look at you, they see right through you. And yet they are so present when they speak, it's as if they connect with the very core of your soul. Being around them, you hate to leave. You can't explain why, but there is this feeling of love and acceptance in their presence that keeps you there."

"So, why are you not with one of these men?"

"Because another cannot give me enlightenment. I must do the work myself."

"How true," said Jesus.

"And you," asked the old man, "what are you doing, traveling down this river bank on a donkey?"

"I am searching for the same experience as you. But I do not feel the need to give up my clothes, my donkey, or the money which buys me food."

"I do not judge you for that," said the white haired Jain.

"Neither do I judge you," said Jesus.

"Do you expect to find this state?" asked the naked man.

"I am not sure one can find it. One can look, and there is satisfaction in looking, but the state of which you speak, I believe, just happens of its own accord. Like a fruit, it drops when it is ripe. So, I cannot say that I am searching, but I am ripening."

"I like that. I like the way you put it. You have a way with words. You should be a teacher."

"To teach is admirable, but to listen and to learn is also admirable."

"So it is."

The rest of the day passed and Jesus felt no desire to leave this naked, withered, white haired man. Jesus felt this man could save him years of search. So Jesus decided to spend some time with him.

"What is your name?" asked Jesus.

"Neti Behapho," said the man.

"Well Neti, do you mind if I spend some time with you? Maybe we can ripen together?"

"My vow is to be alone. But neither can I refuse you. So, if you follow where I go, we will be together."

"Very well," said Jesus, "I will follow you."

"You must stay alert," said the old man, "for when I leave, I will not call you."

"I will remain alert. You will not catch me sleeping."

And so a deal of sorts was struck. The man sat on the rock all

day and mediated. Jesus did the same. Eventually, Jesus grew tired
and lay down to sleep. The old man remained still, seated in a
lotus position. Jesus slept until he heard some movement. Peeking
through one open eye, Jesus saw the old man get up and start off
down a path into the jungle. The sun was just coming up and
Jesus followed. The man made no acknowledgment of Jesus' presence as he continued on the path.

The man walked all day, stopping only to pick berries and
fruit. Jesus followed suit and learned that there were many fruits
and vegetables that could be eaten along the way. Sometimes they
passed groups of women carrying firewood or water on their heads.
The women looked at them, sometimes they giggled, smiled and
turned their heads. But not always—they were used to such sights,
but Jesus could see that the old man's nakedness did touch some
part of them.

For two weeks the old man walked. Jesus stayed with him,
even though he had to give up his donkey along the way. When
the old man stopped, they talked. Neti told Jesus that he was
going to some caves, deep in the jungle, where only ascetics lived,
meditating day and night. "This," said Neti, "is where you will
find yourself." Jesus listened and did not choose to argue. He was
open to whatever was there to be experienced.

Over the next few days, the ground grew more rocky and the
vegetation less dense; then suddenly, they topped a ridge, and
there, across a deep ravine, Jesus saw some thirty to fifty caves,
opening from the mountainside. There were smoking fires in front
of many of them and the smell of simple food wafted up to where
they stood. "This," said Neti, "is the Place of the Living Dead."

"What does that mean?" asked Jesus.

"It means that these people have been written off as dead by
their families. They have renounced everything and come here to
meditate until they die or reach nirvana. Only a few know this
place. You must not tell another soul unless you feel they will
respect this attitude. I feel you will, therefore I have brought you

here. I did not invite you, but you have followed. You will have
the peace here to find what you are looking for."

Neti and Jesus strolled down the hill and into the camp. No
one came rushing up to greet them. No one even smiled to acknowledge their presence. Except for a turned head here and
there, Jesus wouldn't have known that these men even noticed
him.

"We must search for an empty cave," said Neti. Jesus followed
Neti as he walked up and down the narrow paths, peeking into
the mouths of the caves. Finally, Neti said, "I think we may use
this one. Do you see that no fire has been lit here in a long time?"

"Yes. I trust your judgment," said Jesus.

Neti instructed Jesus to go get some straw and tie up one end
so they could use it as a broom. Having done this, Jesus swept the
small cave clean. The floor was stone, as were the walls, and it was
cool inside, out the heat.

"You may now meditate in peace without disruption as many
hours a day as you like," said Neti. With that, he sat down in a
lotus position and closed his eyes. Jesus sat for awhile and then
went out to wander around the camp. He saw numerous men,
most of them naked, some with only loin clothes, doing various
small chores or meditating. There were nods of the head from a
few, but other than a mumble, nothing was said.

Jesus spent the next six months meditating and getting to
know the men of the camp. What Jesus noticed was that these
men were deadly serious. They truly had given up everything.
Jesus was glad that he was here at a young age. That way, he hoped,
"I will learn how to live my life before I am too old."

Jesus was amazed and appalled at the same time by what he
saw in the camp. He did not see many young men sitting in or
around the caves. Most were over thirty-five. He thought, "It must
take a man a few years to get dissatisfied with the life he has put
together. Then, to escape, he comes here." But Jesus wanted to
start his adult life from a point of deep internal reflection now.

Most of the men were thin to the point of looking death right in the eye—living skeletons, with only a token coating of flesh. Many of them meditated so many hours a day that they hardly recognized anyone, even those they had been sitting next to for years. Very few of them noticed Jesus as he walked around. So Jesus had ample opportunity to look and listen. He found that he could approach most of these men and sit quietly in front of them as long as he liked. In doing this, Jesus was able to get a good look at their condition. In examining their facial expression, he could get a feel for where they were emotionally. Jesus did not want to end up in this condition, still searching, when he was old.

One day, Jesus asked Neti, "what are all the buzzards doing sitting on that ridge of the cliff, there, above the caves?"

Neti explained, "When one of these men die, the body is taken up to the ridge and left on a large flat rock. The buzzards clean the body in a matter of hours. There's no mess, no stink, no fuss. It saves time and effort for there are no burials here. It is assumed by all who die here that they are not the body anyhow, so what happens to it is of no consequence."

"But what about the relatives?" asked Jesus.

"Most relatives have long ago given up on the whereabouts of these men. Often, these men haven't spoken to anyone in years. Who's to know?"

In time Jesus observed that this was true. He even helped carry several bodies up to the rock. One time, Jesus stood close by and watched the buzzards as they picked a body clean. Although it was difficult, it brought detachment, which gave Jesus the capacity to see from a mental distance. It certainly gave him a perspective the average person wouldn't easily grasp. It also allowed him to understand the perspective of the great yogis.

Neti and Jesus stayed, settled in their cave, and no one challenged their claim. Later, they learned that some months prior to their arrival, an ancient yogi who had been there for years, had died. Interestingly, the way the men lived here, once a body was gone, there was not much left to show that the man had ever existed.

Jesus meditated several hours a day, but he did take breaks to wander, to eat and sleep. Some of these men never did. Jesus did not practice severe deprivation, trying to prove that he was worthy of God. For some of these men did torture themselves. Some had atrophied limbs because they had not used them for years. One group had held their right arms, raised above their heads for so many years, the limbs were totally atrophied. They pointed, like sticks at the sky, stiff and useless from their shoulders. Was this what God wants? Jesus thought.

One day, in wandering around the camp, Jesus wandered deep into a cave that seemed to have a number of inhabitants. This was unusual, as most of the men here lived alone. Jesus approached in order to see why these men were together. Jesus had seen these men individually about the camp, so they did not stop him from approaching. Jesus found himself deep inside the cave where he stumbled into a room, lit with candles and oil lamps. Several men, stooped over crude yet sturdy desks, were writing text.

Jesus approached respectfully, and standing next to one man, watched as he wrote. After a while, the man looked up quizzically. "What are you writing?" Jesus asked.

"I am writing the history of these men, how they live, what they do, what they experience, what they say."

"How wonderful! It is so good that you do this. Are you assigned by the government or some authority to do this?"

"No, I and these others here have taken this task upon ourselves. You see, we do not have the stamina to sit as they do, but we would like to record what we can of what they achieve for posterity's sake. What is discovered here may be of value to many, long after they are gone. This method is how we come to have the Vedas. Someone took the time to write what the sages spoke."

"I see," said Jesus.

"For us, we value so much what these men say, that we write it down and study it. I guess we're the intellectuals. We call our work Jnana Yoga, for we use the thinking mind. Jnana means, 'the path of knowledge or self inquiry.' We don't meditate by the hour, but use our thinking. But we can learn from these meditators. We do not want to loose what they discover, for they would never write it down. Their words recorded here, make faster progress for those of us who like to read. We just happen to like the intellectual challenge. Sitting is too boring. A number of the men who have lived here have reached enlightenment. We don't have the heart for constant sitting, but we are good observers and recorders."

"You have texts of their experience and thought?"

"Oh yes, many of them."

"And what would one have to do to be able to read them?"

"First you must be of service."

"Is there anything I can do to be of service?"

The old clerk thought for a moment, then said, "Yes, we will be needing more supplies soon, pens, ink and parchment. You could fetch them for us. There is a village two days from here where they can be bought. If you would make a trip for us to get them, we would gladly let you read the texts."

"I will do so," said Jesus. And so it was that Jesus set out on his first trip away from camp in several weeks. He was glad to do so, for although he enjoyed meditation, he was young and craved experience. The clerks had given him funds, food and the name of a merchant in Topa. The only restriction Jesus was given was to be sure he did not talk about the whereabouts of the caves. "Only few know of our existence and we do not want crowds," said the clerk. Jesus agreed to this and set off for Topa.

It was good to be away from the camp. Jesus enjoyed the jungle, the screech of monkeys, the songs of birds and the villagers he passed. After the second day, as he approached Topa, he began to see men and women, gathering wood, fruit and wild greens. He was able to talk and speak with people that were open and friendly. He was given directions to the merchant, Bingwa's, stall.

Jesus found the stall and purchased his goods. But Jesus stayed in the village for several days. He watched the local festivals, the dances, the celebrations. The variety of these he found fascinating. He made friends with a number of families there and they fed him. But, as the supplies were needed by the cave clerks, Jesus left, returning the same way he had come.

Having left in the morning, Jesus eventually became aware that a young woman was following him. Finally, he put down the large pack he was carrying and walked back to where he knew the girl was hiding. He found her, squatting behind a large tree. She was thin, wiry, and dark skinned. Her features were delicate. She was poorly dressed, and yet, still attractive.

"What are you doing, woman, following me?" She didn't move for a long time, but cowered, staring up at him with large expressive, dark eyes. Finally, she spoke.

"I have no family in the village. My family drowned in a ferry boat accident and only I am left. We were traveling to a shrine which is not far from here. I am low caste, and no one will take me in. I have nowhere to go. The people of the village only tolerate me. No one wants to feed me or take care of me. I am alone and stranded. No man will even touch me.

"At the village, I saw you and asked about you. They say you have no one and that you are also alone. Since you have no one, I am following you. I heard that you did not say where you are going, but that it is not too far. Maybe I will fare better there?"

"But you cannot follow me! Where I go there are no women!"

"But then there must be need of one?"

Jesus thought about this before answering. "I don't think so. I really wish you would go back."

The woman just shook her head, passively. Jesus could see she wasn't returning to the village. So, he took off, back down the path, picked up his parcels and proceeded. Periodically he looked back and could see that the woman was still following him. She followed him all day, and as night fell, Jesus turned and motioned to her to catch up with him. She did.

"You may come with me," he said. "But you will have to stay on the outskirts of the place I go to. I will come to you if I can get permission for you to stay."

"Thank you, kind Sir. May I call you by your name? I heard in Topa that you are called Jesus."

"Yes, you may call me Jesus. What is your name?"

"I am Pupal Murati."

"Come Pupal, you may stay close to me tonight."

Jesus made a fire and cleared some space for them to sleep. In the morning, Jesus woke early and they continued their journey to the caves. At the ridge above them, Jesus searched until he found a very shallow cave, but high above the others. This cave was not part of the camp. Jesus didn't think Pupal would be noticed here. He took his knife and with sticks and vines, made a gate for the mouth of the cave.

"Pupal, you may stay here. I will go on alone to the caves below. I will bring you food. But you cannot come into the camp, as they would throw me out."

Jesus took the supplies he had purchased and walked back into the camp of caves and yogis. The self appointed clerks were glad to see the supplies, and for the first time, allowed Jesus to actually sit alone and read the texts. What a thrill it was to do so. And so, Jesus learned much in the East which he would later bring to back to Israel. He learned from the texts and he also learned from Pupal.

(20)

Enlightenment

Jesus dug into the texts. He found some of it mundane, some of it pedantic ranting. But now and then he would find extremely delicate and subtle passages. The experience of reading these passages affected Jesus deeply, etching itself into his very being. He cherished the new and profound insights he caught. Over time, with the help of the scribes, he learned to read the oldest texts in the ancient language, Sanskrit. The scribes helped Jesus understand the subtle meanings, clothed in the delicate shading of the language. He had to master hundreds of different words, each describing an aspect of consciousness. Jesus had many long discussions with the clerks on the meaning and interpretation of certain passages.

Of all the kinds of yoga practiced, Jesus was most taken with Jnana yoga. It was this yoga, Jesus felt, he would have to understand, to get beyond his own mind, to find a space beyond thought. Although Jesus had periods of mystical awareness, it was not always there. He could speak of the understanding he had from his mystical experiences, but he wanted to gain permanent access, to live entirely from it.

That space beyond thought, he could not easily maintain. He understood that it is was a space beyond all conditioning, all thought, beyond space time and outside of personality. In this camp, for the first time, Jesus heard of and began to understand, the art of Jnana yoga.

Jnana yoga, as Jesus began to grasp, was the effort to push the thinking mind to its edge and then beyond that boundary into no mind, no thought, beyond the person that experienced thought. He was told that this was the most difficult kind of yoga to do but that a person with a very strong mind often found it to be the only method that ultimately worked.

The scribes in the caves were the ones who explained this rare yoga to him. They had the time and the intellectual curiosity to enjoy explaining things. Jesus listened to everything they told him about it. He studied all the texts he was told might help him understand. As the practice demanded, Jesus pushed his own thinking to the limits. He did not run from any thought, no matter how degrading or how frightening. He persisted in this new task until the meaning of words fell apart and all context was lost.

When Jesus wasn't studying the ancient texts or discussing their subtleties with the clerks, he went to visit Pupal. Six months had passed since she had followed him to the caves. Jesus had rebuilt the front entrance to the cave using stone and mud. He had made a solid wood door in the center, using the skills he had learned from his father. Pupal was thrilled to have these improvements. She was pleased to have a home of her own. Jesus was spending more and more time with her.

Pupal had cleared a large area around the entrance of the cave and was now growing food. Jesus helped her tend the garden and spent many quiet evenings with her. He felt secure with her. She was a quiet source of strength and trust.

In time, Pupal became pregnant and Jesus knew it was time to stand up and put his relationship with her in the open. He spoke with Jalal, the head clerk of the scribes. Jalal had become a good friend. He laughed when Jesus told him about Pupal.

"Do you think we don't already know?"

"I wasn't sure," responded Jesus.

"We are far more aware than we let on. You should know that."

"Yes, I certainly do now. I need your advice. How do I get the council's approval for Pupal to remain here without conflict for me or her? I want her granted permission to come down here. The lower camp should not be off grounds for her."

Jalal told Jesus that he would present his request to the council. It had taken Jesus many months to discover that there was a council in the camp. He was continually discovering that a lot more went on in the camp than appeared on the surface. Though these men appeared to pay no attention to what was happening around them, they did observe and they did know.

"We have suspected for a long time," said Jalal, "that you had a woman living up on the ridge. At first some of the men were angry. But, in time they got used to the idea. Especially, considering your youth. Anyhow, you are well liked and useful to the camp, you gather wood, food, and go for supplies. We have no one else willing to do that. Whatever woman you have up there, she has not stepped outside her bounds. She has not come down here, nor shown her face. So, I will tell the others what you have told and see if we can get their permission for her presence down here."

"Thank you, Jalal, I am ever so grateful."

And so it was that Jesus gained access to the camp for Pupal. Months and years passed and Jesus and Pupal lived in peace with the men of the caves. Pupal had several children and they often played with the old men, who slowly adopted them. When the yogis weren't meditating, some of them found time to play. Pupal thought it was good for the men, to have their meditation broken, especially by the laughter of children. Pupal took care of the children, and sometimes, took care of a dying yogi. She was equally competent, caring for Jesus and listening to him talk about his experiences. As a child of India, Jesus found her quite adept at understanding and discussing internal subtleties: meditation, prayer, enlightenment.

Jesus read a lot of texts that mentioned seeing the light. The light was variously described, but all agreed, it was a light that could only be seen with the third eye. In the light, the third eye became apparent, somewhere between the eyebrows.

It was an internal eye, one that could be seen with the eyes closed. Jesus wanted to see this third eye at will. He was familiar with the mystical state and sometimes he saw light and patterns when his eyes were closed, but he knew there was more.

In speaking with some of the most awakened one's, Jesus learned much. He learned that eventually, on complete development, with all the chakras open, a white light could be seen, even with the eyes open, covering everything. This light connected everything in the Universe and it's presence surrounded all objects.

Jesus was told that the third eye was a shift in brain pattern that allowed one to see a new spectrum of light. A light that was rarely seen. Advanced yogis spoke of a white light, very intense, but not blinding. The light emanated from everything, the ground, plants, animals, people, the sky. And this effusive light, connected every object in the universe.

Jesus had given up trying to force the light, as he had learned, over and over again, that all one can do spiritually, is ripen. One cannot force the door open. Ripeness was all. In time, whatever experience one was ready for, just happened. So Jesus learned to be patient. Demanding results was counter productive.

One evening, when Jesus was meditating outside Pupal's cave, the light burst forth. Jesus was shaken to the very core of his being. His body shook with convulsions. His head felt like it was going to explode and tears burst from his eyes, like a dam had broken. But the tears were full of joy and the universe opened up.

The light was now inside and outside, everywhere present. The glory of the earth was resplendent. After hours in this bliss, Jesus recalled, that just prior to seeing the light, he had finally felt all thinking cease. Thought had stopped, utterly of it's own accord, defeated. It wasn't a forced stopping, or a pushing away; it was simply thought, realizing for itself that it was at its limit. When all thought had stopped, Jesus was thrown into another dimension.

This was a dimension of complete and total otherness. But the otherness was somehow him. White light emanated from him, from the ground he was sitting on and from every object close or far. The light was there, whether his eyes were open or closed. With this light came the intense awareness of the Absolute, more powerful than ever before.

Jesus was familiar with the sense of the Absolute, but the knowledge of it was now permanent. He remembered that as a child, this state would come over him now and then, but as he grew into adulthood, it had become harder to find his way there. But since he had persisted, and disciplined himself, to regain this grace, now it was his.

Six months prior to seeing the light in its fullest form, Jesus had touched into some deeper experiences that helped pave the way. One night, while rubbing his young daughter's back as she fell to sleep, something special had happened. As Jesus felt the deep love he had for his daughter, he was suddenly aware, that he was absolutely surrounded by awesome unfathomable beauty. That he had always been surrounded by this awesome beauty, and always would be, whether he was aware of it or not. Jesus had remained in this state for some time. As it faded away, Jesus believed that there was no way for him to remain a person, an individual and remain in this state. He was not ready for the final explosion.

He experienced the Absolute again one night while making love to Pupal. It was not he, the individual Jesus, making love to a woman, but the experience of universal man with woman. Jesus knew absolutely what every man who had ever lived, or would live, experienced in relation to woman. The experience gave Jesus the awesome feeling of being eternal. Love incarnate.

Another time, Jesus was so taken with his own thumb, how it worked, how simple yet profound, that he found himself in the mystical state. It had been only after numerous of these experiences that Jesus saw the light. In seeing the light, Jesus finally let go of his own personality and traveled beyond, without limit and without pulling back. It was nirvana.

Since seeing the light happened in front of Pupal's cave, he was able to stay in this altered state for days. As Jesus was getting used to it, Pupal brought him food and water. When she had to,

Pupal fed him, for Jesus was in such an ecstatic state that he could stare at a blade of grass for hours, overwhelmed with the beauty of it, forgetting to eat.

When Jesus didn't show up for several days, down in the lower camp, poking his head in the books and bothering the clerks, they came looking for him. When they found him in his ecstatic condition, they knew what it was and immediately started to record his story. One of them stayed and watched, taking notes: how long he sat, walked, slept, what he ate, drank and said. All was recorded. The clerks changed places when one was exhausted and the observations and writing continued uninterrupted. From that day on, according to the scribes in the caves, Jesus was enlightened.

When Jesus grew accustomed to this mystical state and could come out of it and talk, he did so. One of the first things he did, was to go back to the texts the clerks kept in their library and interpret them for the scribes. Jesus now understood everything immediately, without thought, for he knew the space the words came from. That space, Jesus knew, could not be described in words, but the attempt could be seen and recognized.

One thing the scribes and others noticed about Jesus, was that he was not passive. Jesus did not take his enlightenment, and just sit with it. Although the bliss could be seen in his eyes, he put the energy to use. He spoke, he interpreted and he worked. He gathered wood, helped carry the dead to the funeral pyres, lit fires, carried water, dug vegetables—whatever was needed for the good of the community.

Men of the camp began coming to Jesus for advice, asking questions, wanting to know what his method was. Jesus did the best he could, but from the vantage point he now had, he could see that ultimately, there was no method. So Jesus returned to his old standby, now perfected, of telling parables. He told parables daily and often, leaving the men who asked questions, pondering them. Jesus knew, when any one of them were truly ripe, he would experience the Absolute, just as he had.

It was after his enlightenment that Jesus began traveling away from the caves to speak again at temples and mosques. For he could not contain the awesome oneness and security he felt. He was pressured by his bliss to share it. He still suffered when hungry and grew tired when deprived of sleep, but there was a space that he lived in, where none of this mattered. He felt as if he had swallowed up the whole world; it was him.

Jesus knew and respected others' feeling of separation. But for Jesus now, no one was separate, all were just extensions, or other versions of himself. This was not just an intellectual understanding, but a felt reality. All fear was gone. What he had in place of fear, was wisdom. Jesus did not seek out trouble, but where it was necessary to speak, he did. He spoke the truth, regardless of place or circumstance. Other's felt this lack of fear in him and were attracted to his loving presence.

At the temples, Jesus spoke often of what he called, "The all pervasive I amness." To a gathering of more than two hundred religious leaders, he gave the following talk.

"Dear brothers and sisters, we are gathered here in the great mystery that is our oneness. Some of us know what is beyond the mystery, but cannot express it. I know you try and I try. This my friends, will be another failed attempt to do so, unless, whoever you are, you experience for yourself, the ultimate reality.

"Now, each of us present here, knows absolutely and completely one thing, our sense of presence. Each of us can confidently and readily say, 'I am.' Now, the fact that we can say that, is not overly impressive at first. We use the phrase every day. But at subtler levels, this presence, this 'I amness,' takes on much more significance. For, as we look deeply into the question of our identity, the place from which we say 'I am,' everything that is superficial, individual, personal, recedes. The thoughts by which we would pin this 'I amness' down, seem to flow away, like water between our fingers.

"For there is no permanency, even to our self definitions. We are first a baby, then a child, then a young adult, then an older adult, and so on. Yet at each point, we say 'I am.' Does the first 'I am' of youth, to the last 'I am' of old age, refer to the same person? No, these personal definitions have changed. So, this 'I am' is deeper than our temporary self definitions. I say, that our 'I amness' is simply the presence of God, and it is His presence that allows us to say, 'I am.'

"The deepest experience of 'I am' is to know God. For it is God in you and me, whose presence provides the ground. It is God's ground of being from which we emanate and have our being, our 'I amness.' I challenge each and everyone present to investigate this 'I amness' and see for yourself that ultimately, the only sure definition any one of us can make, is this: 'I am God.'

"This, my brothers and sisters, is the ultimate teaching. That we are all God, manifestations of the One. Though one cannot prove it to another, those of us who have had the experience of oneness, of non-duality, the mystical union, we know and we cannot be dissuaded."

The crowd applauded with clapping and shouting, even some spontaneous dancing. It was so different for Jesus here in India, for when he spoke, he was well received, appreciated. So unlike his reception in the homeland, where as a child he was labeled a blasphemer, a heretic, a crazy boy.

Another time, Jesus was invited to a address a town council. There were a lot of traders, merchants, and wealthy business owners there.

"Tell us something about business," one man said. "Is business part of God's plan?"

Jesus thought about his relationship with Maleb and how they had both benefited. He began. "There were two men, each living in a town, each wanting the best for himself and his family. One day a stranger came into town leading a caravan. The caravan stopped and the owner of the goods and animals wished to go into the mountains to meditate. So he asked two men to watch over his animals, his goods and his money. He said to them, 'Be good stewards. Use what I give you wisely, invest it as if it were your

own. When I return, I will give each of you, half of the increase.'
The two men quickly agreed.

"Now, the first man took good care of the animals he was given and invested the money he received, wisely, as if it were his own. He slept well and as his stature increased, his family prospered.

"The second man, being selfish, said to himself, 'This man will never return, for he will be lost in the hills or enter nirvana and have no need of money.' So he took the goods and animals and sold them in town. The money he received, he squandered without regard.

"In time the owner of the caravan returned to town. The first man returned to his lender, the offspring of the animals left in his charge and all the money he had made. The caravan owner, as promised, gave half of all the increase to the man.

"The second man, hearing that the caravan owner had returned, tried to flee. He knew the townspeople would come after him. They were afraid that the caravan owner would come after them for his goods. They caught the fleeing scoundrel and killed him."

There was a hushed silence in the meeting hall. Then a short stocky man began to clap. Soon others joined in. When the clapping was over, silence returned. No one asked another question. Jesus could see that he had struck a chord. The businessmen loved the parable and Jesus hoped some of them would take it to heart.

Jesus told this parable everywhere he went, and every time he told it, he thought of his friend Maleb and prayed that he was fairing well.

It wasn't long after Jesus left the caves to preach that he could not go far without crowds. A number of young men gathered around him, repeating his lessons, listening deeply to his teaching. Soon they were helping with the crowds. So Jesus appointed some among them as disciples. He sent them ahead of him to make arrangements and prepare his way. Jesus traveled on foot, on camel, on elephant, whatever was provided. He taught all along the rivers and byways of the land. His reputation increased with every talk.

Jesus returned to the caves as often as he could and spent time with Pupal and his children. It became more and more difficult for Jesus to return there, for crowds wanted to follow. Out of respect for the yogis there, he was careful never to announce his coming.

The clerks and their apprentices in the caves took care that neither Pupal nor Jesus' children came to any harm. Within a year of beginning to teach, Jesus' fame had spread throughout India. But Jesus' heart grew heavy with longing to see his mother and father before they died.

So, with care and patience, he let Pupal know that he would be going back to Israel and Egypt. She knew that meant he might be gone for several years. It was hard for Pupal to accept, but she too was committed to Jesus' mission. She had children and she was not about to take her children on a trek to Israel.

"Jesus," she said. "It was you who gave me refuge, hope and children. You brought me to this place where I am now well established. Look how I am cared for while you are gone! These yogis have adopted me and your children. This is now my home. The children have many men to help care for them. I will miss you, like I miss my parents, but I have no parents to visit. So go, go see your parents. Tell them about me and your children and your life here. I give you my blessing to go."

So, one day, early in the Spring of his twenty-ninth year, Jesus left with a small caravan, heading West, back to Israel and Egypt. Maleb, Jesus knew, had long since returned to Hemis. He hoped to stop there and see Maleb. Jesus hoped take his own caravan to Israel from there.

Jesus thought most of all about Chaila. Would she still be there? Had she worsened and died? He did not know. Would she want to go to Israel with him? Would she be well enough? Jesus pondered these things.

Jesus was still young, and already full of light. He was ready to bring the message of enlightenment to the Jews. With all his heart, he wanted his own people, to experience the freedom, the joy and inner authority he felt.

(21)

The Return to Hemis

The caravan wound its way back along the Silk Road, past towns and villages, along rivers and lakes, through valleys and mountain passes. In the evenings many people gathered outside Jesus' tent to hear him talk. Jesus answered questions, spoke of right judgment and told parables. The people loved the parables and discussed them amongst themselves. During the long daily treks the travelers argued over who had the right interpretation. Jesus listened, but he did not intervene, he enjoyed the debates. However, if one of them came to him alone, wanting clarification, he would give it.

One evening the caravan stopped beside a mountain lake. As the men were fishing for their supper, one of them turned to Jesus. He was an older man, a good story teller, who was, none the less, in awe of Jesus. "Tell us a parable," he said. Jesus thought for a moment, then, with a willing smile, began.

"There was once a newborn fish. At birth he was about the size of his brothers and sisters. But this fish had a deformed eye. Because of this, it was difficult for him to catch enough food: his aim was off, his eyes out of sync. As the others grew bigger, he stayed small. Now, the fish knew that soon, he would be food for the bigger fish. Faced with this situation, the fish decided that he would be better off with one good eye, than two that were out of sync. So, the little fish rammed his bad eye into a stick jutting into the water, tearing it out.

"With the bad eye gone, the good eye was distortion free. The little fish was now able to catch more food to eat and began to grow. He stayed close to the bank, where the bigger fish couldn't maneuver. With his good eye he could see insects resting on branches hanging over the water and he learned to leap out of the water and catch them. Soon, he was not dependent on what fell into the water, but caught his meals from above. Eventually the one-eyed fish was the biggest in the pond and could swim anywhere he pleased."

The old story teller loved the parable and thanked Jesus. The parable caused a lot of discussion, especially because of the fish tearing out one of his own eyes. Those, who were aware of some major flaw in their own personality, began to suspect that Jesus was talking about them. The serious ones began to ask Jesus what they could do about such issues. He would speak with them, telling them, "Just be aware, that is enough. Awareness will bring change." Jesus never pointed out anyone specifically for chastisement or criticism. But from this parable and others, many found cues that helped them rise above their own limitations.

After a month of hard traveling, the caravan reached Hemis. Jesus took leave of the caravan and rode up through town on a small donkey. As he passed through town, Jesus looked for Chaila. Where was she? What might she be doing? He hoped to see her soon. When the town's people recognized Jesus, they were all very excited. Their Bodhisattva had returned. They began to yell.

"What news?"

"What stories will you tell?"

"Are you here to stay?"

Jesus yelled back, "You'll have to wait. Where's Chaila?"

"Someone's gone to tell her. She'll be here," someone yelled above the crowd.

Chaila, approached the gathering that was slowing Jesus' progress. Seeing him, she leaped up behind him on his donkey. She put her arms around Jesus' waist and hugged him as hard as she could. She pressed her cheek against the back of his neck. Jesus, tired as he was, smiled. She rode with Jesus all the way to the monastery, peppering him with questions. "How long are you going to be here? Have you eaten? Can you eat with my family tonight?"

"I'll have to eat at the monastery tonight. It would be too big a breach of protocol to do otherwise. Give me a couple of days."

"All right. But I must see you soon! How long are you going to stay?"

"I will stay the summer for sure. But, I am on my way back to Israel to see my family. I will want to leave before winter sets in."

"Take me with you to Israel," she begged, holding him tight. "I am better now and can help. I'm strong again."

Jesus turned his head around, looked at her and smiled. "Dear one, how did you get better?"

"I traveled to Katsari and consulted with an old man there, an herbalist. He prescribed some Ginseng, mixed with a special blend of his own. It helped wonderfully. I feel so much better."

"That's great," said Jesus. "I am pleased."

"So, you are taking me with you to Israel, aren't you?" The donkey was slowing with the uphill climb. Jesus could feel the wetness of the donkeys skin.

"That could be a dangerous trip and a hard life, keeping up with me, for I intend to teach. I will not be staying in one place for long, because I want to reach many of my people."

"But I have waited all this time, and now you are here. I do not want to be left behind again." Jesus nodded that he had heard her, but he said no more.

At the entrance of the monastery, a group had already gathered. A gardener had recognized Jesus and run up ahead, informing everyone he met, "Jesus has returned!"

Jesus turned again to Chaila. "Dear one, I cannot talk further now, but, if you want to go to Israel with me, I will not stop you."

"Thank you. Thank you," said Chaila, hugging Jesus tightly. She breathed in the smell of Jesus' clothes. The joy and love that smell brought back were immense. She could hardly wait till she could have him all to herself.

The headmaster of the monastery was now quite old and could not come down to greet Jesus. So, the monks were pushing and urging Jesus to come in and go to the abbot's quarters.

Waving "Goodbye" to Chaila, he was swallowed up into the mass of shaven heads and ochre colored robes. The sights and smells of the monastery brought Jesus a sense of belonging. This had been his first home away from home. He loved these monks with all his heart. They hoisted Jesus onto their shoulders and Jesus was whisked up to the master's chambers, his feet never touching the ground. They cheered as they put Jesus gently down at the abbot's door. A cheer came up from the crowd, letting the abbot know that Jesus was here.

Jesus walked in and bowed while a young boy closed the door behind him. As soon as the door closed, the room was silent. Jesus knew that out of respect for the Abbott, no monk would yell or speak loudly in the vicinity of the abbot's quarters. Jesus looked at the old monk, sitting in a lotus position on a raised wooden platform. There was a broad grin across the weathered face. He had a wide, round face that carried the smile well. The eyes smiled too.

"Dear enlightened one," said the headmaster, "It is so good to see you again. How have you fared?"

"Very well, Sir," said Jesus. "I am ready to take the message of Oneness back to my own people."

"I knew it would come to that," the monk said, "but, do stay here a while and teach. We have need of you. You must tell us of your travels, your experiences. Please, stay and give some talks."

"I suppose it is my duty to share what I have learned, and I am glad to do it."

"There are many young men here now who have never heard you speak. You must teach them before you go."

"I will," said Jesus. "Then I will go to my people to bring them the message." The old monk, wise beyond his years, was quiet for a long time. Finally he spoke.

"Are your people ready for this message? Will they be receptive to this teaching?"

"I don't know. But I can't resist the urge. Don't our own doctrines say, 'Do the right thing without attachment to results?'"

"I should have known better than to ignore our own precepts when questioning you. Are there not places that would be more receptive to your message? Maybe they deserve your message more."

"That may be. But I have a personal reason as well. I have not seen my parents for many years. Perhaps there is not much time to see them. For they are older now. I wish to see them before they die."

"That is understandable. I cannot argue with that. My own parents are gone and I still miss them."

"Yes," said Jesus, "I'm sure you do."

"About your homeland. I have heard that the Jews are very protective of their religious beliefs. Even the Romans leave their religion alone. Won't your elders reject you, as one come to destroy their claim of superiority?"

"I do not know what their response will be. But, is that the issue? For, as you know, the right thing is to be done, the result is theirs."

"True. But should you waste your time and possibly your life? I have heard that they are not as tolerant as we are in the East. You will not be excused as a foreigner, for you are a Jew!"

"Yes, I am a Jew, but I have always been a foreigner. Even as a child I lived outside my homeland. I can't change that, nor can I abandon my mission. For my mission is of God. My inner eye is wide open. It cannot be closed. The light beckons me to return."

"Ah, so it does. We have many who are enlightened but do not see the light. You have seen the light. Tell me about it."

"I see a white light gently covering and joining all. At first it was hard to take because it was so different. But, since it is all around me most of the time, I have gotten used to it."

"Do you see," said the Abbott, "a strong, surging light, flowing between the two of us?"

"Yes I do. And I know already that you have given me your blessing."

"How true. You do have my blessing. But you also know that it is my duty to question you, to be sure that you see what you are getting into, and that you are ready to accept the consequences."

"I accept all consequences. I am free. I am one with my destiny, in that there is complete freedom. I am not afraid, for I am aware that I am already eternal. I cannot die. I no longer identify with this body, this mind. This body is only a shell, a particular shell named Jesus. It is not me. For I am in my Father, and He in me. We are one."

"I see you have the true spirit, the non-duality of the One. How blessed you are. Tell me more."

"Well, what is essentially me at the core, is God the Father, Mother, Mover, Shaper of all. I know it beyond all shadow of doubt. I and the Father are one, I am everywhere, in all things, in all people. I can forgive even those who condemn me, for I see myself in them."

"You are truly ready for any task, the teaching spirit is full in you. I am no longer afraid for you. You have my blessing to go. I can see you are beyond your little self, one with the One Self. Peace. Now let us go eat with the monks, they are eager to visit with you."

Jesus went down the stone steps, holding the elder's arm, so he would not stumble. The great meeting hall was full of monks, waiting to see their friend, or see for the first time, one of whom much had been spoken. Jesus bowed, smiled and touched as many as came to him, showing each reverence and respect. It was hard for him to carry on a lengthy conversation with any of them, for there were so many that approached, wanting to be close to him, if only for a moment.

After supper in the great hall, the monks sat at their tables, excited, expectant. So Jesus rose and spoke to them. First, he told them of his travels and experiences in India, of the men in the caves, of the scribes, of the strange temples and practices to be found in that vast land. Finally, when the stories and anecdotes were finished and it was quiet, a young monk stood up.

"Please Sir, give us a summation of what all our religions, all our searching is about. I have suffered greatly wanting to know which authority is the highest."

"Of one thing I am certain" said Jesus. "What joins all religions, practices, penances, whether judged good or bad, is longing for return to the One. This longing, due to our sense of separation and lack of insight, comes forth in an infinite variety of ways. In our zeal to perfect ourselves and reach the One, we forget the source of the longing. That source is the same in each and every one of us. The same in all religions.

"For example, one man may want a donkey, another a camel, another a horse. All are used for travel, but is one better than another? It depends on the circumstance. The animals desired are different, but the desire is the same. The desire is one, the root, source, the same. It is so obvious. Yet, we do not recognize the source in each other, looking at the surface only.

"So, we squabble over which is better, the camel, the donkey or the horse. But each has its place and each its burden to carry. I have seen every kind of practice, technique and form of worship, from sexual Tantric yoga, to severe ascetic self torture. From one extreme to the other there is longing. Longing for oneness, communion with the one consciousness that manifests us all." Jesus looked around as if he were finished.

The young monk stood up again. "Please sir, tell us more."

Jesus paused and looked around the room. The hall was very large. The open windows gave a view to the mountains. Jesus felt supreme peace, and though he was very tired, continued.

"For me, at the purest level, there is no argument between any religious practice. Each is a vehicle. Beneath the surface, whether indulging in sexual practices or sitting on a bed of nails, the same quest is there. I see no practice as superior, but all aiming for the mark. There are too many misses, as if the target were not clear. But there is no sin, only missing the mark. Humankind has been missing the mark for too long. The target must be put in plain view and the bull's eye must be hit.

"As I studied and traveled, I began to see less difference and more of oneness. As individuals we have our uniqueness, but we are only ripples on the surface of the One, the vast ocean of Self. Individuals are that Self in a particular form. But we fail to see beneath our own particularity to let the One shine forth. So, we maim ourselves, maim and kill others, all in the name of God. This self mutilation, self condemnation must stop. Evil is not in the other man, the other religion, the other God. It is in our own lack of depth. God is one, though we may worship Him in different forms."

The Abbott looked at Jesus, a wonderful and gracious look on his face. "Please continue," he said.

"For us who truly know, we do not look upon ourselves as superior. If you see the truth, thank God in all humility and volunteer your services. But do not go forth arrogantly, with a big head and a superior spirit. For there is only one spirit, one consciousness, one source. And that One is here present.

"I look out upon you and say, there are no listeners here, only listening. There is no speaker here, only speaking. For the listening and the speaking are both aspects of the One. The One communing with Itself."

Another monk stood. "I beg you, tell us about the light. Do you see it? What does it do for you?"

"As I look out over this room, I see a white light pervading every object and every body present. The light I see, emanates from the floors, the walls, the tables and chairs. Can I say then that the presence is not of the Earth? Or that the presence is not alive in the Earth? I cannot. The light prevents separation, division, denial.

"The light mentioned in your texts, the Hindu texts and the Hebrew texts, is the source of all. All is light, manifested in form; some appears fluid, some solid, some living. But the light is all. When I die, my light will merge with the light of the Earth, the light of God, the light of consciousness. I am the light of the Universe. How then can I fear death? For truly, I tell all of you, I am already eternal. I have no fear of death. Death is not even real to me."

A hush grew over the crowd. Jesus looked at the monks with deep affection. How well they listen, he thought. Can I not tell them all I know?

"People often claim to see a distance in my eyes, yet still they experience my presence as loving. The explanation is simple. My love is not personal, for I see no difference among people. Personalities are shells of the One. I am one with the One, and loving one is as good as loving another. Some, especially women who are attracted to me, get annoyed with my love for all without distinction. It irritates them, makes them jealous. But what am I to do? Deny the deeper reality? Is loving one better than loving another? It is not possible for me." With these words, Jesus paused.

A young monk at the back of the room stood up. Jesus acknowledged him and motioned that he speak.

"Are you the reincarnation of the Buddha or the reincarnation of some other?"

"I am both and neither. Your question is missing my point. Let me try again to state my position, maybe I can make my understanding clearer. Listen closely, for I am saying that there is only the One. Who then is reincarnating? Do you see where I am going? The essence of what I have spoken tonight is that the embodied person, you or me, is a manifestation only, of The One. At death, you return to The One, as the One, no longer separate?"

"I'm trying to understand, Sir," the monk answered. "Please say more."

"The enlightened one's have joined with the One. There is only the One. When your soul is enlightened, it joins the One and does the will of the One, for, in joining the One, one cannot do otherwise. Our shells, these so-called personalities, which are conditioned limitations, do not reincarnate. For example, the shells in the ocean are inhabited by shell crabs. When one of these crabs outgrows its shell, it finds another, a larger one. Our personalities can grow and leave the smaller self behind.

"As you grow, and if you persist, your little mind will die to its small encasement. Then it wanders, homeless, like the crab looking for a new shell. When your mind embraces a larger idea, broader concept, that becomes its new shell. Ultimately, neither the old shell nor the new one is you. You are the presence, the 'I Am' behind the old concept and the new. When you are enlightened, you will not take any shell to be yourself. You are the One, the presence that was in the old shell and the new.

"As for me, being a reincarnation of the Buddha or some other is not relevant. There is no personality that could be reincarnated. The shells are left behind. But the spirit of the One, which animated both, is present in me. So I am both and neither. I am the One, ever present, ever new. The One and only One, the One of all.

"This personality you see here, through which the One now speaks, is only a shell, a convenience. The presence of the I Am is here, and that never changes; though it may speak through different shells. You listen to me and consider me a great teacher. But this is because I have given up all shells"

The monk who had been standing during Jesus' answer to his question, sat down. He was humbled and absorbed in his own thoughts. The room was silent and no one else stood or asked another question. Jesus said, "I am tired now. I will speak again tomorrow and answer any other questions then. As for the man who asked me the question about reincarnation, he was brave, and should be honored, for I know that he truly needed his question answered in order to grow. We should all be so brave. Let none of you be afraid to ask questions. I have asked many questions of many men, both unenlightened and enlightened. Each and every one of them helped me along the path."

Jesus left the hall and returned to his room. The moon was shining down from above the mountain peaks and a clear blue sky stood as a silent backdrop. Jesus lay on his bed and the otherness that was now his constant companion, enveloped him. Every fiber in his body felt a surge of ecstasy and rays of light pierced his body from every object in the room. The light in Jesus body, absorbed the light and then returned it to the object. Jesus felt one with the presence and the presence was all around him and in him. He was at peace.

Over the next few months, Jesus spoke daily in the dining hall of the monastery. He gave talks, answered questions and was revered by all. During the day, he took long walks in the hills and visited the town below. Scribes took notes on all of Jesus' talks, writing down everything that he said and did.

In the village, at the well and in the market, Jesus visited with the women, speaking with them the same message he gave to the monks in the monastery. The women loved the authority with which Jesus spoke and hung on every word. Those who believed he had special powers were often healed. Jesus was often unaware of this, but those who were healed, told their stories and Jesus' fame spread.

Jesus met Chaila up in the mountains at a rendezvous she had chosen. It was hard for Jesus to get away, as he was very popular and people seemed to have no qualms about following him wherever he went. It was early in the morning and Jesus had walked up the steep mountain path, taking in the fresh air and the smell of the little mountain flowers. Chaila was waiting for him, sitting on a rock next to a clear stream taking melting snow to the valley. She rose to greet him. They embraced for the longest time, like they used to, before he had left for India.

"I am still not married and I am still waiting for you to take me with you," Chaila said, looking up into Jesus' eyes.

"I know. You have been pestering me all summer. I have not ceased to tell you what difficulties I may have. Why do you insist?"

"Because I love you and want a yes from you. Take me with you."

You're far too independent for most men. I know. We'd have to liberate them first, to get one to appreciate you."

Chaila smiled, "Yes we would. But you're already there."

Jesus smiled. "Your willingness is quite endearing."

"Shall we start the liberation in Israel?" she said, smiling back.

"You never give up, do you?"

"No, Jesus, I never do. If I had given up, I would be dead now. I told you I would wait for you. And I have. I didn't want to be dead when you returned. So, I have regained my health."

"I am so pleased. How did you find out about the herbalist you went to?"

"From a monk who came here to study. He told me he had had a similar illness. He described the herbs and the old man that had prescribed them. A sage who lived near his village. I went and was also cured."

"It's a shame you have no children to keep you here."

"Your message is my child. I will carry it with you."

Over the summer months they had told each other all that they had done and experienced while apart. One day, as they walked along a path among the pines, she told him again, of her deepest wish.

"I wish to go with you to Israel. I was sick and could not go to India with you, but if I had been well, I would have been with you all this time. I have lived here, waiting for you. Although I have had other men, no other has the place in my heart that you do. Besides, no man will have me for a wife because I am barren. So all here are agreed. I cannot have a normal life, I might as well go with you."

"Your independence and willingness to stand where your heart is, makes you one with me. I hear you."

"Since I have no children and cannot bear children, I would be no burden to you. But if I go with you, I could be of great service. You will be traveling about, speaking to crowds who will press upon you and take up your time. You will need someone to make your way easy, to comfort you and please you. I am healthy now, with no attachments and can keep up with you—put up with you. You know how badly I wanted to go with you to India, but neither you nor my father would let me go in my condition.

But now I have my father's blessing and all I need is yours. I am no longer a young woman. There is no future here for me. Let me come with you."

"Chaila, you know that while in India I lived with a woman for eight years. She has children of mine. Some day I will return there. Tell me, doesn't this make you hesitate?"

"No. It does not. Do you think I have waited all these years for your return only to give you up? My heart has always been yours. I too have known other men, but none own me. You are the one I wish to follow. It is for you that my soul longs. I do not ask that you marry me, only that you take me with you.

"I want to support you in any way I can. I am an odd woman, for I know no jealousy. I could go with you to India now and meet your woman there. I would feel no anger toward her, but only love. For I know she cared for you and your children. I could care for your children by her and treat them as my own."

"You are truly a unique woman," said Jesus. "Yet I am concerned for your safety. Should you come with me to Israel, I fear you might be harmed, for I may not be well received."

"All the more reason for me to be there. I will care for you, mend your clothes, fix your food. I will stay where you ask and serve whom you ask me to serve. There is nothing more precious to me than helping you spread your message of oneness. Do you not see that I feel the oneness too?"

"Dear Chaila, I not only know it, but I can see the light pouring from you like shafts of love spreading in all directions. Are you certain you have your father's permission?"

"Yes, I do. As soon as you returned to Hemis I spoke with him. I told him that unless you forbade me, I was going to go with you wherever you went. Not only did he say yes, but he was glad to hear my request. For, though he loves me, I am not the kind of daughter a businessman and town leader wants. He loves me, but I cause him grief."

"Very well, Chaila, you may come with me when I go. You will be my first disciple."

"I accept," she said, "with all my heart and mind and soul. You will not regret this." She gave Jesus a big hug.

"How can I refuse you," said Jesus. "My father accepts you. His light shines in your eyes and heart. Come. Let us plan our trip and see if Maleb Moab wishes to come along."

So, Jesus and Chaila renewed their love and made plans for the trip to Israel. Chaila was invaluable for Jesus and through her father's connections, the necessary arrangements were made to put together a successful caravan. Maleb did not come along, but over the next three years, Chaila was the mainstay, working in the background, as Jesus brought all he had learned to his people in Israel.

(22)

Return to Israel

Months had passed since Jesus' return to Hemis. He had been busy at the monastery and had found little time to meet with Maleb Moab. But Maleb was patient. He knew Jesus would come to him to plan his departure. There would be time then to bring each other up to date. On a sunny clear day, Jesus arranged to meet Maleb at his home. When Jesus arrived they embraced heartily. Maleb was glad to see Jesus, understanding that Jesus' first responsibility had been to the monastery. He did not begrudge the fact that so much time had passed.

"I heard a parable from someone," Maleb said, "about the good steward and the pack animals left in his care. It is attributed to you, and I heard it several months before you got here. Your stories, as well as your fame are spreading fast, even ahead of you!"

Jesus smiled. "So it is. And how have you fared? How are you and your family?"

"I'm fine and all in my family are well. I am truly blessed. With the loan of your animals, I have become fairly well to do. Thank you."

"What is my financial situation with you now?"

"You are doing very well, indeed. Your animals have bred and prospered. The camels you own now number over a hundred. Many of them are traveling in caravans right now. Your sheep number over two-hundred and you have forty goats. The land they graze on is yours. I bought it with the profits. Your funds, what I have made from sales and trades of your stock, I have in gold, more than enough to finance several caravans. You could retire, stay here and mediate, never work another day. But, if you must go, say the word and I will arrange a caravan for you."

"How soon can we have one put together that can go all the way to Israel?"

"A matter of weeks only, and you do not have to wait for another group to team up with. You have enough pack animals to leave with your own caravan. I can get volunteers to make the trip by making an announcement today in the market."

"Very good Maleb. Make an announcement. I intend to leave in three weeks. And you Maleb, can you come along?"

"No, I will not be going. I am settled now, thanks to your generosity. I can run my business from home. I have land, as well as animals, and money coming in from my own expeditions. I am no longer the middle-aged man you once knew. I am growing old. I get around fine, no complaints, but such a long journey is for younger men. You will not need me."

"That's too bad. Your company would be a blessing. I've hardly had a moment alone with you since I returned. A caravan trip would provide the time. Oh well, I will miss you. What can I say? Who would you recommend as leader? Someone I can trust, for I do not want the responsibilities of being in charge of the caravan."

"My youngest son is in need of training. He is younger than you, but he's traveled with me and my older sons many times. He would be a good choice."

"A good steward deserves his rewards. Your son will do fine. Would that be Shiguam Moab?"

"Yes, he is my youngest child, but now grown. He is ready. This trip will make a man of him!"

"Very well. In three weeks I will leave with him for Israel. Wherever you wish the caravan to go, after I get to Nazareth, is up to you. I will have no need of the caravan in Israel. And I hope to return here to live someday. Pray they do not kill me!"

"Heaven forbid. Please return to comfort me in my old age."

"I would love to Maleb. But there is great risk. I may have a rough time back home. And if my family has not returned there, I will be going on to Egypt. Though I am loved here and in India, I may not be so easily accepted in Israel. What prophet is respected in his own land? They will be saying, 'Who is this man from Nazareth, that hasn't even bothered to stay in his own country? One who abandoned his mother and father, whose brothers and sisters we know.' No, Maleb, I think I will have a rough time in Israel."

"But the Romans. They're very pragmatic. Maybe they will protect you!"

"If it pleases them, they will. But the Jews have special compensations from the Romans. They are free to have and practice their own religion. The religious elite have considerable sway. They could do me harm."

"No more of this talk. I will see you again, God willing."

In three weeks time, Jesus' own caravan set out for Israel. Chaila was with him, traveling for the first time, far away from home. She was the happiest she had ever been. Maleb's son was in charge and Jesus was free to ride at ease, taking in the scenery, talking with Chaila and listening to the banter of the camel drivers. He felt the presence of God continually, and he spoke from that space with all who came to him. At night he told stories and parables, delighting everyone. In the towns and villages where they stopped, he spoke, and many were amazed at his teaching.

When they finally arrived in Israel, Jesus found the condition of his people appalling. For though there had been concessions from the Romans, the populace was poor and downtrodden. Only the business elite, the Pharisees and Sadducees, and those with political connections fared well. The men in the street were poor, overburdened and angry. Jesus could see that the Jews were ripe for rebellion. He did not want to get caught up in that, for his mission was different. He decided not to speak publicly to the people of Israel until after he had arrived in Nazareth. There he hoped to get word of his Mother and Father. He had heard nothing since leaving years ago. In Nazareth he thought, the relatives would have word.

On arrival in Nazareth, coming up to Joachim's estate, Jesus was caught off guard by the sight of an older woman, a woman that looked amazingly like his mother. She ran to his camel crying, "Jesus, my son! Jesus, you live!"

"Mother, is it you? You are here?

"Yes! Yes! I am here!"

"I am so pleased. I thought you would still be in Egypt. Now I don't have to go there. Where's Dad?"

"I'm here, but your father is gone. He passed away two years ago and we returned here. Now you are back too, as if from the dead!"

Jesus dismounted the camel and held his mother tight. "You are home, and I am home, and Joseph is with our Father; so he is present too. We are not abandoned." Mary broke into tears and wept on Jesus' shoulder. He held her tight until her sobs subsided.

"Tell me about father. What happened?"

"There was a plague in Egypt and many died of fever. Your Father was one of them. I held him in my arms as he died. His last words to me were, 'Tell Jesus when you see him, that I love him, and that he made my spiritual life complete. And you Mary, Jesus, and the other children, were my pride and joy. Leaving the community was never a regret.'"

Jesus said, "I feel his presence here. Have you fared well?"

"I am glad to be home, but I miss your father very much. He is the only man I have ever known and I do not wish to know another."

"My brothers and sisters, are they all here?" Jesus pointed to the group around him, many whom he did not recognize.

"Yes Jesus, they are. Let me introduce you."

Mary introduced them all, some Jesus recognized and some he did not. Several had been quite young when he left, and they were now all grown. His sisters were all married now, the youngest one since returning to Israel. Most had children of their own. Jesus was introduced to them as well.

Jesus introduced Chaila to them, explaining that, for all practical purposes she was his wife, and that he expected them to treat her as such. He did not, however, go into detail about the circumstances of their relationship, or that they had not been formally married. To his family, Jesus was somewhat of a foreigner, and Chaila was obviously foreign, so they were not overly concerned with her status.

There was a big feast that night, with drinking and dancing, and stories told by all. That night, as Jesus lay in bed with Chaila, he thought about the occasion of his return and what lessons it might contain. The parable of the prodigal son came to him. But he decided not to speak it here. Neither did Jesus tell of his wealth, back in Kashmir. He did not even tell his family that the caravan with which he had come, was his.

(23)

The Message Within

Soon after his return to Israel, Jesus heard frequently of a man named "John the Baptist," a Nazarene, unshaven, dressed in camel hair, with the look of a wild man. He lived an acetic life, traveling the back roads, living on insects and honey. He was often dirty, sweaty, with locusts in his hair.

He was known for his ministry, baptizing many at the Jordan crossing, crying, "Repent, for the Kingdom of heaven is near. Repent of your sins and be baptized. Present yourselves before God, cleansed and open to Him. I announce a new teacher. He is coming after me, yet will be preferred above me, for he will speak as one with God.

"In the beginning, God's thought created this world. Now His very word will be brought to us in person. For he who comes after me will speak from the heart of God. He will speak with wisdom and full authority. His light will be visible to those with spiritual eyes, his words, heard by those who truly hear. Those with inner eyes will see miracles and know that he has come to show the way. For the Kingdom of God is at hand and the Way Shower is near.

"I am here to clear the way for he who comes after me. For he is greater than I, with insights that will open the very gates of heaven. Though I call him 'The Son of God,' he will call himself, 'The Son of Man.' And you shall know him by his words and deeds as one who has the authority to point the way. Repent and be baptized. For though I baptize you with water, he will baptize you with the Holy Spirit."

Now in Nazareth, Jesus heard a great commotion over the words of John. So he began to ask about John, where he came from, and why he was preaching? Mary informed Jesus, "John is your cousin, born just a few months before you. Elizabeth, his mother, dedicated him to God, for she had been barren for many years. She prayed for a son and pledged to God that should she bear a son, he would be raised a Nazarene, dedicated to God. As you know, such a promise is common among our barren women.

"As a Nazarene," Mary continued, "John led a secluded life, away from common people. But the call to preach got hold of him and led him to the Jordan crossing. For months now, people have been gathering there, waiting to cross, listening to him preach and being baptized."

Jesus found Mary's tale intriguing. A short while later, while talking with the local priests, he asked them, "Who is this man, John?"

"We have sent messengers to him asking, 'Are you the Christ?' and he said, 'No.' And we asked him, 'Are you Elysia, or Elija, reincarnated?' And he said, 'No, I am not.' So we asked him, 'In whose name do you Baptize?' And he said, 'I am a voice crying to all, straighten your path, for the Lord is coming. I baptize with water which is symbolic, but there is one in your midst who will soon reveal himself. He will bring the Spirit. He will rise above me, for I am not fit to unfasten his sandals."

Jesus asked the priests, "Who do you think he is?" They answered, "We do not know, but we are afraid. For John is bringing multitudes out to hear him, and they are being baptized by the thousands. If he should point to this one, or that one, and say, 'Behold, this is the Christ,' the people will believe him, and much trouble could result. We don't know whom he will point out, and if the man he points out is not one of us, how will we control him?"

"Do you propose to control the son of God?"

"Don't be insolent, Jesus," said one of the elders. "Don't you see the precarious position of our people. We leaders of the church are responsible for keeping the peace. This is our pledge to Rome. If we break this pledge, the Romans will take away our privileges. Our religious freedom depends on keeping things under control. We cannot have wild men preaching and stirring up trouble. We are responsible to Pilot, not the people!"

Jesus was dismayed at their arrogance and concern for Rome. "So whom of your own people will you not sacrifice to appease the Romans?"

"Is it not wise to sacrifice one, or even a few to save many," they said.

Jesus answered them, "Your hearts are prejudiced against the truth. Your own eyes and ears are therefore of no use. For neither one nor many is meant to be sacrificed to Rome. All are the children of God, our Father." With this statement, Jesus left the priests and went into the wilderness to seek out John. Chaila came with him, bringing water, bread, cheese and figs. It was a long dusty walk.

Now, when Jesus and Chaila approached the river, it was around noon. The sun was shining hot and people waiting to cross were sitting in great numbers along the bank. Some were there to cross and some had come to hear John preach. John was passionate and fearless, attracting many who were uplifted by his message. Jesus listened to John preach and was impressed with his passion. He determined to speak with John personally and share his commitment to a better way of life. He left Chaila's side and stepped forward out of the crowd to be baptized.

As Jesus approached, John became quiet and looked at Jesus, deeply, for several minutes. Being sensitive, with extraordinary perception, John recognized that before him was a man of tremendous authority and strength. As John looked into Jesus' eyes, John thought, Could this be the one? So he moved nearer, to see Jesus' eyes more closely. The two of them stood, face to face, eye to eye, neither one blinking. John sensed that this was the man he had been expecting. John reached out and held Jesus by the shoulders and closed his eyes.

In his mind's eye, John saw a light around Jesus and a dove coming out of heaven, descending on Jesus' shoulder. An inner voice said, "This is the one of whom you preach. This is the one bringing light, wisdom and the Holy Spirit to all."

John opened his eyes and said to Jesus. "Who am I to baptize you? You are already filled with the spirit. You are the one of whom I have proclaimed, 'Lo, there is one who comes after me, who will bring the Kingdom of God.'"

But Jesus said, "I am a son of man as you are. You have your mission and I have mine. It is right that I acknowledge you, as you acknowledge me, for our mission is the same." So John acquiesced and baptized Jesus. And when this was done, John raised his arms toward heaven and announced.

"This is he, of whom I have proclaimed, 'Behold, a son of man, but one who holds the light.' This is the one to whose authority I submit. For though he is the son of man, yet he is one with God. He will teach you to pray and to see the wisdom of the light. Listen to his words, for he speaks with the authority of God."

When the people heard these words, they rushed forward to Jesus, asking him to teach. Chaila sat on the bank and smiled, for she knew what was coming. She hoped that Jesus' reception here would be as great as it had been in Kashmir. Jesus stood on the bank of the river and spoke to the people.

"We are the sons and daughters of the Most High. Yet we lower ourselves and ignore our divinity by denying this truth. We look to others, the Pharisees, the Sadducees, the Levites, the Nazarenes, to John, to replace it. Who among us will take a stand in his own Godliness and know God directly? I tell you, the Kingdom of God is neither here nor there. But it is all around you. The very grass beneath your feet and the lilies of the field proclaim God's glory. How can you deny it and look elsewhere? You need look no further than the soles of your feet, for within each of you is the light, the glory and the power of God. I do not point to the glory of God as mediated by anyone, but as it rests, hidden in each of you. So look no further, go home, sit in the quiet of your own space and you will know God."

When Jesus was done speaking these words, he said no more, but left, returning home with Chaila. The people on the banks of the river who heard these words were astounded at them. For Jesus spoke with an authority that none of them had ever experienced. As they sat, stunned, watching Jesus walk away, John yelled above the crowd. "Behold a lamb of God, who knows the way."

Now some in the crowd, having heard Jesus' words, followed him at a distance to see where he would go. When Jesus noticed those that were following him, he stopped and turned around.

"What do you seek, gentlemen?"

"We seek more of your wisdom, for you speak with authority."

"I live in Nazareth and I am returning there. Who wishes to walk that far?" Two men stepped forward. "Very well, come with me. My name is Jesus, and you?"

"I am Andrew."

"I am Simon, Andrew's brother."

"Very well, follow me."

So Andrew and Simon followed Jesus home. They told Jesus all about John and his preaching. "We have followed John since the beginning of his preaching. But since you are the one of whom he speaks, we will follow you."

That night in Nazareth, Jesus spoke to a group of commoners who had gathered on a hillside to listen. His message was for these who were open and receptive, and he enjoyed teaching. He did not like the meaningless arguments with the priests at the temple. He was aware that the rabbis did not want to hear his message. But the people, like those here, were longing to hear a message of hope and authority, showing them their own inner strength, their own inner peace and glory.

"John came to you announcing one who would bring you 'The Kingdom of God.' Many of you followed John, believing that he spoke of the Messiah, one who will lead the land of Israel to freedom. I say to you that I am not that Messiah, but a son of man. The true Messiah is not a person, but a message. The message is this: There is a way to God in each and every one of us. That way leads to freedom. Each of you is a manifestation of God himself. John was the announcer, but I am the way-shower.

"When you know the way, you too will be way-showers. What I know, you can know also. What I do you can do also. For the authority with which I speak is not my own authority, but authority from the source. That source is God, abiding in each of you, in your core. We have all hidden from and denied our source for too long. We look outside ourselves for it. Yet I tell you, it is inside, and when you look inside, you will find God to be yourself."

And so it was that Jesus' ministry began. People flocked to hear him. His message was well received, for Jesus did not point to himself or seek his own glory, but spoke constantly of the Father, present in everyone. He did not speak down to the people as the rabbis and priests, but spoke up to them, lifting them up as he spoke. And many wondered at his teachings and spread the word that among them was a great teacher.

The priests and rabbis soon heard of Jesus' teaching and sent messengers, asking him, "Are you the Christ, the Messiah?" Jesus knew that this was a trap. He did not want to fall into their hands. So he told the messengers. "Those who have open ears and open eyes will hear, see, and know. Those whose eyes and ears are closed will not."

So the messengers returned with these words and the rabbis and priests were perplexed. For they could not accuse Jesus of anything. Sensing the trouble he would encounter if he stayed, Jesus decided to leave. He did not want to harangue with the religious elite, but bring the message of God to the people. So Jesus chose to go to Galilee, where there would be time for him to talk and teach in peace.

Now, a man named Philip came to Jesus, asking who he was. Jesus said, "Follow me and find out for yourself."

Philip was from Bethsaida, the city of Andrew and Peter. Not wanting to travel without a friend, he found Nathaniel and said to him. "We have found Jesus, a true prophet. We think he may be the one whom Moses called the Messiah. The one foretold in our law, by our prophets."

"Where is he from?"

"From Nazareth."

"Can anything good come from there?" asked Nathaniel.

"Come with me and see for yourself. Let's find out." So the two of them, along with Peter and Andrew, followed Jesus to Galilee.

As they traveled, Chaila would go ahead to the markets, purchasing food and drink, making arrangements so Jesus was free to teach. Often, when she told merchants she was with Jesus, the food she was purchasing was given for free. Some even gave her money. Jesus' message had inspired the people and they did what they could to keep him in their midst.

In the evenings, Jesus and Chaila taught the disciples to meditate. Some of them resented Chaila, as they were not used to women presiding over spiritual matters. One asked Jesus, "Why do you let this woman teach us? Where does her authority come from?"

Jesus answered, "Her authority is the same as mine. Her gift may not be for public speaking and she is a foreigner, but, I tell you her heart is pure. She has greater knowledge of some spiritual things than you will ever know." With that, the disciples knew his message was for everyone.

One day, while Jesus was sitting in the shade of a fig tree, he asked his disciples a hard question. "Who do you think I am?" They were afraid to answer him, though they knew that many called him the Messiah. So they were circumspect in answering him.

"Some say you are the Messiah. Some say you are Elija reincarnated. Some say you are a magician."

Jesus answered them. "I am the true light, the son of man and the son of God. I come from Him, and I am in Him, and I bring His message to you. Be not afraid, for you will see great things. For there is authority coursing through me, solid as a rock. I do not speak of myself, nor of others, but of Him who sent me. He who is present in all of you, but whom you do not recognize, that is the One of whom I speak. When you unveil your inner light, this you will know."

This was one of Jesus' teaching methods. To question, to cajole and to speak in such a manner that each who heard him could not look for answers anywhere but within his own heart.

Jesus asked Nathaniel. "Do you believe that I come to bring the presence of God because of what you see or because of your own inner experience?" Nathaniel was a man without guile and Jesus knew he would get a straight answer.

"I only know what I have seen."

"You are an honest man, Nathaniel. But the day will come when your heart will open like a ripe peach. Then you will know that God is the messenger and that it is from the One that I speak. You shall see greater things soon. You will see that heaven is on this earth, ascending and descending through man."

(24)

Nicodemus and Mystical Awareness

There was a wedding feast in Cana, a city of Galilee, and Mary and her relatives were invited. So Jesus, Chaila and his disciples were welcome and they came. Since Jesus was gaining popularity among the people, the wedding party was pleased to have such a distinguished person present.

Now when Jesus came to the party, he brought with him wine that had been given to him. But he told no one and kept the wine aside. Jesus and his disciples ate and drank heartily with the wedding guests until all the host's wine was gone. Mary came to Jesus and said, "Look, the wine is gone. Is there nothing we can do?"

"Give me a few minutes," said Jesus. "I have brought wine and I will fill their vessels. So Jesus and his disciples went to the pack animals they had brought with them and unloaded the wine. Chaila was glad to get rid of the wine, for though much was given to Jesus, she had no place to store it. Taking the wine to the kitchen, they poured their wine into the vessels of the host. When this was accomplished, Jesus called his Mother.

"See, I have filled their vessels, call the servants and have them serve it to the guests."

So Mary did as she was told and called the servants. When the servants tasted the wine they said, "Behold, this wine is better than the last. Let us serve it at once and we will make our master very happy." So the servants served the new wine. Soon guests came to the master and said, "Usually the best wine is served first and only when the guests are well fed and pleasantly relaxed is the poorer wine served. But you have saved the best wine for last."

So the master asked the servants where this new wine came from. But the servants did not know from where it came. They told the master, "The vessels were empty and only Jesus was in the room when we found the vessels full again." So word spread among the party that Jesus had made wine from water.

In the morning, Jesus and his disciples left and returned to the hills where he was teaching. It was only weeks later that Jesus heard the rumor that he had turned water into wine. Jesus denied it, but it did no good, for the common people were enamored with Jesus and believed what they wanted. Chaila was glad to see Jesus' stature grow, but she was amazed at how easily rumors started and how quickly the spread.

When the crowds grew too large, Jesus and his disciples moved to other areas. Teaching along the way, they passed Capernaum and on to Jerusalem, for Jesus wished to participate in the Passover. Though Jesus was familiar with the Passover, he had been away for many years and he relished the idea of experiencing a truly Jewish holiday. He remembered his father and the times spent celebrating the Passover with him.

Chaila had arranged with friends of Jesus, a place for them to stay in Jerusalem. He and Chaila, wishing to take a break from the crowds, went in secret, together, to the family that had put him up, years ago, near the temple. He had been only a boy then, visiting the temple alone, and now he wished to thank the family for their generosity.

He found the home. The daughters, now married, were living nearby. He introduced them to Chaila and told them of his travels since he had last seen them. They were delighted with his stories and told him what went on at the temple. He heard from the family what a racket the purchase and sacrifice of animals had become. They told him, "Those of us who live near the temple no longer even participate, for we see too clearly what goes on. The priests and money changers make bundles of money while the poor and truly religious are taken advantage of."

Jasmine, another daughter, said, "The priests are out of touch with the people, serving their own interests and those of Rome."

Jesus was very upset when he heard these words, for he loved the common people, and he understood their simple faith. He knew this family's description of what went on was genuine. Jesus was angry that the Pharisees and Sadducees were taking advantage of the people. Jesus said, "I will challenge what is going on here. Believe me, they have no idea what I can do. Who, in the name of God, could do this to our people?"

Chaila was frightened by Jesus' words. She wanted Jesus to teach, but the Jews could be a rowdy lot and she didn't want Jesus physically harmed. "Please Jesus," she said, "Don't put yourself in danger. Speak to the people. Don't challenge the priests."

"But I must. Who else will do it?"

Chaila had no answer. The rest of the day and evening were spent eating, talking and resting. In the morning, Jesus was met by other disciples who had heard where he was. They went together to the temple. Chaila watched from a short distance.

There, crowding out the places where people might kneel and pray, were traders and money changers. The temple had become a trading camp rather than a place of worship. Jesus asked the money changers, "Can you not do business elsewhere? What you are doing is shameful. Is this not a place of worship for the people? Where is the place for quiet prayer and contemplation? I see and hear only the sounds of bartering and trading, the sound of money clinging in your pots. Where is the peace of God?"

The money changers laughed at Jesus. "Who are you to come in here like this asking us to leave? Do you have authority from the priests?"

The money changers' arrogance infuriated Jesus. The veins on his forehead began to fill with blood. He picked up some cord used for tying up sheep and cattle and wove it in his hand until he had a heavy rope. When the traders and money changers saw the look on Jesus' face, they were frightened.

"What are you doing?" they asked.

"If you will not leave after being politely asked, I will show you by what authority I speak. This is a place where people come to worship and you have turned it into a place of greed!"

With that, Jesus took the heavy rope in his right hand and began to drive the oxen, sheep and goats from the temple. Some of the traders tried to stop him. But Jesus and his disciples pushed them away. When the animals were driven out, Jesus went over to the tables of the money changers and turned their tables over, spilling the coins on the ground.

The vendors of doves looked at Jesus and said. "Are you going to drive us out too? By what authority?"

Jesus answered, "By an authority which you do not know. The temple of God does not rest on the authority of priests and rabbis, nor of this place. The temple of God is in us and it is by that authority that I act. You are disgracing God by abusing His people. Go, and do not come back!"

The vendors fled before Jesus and his disciples and many people cheered, for Jesus had done what many of them would have liked to do. The rabbis who beheld this scene were afraid. Jesus had challenged their authority and had made them look like fools. They saw that many people were glad to see the money changers thrown out. They waited until the traders and money changers were gone and the crowd was quiet before they approached Jesus. They said to him, "We have sent for the guards. If you are here when they arrive, we will have you arrested."

"I will leave for there is nothing more for me to do here. Remember, these temple grounds are no more hallowed than any other place. This is just a place for worship. God's temple is in the heart. As for me? I will go directly to the people, for you disgrace yourselves and God by defiling this place and leading my people astray. You are a disgrace to my Father. You may have this place, but I will have the people's heart."

"You are an insane blasphemer," yelled one of the rabbis. "Keep this up and you will not last long!"

"And you have turned our faith into a political circus. Spreading fear of God and Rome! God is not to be feared, but praised. If this temple fell, within three days, I would uplift more people than you have here today. This temple is of stone, yet I replace it with the true temple of God—the heart of man!"

Jesus left and hurried toward his friends' house near the temple. Chaila waited behind to be sure no one followed him. She grabbed the arms of several men following Jesus, delaying them by asking, "What is going on?" When she was sure no one had seen Jesus enter the home, she quietly let herself in. She felt that she had successfully protected Jesus from those who might have brought guards after him.

The rabbis at the temple gathered to discuss what had happened. What did he mean about tearing down the temple? How could he rebuild it in three days? Is he in on a conspiracy with the Romans? They knew well that in other parts of the world, the Romans did tear down churches and temples. They thought, Jesus intends to have the Romans tear our temple down. Not only is this man dangerous, but he is crazy. So the Pharisees and Sadducees began to watch and listen for Jesus, to arrest him, for he demonstrated and acted on his own authority.

Jesus stayed in the house provided by his friends and sent his disciples out in separate directions. He did not want them drawing attention to him or themselves after this event. The next day, when things were quiet, Jesus left and went to another home, meeting up with his disciples on the outskirts of town. His disciples were still amazed at what they had seen the day before. They loved what he had done, but it also frightened them, for they saw that Jesus was fearless. Some of them spoke with Jesus, telling him to stay away from Jerusalem. Jesus agreed to do so, for it was not his wish to endanger any of them.

During the night, while Jesus was still keeping a low profile, a Pharisee named Nicodemus came to see him. The man of the house was afraid to let Nicodemus in, but Jesus woke and said, "Let him in." Chaila went to the door and telling the owner, "I will take care of this," let the man in. Nicodemus stepped in and Chaila led him to Jesus' room. By the light of a candle in the middle of the night, this Pharisee, a leader of the Jews, squatted before Jesus, asking him questions.

"Jesus," he said, "we Pharisees know that you are a great teacher. Many of us are afraid of you, for you speak with such sincerity and authority that none can deny it. But we do not know from where your wisdom and authority come. Please tell me, for I want to know the truth. I am no longer a young man and I have studied the scriptures all my life, but I have never understood what you speak of so easily. Please help me."

"What exactly is your question?" asked Jesus.

"I want to know, where is the Kingdom of God, here or up there?"

"Nicodemus, the Kingdom of God or heaven, is neither here nor there, because it is everywhere. The whole universe is the kingdom of God, but men do not see it."

"But I do so want to see it, to know it. Show me how?"

"Well Nicodemus, I see your sincerity, so I will answer you. But keep in mind, the truth of this is beyond what you can think. It requires that your very soul be born again. For the Kingdom of heaven is an awareness that sprouts within a man. And this new awareness changes everything. All is tender, fresh and new. Nothing is misunderstood."

"So how do I gain this awareness? What do I do?"

"It is like being born again," said Jesus.

"Look at me! I'm an old man. Can I be born again? Return a second time to my Mother's womb and be born?"

"Listen Nicodemus. First a man is born of the flesh, thrust with water from his mother's womb. This birth is into the material world with a physical body. God manifests as a body in space and time, a certain span of years, with a beginning and an ending. But when you are born again, it is the birth of Spirit, the awareness of oneness, non-duality. This is a birth that breaks the space-time barrier. Then you know yourself, as you truly are, Spirit. It's like swallowing the whole world. The world becomes you! There is nothing left but yourself, everywhere, always. You no longer identify yourself with this body-mind, but with Spirit, that which is eternal. With this identification comes the experience of eternal life."

"I do not know how to respond. You have spoken way over my head."

"What I say is not something to be accomplished overnight. It may take a lifetime, but even if it does, it is still worth pursuing. You come here asking where this Spirit is. I tell you, it is like the wind. It blows where it pleases and you hear its sound, but you do not know from where it comes nor where it goes. So it is with every man, born again in Spirit."

"Tell me more, Master, for I do not yet get it."

"You are a teacher, a leader of the Jews and yet you do not get these things! Surely you need to open your heart. I will tell you again. You are not this body, you see here, nor are you the personality presently here asking questions. You are the Supreme Consciousness itself, restricted and limited by it's own volition, to this body and personality. Your questions are the desire of that Supreme Consciousness to know itself. When you do, there will be no more questions. You will be mute with understanding."

"So where does eternal life come in?"

"Once you have mystical awareness, you know you already have eternal life; the question is then no longer valid. Your identity changes from little self to big Self, God, the Universe. With that identity, you will know that you always have been, are, and always will be, eternal Spirit."

"And this is all?"

"Let me say this another way. The power to know eternal life is in each and every man. It is a level of awareness that is beyond the little self, beyond intellectual grasping. You cannot get it for yourself. It is more like letting go than grasping. It is an awareness that comes to one when one is completely open, ready, willing, ripe.

"I tell you, there are many teachers and I am only one of them. When the student is ready, the teacher appears. There are many ripe in the land of Israel. But many will resist my message. The leaders will resist my message because it takes power from the few and returns it to all. The key, Nicodemus, is in every heart. You also possess the key."

"Please Jesus, go on."

"You must understand, until you have this awareness, you will feel condemned. All men feel condemned before they have this awareness. But I tell you, the son of man is here to proclaim this truth. I am only one teacher. Others have come before me, and others will follow, but each brings this same truth, the mystical awareness at the core of man which leads every man home."

"Thank you Jesus," said Nicodemus, grasping Jesus' hands with tears streaming down his face. Nicodemus knew in his heart that Jesus was telling the truth, but he was not sure that he could let go as Jesus asked. But the tears felt good. Jesus felt Nicodemus' tears as a fullness in his heart.

"Farewell, Nicodemus. Have a safe trip home. Remember, I do not lift you up because you are low and I am high, but because I am you."

"Thank you Jesus. Thank you." Chaila led Nicodemus to the door and let him out. She returned to Jesus smiling. She loved his skill with words.

(25)

The Woman at the Well

After spending a short time teaching outside Jerusalem, Jesus moved on with his disciples to Judea. Chaila organized the women who were making sure that Jesus and his disciples were fed and clothed. Jesus often told her that she made his life much easier than it would have been without her. But Chaila needed little encouragement, for she believed what Jesus taught was true.

Jesus stayed in Judea for awhile and his disciples baptized many. Jesus did not promote baptism, but counseled a change of heart through contemplation and meditation. The Jews, even those following Jesus, preferred signs and miracles—something symbolic, something they could see and grasp. So Jesus allowed his disciples to baptize, but he was concerned that many would not go beyond this symbolic act. To be born again was not a simple task.

Now, word of Jesus' disciples baptizing came to John the Baptist and those around him. John was unconcerned and continued baptizing many, quietly in the region of Shalim, near the spring of Aenon. Church elders sent a messenger to question John, hoping to embarrass him, as he was a supporter of Jesus. The messenger, a shrewd man, asked John, "Now we know that a certain man named Jesus of Nazareth was baptized by you at the Jordan Crossing. You bore witness to him proclaiming, 'He will bring the kingdom of God.' Now, if Jesus is that one, why are you still baptizing?"

John, knowing full well what the messenger was up to, answered accordingly. "The baptism that I do, and the baptism that Jesus' disciples do, is no different. Both are symbolic of repentance and the washing away of sins. Jesus' disciples and my disciples are performing the same service for the people. But I tell you, this baptism is of no significance compared to the Kingdom of heaven of which Jesus speaks, for his kingdom is not of flesh and water, but of spirit, a change in the heart of man."

"So, is Jesus greater than you?" asked the messenger.

"No one is greater than another; we each have our task to do. But Jesus' message is at a higher level than mine, for he brings the complete message. I announce the messenger; Jesus brings the message. Neither I nor Jesus bring these things of our own will. Both of us bring you the message of the will of our Father.

"You yourselves bear me witness that I said, I am not the Christ. I am only a messenger, clearing the way for him. Doesn't the bridegroom have a bride? The best man of the bridegroom is glad to hear the bridegroom's voice. He listens and rejoices that the groom has arrived. Thus, my joy is fulfilled. He is destined to become greater, while I, having performed my duty, fade into the background."

The messenger began to see that he was getting nowhere. He tried again to get under John's skin. "So, Jesus' message is greater and he is destined to be greater than you?"

"Yes," said John. "I speak of an earthly place, calling you to pay attention to a heavenly place. But, Jesus speaks from a heavenly place, and if you listen, even you will catch the spark. The spark of the heavenly flame brings you to the awareness of eternal life. It is this of which Jesus speaks. Of this, I am only able to point and say, follow him."

So it was that the elders of the Jewish church could not trap John or start a feud between his disciples and Jesus' disciples. Many came to respect both John and Jesus as they could see that they did not feud, but supported each other. So both their reputations increased with the people of the land. The Jewish elders, the Pharisees and the Sadducees, became very anxious over these two and began to plot to have them killed.

When Jesus heard how John was being questioned he moved

on to Galilee where he had more freedom. John was now getting into serious trouble with the religious elders and Jesus' disciples were gaining more converts than John. To avoid trouble, Jesus and his disciples moved from place to place and town to town. Chaila was always busy, asking Jesus where they would go next and sending messengers ahead so people could gather food for Jesus and his disciples.

In his travels Jesus often walked great distances. He was often surprised at how Chaila could keep up with him. "Are you now completely cured? He asked.

"I believe so. Perhaps it was meant to be, that I was ill, so that you could go to India alone. Wasn't that freedom valuable to you at the time?"

"Oh, yes. Very valuable. I don't think I would have gone to some places or stayed in others, if you had been along."

"That is in the past. I am healthy now, and strong. Don't worry about my strength. The spirit we have in this endeavor is so powerful and joyous, I don't see how I could use more energy."

"That's wonderful, Chaila."

Sometimes, to avoid crowds, Jesus walked out ahead of his disciples. This gave him time alone. While passing thorough Samaritan territory, Jesus stopped by a well in the city of Sychar. There was a field there, which many said, Jacob had given to his son Joseph.

It was late in the afternoon and Jesus was dusty and dirty. He sat on the stone wall at the edge of the well, tired and dripping sweat. He wanted a drink, but he had nothing with which to draw water. As Jesus sat wiping his brow, a woman from the town came to draw water. Jesus watched her as she approached. He could see that she was a beautiful woman, but there was weariness in her demeanor and sadness on her face. She was tall and thin, her eyes looking at the ground. When she drew near the well, Jesus said to her, "Woman please draw some water for me. I'm very thirsty."

Now the Samaritan woman was surprised that Jesus, obviously a Jew, was speaking to her. For the Jews refused to have any dealings with Samaritans. She said to Jesus, "How is it that you, a Jew, speak to me a Samaritan woman?"

Jesus answered, "If you knew my heart, you would know that I see neither man nor woman, neither Jew nor gentile. You would know that I see all men and women as equals in the sight of God."

"How am I to know the heart of a stranger?"

"If you knew the heart of God and the gift He offers, you would say, 'Give me living water,' and it would be given to you so that you would never thirst again."

"How Sir, are you to give me living water, when you have neither vessel nor pouch nor rope with which to draw water?"

"But I am not speaking of this water that is here today and gone tomorrow. I am speaking of a living source of eternal life within the heart of all. Please woman, give me to drink and I will tell you more."

Strangely bemused, but glad to see a Jew willing to speak with her, she lowered her leather bucket into the well and drew water. Carefully holding the bucket, she poured water into a clay cup and handed it to Jesus. Jesus drank the cupful quickly and she filled it again. When his thirst was quenched he returned the cup to her and said. "Everyone who drinks water from this well will thirst again, but whoever drinks the water which I reveal, will never thirst. For the source that I reveal lies in each man and woman and is the source of Spirit, the source of everlasting joy and eternal life."

"Tell me more about this source of everlasting life, this spiritual water, that quenches thirst forever."

"What I have to say, dear woman, is for everyone, not just the few. So, go get your friends and your husband and tell them to come and listen."

"But sir, I have no husband," she said.

Jesus looked closely at the woman. He could see the lines of stress and worry on her brow, the sorrow in her eyes. He could see that her life had been hard. So he said to her, "Dear woman, what you say is true; for I suspect that you have had several husbands and the man you are with now is not your husband."

"You perceive quite well," the woman said. "I will go and tell everyone that a wise man waits at the well to teach us."

"Thank you kind woman. You are blessed."

At this time, Chaila with Jesus' disciples returned from buying food in the market. They approached the well, saying nothing until the local woman left. Jesus' disciples then said to him, "Why do you sit alone with a Samaritan woman, people will think ill of you?" Jesus looked sorrowfully at the disciples. "When will you learn, the law is for man and not man for the law. No man or woman is so low that I may not speak with them and treat them as my equal. Open your hearts, for soon she will return with others and we will share our food."

When the woman returned with people from the village they gathered close to hear Jesus speak. Jesus motioned to his disciples to share the food they had purchased. As the people ate, Jesus spoke to them in a quiet voice.

He said, "We Jews are not superior to you Samaritans, nor is any race or creed superior to another. Each person, each race, is but an aspect of God. His presence is everywhere, constant and unblinking, behind every face of every creature, everywhere. Where God is, so also is eternal life. But this is not an easy thing for us to grasp. For eternal life comes only to those who can let go and let God. For life belongs to God and not God to life.

"We ourselves cannot take a piece of God and claim it for ourselves. The truth is, we have to give ourselves up to God. It is not we who grasp God, but God who grasps us. But we must allow Him to do so. Then He lets us know that we are His very presence, His very Self. This truth, of the living water, of spirit in each of us, will guide us to this awareness, if we let it. For God is spirit, and those who worship Him, must worship in spirit and in truth. Peace be to you my brothers and sisters of Samaria; may we never be strangers again."

The people who heard Jesus' words were amazed. Who was

this man that spoke with such authority? Who is this young man who speaks like a man of twice his years? Though tired, the people could see that Jesus appeared quite strong, full of energy and life.

"Who are you?" they asked. "Are you the Messiah?"

"I will not tell you who I am, for I would be accused of blasphemy. But I will tell you who you are; you, your brothers and sisters, the Jews, and the Gentiles alike; all are God, present here, Himself. He is knowing and experiencing Himself through you. Truly I say, I am in you and you in me. We are all in the Father, present, here and now.

"There is in reality, no you, no me, for our bodies and minds are only the gross or superficial form of God. There is only one presence here, one being manifested in various forms. There is no duality of you and me. The separation is a mirage. There is in reality, no speaker, no listener, only speaking and listening. For only one, the One, is truly present."

The sincerity with which Jesus spoke was undeniable. The men, women and children, were awestruck, dumbfounded beyond comprehension. An older gentleman stepped forward and said, "How can you speak like this if you are not the Messiah come to free the Jews?"

Jesus answered, "The Messiah is not the only one with wisdom. And wisdom is not left to the future. There have been many world teachers, but the world rejected them. The world may very well reject me, for I teach the ultimate truth, the ultimate state of reality. But I tell you, and you must hear me, I am not the only one who has taught this truth, nor will I be the last. I tell you, any one of you who inquires deeply enough, asking, 'Who am I,' will know what I know, and be one with that understanding. You will do the same wonders I do and even more." Jesus spoke these words, not solely for the Samaritans, but also for his disciples, for though they followed him, they did not yet fully understand.

The old gentlemen who had asked the question, just stood with his mouth open, for he could think of no response. So Jesus continued. "I can see that what I say is very difficult for you to understand. Forgive me, for I do not wish to confuse, nor to appear condescending. For me, what I teach is elemental, pure and simple. Reality is ultimately, as plain and clear as the sky above. But there is a veil between where you are and where I am. It is a veil that each and every one of us keeps and maintains, for we do not see how to live beyond the veil. Therefore, I do not condemn you, nor accuse you of sin. But I ask each of you, find the veil and remove it; then what I say you will understand. However, and this is a warning, once you remove the veil, your life will not be yours, for you will belong to God the Father, and thus to everyone."

The crowd was now some fifty people of various ages. They could not express what they were experiencing, for Jesus was speaking to a level of consciousness they barely knew. But the clarity of his talk, the conciseness of his words and the authority with which he spoke, was compelling. Each one, knew in his heart, that indeed, they were in the presence of pure spirit, a clear knowing, a reality blissfully secure, serene and permanent. They begged Jesus to stay with them for a few days and Jesus agreed to do so. He and Chaila went and stayed in the home of the Samaritan woman. She found lodging for the disciples amongst her friends.

Jesus told stories to the children and parables to the men. The women he encouraged to stand up for themselves and to value their contribution. "Bring your children to me and let me teach them, that they may grow up to live in the very presence of God. Not a God up there in the sky or over yonder at the top of that hill, but present in their very souls, with them always."

These words made the women love Jesus all the more and many wanted to follow him. But Jesus told them. "Women, stay with your men, for I travel constantly and know not where next I will lay my head. Your children, your brothers and sisters and your parents need you here. Just practice the presence of God in your heart and you will be with me."

The women appreciated that Jesus did not turn them away. He did not speak down to them or treat them condescendingly. He spoke to them as equals, which was very unusual. So the majority of Jesus' followers were women and wherever he went he was always provided for. And Jesus was well received outside of Israel, by Gentiles and Jews alike.

Jesus' disciples did not always see Jesus eat, as he was busy speaking with the people, day and night. Though food was present, Jesus often did not have time to eat. In their frustration, they said to him, "Jesus, stop and eat, for you have need of food and rest."

But Jesus answered them, "I have food to eat which you do not see." They said to themselves, "What? Has anyone seen him eat today? Has he eaten and we did not see it?" Again Jesus responded, "My food is to do the will of the One; to finish His work in me and share that light with all. There is an enormous energy flowing through me which you do not see. This energy nourishes and sustains me. If you were aware enough, you would sense a stream of light, entering through the crown of your head. Believe me, there is more to this life than meets the physical eye."

The disciples just shook their heads and wondered what this energy was and what it must feel like. Jesus understood their concern, but wanted them to experience the energy for themselves. So Jesus told them a parable.

"Do you not say after planting, in four months we will harvest? Lift up your eyes. Do you not see the fields, turned golden yellow, ready for harvest? There are other fields which you cannot touch with your eyes, they too are ready for harvest. He who reaps those fields, yet unseen, receives more than wages, for he gathers the fruit of life everlasting. Just as the sewer and the reaper rejoice together, for they both have gained, just so, he who shares eternal life, joins with all in the One. For them, the whole creation sings.

"In regard to spirit, the saying is true, one sows and another reaps. I send you to reap what others have planted, just as I reap where I have not sown. But you may still rejoice when the One blossoms, where you have neither sown nor labored. Ultimately, there is only One laborer and One Self, you only appear to be doing individual labor."

The disciples did not fully understand, but they listened and

took from Jesus' parable what they could. Chaila, knowing this
subject well, found herself amazed at how difficult it was for many
to understand the ultimate simplicity. Chaila walked ahead with
Jesus as they left the town. After an hour's walk, the two of them
sat down on a grassy knoll, waiting for the group to catch up.
Chaila felt the grass beneath her and the freshness of the land.
"You know Jesus, I am still in awe at your ability to use words and
parables. But how can this be so difficult?"

"Chaila, this is all to the glory of God. For, if the One cannot
hide from himself, how can he know himself? He is lost among us,
and when we find him, we rejoice. Were we not lost, how could we
be found? How could God play?"

"Oh, I see, Lila, the play of God."

"Yes, Lila. You know, stuck in our little selves, this all seems so
serious, so dreadful, but, from the highest point of view, knowing
all the illusion will end, it's just a game."

Chaila laughed a hearty belly laugh. "Please Jesus, don't talk
like this here. Others will not understand. They will find you
cruel, insensitive, deranged. To you this is all so simple, but really,
this is very subtle stuff. Be gentle with them."

"I try, Chaila, I really do. Don't you see? My parables are a
way to leave them with the idea, so they can get it on their own,
discover the subtleties for themselves. I am so glad that at least I
have you to share this with. I am truly thankful that you came
with me."

"Thank you Jesus. I too am glad I came." As the other disciples approached, Jesus and Chaila rose and went with them.

Many of the Samaritans who heard Jesus that day, believed he
was a man sent of God, and many believed what he said, though
they did not fully understand. As Jesus moved on to other towns
and villages, word had spread before him. Wherever he went, crowds
gathered and listened to his talks. Many were healed personally,
for he gave them hope, dignity, and self worth. Some even believed
his presence had cured them of long standing illnesses. So people
came to Jesus to be healed physically as well as spiritually.

With those who wanted to be cured of physical illness, Jesus was very careful. He would pray for them and bless them, but he always said, "According to your faith may you be healed." For Jesus knew that many were healed of illnesses due to stress and worry and that these could be cured by words alone. Jesus did not claim to be a healer and he didn't want healing to overshadow his message of life everlasting.

(26)

Jesus Visits Qumran

After leaving Samaria, Jesus and his disciples traveled the countryside, stopping wherever people gathered. As in Samaria, one of the most common meeting places was at the village well. On a particularly hot day, Jesus and Chaila, who had gone out ahead, as was often their custom, stopped at a well to rest. This one in a valley, below a village that sat on a hill, was nearly deserted. At the well were two monks, an older one with graying hair and a younger one. The elder monk was giving instructions to the younger one, who was listening intently.

Jesus and Chaila, who were within earshot, listened. They were both quite interested in what the monks might be discussing. The monks were white robed, obviously not Pharisees or Sadducees. The two, deep in conversation, paid little attention to Jesus or Chaila. The elder monk was talking about some esoteric texts dealing with God as the Unknown. Surprised by how well the monk was doing, expounding his ideas, Jesus nudged Chaila to speak.

"Where are you from?" Chaila asked.

The two turned toward her, surprised that a woman had spoken to them first. They looked to Jesus to see if she was out of line. But, seeing that Jesus made no disapproving gesture, they responded. "We are from Qumran," the older man said.

"Qumran?" said Jesus.

"Yes, it is a monastery not far from Jerusalem." The older monk studied the couple before him, noticing that the woman was obviously foreign.

"I have heard of Qumran," said Jesus. "My Father was from there. He spoke very highly of the place."

"Your Father was from Qumran," the older monk said, warming up with interest.

"Yes. But he left a long time ago."

"What was his name?"

"Joseph. Joseph of Bethlehem."

The old monk knit his brows and thought a long time. Finally he spoke. "I did not know him well. I don't think he stayed long after he was first sent out to teach."

Jesus smiled, "I can vouch for that."

The monk looked at Jesus, perplexed. "Anyhow, I remember he was the master carpenter. There are still many items of his in use. I was not a close friend of his, but I am sure some of the other monks would remember him better. We are returning tomorrow. You are welcome to come with us and visit."

Chaila turned to Jesus, "Let's go. It would be a fun change. You have never been there, have you?"

"No, I haven't. If you really want to go, let's do it. I might find it refreshing."

"We often find ourselves in the minority," said the older monk, "But, if your father came from there, I doubt you would find us too strange."

"Strange? I doubt it," said Jesus. "It would be a welcome relief. I too am often in the minority." Chaila nodded her head approvingly. "I do speak out," Jesus continued, "and many come to hear me, but I do have my detractors."

"Have we heard of you?" asked the younger monk.

"This is Jesus," said Chaila.

"Jesus! I've heard of you. You're the one who gathers great crowds. People come for miles just to hear you."

"Yes it's true," said Chaila.

Again the monks looked at Chaila and then at Jesus. Again they caught no disapproval from him. "What do you talk about?" asked the younger monk.

"The One. Our true Father as you would say in Israel."

"Very good," said the elder monk.

"What's your name?" asked Chaila.

"Chaim," said the older one. "And this is Michael."

"My name is Chaila."

"Do the Pharisees and Sadducees cause you much trouble?" asked Jesus.

"No. We stay out of their way. We're happy to stay in Qumran where we can practice in peace."

"That's wonderful," said Chaila. "What do you practice? Do you meditate? Chant?"

"Both and more," said Michael with a smile.

"What mystical texts do you have?" asked Chaila.

The monks looked at Chaila, surprised that she even knew the word. "Yes," said Chaim. "We do."

"Have you heard of the Bhagavad-Gita?" she asked.

"Yes. We have a copy. We have a number of foreign texts. We feel they deepen our own understanding of the Torah."

"Excellent," said Chaila.

The discussion continued for several hours. By the time they were done, Chaila and Jesus had agreed to accompany the two monks to Qumran. Chaila was eager to take a respite from the constant travel. Jesus agreed to go, but warned the two that they would have to travel slowly, as he would be speaking along the way. The two monks weren't on any strict schedule so they were not opposed.

When the other disciples caught up with the four of them, they were introduced. The motley band of men and Chaila, slowly began the walk towards Qumran. Jesus hoped the Pharisees would keep their distance and not interfere as Qumran was very close to Jerusalem. As the sun fell toward the horizon, they kept a steady pace towards Qumran.

It was several days before they arrived. As Jesus had warned, crowds formed along the way. He stopped and gave talks, denying no one. The monks were surprised at how easily Jesus traveled. He was always fed and clothed and always had a place to sleep. Michael noted to Chaim "We are much better off traveling with Jesus than by ourselves. We have never been so well provided for."

On a cool morning, Jesus and the monks arrived at Qumran. They had bypassed Jerusalem to keep the crowds down. They were tired and ready for a break. Michael said, "Don't worry, the crowds will not come to Qumran. They know better. We are very selective."

Jesus wondered if anyone there would remember his father. He knew he would enjoy hearing some descriptions of his father as a young man. He wished that Mary could be here. As they approached the gate it opened. The two monks, Jesus, Chaila and six disciples, entered.

Jesus was immediately aware of the stillness. There was a spirit to the place, different from the Viharas, but still, a spiritual essence. He felt right at home. They were taken to the kitchen and dinning area for water and fruit. As they sat eating, Jesus asked, "Is Caleb still here?"

The cook was surprised. He looked at Jesus in disbelief. "Why no, he died long ago."

"Oh, I'm sorry," said Jesus. "I used to know someone who knew him, a long time ago." Looking at the large table they were sitting at, Jesus inquired, "And who built this table?"

"There used to be a master carpenter here. I don't recall his name. But, all the great pieces here were made by him. His name is on a plaque in the carpenter's shed. You can go have a look later."

"I will," said Jesus.

After they had eaten, Jesus got directions from Chaim to the carpentry shed. He and Chaila walked there together. The others with them went to the meditation hall to sit in on the morning session.

The door to the shed was wood, heavy, worn, but its precise woodwork could be seen. Someone had put their soul into it. Looking around, Jesus found a plaque, it read, "JOSEPH OF

BETHLEHEM—MASTER CARPENTER." Jesus' eyes grew moist and Chaila saw a tear trickle down Jesus' face.

Chaila reached out and squeezed Jesus' arm gently. He turned to her and smiled.

"How wonderful that you can be here," she said.

"Yes," said Jesus. "My father took a lot from this place. He passed it on to me. I'm sure he left much of himself here too. His spirit is in the wood. I feel it."

There was an older man, small, wiry, sitting in a chair at the back of the long shed. Jesus approached him. "Do you remember Joseph?"

Shaking his head as if from reverie, the man thought for a while, then, as if shaken back in time, he answered, "Yes."

"What was he like?" asked Jesus.

"Let me see. He came here about the same time I did. We were both orphans. He was from Bethlehem. I was from Jerusalem. He was a good friend of mine and the best carpenter this place ever had. That's why there are still so many of his pieces still around. We care for them like museum pieces. They're just so good. Here, follow me. Let me show some of them to you."

With that, the man rose from his chair, grabbed a staff and headed for the door. "Come on," he beckoned.

Chaila and Jesus followed. He led them to the stable area. "See the fencing here. Still, in good shape. No one makes fences like this. Look at these posts! See how we keep them oiled. It keeps them from rotting in the sun. Look at these benches. Aren't they something?" The man's joy at describing his old friend's work was obvious. It was Chaila now who had tears running down her cheeks. Over the next several hours they were shown doors, chairs, troughs, tables and carvings, all made by Joseph. Jesus' heart was full.

"Why are you so interested in this carpentry?" the man finally asked.

"He was my father," said Jesus.

The man stood still. Then he came over to Jesus and gave him a big, long, hug. Jesus took in the man's joy and compassion. The man, Chaila could see, seemed like a child again.

"You have been so kind to show us around," she said.

"He was my friend," said the man. "Tell me what happened to him?" Jesus told him Joseph's story. His life in Egypt and how he had died of plague in Egypt. The man wept. "I would so love to see him again," he said. "To say goodbye."

"You've done enough," said Jesus. "God bless you."

When they returned to the shed, the man told Jesus all about his father. How he carried himself. How he prayed, meditated, worked, played. It was a wonderful tale. Chaila enjoyed hearing from another about Jesus' father. For Chaila knew already, that the world would never be the same.

After spending several days there, looking at the library, the books, and joining in the prayers and meditations, Jesus, Chaila and the others, parted. Jesus was again eager to continue his talks. There was a pressure in him that Chaila sensed deeply. It rarely left Jesus and he could not help but respond. She felt renewed by their stay and she could sense that Jesus too, was refreshed. They were ready.

(27)

The Pool at Bethsaida

Jesus left Qumran and returned to Galilee. He liked the area, especially the seashore. When the crowds grew too dense he could get away from them by taking a boat. Jesus was very careful to stay away from Nazareth, for though his family was there and they loved him very much, they had a difficult time with the multitudes and the attending troubles of his talks. Jesus told his disciples that the saying was true, that "A prophet is never honored in his hometown. They cannot see beyond the child they once knew. They remember all too clearly the character they knew before he became a prophet."

The people of Galilee welcomed Jesus. They had often heard of his travels and great speaking ability. They were curious to see and hear him for themselves. In Cana, where Jesus was staying, his reputation was well known, for it was told that he had turned water into wine. While there, a certain servant of the King, heard that Jesus was near and came to see him.

Now, this man was well known to the people and he risked his stature with the King by coming to see Jesus. For Jesus was also an authority, though of a different kind. The man, tall, with an intelligent face and a mole on his cheek, stood before Jesus and said, "Jesus, please come with me and heal my son, for he is gravely ill." The man's right eye twitched with nervousness for he felt the power of Jesus' presence.

Jesus felt compassion for the man, but he was disturbed by all the requests for healing being made of him. He turned to the crowd and said, "Look how this man comes and asks for a healing. I am glad to help where I can, but healing the physical body is not my primary purpose. I am here to bring peace, the knowledge of eternal joy and openness of heart. Do not be distracted by these healings which occur around me, for they will distract you from my message. It is easy to believe when one sees apparent miracles. But I do not want you to believe because of miracles, but because of what you experience in your own hearts."

Jesus turned to the King's servant and said. "Go. Your son will be healed according to your faith." The servant thanked Jesus and went on his way. Now as he was on his way home, his servants met him on the road, saying, "Master, your son is well." The King's agent then asked his own servants, "At what time did this happen?"

"Yesterday, shortly after noon the fever left and he rose from his bed."

The King's servant knelt on the ground at the very spot where he heard the news and thanked God. He knew his son was healed at that very hour, when Jesus had said, "Go and your son will be healed according to your faith." The man and his servants rejoiced together and returned home. On the way they told passers by and anyone they met of the miracle that had happened. So, Jesus' stature and reputation grew.

A day of feasting for the Jews was approaching and Jesus wanted to join the celebrations in Jerusalem. Though Jesus had avoided Jerusalem, taking his message to the common folk in the towns and villages, he wanted to be there for the feast and celebration. Chaila went ahead of him to arrange a place for them to stay. Because the crowds were getting too great to handle, he took his disciples to Jerusalem, quietly by a back road.

In Jerusalem, by the sheep market, there was a baptismal pool called Bethsaida. The sick, lame, blind and others with all types of ailments, came to this pool to be healed. The stature of this pool was great, for there was a belief that at a certain time an angel stirred up the water. It was believed that whoever was able to enter the water first, would be healed. Now Jesus was speaking near the entrance of the pool and he noticed a man lying on a mat, who had been ill for years. Jesus asked the man, "Why is it that you have been coming here for years and yet you are not healed?"

"I am a poor cripple and I have no one to lift me and carry me into the pool when the water is stirred up. For, as soon as the water stirs, another rushes in before me."

"Do you wish to be healed?" said Jesus.

"Of course I do!" said the man.

"Then quit lying there, your faith can make you well. Not I, but your faith. Do you have faith?"

"Yes I do."

"Then rise, take up your mat and walk."

The man looked at Jesus, startled by his commanding words, for Jesus spoke with authority that no man could deny. As Jesus stood before the man, looking intently into the cripple's eyes, the man could resist the command no more. Slowly, hesitantly, he pulled himself up on one knee, then the other, then lifted one leg and then the other. The man stood. Staring in awe at Jesus, he slowly bent down, rolled up his mat and put it under his arm. Turning to walk away, he said, "Thank you Sir. Thank you!"

Jesus said to him, "Tell no man that I healed you, for it is not so. It is your faith that has healed you. Do you hear?"

"Yes, I hear, I will tell all, faith has healed me."

As the man walked off some elders of the Church were passing nearby. Not having seen what transpired, they accosted the man carrying his mat and said, "Who are you to break the Sabbath like this, carrying a mat?"

The man said to them. "Who are you to question me? That man over there just healed me. I have been a cripple for thirty-eight years and now I walk. What am I to do, walk away and leave this mat, which has been my only comfort for years?"

The elders were incensed at this beggarly man speaking back to them in such a manner. But they could see that the man was serious. So they asked him, "Who is this man that healed you?"

"He is over there, in the midst of that crowd. I do not know who he is. But he spoke with great authority, a true man of God, a prophet. Who am I to ask his name? I am thankful that I can walk. That is enough. Go see for yourself who this man is." So the elders went to the edge of the crowd and pushed their way to the center, where Jesus stood preaching.

"Sir," one of the elders shouted. "Are you the one that healed the cripple over there?" They pointed the man out, carrying his mat. Jesus turned and he could see by their expressions that they were not pleased. Jesus said. "Of what concern is it to you that a crippled man is able to take up his mat and walk?"

"It is the Sabbath and to work on the Sabbath demeans it. Can God send us the Messiah and save us, the Jews, if we do not respect the Lord's day?"

Jesus turned to the elders, amazed at them. "All days belong to the Lord, not this one or that one. If a man carries his mat on the Sabbath, do you think God is concerned? I tell you, God is more pleased with the faith of that crippled man than he is with your self righteousness."

The elders were now incensed. They had not reckoned to be in the presence of one with such authority. "By what power do you heal?" they asked.

"I do not heal. The cripple healed himself by the conviction of his own faith. It is no different from any others who are healed here. Do you believe that an angel stirs the waters here? If that is so, why would an angel limit his healing to the first man who can step into the pool when the water is stirred? Wouldn't an angel, if present, heal one and all? As it is, men fight and quarrel over who will be the first to enter. God does not work like that."

The elders were speechless, so they turned and left. They had no answer for Jesus and they could see that they had met their match.

Jesus turned to the crowd and said, "Truly, I tell you, the son of man can do nothing of his own accord, but only what the Father wishes. I can do nothing on my own account but only what the Father shows me to do. For the Father is in me and I in Him and together we work as One. You also are one with the Father, but you do not know it. God's presence is here. For he who is one with the Father is not himself, but the Father only."

The people at the pool were amazed at Jesus' teaching. They could not fully comprehend what he was saying, but they felt secure, listening to one with such authority.

"Every man should honor himself, for it is only in this manner that the Father is honored. For each and every one of you is the Father, multiplied and hiding behind a myriad faces. Behind each face is the One, the Father, the Source. So, love one another, for the one you see is none other than yourself."

"How can this be?" the crowd asked.

"God is here because you are here. He sees because you see. Be not amazed at these teachings, for they are true. But you must step outside yourselves for a moment. Then you will see. I do not judge you, for you are no less than myself. This is what I see and this is what I say. You too can have the knowledge of eternal life. But first you must let go of yourself and become one with God. For that is your true state which you have forgotten. I do not do my will, but God's will and if you felt as I do, you too could do nothing but God's will."

"Who then was John the Baptist?" one of them asked.

"John the Baptist was a blazing light to point the way. But the one who points to another is not fully realized. So John could not say, 'I am in the Father and the Father is me.' But John could point to a higher path and that he did. John's work and my work are to the same end. But John does not have the understanding of oneness that I have. So, though John came before me and cleared the way, I show the way more clearly.

"You flocked to John, for his message was clear and simple. You had a symbolic baptism in water with which you could identify and this was satisfying. But I point beyond all symbols, and to grasp what I am saying, you have to lose yourself. And which of you is willing to take that risk? But I say to you, any who do not risk beyond themselves, will know death, but those who risk themselves into that which is beyond the little self, will know eternal life.

"I tell you, my testimony is greater than John's. For the work which John started, the Father has given me to finish. The work which I do testifies concerning me that the Father has sent me. Those of you who can hear, hear. And for those of you who cannot, I do not judge. For neither does my Father. But work on this, for it is my Father's good pleasure to give you the Kingdom. The Kingdom is here and now and for one and all. My message is only this, partake of the oneness that is present and know eternal life."

Jesus left the crowd standing in awe at his words and he left Jerusalem, for he knew the scribes and priests would be coming to question him. He knew that their hearts were closed and that there was no point in arguing with them.

The men who had questioned Jesus went to the rabbis and informed them of what Jesus had done and said. The church elders then began to make plans to get rid of Jesus, for he was undermining their authority. But Jesus and his disciples returned to Galilee and stayed by the sea. There people gathered on the hillside and he spoke to them from morning till night.

When evening came, Jesus asked the disciples what there was to eat. A boy had brought a few small loaves of bread and some fish for the disciples. Jesus knew that if he and his disciples stopped to eat, the people would also get out their food and eat. So Jesus quit talking and took the loaves of bread and the fish and blessed them and thanked God for His abundance. Then he broke the bread and fishes and ate with his disciples. The crowd, seeing that Jesus had stopped to eat, brought out their own food and ate also.

Now, as night was falling and Jesus and his disciples were always in need of food, the crowd passed around a basket and put in it all the food that was left. For, they were all returning home, but Jesus and his disciples were far from home. When the people had all gone home, Jesus and his disciples counted what had been left for them. There were twelve baskets of food: fish, cheese, wine and bread, enough for Jesus and his disciples for several days. But rumors spread and many believed that Jesus had fed the crowd.

As his fame spread, people began to say that Jesus was the Messiah. Many wanted to anoint him King of Israel. But Jesus refused this, telling the crowds that his Kingdom was not a country or a territory, but the Kingdom of God, hidden in every man's heart. One day, to get away from the crowd, Jesus went down to one of the boats on the shore, and went to sleep.

Some of the disciples, thinking that Jesus had gone ahead, came down to the boat and headed out to cross to Capernaum. The sea grew rough and the light on the water was strange and eerie. Now, as the disciples grew concerned that they were in danger, several of them cried out over the waves, "God save us! Know you not that we are the disciples of your servant, Jesus!"

In their fear, peering through the eerie light, several of the disciples thought they saw Jesus walking on the water. This sighting calmed them down and the night passed. Towards morning, one of the disciples who had been unable to sleep, finally felt drowsy. He went to the head of the boat and pulled up some canvas to make a place to sleep. There, under the canvas, fast asleep, was Jesus. "Master!" the disciple cried, "How did you get here? Did you not see the torment of the sea? Did you not hear our cries?"

"Dear one," said Jesus, "I was very tired and I neither heard the sea, nor you."

"Did we not see you walk across the water?"

"No," replied Jesus, "I have been here all along."

The disciples would not believe him, for several of them swore they had seen him walking on the waves. Though Jesus denied their claims, they held fast to their belief. This incident too, became a legend, and Jesus' fame spread far and wide. Jesus himself grew concerned, as his message was being lost in rumors of miracles and healings. However, as much as Jesus tried to downplay these stories, they persisted.

Jesus did not want his message of enlightenment to be lost while stories of miracles persisted. But the people were longing for a Messiah with miraculous powers that would set Israel free. For them, Jesus was the Messiah, and though Jesus did not condone that interpretation, for many, that was the only message they received.

(28)

A Talk on Mystical Oneness

Jesus had left the place where he preached to the multitudes and had come to Capernaum hoping to find peace and solace. Chaila was also tired and encouraged Jesus to speak to smaller groups. She was having a difficult time helping Jesus free himself from the crowds, to eat, to sleep, to meditate. Jesus enjoyed speaking to smaller groups, for when the crowds grew too large, intimacy was lost. So Jesus, with Chaila's encouragement, moved frequently, keeping people wondering where he was. People searching for Jesus, wanting to hear and see more, found him in Capernaum and begged him to teach. So Jesus found a tree stump standing three feet off the ground and from there, where all the people could see him, spoke to the crowd that gathered.

"I know that those of you here are blessed with true ears and true hearts. You are not here only to see miracles and chat with friends, but to hear the word of God. I tell you, listen with your heart and through my words, you will hear the word of God. For the word of God is already in your hearts, though it may be hidden.

"Do not labor for food which grows old and rots, but seek food which endures, spiritual food that leads to the oneness of eternal life. The son of man teaches that we are twofold, both sons of man and sons of the One. I can say nothing that is not of the Father, for I have given myself to the Father so that he may shine through me to you. I am in the Father, you are in me, and we are one."

Someone asked Jesus, "What can we do to gain insight and inherit eternal life?"

Jesus answered, "All who come to me and listen are doing God's work. If you hear the message I bring you, you will be able to do nothing but God's work. For my lips are sealed to anything but that which comes from my Father. Moses brought you manna from heaven, but the true bread is of spirit and comes from our Father.

"I give you the true bread which is the word of God. He who understands my message in his own heart will know eternal life. The one who hears will never thirst again, for there is an indwelling source, your true heritage, a living spring of eternal spirit. Once known, this source will take away your fears and though your body die, you will not know death.

"Everyone whom the One leads to me, I will not deny. I come, not to do my will, but to do the will of Him who sent me. I do not speak of my own authority, but with the authority of God. You who hear with your heart will know with the same authority that I know. You will have no further questions of me, for you will have your own answers. Listen then to your own heart, which my words are meant to open. And when your heart is open, you too will know what I know."

Jesus left the crowd and walked away. He met Chaila in a house in the city and stayed with her there. Jesus and Chaila made plans for his future travels and Chaila begged him to leave Israel, for she believed he would be arrested. But Jesus felt that his message was not yet complete. So, Chaila went ahead, finding food and lodging for Jesus. Wherever they went, Chaila arranged a place for them to rest. So, unlike the priests and scribes, Jesus had no constant abode and was able to travel easily over wide areas.

On the Sabbath, Jesus spoke in the Synagogue at Capernaum. Jesus was challenged by the rabbis, but Jesus' authority and understanding overshadowed them. Jesus chastised them for wallowing in darkness.

They asked Jesus, "Who are you, that you interpret the scriptures in this manner?"

Jesus replied, "And who are you to speak with so little under-standing. You are the blind leading the blind. You should be quiet and listen to your hearts. Then you would have the authority that I have. For it is the spirit that manifests life. The flesh is of tempo-rary use. The words I speak are of eternal spirit, life in the One."

To the crowd Jesus said, "Beware of these priests and rabbis, for they speak of that which they do not know. Listen to them, but if your heart does not respond, let their words be like water slip-ping from a duck's back. I tell you, their words cannot take root. For they are shallow. When your own heart hears, you will not look to the priests and rabbis for God, but you will know for your-self. Then you will speak as I speak and know with the certainty that I know. I do not condemn these church elders, but their very own hearts condemn them, for the words they utter are like grass to be thrown in the oven and burned. But the knowledge in your heart that can be found, will be like a river flowing through you. What I say, you can know too. What I do, you can do. In that day when everyone knows the truth, the world will be set free, and no neighbor will accuse another or hate another, but all will work together as one body, which in truth we are."

The church elders wished to throw Jesus out of the temple, but they dared not, for the crowd loved him. And when they chal-lenged Jesus, they could not stand the light. So in the dark of night, in dimly lit rooms, the elders made plans to do away with Jesus.

Hearing of the plots, Jesus left the area and traveled in and around Galilee, speaking to all who came to him. Many were healed just listening to his words. But Jesus took no credit for the healings. If anyone tried to thank him, Jesus said, "It is not I that has healed you, but your own faith, your own inner spirit. As you have be-lieved, so you have received." Many people loved Jesus, for he took no glory for himself.

Now Jesus sent out his disciples telling them. "I speak in the open before the people the priests and the elders. For what man does a thing in secret when he is eager for it to be known? I have hidden nothing. If you speak for me, show yourself to the people, do not be afraid."

So the disciples went out and spoke concerning what Jesus preached. Many who heard, felt the spirit and were moved, but others resisted their own heart's longing and heard not. These, then spread evil rumors about Jesus and rebuked those that spoke highly of him.

In time, the great feast was due, and Jesus went quietly to Jerusalem, for many wanted to harm him. In the middle of the feast, unannounced, Jesus went to the temple, stood up and preached. He read from the scrolls those passages he wished to teach. Now the rabbis and the people were amazed that Jesus, not an elder or a member of the priestly order, could read, quote, and interpret the scriptures. His interpretation and manner were far above the teachings of the rabbis.

"Who is this?" the elders mumbled among themselves, "Who can speak like this, with such authority, and use our own scriptures with so much insight?"

Jesus, knowing what was in their hearts, answered. "My teaching is not mine, but is His who sent me. He who does the will of the One, will know whether my teaching is from that One. I do not speak of my own account. He who speaks from his own limited view, seeks glory for himself, but he who seeks the glory of the One, is true, and there is no deception in his heart.

"Do not judge by the letter of the law, but the spirit of the law. For spirit is a moving thing, alive and indwelling. Do not judge according to appearance, but judge by spirit. If any man thirsts for spirit, let him come to me and drink."

People were divided because of Jesus' words. Many understood the significance and believed in what he said, but others did not. Many arguments arose as to who he was. "Was he a reincarnation of a prophet? If so, which one? Was he Christ, the Messiah?" So the elders sent soldiers to arrest Jesus, but they could not get close, for the crowd was too big. The soldiers could see that the crowd of people loved and respected Jesus and they were afraid. They returned to the priests saying, "We could not arrest him, for he is too popular and we ourselves would be harmed."

A few weeks later Jesus again went to the temple and sat down amongst the people and taught. While Jesus was speaking, a woman was brought to the temple to be stoned, for she had committed adultery. The Pharisees and Sadducees saw that this would be a perfect occasion to place Jesus in a bad light. For if Jesus defended her, he would be going against their laws. So they brought the woman into the midst of the crowd and held her before Jesus.

"Teacher, this woman was caught in the very act of adultery. The law of Moses commands that a women such as this should be stoned, but what do you say?"

Jesus bent down and doodled in the sand, thinking what he might say. For he knew that if he did not respond well to this test, the Pharisees might very well have grounds to arrest him. The woman being held, looked pleadingly at Jesus, for she knew that she was about to die.

Jesus stood up and looked over the crowd. He paused and let the silence pervade. Everyone had their eyes and ears on Jesus. He looked straight into the eyes of the Pharisee that had asked the question. In a loud voice, Jesus said, "Let him who is without sin cast the first stone."

Silence reigned. Jesus sat down again and doodled in the sand, making lines and circles. One by one the elders left, the one who had challenged Jesus left first and the others followed. All who had accused the woman were now afraid, for no one could answer to Jesus' authority. The woman stood alone. Jesus looked at her and said, "Woman, where are those that accused you?"

"They are all gone. No one is left to condemn me."

"Neither do I condemn you. Go woman. God is with you."

The woman rose, came to Jesus and hugged him tightly. "Dear Lord," she said, "surely you are God come to earth. Blessed be your name." Jesus looked at the woman and pointed away from the center of town. "You should go woman, before they change their minds and come back looking for you. But after this day has passed, you are free, for they will not try you again."

The woman let go of Jesus, turned, and walked hurriedly away. To those that remained Jesus said, "I am the light of the world. If you hear what I say and feel it in your hearts, you too will be a light unto the world. If you follow me in your hearts, you will not know darkness, but light everlasting."

During another meeting at the synagogue, a Pharisee said to Jesus, "Your testimony is not true because you testify concerning yourself."

Jesus answered saying, "Even though I testify through this body, my testimony is true, because I know I came from the One and will return to the One, but you do not know where I come from or where I will go. You judge according to the flesh, but I judge no man. If you sense that I am judging, look into your own hearts, for it is the One in you, that you transgress.

"Your own law says that the testimony of two men is true. I testify concerning myself and my Father who sent me, also testifies through me. Therefore my testimony is true."

They said to him, "Where is your Father that we may have his testimony?"

Jesus answered, "You know neither me nor my Father. If you knew me, you would know my Father also. Therefore, since you are not capable of receiving my testimony or my Father's, you are not capable of judging me."

This angered the Pharisees and they wished to arrest him on the spot, but they dared not. Knowing what was on their minds, Jesus said to them, "When I go away, you will be in darkness with no one to show the way. Since you are incapable of listening to your own hearts, you will die in your ignorance and never know eternal life. Where I go you cannot go, for your hearts are closed. You are stuck in this manifestation, but I am not. You are of this world. I appear in this world, yet I am beyond this world.

"You may condemn me, but your judgment is false, for I speak of the One who sent me and I speak only that which the One puts in my heart to tell. The One is with me and never leaves me because I always do what pleases that One. You may kill me, but the spirit which I am, you cannot kill. That spirit, though my body die, remains."

To those that believed in his word, Jesus said, "If you take my word to heart, you are truly my disciples. You will know the truth and the truth will set you free. For I come that you might have life and have it more abundantly. For the spirit, when it is in the world, brings light and life into the world in all its fullness.

"Whoever commits error is a servant of error, but he who is free in spirit, knows no error. He is immediately forgiven and forgives himself. If you knew and loved the One, you would love me also, for I am joined without barrier to the One. I am manifest by the will of the One as a separate soul, but am truly only that One.

"Truly I tell you, before the world was, I was. But you do not understand this, so you judge me to be crazy, insane, dangerous. But if you were joined with the One as I am, my words would sing in your heart and you would praise God with every fiber of your body."

At this the Pharisees took up stones to kill Jesus. But the crowed pressed in around Jesus and they could not throw a stone to hit him. Jesus turned to his followers nearby and motioned to them with his head. Together, moving as a throng, they left the temple and Jesus went to the place that Chaila had found for him and he stayed there quietly. None of Jesus' friends told anyone where he was. Thus it was, that Jesus was able to continue his ministry, because the Pharisees could never find him alone, where they could do him harm.

(29)

A Talk With a Blind Man

When Jesus was leaving Jerusalem to return to Galilee, he passed by a man who was blind from birth. The disciples knew the man, for he was always begging at the gate where people had to pass. So Jesus' disciples asked him, "Teacher, who sinned, this man or his parents, that he was born blind?"

Jesus answered, "Neither he nor his parents sinned. It is an error in thinking to condemn people such as this, for it is not by sin on anyone's part that sickness and disease are present. One must know that God is simply working out his presence, here and now, in you and me, and in this blind man. God is not limited by one man's lack of sight, for God has many other eyes.

"I tell you, God has put himself in human form so as to know Himself. Were there no vulnerability, no needs, love could not exist." Jesus turned to the blind man and said, "Do you believe that your blindness is because of sin?"

"No sir. I do not. For my parents are kind and I lead a quiet honorable life."

"Do you see what others do not see because of your blindness?"

"I see and feel things that others do not. I have eyes that see, but not these empty eyes on my face."

Jesus turned to his disciples and said, "This man is not blind. You are judging by appearance only. He has eyes you cannot see and insight which you cannot perceive."

So Jesus passed by and many were amazed at his teaching. A

Pharisee standing nearby accosted Jesus and asked, "How can you say such things? For we know that sin is the cause of disease."

Jesus answered the Pharisee, "You are more blind than this man, for you say you see, yet you do not. I tell you, man is not punished for his sins, but by his sins. Furthermore, though many appear to come short of the glory of God, we can only say that they have missed the mark. One cannot condemn any man. But many, such as you, condemn yourself, for you claim to see and understand what you do not. In your blindness you lead many astray. Whereas, God allows this one man to be blind, you are the cause of blindness for many."

The Pharisee was not going to stand for this disrespect. He threatened, "I will have you thrown out of the church, for you are a blasphemer!"

Jesus answered, "Only one who knows God can accuse me. Since you do not, your accusation is false. Get away from me you snake! Crawl back to your brothers and join them in your ignorance, for they will hear you. But you cannot hear me, your heart is as rigid as the stone of your temple."

So the Pharisee went off searching for the elders to complain of Jesus' teachings. Jesus went out of the city and warned the people with him, "Stay away from the Pharisees, for they are out to do harm to any who follow me."

After several days journey, Jesus was back in Galilee and crowds came to him. He told them a parable. "Only a thief enters the sheepfold by climbing over the fence. The true shepherd enters through the gate. To him the doorkeeper smiles. He calls his sheep by name and they follow.

"He leads his sheep to pasture and they follow him because they know his voice. The sheep do not follow a stranger, but flee, for his voice is strange.

"I am the door for the sheep. All who have come before are bandits and thieves if their sheep could not enter the Kingdom of heaven. I am a door, if any man follows me, he will know life eternal and the whole world will be his pasture. A false teacher is a thief, stealing the truth, killing and destroying that which should guide one home. I have come to Israel to show that you may have life and have it abundantly."

"I am a good shepherd, for I listen to the One. I am eternal, though I risk this body for the sake of my sheep. When the hired hand sees the wolf, he runs, for he is not one with the sheep. The wolf scatters and kills the sheep. I am a shepherd for the One. I know my own and they know me. The One knows me and I know the One. I place my body before you and bring this message, for you are my sheep.

"I have other sheep of other lands that I must gather. When I have gathered all that can hear my message here in Israel, I will go to other places, to the Gentiles of all nations, that they too, may hear the good news. For the true flock is one, whether of this nation or other nations, of this race or another. All are of the One, as I am in you and you in me.

"This is why my Father loves me, because I give this small self, this appearance of body and personality, to Him. There is one universal self. No man asked that I give up this small self to take on the work of the one Father. I lay it aside, of my own will, like unneeded clothing. How long I can teach in Israel is uncertain, for the church leaders want to kill me. I do not seek to suffer, nor do I wish to die. But I am willing to risk, to suffer, to die for my sheep. Hopefully, I can go on and teach in other places, but it is God's will, not mine which will prevail."

As the words of Jesus spread like a flood over flat land, the Jews of various sects debated who this man was. To the Jews, this was a very serious matter, for among them was a belief that only if a number of them were pure enough, keeping the laws of Moses, would the Messiah come, a Messiah who would be King and free the land of Israel from all oppressors. For many of the Jews, any individual who threatened this possibility, deserved to die.

The debate had many sides. There were those that considered Jesus truly insane. For these, Jesus was not a threat, because if he was crazy or perceived as crazy, it didn't matter what he said. However, this argument was hard to sustain, for the multitudes hung on Jesus' words, regarding him variously, as Elija reincarnated, the Messiah, or a God. If he were insane, why were so many following him?

Another argument was that he was a political activist, a zealot, trying to overthrow the Sanhedrin to his own ends. A third view was that he did have some internal or higher authority. But, either way, if he caused a rebellion, the Romans would take over entirely, denying the religious privileges they now enjoyed.

When the time of the feast of dedication came, Jesus went to Jerusalem, to the temple, where he stood and preached on Solomon's porch. The Jews of the temple, those with a vested interest in keeping things under control, accosted Jesus. They said to him, "How long are you going to keep us in suspense? If you are the Christ, tell us plainly!"

Jesus answered them, "I have spoken openly, but you do not understand. I am not come to rule Israel or any people. I am not the one who has put on the mantle of the Messiah. The people have placed this burden on me and I have rejected it. But I cannot stop them, for they believe what they will, just as you do. My kingdom is not of this world and it is not solely for the Jews. My kingdom is the kingdom of God, an inner kingdom of spirit, of life, even unto life everlasting."

"You blaspheme!" one of them yelled, "and take the place of God for yourself. You ought to be stoned." Those surrounding Jesus were emboldened by the man's accusation. Many picked up stones and held them in their hands to stone him.

Jesus said, "I tell you truly, there is no reason to fear me, for I did not come to take power in Israel. My task is to spread the will of God. Though you cannot see it, the Father and I are one. My words are not my words, but my Father's. I am not the King of the Jews, but the King of Spirit, for the One has given me the task of bringing His Inner Kingdom to the Jew and the Gentile alike. As for these stones in your hands. I have no fear, for if I am to live or die, it is not in your hands, but only in my Father's.

"But you cannot hear me, because you are not my sheep. If you were my sheep, you would hear my words and take them to heart. But my sheep do hear me and see into eternal Oneness. Neither you, nor all the elders in the land, nor the power of Rome, can snatch them from me. The One has given them to me and no one has the power to take them away. Should you stone me and my body rot right here on the temple grounds, my Kingdom remains."

At these words more of the crowd picked up stones. "You will die today for being a blasphemer!" they yelled.

"You cannot harm me for the Father and I are One." I have shown you many wonderful things. Who have I harmed? For which of my good works do you stone me?"

The Jews said to him, "It is not for good works or bad that we stone you, but because you blaspheme. We can see that you are only a man, yet you claim to speak for God."

Jesus said to them, "Is it not written in your law, by King David himself, 'Know ye not you are gods?' If he called us Gods, because the very heart of God is in us, and you believe the scripture cannot be broken, why do you condemn me if I say, the Father and I are one? Do I blaspheme, just because I say, I am the son of God. We are all the sons and daughters of God."

When Jesus said this, there was a hush in the crowd and those that believed in Jesus' words came forward and made a human shield around him. Chaila always made sure that there were followers nearby and when Jesus was in trouble she urged them forward so they could protect him. Surrounded by his followers, Jesus walked from the temple and no one dared to throw a stone.

Jesus left the city and went to the Jordan crossing where he had first met John and been baptized. There he stayed, and many came to hear him. And when Jesus spoke, the people said amongst themselves, "Though John did not perform miracles and though he did not say what this man says, yet everything John said about him is true."

Again, the crowds became too large and speaking to them was

difficult, so Jesus and his disciples left the Jordan crossing and
headed back into Judea. Chaila and the disciples tried to dissuade
Jesus from going to Judea, for there were many there who wanted
to kill him. But Jesus said to them, "Are there not twelve hours in
a day? If a man walks by daylight he will not stumble because he
sees the light of this world. But if a man travels at night, he will
stumble because there is no light.

"The kingdom of heaven is my light and wherever I go the
light sustains me. So I may go where I will, and because I am in
the light, no harm can befall me unless it be the will of the Father.
Since my will and my Father's will are one, I have no fear."

The disciples were emboldened by these words and followed
Jesus to Judea. But the disciples were afraid for Jesus and themselves. When they came to Bethany, a woman named Mary came
to Jesus saying, "Come quickly, for my brother Lazarus is dying."
So Jesus went to their home and went into the sick room.

"Are you Lazarus, the one who is ill?

"Yes. I am not well, as you can see, for I have a fever and no
strength and I fear that I will die."

Jesus answered, "Lazarus, though your body lose its life and
be buried in the ground, yet you will not die. For your spirit is the
Spirit of God, which cannot die. Mark my words, have no fear of
death, be calm. For if it is God's will that he take you home, go
willingly, for the Kingdom of God is eternal. And if you live, praise
God with all your heart and all your mind and all your strength."

"Thank you Jesus. Thank you. You have calmed my spirit."

Jesus got up from the sick bed and went to Mary and said,
"Dear woman, be at peace, for it is only God's will that will prevail. Whether your brother lives or dies, he will rest eternally with
the One."

Mary, hearing Jesus' words, grew calm. His very presence was
reassuring. Mary went in to see Lazarus and saw that he was at
peace. Chaila also spoke with Mary and comforted her.

Many people came to Mary and her sister's house, for they
wanted to see what would pass. And Jesus spoke to those who

came, saying, "I point the way to the eternal kingdom within. If any man hears my words and understands, he will not know death. I speak as the One, the Truth, the Light."

Many said, "Surely this is a son of man, but also a man at one with God. For no one can speak the words this man speaks." And word spread that the son of God was present here on earth.

In several days, Lazarus' strength returned and he left his sick bed. Many were amazed, for they thought surely, Lazarus would die. And those at some distance, who assumed that Lazarus had died, when they heard that he was well and that Jesus had been there, told that Jesus had raised Lazarus from the dead.

When word reached the Pharisees that Jesus was raising the dead, they became fearful. Though they did not believe Jesus could do these things, the people did. So Jesus was a threat. They were concerned that when Jesus spoke in the temple, even they could not argue with him, for Jesus was as subtle as a rainbow and just as bright. His light shone like a beacon on a hill at night. So they plotted how to seize him in secret and have him killed.

The Pharisees knew that their special privileges from Rome were in danger and that their privileges would be taken away if there were disturbances. Jesus, though he did not claim to be a leader of Israel, but a leader of the Spirit, was causing great disturbance. The leader of the priests for that year was a man named Caiaphas and it was his responsibility to keep the Jews in line. He said to the Pharisees, "It is better that this one man should die, than he stir up trouble for all of us. For if he stirs up the people and the Romans are offended, we will all be killed." So they determined to find charges against Jesus, so that he could be taken to the Romans, who alone held the power to condemn a man to death. Jesus, hearing of plans to kill him, stayed away from Jerusalem, living in the wilderness, in the province of Ephraim.

The Jewish Passover was at hand and many from the country-side went up to Jerusalem before the feast to purify themselves. The church elders and their supporters were looking for Jesus. At

the temple they kept saying to one another, "Surely, he will come
to the feast." The high priest and the Pharisees put out the word
that if any man knew of Jesus' whereabouts, he was to inform
them, that they might arrest him."

(30)

The Last Teachings in Jerusalem

Six days before the Passover, Jesus came to Bethany where Lazarus and Mary were having a banquet. This was in celebration of Lazarus' return to health. Jesus and his disciples arrived at the feast and Jesus was placed at the head of the table, for he was the guest of honor. After the meal, when everyone was full and relaxed, Mary, wanting to show her appreciation for what Jesus had done, brought out a small stone bottle of rare plant oil. The perfumed oil was expensive, with a delicate scent, and she bathed Jesus' feet with it.

Mary was dressed in her best silk dress, deep maroon, with a low cut front. Her hair was pulled back and clasped behind her neck. Holding Jesus' feet, she turned him around so that he faced her. Kneeling at his feet, she spread the perfumed oil over them with her bare hands. She rubbed the excess off with her hair. Jesus said not a word. A soft breeze stirred the air and the house was filled with the fragrance.

Judas of Iscariot, one of Jesus' disciples, was furious at what he saw. He turned to Jesus. "Why wasn't this oil sold and given to the poor? It could have brought three hundred coins."

Jesus turned to Judas, "Why do you begrudge this woman her joy? It is her good pleasure to show her appreciation in this way. My Father in heaven would rejoice if we were all so thankful. Many are blessed, but few acknowledge their blessings. Is Mary's brother not healed? Your anger is unjustified. The poor you have with you always, but I am here only a short while." Judas sat, not daring to say a word, for he knew that no one would back him. Disgruntled, he turned away from Jesus and mumbled into his bread. A number of the guests smiled, for Jesus had spoken eloquently.

As word of the banquet spread, many came to see Jesus. Some said, "Come see the man who can raise the dead." Crowds gathered and Jesus came out and blessed them, shaking hands with many. Eventually, word got to the Pharisees. When they heard that Jesus was there, eating and drinking with Lazarus, they sent soldiers to arrest him. They sought to kill Jesus and Lazarus too. For, because of Lazarus, many were following Jesus. But Jesus was told that the Jewish guards were coming and left for Bethany. Once he was out of town, he went openly to Jerusalem, speaking as he went. Many were with him and no guards dared to follow. They were outnumbered and Jesus was extremely popular. When Jesus arrived at Jerusalem's main gate, people saw him and were thrilled. Many began to cut branches from palm trees to wave in the air. The atmosphere around Jesus grew intense, some shouted "Hosanna! Blessed is the King of Israel, who comes in the name of the Lord."

A wealthy man bowed before Jesus and gave him a donkey to ride. Jesus mounted and rode amongst the crowd pressing in on him from either side. The crowd grew, for when people asked, "Who is this? What is going on?" they were told, "This is the man who raises the dead and turns water into wine." So more gathered to see this man riding on a donkey.

Men and women, Gentile and Jew, had heard of Jesus; so they gathered. The Pharisees, seeing the crowds, were afraid, for their stature and control over the people were threatened. But they could do nothing while Jesus was surrounded by adoring crowds. Jesus stopped at a crossroads where people had gathered, stood on some steps above the crowd and spoke.

"Listen! Unless a grain of wheat falls to the ground, letting its seedling self die, it will not become a plant and bear fruit. So it is with man. If a man loves his apparent self, he will lose his true self, but if he has no concern for that apparent self, which is of the world, he will gain a new life, joined to the One, knowing eternal life. For one who clings to this world will die, but one who sees the spiritual will not know death."

"If any man hear me let him follow me. For where God is, there am I also. All God's servants hear me and together we honor our Father's home, the kingdom within. You glorify me today, but I tell you, the glory is not mine, but my Father's, for it is He who sent me and causes you to hear. Glory be His name!

"The light of this world is always here. But someone who points the light out to you is not always here. So, when there is a teacher, one who knows God and is one with Him, listen to him! For the ripe fruit falls from the tree and brings life to others. I am the ripe fruit, and he who eats of my fruit, will know the light."

Now, many of the leaders who had not heard Jesus before, were amazed at his teaching and his authority. Many came to believe that he truly was a messenger of God. But though they believed, they were afraid to speak aloud, for they were afraid of the Pharisees. For with Jesus' authority, he could speak in public and not be harmed, but for those without such authority, there was no protection. So they believed but were silent.

Though many were silent, many cried out. "Speak! Speak!" So Jesus, pleased that the people listened, spoke again. "He whose heart is open to me, knows not me, but sees the One of all. If your heart responds, you know the One who sent me. I have come to Israel as light, so that whoever hears me and understands, will leave darkness behind. He who casts aside my words for lack of effort, only condemns himself. For, I do not condemn, nor do I judge, for I speak, not to judge the world, but to free the world."

"I tell you, he who oppresses me and does not receive my words has pronounced judgment on himself. For the message is sent, it is up to each individual to receive. I do not speak to honor myself, but to honor the One. That source compels me to speak and I only say what the Source reveals. The One is life everlasting! Join me in that presence.

When Jesus grew tired he had his disciples clear a path for him. He ran the gauntlet, escaping the crowd. When he and the disciples were free, they went to a room Chaila had found for them, where they could meet in private. Before supper, Chaila took Jesus aside and suggested that he speak further with Judas, for she could see that Judas was still disturbed. While they were gathered in the room, Jesus took the opportunity to address him.

"Judas, I know that you were offended by Mary, that she washed my feet in expensive fragrant oil, I wish to show you that there is no offense. Showing affection is a blessing, but receiving graciously is also a blessing. As Mary anointed my feet with oil, so I will wash your feet." Jesus walked to a table in the corner of the room and took a pitcher of water from it. He picked up a cloth from the basin and looking at Judas, said, "I will wash your feet clean."

"Not me first," said Judas. "Do someone else first." Judas was appalled at such a display of affection. "This is like servitude," he said. He watched in horror as Jesus washed, one by one, the disciples' feet. When Jesus came to Peter, the disciple pulled back, "Teacher, I cannot let you wash my feet!"

Jesus answered, "What I do, you may not understand, but someday you will. I do these things so that you may feel what I feel and know what I know, for we are all servants of the One. I do this so that you know that I am not higher than you, nor you higher than anyone else. For God only is present here. Though we appear as many and separate, we are truly one, one in Him who is present everywhere, in everyone and everything. There is only one power and one presence in the universe, God."

Peter was astounded by these words, for though he loved Jesus and thought him wise, yet he did not fully understand.

After Jesus washed Simon Peter's feet, he turned to Judas. "You too Judas, for we are all one family." Judas acquiesced but was extremely uncomfortable and turned his head so as to avoid looking Jesus in the eye. When Jesus was finished he sat down.

"Do you understand what I have shown you? You call me friend and teacher and what you say is true. But I am not the only teacher, nor the only Lord, for we are all the sons of God. If then, your friend and teacher washes your feet, take my example and do likewise for others." I have done this so that you may understand, in the sight of God we are all equals.

"In reality, no servant is greater than his master and no disciple is greater than the One who sends him. If you feel this, you are blessed, for you know the joy of non-duality." After these words, Jesus ate with the disciples.

Judas pulled himself aside, feeling disgusted with what had gone on. He thought, I have followed this man to gain stature, not to learn to wash feet. This is beneath me! Aren't I better than a servant? He rose and quietly slipped out. Jesus noticed him leaving and feared he was up to no good. Jesus knew that Judas was through with him and would soon be going to the temple to see the Pharisees.

Jesus knew he would not be able to stay in Jerusalem much longer, for with crowds and attention so prevalent, he was courting danger. He knew the Pharisees were plotting to arrest him. He had considered this possibility many times and had decided that he could not continue his mission much longer in Israel. Soon he would leave and return to Hemis. In view of this, Jesus spoke to his disciples.

"I may not be able to preach in Jerusalem much longer for the crowds are becoming too great. The church elders will not tolerate my presence much longer. They have powerful friends who will do their bidding. The Roman governor listens to the Sanhedrin and even I cannot prevent what they may be planning. Therefore, I tell you now, I can only stay in Israel a short while longer. When I go, I will be going far away, to a place unfamiliar to you. A place where you would find it difficult to live; for you would be without home and family. As for me, I have lived in strange lands since I was a small child, it is not a burden for me to live elsewhere.

"Since I will be leaving soon, I am going to give you a new commandment. This I leave as a blessing and a code of conduct. Love one another as I have loved you. For if you love one another as I have loved you, the message I have brought will be witnessed among you and my message will not be lost. The kingdom of heaven, which I have displayed for you, brings love, non-duality, the insight that all is One."

The disciples were dismayed at this talk by Jesus. They urged him to leave the danger of Jerusalem and hide in the hills. So Jesus took his disciples to the hills and began to instruct them as he never had before. Avoiding the crowds, he was able to focus on his disciples, making every effort to bring forth in them the light he knew.

He said, "Believe in me and hear what I say, then, though I leave, my presence, which is God's presence, will be with you. If God be with you, then I am with you also, and you will not be alone. In my Father's kingdom there are many rooms—rooms for all nations and all races. I came here to prepare Israel for its place in my Father's mansion. When I go, I will prepare other nations for their places also. All nations, all religions, have their place in my Father's mansion. None are excluded. The kingdom of God is one, for God the Father, is the One of all.

"He who has seen me has seen the Father. If you have seen me, the Father is in you, and you need no longer depend on my presence. For my presence is but His presence in the flesh. His presence abides in you also, though you may not recognize it. I show you the light, but you are light also. You truly are one with me and the Father. You will miss me, but you will not be abandoned, for I and the Father will be indwelling. And he who knows the Father as I know the Father, will do the works that I do, and even greater. For whatever you ask that is of our Father's will, that you will receive.

"Any man or woman can come to the Father, but the way is hidden, for we are in the flesh. Whatever religion, whatever creed, whatever path, all search for the One. I point the way as others have pointed the way before. Others will come after me also pointing the way. So, fear not; I am always with you. When you are lonely and afraid, go within and you will find me. Search out that presence in your heart and you will never be alone."

Now when the disciples heard these words, they were afraid.

They knew that the situation was getting difficult for Jesus and that it was getting harder and harder for him to travel in Israel. But they did not want him to leave.

Jesus said, "When you have the spirit, the oneness with God which I show you, you will feel it, and it will be as real as the ground beneath your feet, as close as the palms of your hands. But others will not see it, for they are caught in the manifest world. But they will see the effects in you, for you will be different. Some will revile you, but others will come to you in secret, saying, 'Please tell me what is this spirit that you have?' Those, you will be able to show the light, for they ask with open hearts.

"I tell you again, I am going away. I intend to go back to Kashmir if that be possible. But let me make this very clear. Should the Pharisees arrest me and try me, it is possible that I will be condemned to death. This is a possibility! So you must be prepared. As for my death, should that be ordered, be assured, I am not afraid to die. Though, like you, this body may suffer; still, I have no fear of death.

"So, you must be prepared, for either way, I will be leaving you, and where I go you cannot come. Should I make it to Kashmir, maybe years from now, I will return. But this I cannot promise, for there are many people in other nations that are ripe to hear my message. When I am gone, remember me. In remembering me, remember the One, for I come not for myself, but to reveal the One. Peace be to you always and forever."

Several days later, after Chaila had led the group in a lengthy meditation, the disciples asked Jesus to talk to them again. They wanted reassurance of who he was and what his message was. They asked, "Speak to us that we may calm down. For we are afraid."

Jesus thought for awhile knowing that a parable or story would be more easily remembered after he was gone. He told them this parable.

"I am a spiritual vine and my Father is the source. Every branch of me that does not blossom is cut off, and the one which does bear fruit, is pruned so that it may flourish and produce more

fruit. You are the pruned branches because you have willingly received the message I have given you. Stay faithful that the One
prevail in you. For the branch is not alone and bears fruit only on
the vine. So friends in Spirit, you too must stay in touch, for when
you abide in the One, the outer reveals good fruit only,

"When you are one with the Presence, which is who you really
are, the world will seem to do your bidding. What would make
others suffer, you will accept, for your suffering will be transformed.
Though you be condemned to death, you will go to your death
happy to be rejoining the One. I tell you, without this body of
flesh, there is no distance between you and the Father. Your oneness will be complete.

"Just as the One loves me, I have loved you. Share my love. I
have spoken to you that my joy may grow in you and that your life
may be full. Remember my example, love one another as I have
loved you.

"I will no longer call you servants, because a servant does not
know his master's mind; but I will call you friends, because I have
shared with you all that I have received from the One. By choosing
to follow me, you have chosen your true Father. Therefore, we are
one in spirit and in truth. As I am my Father's fruit, you are my
fruit, and after I am gone, you will also bear fruit.

"If the world does not understand you and seems to reject
you, accept it and forgive them, for the world rejected me first. If
you had remained in the world, no one would fear you, for you
would be understood. But since you are drawn out of the world
into the One, many will not understand. They will revile you and
condemn you. So be wary yet kind."

(31)

Jesus Is Arrested

Judas was convinced that Jesus was no longer worth following. His idol had forsaken a heroic stance and debased himself. Judas wished no longer to offer his support. Being a practical man, he pondered his situation to determine the greatest possible advantage to himself regarding his knowledge of Jesus. It would be easy, he thought, to turn Jesus over to the Pharisees. To leave the disciples and be able to hide, he would need traveling money. He felt justified, in whatever he might do, for Jesus had let him down. Judas told himself, I will go to the Pharisees and claim I want to help protect others from being led astray by Jesus.

He knew the disciples typical movements, so he could help the priests find and arrest Jesus. With Jesus out of the way, the money purse he carried for the disciples would be his. He planned, still sitting with the other disciples and scratching his beard, to keep the purse and add to his funds with what the priests would pay him.

The best way to break away and be safe would be to get Jesus arrested. With him out of the way, who would be looking for the purse? So, Judas excused himself and walked the winding streets of Jerusalem, head bowed. He went to the home of a Pharisee he knew, demanding money to lead them to Jesus. He informed them that he could lead them to Jesus in the night, when he and his disciples would not be surrounded by adoring throngs.

Jesus and his disciples, unaware of Judas' activities, had gathered for the evening, outdoors in a common garden. There were no more than twenty altogether. Judas, knowing where they were likely to be, led the soldiers sent by the Sanhedrin to the place. Holding torches so that they could see, with weapons drawn, the guards approached Jesus and the disciples.

Seeing the torches, the soldiers and the drawn weapons, a number of the disciples, including several women, ran into the night. They knew that soldiers coming in the night, whether Roman or Jewish, meant to do them harm. But Jesus and a number of disciples stayed to face the guards.

Judas, standing back behind the guards, whispered in one of the soldier's ears, "Jesus is the tall one. The one with the white robe." When the group of soldiers drew near, Jesus stepped forward and asked loudly. "Who are you looking for?"

"Jesus of Nazareth," said the leader of the guards.

"I am he," said Jesus.

So the guard went forward and with the others grabbed Jesus and forced his hands behind his back. Quickly they tied his wrists with rope. As they did this, Simon Peter demanded loudly, "Why do you arrest this man? On what charge?"

"Blasphemy," the guards answered. "Step back and do not challenge us or you will be arrested too."

Jesus turned to the remaining disciples, Chaila among them, and said, "Do as they say. Do not try and defend me, for they are armed. There is no need for any of you to be harmed or accused with me. Your work remains. Do as I say, go!"

But Chaila, not wanting to lose Jesus again, responded, "I will not leave you. I will not cause trouble. But let me come with you, for I cannot leave you."

"I beg you to go," said Jesus, "Please don't follow."

But Chaila was not dissuaded. She stood her ground as the other disciples left. The head guard turned to Chaila, "Woman, you may follow at a distance, but if you impede us, you will be arrested."

"Do not worry, Sir, I will not impede you. I simply want to know where you are taking him." With that, the guards took Jesus by the arm and led him away. Chaila followed at a distance, keeping her word not to cause further trouble. Even now, though worried, Chaila believed that things would turn out right.

She believed that Jesus could not be held for long, for though he challenged the religious elders, he did not challenge Rome. His kingdom was not political. Neither did it concern land or property. His talk and his actions were for the spirit of man, not possessions, politics, or status. So, though she was frightened, she was not entirely without hope. In the three years she had been in Israel, she had seen very clearly how the Romans dealt with their subjects. They were, as far as she could tell, very careful how they treated people in regard to the law. They were firm believers in law and order and Jesus had not challenged or offended their rule. The Sanhedrin, however, could punish Jesus, though they could not, on their own, condemn Jesus to death.

Chaila followed until the group came to a halt before a large private home not far from the Synagogue. She hid herself in the shadows of a house across the street. But someone inside the home, aroused by the torches and the commotion, came out to see what was going on. Chaila, seizing the moment, pointed to the house across the street and asked the man, "Who's place is that, where those men are entering?"

"That is the home of Hanan, the Father-in-law of Caiaphas, the high priest for this year."

"Oh thank you sir. Thank you."

Chaila stayed in the shadow of the house across from Hanan's home, watching. She wanted to see if Jesus would be kept there or moved to another location. All the lights were on in the house, and Chaila could hear yelling and the clanging of metal and chairs.

Inside, Hanan was questioning Jesus. He was determined to find a reason to have him turned over to the Romans for treason. For, except for spontaneous stonings, which Rome never found out about, the Jews were not allowed to condemn a man to death. This, the Romans kept under their jurisdiction, at their own discretion and judgment.

"Are you Jesus of Nazareth?" Hanan asked.

"I am he."

"Do you know the disturbance you are causing among the people? Are you aware that you may cause many to die because of your insolence?"

"I do not stir up the people. I teach them only of the Father. It is your response that is causing the people to stir. No one but you and your minions has attacked me or threatened me."

"How dare you speak to me this way! I represent the highest levels of the Jewish law."

"There is none high except our Father. It is He whom I follow."

"So you deny my authority completely?"

"If you had the authority of my Father, you would not speak to me in this manner?"

For his insolence, a member of the guard struck Jesus across the face with the back of his hand. "What is your doctrine?" asked Hanan.

Jesus replied, "I have spoken openly throughout Israel, even in the synagogues. I have kept nothing secret that God revealed to me. Why ask me? Ask those who heard me. You know what I have taught."

"I ask you here in front of these men, so that we can verify what I have heard, that you are blasphemer."

"If I have spoken against the One, testify to it. But, if not, why arrest and abuse me?"

"Will you not answer me?"

"I ask you this, how can I blaspheme against my Father when I speak only what He tells me to speak?"

"You have spoken enough, no Jew may say to us, 'I speak for the Father.' You have said enough for me. I am sending you to Caiaphas. He will know what to do with you!"

With that, the guards took Jesus under the cover of night, to Caiaphas. Chaila followed and again stood outside the place where they held Jesus.

When Caiaphas entered the room, he looked sternly at Jesus and asked, "What have you to say for yourself?"

"I have nothing to say to you. You have already condemned and arrested me. Shall I honor your court, held in the dark of night, like a pack of hyenas?"

"Enough already, I need hear no more from you. You cannot talk to the high priest this way. For if you speak this way, your followers will speak this way, and there will be no Jewish authority left to deal with the Romans. Your actions, if left unchecked, will put us all in danger. Send this man to Pilate!" he yelled.

By the time the guards and Caiaphas were done with Jesus it was morning. As the guards drug Jesus out onto the street, Chaila watched. She was numb from having been up all night, and stunned at what she saw. But, she did not give in to fear. She stayed alert, and once again, followed the guards and Jesus silently, staying well behind in the shadows.

They took Jesus to the Praetorium and waited outside. For they did not want to go in, as they might be defiled by the gentiles. So Pilate was summoned and he came outside and stood on the steps. "What accusation do you bring against this man? For I have not heard of him."

"We bring this man to you because he is evil and stirs up the people. He is a disgrace to us and we want him silenced."

"So, if he is causing a disturbance among you, deal with him yourselves. You have the authority to put a man in prison."

"But we do not want prison for this man. We want death. We want him sentenced to death. We do not have the authority to do so."

Pilate then motioned the Jewish guards to let Jesus go. Then Pilate nodded his head that Jesus should follow him. So Jesus followed Pilate into the Praetorium. The Roman guards followed.

Pilate called Jesus aside where the guards could see but not hear their conversation.

"It is not often that the Jews bring someone to me asking for the death penalty. What have you done?"

"I have offended them, for they follow the letter of the law, but I follow the spirit of the law."

"And what is the spirit of the law?"

"Love."

"Love?"

"Yes the spirit of the law is love."

"And they want to condemn you for this?"

"Yes. They are offended, for I have authority from God to speak the truth. They speak with the authority of the Jewish law, but I speak with the authority of God. Since they cannot match the authority of my Father, they condemn me."

"But they want you condemned to death! This is a serious charge."

"Yes, serious. But I have no defense."

"Why say you, that you have no defense?"

"Because I can no more deny my Father's word than cut off my own head. My Father and I are one."

"You speak of God, not your natural father?"

"My natural father is dead. God, my Father, my Mother, my very soul, is of whom and through whom I speak."

"So, have you stirred up the people and asked them to rise against your priests and rabbis?"

"No. I preach love and forgiveness. I speak of God who is in the hearts of all men. That God is free, not bound up in religious law, rules and regulations, causing people to suffer. They have turned the temple of God into a place of business and abuse the people, claiming piety."

"Therefore, they want you out of the way because you are challenging their authority."

"Correct."

"But you are not proclaiming that Israel should be free of Rome?"

"No. I preach that Israel and all peoples should be free to worship God in their hearts, in their own way."

"I know the Jews have prophesies regarding a Messiah. Are you that Messiah?"

"I am a messenger of God. I am not wanting to be king of the Jews. For my kingdom is a kingdom of the spirit, a kingdom of love. It is not a political kingdom."

"So what do you think of Rome?"

"I say, give unto Caesar what is Caesar's and give unto God that which is God's."

"I see no treason in this. You seem reasonable enough to me, though you may be a bit touched in the head to get the Jewish elders this riled up. Why haven't you left the country?"

"I have been thinking that it was time I did so. But my timing seems to be off. I didn't expect that they would arrest me this soon. I thought I had a little more time."

"Stay here. I am going to talk to your people. Maybe we can strike a deal."

So, Pilate went out to the steps again and spoke to the Jewish elders gathered there. "Who is this man that you want condemned?"

"He says he is King of the Jews."

"But he tells me his kingdom is not of this world. You may have a crazy man here, but I see no threat of treason."

Then the crowd that had gathered, summoned by the Sanhedrin, started shouting. "No one is allowed to call themselves, King of the Jews." Pilate's voice was drowned out by the crowd, so he went back in and stood before Jesus.

"Are you wanting to be King of the Jews?"

"I told you, my kingdom is not of this world. If my kingdom were of this world, my servants would have fought these people and your soldiers as well. For they would not want their leader killed. But since my kingdom is a spiritual kingdom, you see no one raising a finger or unsheathing a sword."

"Your words ring true."

"I tell you, I came into this world to bring the truth, and I have done so, even unto this."

"Tell me, what is truth?"

"That you and I are one in the Father."

These words shook Pilate to the core, for he had never heard such words uttered before, nor had he ever been spoken to with such authority. Whether this man was sane or crazy, Pilate could not tell, but the authority with which he spoke was undeniable. Pilate began to sense what the Jews were afraid of, for no man had the authority with which this man spoke.

Pilate determined to try and thwart the Jews' efforts by punishing Jesus himself. To Jesus he said, "I will make one last attempt to save your life. I am going to have you flogged and sent before your people, making a humiliating joke of you. Maybe this will be enough to dissuade them from asking for your death."

Jesus sat impassively, saying nothing.

Pilate ordered the guards to take Jesus to the courtyard and have him flogged. As this was in progress, Pilate went to his own quarters and fetched one of his own robes, a purple one signifying royalty. He returned to the area where he had spoken to Jesus and waited for the soldiers to return with Jesus. When they brought him back, he put the robe over Jesus' shoulders.

Though Jesus could hardly stand, Pilate brought him out before the crowd. With his own knife he cut twigs from a thorny bush growing nearby. Twisting the twigs, he made a crown of thorns and placed it on Jesus' head. "I give you the King of the Jews," he shouted. Then Pilate had the soldiers turn Jesus around and Pilate stripped the robe from Jesus' back so they could see that he had been flogged. "Here is your King! I release him to you!"

But the crowd yelled back, "Kill him. Kill him."

When the crowd finally stopped, Pilate said to the people before him, "I find no guilt in this man. He challenges neither me nor Rome. He does not even claim to be your King. There is no cause to condemn this man."

But again the crowd yelled, "Crucify him. Crucify him."

Becoming afraid, Pilate turned again to Jesus. "What have you to say? They want to crucify you." But Jesus looked up toward the blue skies and did not answer. Pilate said to him,

"Will you not speak, even to me, who has the power to release you or to crucify you?"

Jesus answered, "Except that the One permits you this authority, I would not be here. It is in his hands, not yours."

Even more than before, Pilate was filled with fear. He had never encountered a man, confronted with death, exuding such confidence and serenity. More than ever Pilate wanted to release Jesus, even to have him escorted out of the country. Pilate turned to the crowd. "I am going to release this man. He harms no one."

Now Caiaphas stepped forward, whom Pilate knew was the high priest for the year. So Pilate listened as Caiaphas spoke. "If you do not condemn this man, you offend Caesar, for whoever would be king, challenges Caesar."

"You ask me to crucify your king?"

The crowd, following Caiaphas lead, yelled, "We have no king but Caesar! We have no king but Caesar!"

Pilate knew that his game was over. It would not be possible now to save Jesus without threatening his own career. He called to the soldiers at his side and asked that he be brought a bowl of water. When this was done, he stood above the crowd on the pavement stone and said, "I wash my hands of this affair. This man offends no one. Only your arrogance is threatened. I deliver him to you. You may crucify him, but his blood rests on your heads."

With these words Pilate instructed the soldiers to take Jesus and have him crucified. So Jesus was delivered to them and was led away. Chaila, still numb, her mind whirling, followed a short distance, but then, realized she needed help.

(32)

Crucifixion

Chaila ran from the scene, horrified. She ran all the way to the upper room where she knew the disciples would be. It was a secret place in the home of a family who quietly supported Jesus and his disciples. Their secrecy had allowed Jesus to stay in Jerusalem undisturbed. Chaila bounded up the stairs and burst into the room. The Essenes, Chaim and Michael, were there. They had come to Jerusalem for the Passover, and wishing to see Jesus, had come to the home looking for him.

Seeing her friends, Chaila blurted out breathlessly, "Something must me done! Jesus has been condemned to die!" The disciples who had been with Jesus in the garden were gathered here along with other followers. Chaila was the first to bring news since Jesus' arrest. All were shocked that things had progressed so rapidly and that the situation had turned so dire.

Chaila told them all that had transpired. She quickly described Pilate's efforts to free Jesus. How he found no reason to condemn Jesus and that despite his efforts, Jesus had been turned over to the Jews for crucifixion. "Centurions at this very moment are carrying out the crucifixion!" she said breathlessly. Chaila was glad to see the two Essenes. But what could they do now?

There was no time for despair if anything were to be done. Considering the impossibility of their efforts, Jesus' friends were unable to think of anything they could do to stop the crucifixion. The disciples told Chaila, "We are afraid to go to Golgotha. We fear for our own lives!"

Chaila turned to two Essene monks among the group. "Is there nothing you can do?"

Chaim, who had been with the Essenes for many years, answered. "I don't know if we can save his life, but I know what might make it possible." Every head in the room turned toward the older monk. Did he have powers they did not know about?

"Tell us. Tell us what you propose!" cried Chaila.

"We brought a very powerful concoction with us to use during the Passover. The Romans allow a condemned man, even one hung on a crucifix, a drink. Friends or relatives often give wine to those being crucified, as it dulls the pain. It's certainly better than the water and vinegar the Romans carry with them. But we have soma, which is much more potent than wine. We use it in our ceremonies—an herbal drink. It is a powerful calmative and induces ecstatic states. But, it also has the power, in a strong enough dose, to induce a deep sleep. If we could get a strong mixture of this to Jesus, we might be able to save his life. If he passed out, into a death-like state, we could take him down from the cross as dead and revive him."

Chaila and the disciples were speechless. They knew that the Essenes were powerful healers—that they grew and used powerful herbs. But they had never thought of such a use for soma. Chaila, who had lived in the Far East where soma originated was immediately aware of the brilliance of the monk's idea. This would be a far better use of soma than she had ever imagined. She knew this was their only chance.

"Where is the soma? Get it!" She yelled. "We have no time to waste. They are taking him to the Place of the Skull now!"

Chaila's words sparked the monks into immediate action. They ran down the stairs to a cistern, hidden under the lower floor. They retrieved a small earthen jar that held the soma. Rather than wait any longer, the two monks and Chaila left at a run with the jug. Michael grabbed a donkey and helped Chaim up on it, for the older monk could not sustain a run. Chaila managed to grab a clay cup on the way out. Then, along the way, she picked up a

long stick that she could use to hoist the cup to Jesus' lips. They
ran as fast as they could, Michael leading the donkey and Chaim
holding fast to the jug. The heat of the day took its toll. Finally
they arrived at Golgotha, sweaty, but alert.

There was a small crowd gathered beneath the cross. Some
were crying. The Pharisees had left hirelings to watch and be sure
the crucifixions were carried out. There were many people passing
by, for the place of crucifixion was just outside the city. Jesus and
two others, one on either side of him, were already nailed to crosses.
Their bodies were bloodied and sweating in the sun. Jesus' chest
heaved in the heat. Chaila shuddered to the core of her being.
"How could people do such a thing? Especially to one who preached
peace and love. Someone who wished harm to no one."

Chaila and the Essenes approached the crowd. They were careful not to draw attention to themselves. For anyone suspected of
interfering with Roman punishment would be sent away. The three
of them moved through the crowd, trying to look interested, but
not overly concerned. The scene was horrific, for while three men
were dying, others stood around talking and chatting about family and friends.

Chaila looked up at the words over Jesus' head. In bold letters,
in three languages, the sign read: THIS IS JESUS, THE
NAZARENE, THE KING OF THE JEWS. The Centurions periodically pointed to the sign, making fun of the Jews present. For
they knew that Caiaphas had pleaded with Pilate, that the sign
read, HE SAID HE WAS KING OF THE JEWS. But Pilate was
angry at Caiaphas and the Jews for putting him in the position of
condemning an innocent man. So the sign remained as Pilate ordered.

There was blood running from Jesus' head where the crown of
thorns still remained. Blood was streaming from his hands and
feet. He looked exhausted. Chaila could see that the flogging had
sapped most of his strength. He looked as though he might go
into shock. His face was dirty and covered with sweat. He could

barely move his head. But, his eyes were aware, looking with sadness at the crowd beneath him.

When Jesus' eyes fell on Chaila, a smile crossed his lips. His eyes brightened. "Chaila," he called out softly.

"Yes Lord," she said, approaching.

"Tell my disciples I am not going away. Though I die, yet I am with them. For when they touch the Father in their heart, they touch me."

"I will tell them Jesus."

Then Jesus looked at the crowd and those that had condemned him. In a loud voice he cried out, "Father forgive them for they know not what they do."

Even Chaila was amazed at Jesus' forgiveness.

"Jesus," she said, "We have brought you a drink that will take away your pain."

"Chaila," he said, "I am not afraid, I cannot be hurt any more than this. Though my body suffers, I go to the One. So do not fret. I wish I could keep you from grieving but I cannot. I know you will miss me."

"But the drink Jesus. I want you to take some of this!"

"I have no need of wine."

"This is not wine. It is soma. Jesus please, drink it. Maybe you will pass out and live!"

Now Jesus knew what soma was and what it's effects could be. He was silent for awhile. Then he said, "If not for God's will, you would not be here and you would not have brought the soma. Give it to me, I will drink."

Chaila had tied the lip of the cup with twine to the stick she had picked up. Now she poured the soma into the cup and hoisted the stick and cup to Jesus' mouth. Jesus swallowed, knowing what the effect would be. It was very strong and Jesus knew he would suffer no more. When he was finished drinking he raised his head and sighed, "It is finished!"

Within a few minutes, Jesus' eyes closed and his head rolled to one side. His breathing fell to an imperceptible level. For all prac-

tical purposes, he was dead. As the four followers of Jesus stood
there, they heard the Jewish elders saying, "Let us go to Pilate and
ask that the legs of these men be broken, so they can be removed
from their crosses before the Sabbath as required by our Jewish
law."

Just then, Joseph, a member of a wealthy family, whose home
often provided Jesus and his disciples with lodging, stepped forward. He nodded to the others as a sign that he had been told
about the soma. He knew that the only hope for Jesus now, was to
get him down from the cross as soon as possible. It was common
practice for friends to take the bodies of the crucified to be buried.
So Joseph followed the elders to Pilate's residence.

When the elders asked that the legs of those crucified be broken, Joseph spoke up. "Let me have the body of Jesus, for he is
already dead."

In response, with a note of anger, Pilate said, "How can it be
that he is already dead? He has been on the cross only a few hours."

But Joseph, emboldened, spoke again. "The Sanhedrin kept
Jesus up all night and your soldiers flogged and beat him. He was
already half dead when he was nailed to the cross."

Hearing this, Pilate quietly gave orders for a Centurion to accompany Joseph back to Golgotha and verify that Jesus was dead.
He also gave orders that any of those crucified not yet dead, should
have their legs broken. Lastly, he gave permission that Jesus' body
be given to Joseph. So the Centurion, Joseph and the others, returned to the Place of the Skull.

On arrival, the Centurion noted that Jesus' body was limp.
With a wooden mallet, he broke the legs of the other two men, for
they were still alive. Their screams pierced the evening air. Returning to Jesus, he raised his spear and gave Jesus a shove in the side.
The skin broke and blood began to trickle, but Jesus made no
response. The Centurion then motioned to Joseph that he could
take the body.

With Joseph's help, Chaila and the two Essenes lowered the
cross. They removed the nails and lifted Jesus' tortured body from

the cross. None of them knew if Jesus were truly dead. But, they hoped that he was only unconscious. They wrapped his body in a linen shroud, soaked in aloe and perfumed oils, and carried it away.

Joseph had brought the linen in hope that Jesus might survive. If the soma worked as planned, the aloe would help heal the wounds. A short way from Golgotha one of Joseph's sons was waiting with a donkey. They laid Jesus' body over the donkey's back and quickly returned to the home of Joseph and his family. They took Jesus' limp form to the upper room and laid it on a cot in a corner.

Chaila immediately put her ear to Jesus' chest, but she could hear no heart beat. She then put her lips next to his to see if she could feel any breath. She could feel none. She turned to the Essenes, "I think he's dead. I don't think it worked." She was numb with pain. The elder Essene who had suggested the soma stepped forward. He had a concerned yet knowing look on his face. Chaila wondered what he would do. Taking a flat black stone from his pocket, he spoke to Chaila.

"We have experience with soma. One way to check for life, when breathing is this shallow, is to use this." He held up the highly polished black stone. Then he placed it under Jesus' nose. After several minutes he brought the stone up and looked at it carefully. He rubbed his thumb on the surface. He turned again to Chaila.

"There is a slight bit of moisture condensed on the surface. This means that there is some breath."

Chaila looked at the old monk hopefully, not daring to smile, yet still hoping. "When will we know?" she asked.

"It may be a day or two before he wakes up," said the old monk. "However, a sign that he is still alive is very evident. When I touched his body, it was still warm!"

Chaila had not considered this. Now she smiled and rushed over to Jesus, feeling the sides of his chest. "Yes, he is still warm! In my fear and this heat I did not think to check whether his body was warm or not!"

Joseph spoke up. "If he is alive, we must move his body some-where else, for though we have met here secretly, we don't want people coming here seeing that he is not buried. We must move him somewhere else. No one but those of us in this room must know where he is."

Chaila recalled the family who had often befriended Jesus, the family that lived just below the temple. "What about the Shabaz family? They would keep him. No one would look for Jesus so close to the temple!"

Joseph sent the younger Essene to make the request of the family. Chaila remained at Jesus' side. While she waited for the news that Jesus could be moved there, she tended his wounds. She washed them clean with oil and aloe, kissing his cheeks and wip-ing the dirt, blood and sweat from his body. She tasted the salt from his sweat. It reassured her. It was past midnight when the monk returned. "We can take his body there," he said, "They will keep him. They will take him gladly."

So Jesus was once again placed on the donkey. Accompanied by Chaila and the monks, they traveled through the dark alleys of Jerusalem, to the family's home. They laid Jesus on a cot in a back room. All were sworn to tell no one, not even those sympathetic to Jesus' teachings. Chaila and the monks stayed there with him. Joseph remained at his home, telling everyone that Jesus' body was in one of his family's tombs. He told anyone who asked to see the body that he would show it to them later. For now, he did not want crowds of people standing around mourning, drawing atten-tion.

For two days Chaila stayed with Jesus. She could only tell that Jesus was alive because his body remained warm. There were only slight, almost imperceptible signs of breathing. Sometimes, she thought she could hear a soft heartbeat. Chaila was encouraged by the fact that Jesus' body did not grow stiff with rigor mortis.

While Chaila tended Jesus, she asked the Jews about this bar-baric form of punishment, crucifixion. She was told that it could take up to three days for a man to die on a cross. She was also told that they often broke the legs of the condemned to hasten death. Without the support of their legs, those crucified, suffocated from their own body weight. These facts helped keep Chaila's hope alive, for Jesus had been on the cross only five or six hours and the wound from the spear was not deep. Chaila had witnessed the Centurion spear Jesus and knew he had only intended to get a response from Jesus, were he still alive.

Chaila thought to herself, "It is truly a miracle that the Essenes were in the upper room and that they had stored soma in the house. It will be a miracle, indeed, when Jesus revives."

On the third day as Chaila lay on the floor next to Jesus, she heard a low moan. She leaped from her place on the floor and leaned over him. In the light coming from an open window she saw Jesus' head move. Her heart leaped with joy. Again Jesus moaned and Chaila knew he would recover. She clutched his head between her hands and turned his head towards the light. But his eyes were closed. She kissed his lips.

She stood bent over him for more than an hour. Periodically Jesus moaned. Finally, he opened his eyes. There was a far away, foggy look in them. "Jesus! Jesus!" Chaila cried.

After several minutes, Jesus gave her a sign of recognition. The response was vague, but Chaila thought she saw a smile cross his lips. She renewed her efforts to revive him. She got a pot of cold water and gently began washing his body with a damp cloth. She could see that he was responding. Her heart warmed and she smiled at him. Tears streamed down her cheeks.

By mid morning, when everyone was up, Jesus was alert. Due to the effect of the soma, though, he was not quite himself. His responses were slow and vague, but he seemed to be getting clearer by the minute. Finally, with great effort, Jesus said, "Am I not dead?"

"No, Jesus, you are alive," said Chaila.

Jesus, very perceptibly now, grinned. It took the rest of the day for him to comprehend just what had happened. However, as he regained strength and as his blood began to flow, a fever set in

TW

and Jesus began to sweat. Chaila continued to clean his wounds and give him water to drink. Jesus' hands and feet were swollen red, black and blue. His back was raw and also black with bruises.

No one told of what was transpiring in the home. Joseph was informed and kept his own sons guarding the tomb where Jesus had supposedly been buried. Joseph did not want anyone going in and finding the tomb empty.

In time, Jesus was sufficiently recovered to ride a donkey. Arrangements for Jesus to leave Jerusalem were made. Early one evening, his close friends gathered, and in small groups they passed through the city gate with Jesus among them, disguised as an old man. They traveled toward Galilee.

Jesus was absolutely amazed at what had happened. That he was alive was more surprising to him than anyone. The last thing he remembered was being on the cross and taking the cup. Now he was on his way back to Galilee. They traveled several days and went to the home of Simon Peter. There they stayed. But soon word began to spread that Jesus had survived the crucifixion. Some even said that he had risen from the dead.

Back in Jerusalem, when these rumors arrived, the Sanhedrin responded by sending guards to Joseph's home, demanding that he open the tomb. He did, and when there was no body present, the leaders were furious. They brought Joseph in for questioning. But the only thing they could get from him. was that he had placed Jesus' body in the tomb and that he did not know where it was now.

When word got back to Galilee, Jesus told his disciples that he must go. He informed them that he would return to Kashmir and stay there. He gave them the names of the towns where he might be, especially, the Hemis monastery. But he discouraged any from coming with him. Soon, with the help of wealthy followers, a caravan was arranged for the trip. Early one morning, a month after he had been crucified, Jesus took Chaila with him and left for Kashmir.

A crowd followed for some way, but as the caravan began to climb a steep, very high hill, they fell back. Some fell to their knees, praying. Many were waving. For half an hour the crowd watched as the caravan rose to the top of the steep mountain. Chaila, looking back, said to Jesus. "It's a good thing we are leaving, look how you have drawn such a crowd. You have neither spoken in public, nor gone to the temple since your crucifixion, yet here they are. There is no way your enemies would have stayed away much longer."

"You are right Chaila. Yet, I am thankful that I had the time to recuperate. I don't think I could have made this trip without healing first."

It was mid-morning as the caravan reached the summit. From below it looked as if the sun had dropped from the sky to the top of the hill. There in blazing sunlight, the crowd below saw the caravan swallowed up and disappear. Many ran home yelling. "Jesus was taken up! He has returned to heaven!"

In the months that followed Jesus' fame spread far and wide. Rumors flew and grew. Some said he had stepped down from the cross himself and walked away. Others said he had risen from the dead. Whatever the story, Jesus' message and life were talked about. Many believed and asked about his message. The Sadducees and the Pharisees tried hard to squelch the rumors that Jesus had survived or risen from the dead. But their efforts were to no avail. Jesus' disciples knew he was alive and waited for his return, spreading the Gospel as best they could.

The End of Book

Printed in the United States
68276LVS00002B/21